# MIRACLE BABY, MIRACLE FAMILY

## ALISON ROBERTS

# A GP TO STEAL HIS HEART

## KARIN BAINE

**MILLS & BOON**

First Published in Great Britain 2022
by Mills & Boon, an imprint of HarperCollins*Publishers* Ltd,
1 London Bridge Street, London, SE1 9GF

www.harpercollins.co.uk

HarperCollins*Publishers*
1st Floor, Watermarque Building,
Ringsend Road, Dublin 4, Ireland

Miracle Baby, Miracle Family © 2022 Alison Roberts

A GP to Steal His Heart © 2022 Karin Baine

ISBN: 978-0-263-30122-9

04/22

MIX
Paper from
responsible sources
FSC™ C007454

**Alison Roberts** has been lucky enough to live in the south of France for several years recently, but is now back in her home country of New Zealand. She is also lucky enough to write for the Mills & Boon Medical line. A primary school teacher in a former life, she later became a qualified paramedic. She loves to travel and dance, drink champagne and spend time with her daughter and her friends. *The Vet's Unexpected Family* was Alison Roberts's 100th book.

**Karin Baine** lives in Northern Ireland with her husband, two sons and her out-of-control notebook collection. Her mother and her grandmother's vast collection of books inspired her love of reading and her dream of becoming a Mills & Boon author. Now she can tell people she has a *proper* job! You can follow Karin on Twitter, @karinbaine1, or visit her website for the latest news—karinbaine.com.

# MIRACLE BABY,
# MIRACLE FAMILY

ALISON ROBERTS

**MILLS & BOON**

# CHAPTER ONE

Isobel Matthews had fully expected him to be here.

Her brother-in-law. Raphael Tanner.

Rafe...

Of course he was here. He would also have been here in plenty of time—not late enough to have actually missed the ceremony, as Isobel had unfortunately managed to do despite her very best efforts. When the draught caught the heavy wooden door of the church hall and made it slam behind her as she tried to close it, it was also only to be expected that he would turn, along with everybody else, to see who was arriving so unacceptably late.

What Isobel had not expected was this *awareness* of him to be so astonishingly powerful. With no more than a split second of eye contact, memories that were embedded in every cell of her body and stored away in her heart were in danger of being triggered again. She'd been so sure she was completely over this man. That she could have lived the rest of her life without ever wanting to see Raphael Tanner again. Without ever being derailed by those memories again.

That certainty had just been blown out of the water.

It was Rafe who broke that eye contact almost as soon as it happened, turning back to the priest standing beside him, but it was obvious to Isobel that he *hadn't* expected to see her here. The speed with which he looked away and the impression that every muscle in his body had just stiffened was more than enough to suggest that he might have been relieved that she hadn't shown up. That maybe she wasn't the only one who would prefer not to have memories triggered?

The pull was simply too strong for Isobel to look away quite that quickly as she took a breath and gathered her courage to face these people and this situation. She could feel her heart thumping as she registered the difference nearly seven years had made. Rafe's face was thinner and there were deeper lines from his nose to the corners of his mouth. And was he already going grey in his late thirties or was the shimmer from fine raindrops still clinging to those dark waves of his hair after being outside in the driving rain?

Isobel had noticed the still dripping umbrellas propped under the coat hooks in the entranceway of this old church hall but a lot of people were still wearing heavy coats as if they hadn't had time to warm up yet. They were also queued in front of a table laden with cups and saucers, huge teapots and an urn of boiling water, waiting for catering staff to serve them a hot cup of tea or coffee. She'd only missed the graveside part of this service by minutes, hadn't she?

Now she would have to deal with the possibility that having missed the most significant part of this funeral would haunt her for the rest of her life. That the people here would no doubt add it to their existing disapproval of her estrangement from her family. She'd known it wouldn't be easy coming here, but she had no choice but to deal with it so she might as well start by joining the end of the queue and talking to people who'd cared enough to come out in this inclement April weather to pay their respects to Sharon and Lauren Matthews. After all, there were going to be a lot of things she would have to face in the coming days and weeks that weren't going to be easy but when they were sorted she could leave again.

And never come back.

Rafe was ushering the priest to the front of the queue to get a hot drink as Isobel joined the back. With her first impressions already gathered, Isobel could clearly read the emotion behind his features and there was enough sadness there to trigger a fresh wave of the grief that Isobel had been struggling with for days now. Ever since she'd received the shocking news of the accident that had killed both her mother and her sister.

The long, long flight from New Zealand back to England, with the addition of a mechanical fault that had kept her grounded in Singapore for thirty hours, had given her too much time to get below that first layer of grief. Time to sink into feelings of deep guilt that she'd left it too late and that any opportunity to try and repair such badly fractured relationships had been lost. There was a new, unexpected loneliness mixed in with both the grief and the guilt. The only family Isobel had ever known was gone. For ever.

This fresh wash of grief wasn't for what she had lost herself, though. This was empathy for Rafe, which was something else she would not have expected. It was, in fact, beyond disconcerting because it suggested that she cared too much about whether he was happy or not. The way her breath came out in a dismissive huff reminded her that Rafe's happiness had not been her concern for many years. It also made the woman standing directly in front of Isobel in the queue turn around.

She recognised her mother's next-door neighbour and closest friend, Louise, and saw real sympathy in the older woman's eyes.

'I knew you'd come if you could,' Louise murmured. 'Such a terrible, terrible tragedy. I'm so sorry for your loss, love.'

'I feel awful that I'm so late,' Isobel said. 'I came as soon as I could. I should have been here the day before yesterday but we got delayed. And even with this rain I wasn't expecting London traffic to be so heavy so early in the morning.'

'You're here now. No doubt you'll have time to come back here before you go away again.' Louise turned to take a step closer to the table. 'Some things are best said or done in private, anyway, aren't they? It was a lovely service under the circumstances.' She reached for a cup and saucer, already glancing towards the plates further along the trestle table, where club sandwiches, savouries and cakes were being provided as refreshments. 'I must say, Dr Tanner's done a wonderful job of organising everything. Especially when he didn't really have to, did he?'

Didn't he? What an odd thing to say, Isobel thought. This was his wife's funeral. And his mother-in-law's. The mother and grandmother of his sons. Surely nobody would have expected Isobel to have been the person to organise this funeral?

Louise was balancing her cup and saucer in one hand, reaching for a serviette and a sausage roll with the other. 'So very sad,' she added, shaking her head. 'Especially for that poor baby...'

*Baby?*

Isobel had picked up a cup but she didn't move to spoon coffee into it or hold it out for tea to be poured because she was still trying to process what Louise had just said. The twins would be six years old by now, she realised. Why had it not occurred to her that Rafe and Lauren would have added to their family? Maybe there was also a toddler in between the twins and...the new baby. A perfect family, with Grandma just down the road to help with the busyness of so many young children.

An echo of Rafe's voice snuck into the back of her mind.

*'Once bitten, for ever shy in my case. I should be clear right from the start about that, Belle. I'm never getting married again. Or having kids. Never, ever...'*

Not with her, anyway. And it still hurt that her own sister had been the one to change his mind. Even having grown up knowing that Lauren was always the favourite. Always the chosen one if both sisters were available. Even after so many years and a totally new life on the other side of the world, it still hurt and it was only natural for her gaze to roam until it found the person who had been the catalyst for that unspoken competition to have finally become unacceptable. For her life to have fallen apart. Isobel knew she'd have to talk to

Rafe at some point in the next few days as she dealt with her mother's estate but this wasn't the time or place.

Rafe wasn't looking at her this time. He was still standing beside the priest and now Louise was heading towards them, possibly to tell Rafe how impressed she was by his organisation of this funeral. And Isobel found her gaze shifting to the priest because there was something a little odd in the way he was smiling at Louise or, rather, the way that smile was fading so rapidly. He was losing his grip on his cup of tea as well, the contents spilling onto the silk stole and white surplice he wore over a dark robe.

In the same instant, she could see the robe beginning to puddle on the wooden floorboards of the hall as he crumpled, seemingly in slow motion. Slow enough for Rafe to be able to put his arms out and catch the large man to at least cushion his fall.

The dramatic slump and then the unnatural stillness of the man when he was on the floor made it quite obvious that he was unconscious and Isobel's training meant that it was automatic to move in swiftly. To start doing what needed to be done to potentially save a life. Her cup and saucer clattered as she abandoned it on the table.

Rafe was already crouched over the priest by the time she got to his side. He had tipped the man's head back and had his ear close to the nose and mouth, one hand resting on the diaphragm to try and feel for movement beneath the layers of clothing, the other on the neck to feel for a pulse.

'Is he breathing?' Isobel asked.

'No.' The word was terse. 'No pulse either.'

Rafe raised his arm, clenched his fist and brought it down with a hard thump onto the middle of the priest's chest. A horrified gasp could be heard from the group of people, including Louise, who were all staring, open-mouthed, at the unexpected drama unfolding in front of them. They didn't understand that even the small impact of such a thump, if it was delivered soon enough after a witnessed cardiac arrest, could potentially have the same effect as an electrical shock in providing an opportunity for a heart to start beating again.

'Someone call an ambulance.' Rafe had his fingers on the priest's neck again, feeling for a pulse. 'Tell them it's a cardiac arrest and CPR is underway.'

With his other hand, he reached into the pocket of his suit jacket and pulled out a set of keys, turning to give them to the closest person. 'Louise, my car is parked right in front of the church,' he told her. 'Black SUV by the gate. Get my medical kit and the defibrillator out of the back. Hurry…'

'What does a defibrillator look like?'

Rafe didn't even blink. Instead of giving Louise the keys, he turned and looked straight at Isobel.

'*Belle?*'

By way of a response, she held out her hands to catch the bunch of keys and then turned to run to the door that led outside. She could see Rafe positioning his hands on the priest's chest now, one palm flat on the sternum, the other on top, fingers interlaced. He was starting the chest compressions and he knew exactly what needed to be done but the sooner he got his medical equipment the better. CPR alone could keep someone oxygenated and cells alive but it was not going to restart a heart that had stopped for whatever reason. Isobel increased her pace as soon as the door slammed shut behind her again, thankful she had flat-soled boots on and not heels. She could already see the big black vehicle parked by the gate so there was nothing that was going to interfere with her focus. Not even the fact that someone had called her 'Belle' for the first time in nearly seven years.

With the odds well against a successful outcome to dealing with a cardiac arrest, having it happen at a funeral was almost ironic but that wasn't even a background thought for Rafe Tanner as he kept his arms straight and continued the rapid chest compressions needed to keep this man's blood moving. With the priest being considerably overweight and the need to depress the chest by a third for the pressure to have the desired effect, Rafe was feeling the physical effort by the time Isobel came running back with both his medical kit and the small portable defibrillator he always carried.

She was panting a little from her own effort. Her boots were spattered with mud and her hair was wet from the rain that clearly hadn't stopped yet. That golden blonde hair was starting to curl. Like it always did when it got wet…

Good *grief.* Where the hell had that random memory sprung from?

He didn't have to waste extra breath on telling Isobel what to do. She was kneeling on the floor now, opening the lock on his kit. She lifted the lid and went straight for the pair of shears that could cut through any clothing, even leather shoes, but put them down to one side because they would not be interrupting compressions until absolutely necessary. With a speed that suggested the actions were pretty much automatic, Isobel grabbed some other items and wriggled herself into a position at their patient's head. She snapped a mask onto the end of an Ambu bag, tilted the man's head well back and curled her fingers under his jaw to hold the cushioned edges of the mask firmly in place. With a single nod, Rafe paused his compressions so that she could deliver two breaths. With a patient this size, it wasn't always easy to keep a perfect seal around the mouth and nose, or to push air in enough to make the chest rise but Isobel managed both with apparent ease.

'Ambulance is on its way,' someone called from behind Rafe. 'They said they'll be about six minutes.'

'Okay...thanks.' Rafe was slightly out of breath as he began compressions again but he needed to keep them up until the last possible moment when he needed to cut the man's clothing to allow the sticky pads from the defibrillator to be placed on his skin.

Again, without direction, Isobel was doing exactly what was required. She dropped the bag mask, reaching to lift the lid of the automatic external defibrillator, which made it spring to life and immediately begin issuing instructions in a calm robotic voice.

*'Peel off pad labelled one and stick to the skin of the patient exactly as shown in the picture.'*

Isobel had the shears in her hands and was slicing through the thick layers of the white surplice and the black robe beneath, using the fabric to make sure that any sweat was wiped from the skin. There was no need to cut the soft woollen singlet that was a poignant reminder that the priest had dressed himself with only having to stand outside in bad weather in mind, having no idea what was about to happen to him. Keeping their patient warm would be another consideration if the ambulance was delayed for some reason but Rafe dismissed the thought for now. Just like he was easily able to dismiss any thoughts related to Isobel Matthews having suddenly stepped back into his life.

She didn't look at the picture on the pad before pressing it into place beneath the collarbone and caught up with the machine's instructions as she placed the second pad on the side of the chest.

'*Stop CPR. Do not touch the patient,*' the device said.

Rafe lifted his hands and stopped compressions.

'*Analysing heart rhythm.*'

The brief pause felt so much longer than the ten seconds or so Rafe knew it was. Especially when he was kneeling directly on the other side of the man's chest to Isobel and they'd both looked up in the same moment. When they both seemed incapable of looking away before the moment stretched into something significant because it was so much longer than you would hold eye contact with anyone that wasn't an intimate acquaintance. The faint background realisation that they were being watched, and that some of those people might well remember they'd once been an item themselves, did not seem to be enough to break this hold.

Just how many impressions and/or memories was the brain capable of producing in a space of only a few seconds? Enough for them to be indistinguishable individually, apparently, but not enough to completely blur an emotional response. And that response, which was quite surprising after all these years, included a good dollop of anger.

Why had Isobel bothered showing up at this funeral when she'd never bothered doing the right thing in the past seven years?

'*Shock advised,*' the device told them. '*Stand clear.*'

They both looked down to ensure their bodies weren't in contact with their patient. They leaned away from the patient but it also felt as if they were leaning away from each other.

'*Press the flashing orange button now. Shock delivered. Begin CPR.*'

Isobel picked up the bag mask again and positioned her fingers to get a perfect seal around the man's nose and mouth. She held her other hand on the squashy bag, ready to squeeze it when the compressions stopped for long enough. There was no point trying to push air inside lungs if they were being pressed hard from above. Rafe began counting aloud to give her warning that he was about to stop.

'Twenty-eight, twenty-nine. Thirty...' His hands were still touching the sternum but they weren't moving.

Isobel squeezed the bag but the air didn't go in as expected. She could feel it pushing out from the sides of the mask she was holding in place on their patient's face with an audible puff. She heard a shout from behind as she let the bag inflate to try again.

'The ambulance is here.'

Isobel squeezed the bag again and then realised why it wasn't working. It wasn't the chest being pressed that was working against her, it was their patient trying to breathe for himself. Rafe was also aware of what was happening. He put his fingers against the priest's neck and caught Isobel's gaze as he nodded a moment later, to confirm that he could feel a pulse.

This time, it felt very different to that uncomfortably long eye contact they'd had when the defibrillator had been analysing their patient's heart rhythm. Isobel couldn't have said whether that palpable hostility had been all Rafe's or whether he was reflecting what he'd seen in her eyes but she could certainly be confident it wasn't there this time. This was an acknowledgement between two professionals that a job had been well done. That their team work had made a difference to the world because a life had been saved.

It took all of a nanosecond to remember another shared glance that had been the way they'd met that first time. On either side of a patient in the emergency department of St Luke's Hospital, here in Balclutha. During a shift where the department was so run off its feet that the only staff available to answer the cardiac arrest alarm had been one doctor and a nurse who'd just begun working there. Rafe. And Isobel. Sadly, they hadn't been able to share the triumph of a successful outcome that time but maybe that was why Rafe had come to find her at the end of the shift. Why he'd spent the time talking through the case and reassuring her that the outcome was no reflection on her skills.

Why Isobel had fallen head over heels in love, right then and there, with Dr Raphael Tanner.

Oh, help…

She'd kept a lid on all those memories for so long but

they were seeping out through cracks that had been appearing ever since she'd heard the news of that dreadful accident and had widened considerably with the emotional impact of being here at the funeral. At least Isobel found herself capable of breaking the eye contact this time. And, thanks to the arrival of the paramedics beside them, she could dismiss the memory as no more than an unwelcome passing thought.

What helped even more was that the priest was regaining consciousness. He was raising his hand, in fact, as if he wanted to push the mask away from his face.

'Hey…looks like you've done all the hard work for us,' one of them said. 'Good job, guys. Let's get him on the stretcher, get some oxygen on and then we'll get him into the ambulance and give him a thorough check.'

If anything, the rain was even heavier by the time the stretcher was loaded into the ambulance. The paramedics had been grateful for the extra help in getting a heavy patient on board, but it had still taken enough time for them to have got cold and wet. Isobel was shivering.

'You're frozen,' Rafe said. 'You should go back into the hall and have a hot drink.'

Isobel shook her head. 'I'd rather not, to be honest,' she told Rafe. 'I just need some dry clothes. I've got my suitcase in my rental car and I'll go to Mum's house. I'm hoping she's left a spare key under a flowerpot like she always used to do, otherwise I might need to wait for Louise to get home. I'm sure she'll have one.'

'I've got a key,' Rafe said. 'Just in case of an emergency.'

Of course he did. He was the sort of man who'd make sure he was always available to help his mother-in-law. Isobel kept her gaze on the flashing lights of the ambulance as it disappeared around a corner up the road. She wrapped her arms around herself as well, trying to suppress another shiver.

'I might come with you,' he added. 'I'd like to pick up a couple of things the boys left behind the last time they visited her. Then I can give you the key to keep.'

Isobel turned towards her rental car. 'You're not going to follow the ambulance in, in case they need high-level assistance?'

'The patient's stable. He's got an IV line in and he's getting oxygen and being well monitored for his heart rhythm. I know those paramedics and they can deal with another arrest, if that happens, as well as I could on the road. I'll go into the hospital later and follow up then.'

Isobel nodded. 'I expect everyone in the hall will want to talk to you.' She was biting her lip as she began walking away. 'I should also say that I'm very sorry for your loss.'

The incredulous huff of sound behind her made Isobel turn back. She could see muscles moving in Rafe's face and jaw as if he was trying to stop himself saying something. Then he appeared to take a deep breath.

'I haven't seen Lauren since she walked out on me nearly five years ago.' Rafe's voice was controlled enough to sound icy. 'I've seen your mother once in the last six months because I arranged for the boys to visit her. I'm only here to pay my respects to the mother and grandmother of my sons.'

*'I'm doing this because it's the right thing to do...'*

The new echo of Rafe's voice from years ago was simply another memory seeping out of that supposedly secure place. Isobel mentally tried to slam the lid shut more tightly. Starting to ask the questions that were suddenly tumbling around in her head was not going to help anything. She was here to finish things, not start anything that might complicate her permanent escape.

But he had been estranged from both her sister and her mother? What on earth had happened?

*His* sons? Had Lauren walked out on her children as well?

And what on earth had her mother's friend Louise been talking about when she'd mentioned that 'poor baby'?

'Do you remember the way to your mother's house?' It sounded as if Rafe was carefully keeping his tone neutral. 'Or shall I wait so you can follow me?'

'The address the solicitor sent me is the house I grew up in.' Isobel also kept her tone completely flat. 'I think I might be able to remember how to get there, thanks.'

Was Rafe just trying to rub in the fact that she'd been gone for so long? That *she'd* been the first member of her family to walk out on people? To somehow make that whole mess in her life her own fault?

Despite how miserably cold she was, Isobel straightened her back as she walked back to her car. She wasn't going to take the blame here.

Was Rafe actually not aware that what hadn't been his own fault had been Lauren's? If so, maybe that was something else that she could add to the list of things that needed sorting out before she left. It might even be a good way of finding a new lid for that box of memories.

One that was heavy enough to stay closed for the rest of her life.

# CHAPTER TWO

MEMORIES ON TOP of memories.

Isobel knew these streets so well, in one of the largest towns not far from the coast in Kent. The primary school that she and Lauren had attended looked exactly the same. She could hear the echo of her beloved younger sister's demands even.

*'Belle's got braids, Mummy. I want braids too.'*

*'Belle's got a red dress. Why can't I have a red dress?'*

*'Wait for me, Belle. You're walking too fast...'*

Her mother's house, on Barrington Street, also looked exactly the same. Just an ordinary end-of-terrace brick house with small rooms, steep staircase and a tiny garden out the back—the sort of home a single mother with two small daughters was lucky to be able to own. A happy enough little home to outward appearances, perhaps, but it was obvious to everyone that it was her sister who was the 'mini-me' of their mother. The prettiest daughter. The favourite.

*'You don't need braids with your beautiful straight hair. Let's give you a ponytail, darling.'*

*'Of course you can have a red dress, Lauren.'*

*'Wait for your little sister, Isobel. Don't be so mean...'*

There was something to be said for an overload of memories and the emotions they could invoke, mind you. Especially when added to the mix of grief and guilt that Isobel was struggling with. Jetlag on top of that and it was all becoming too much. A curious numb sensation was rolling in like a mental fog to obscure details and muffle emotions and make it easy to step back and simply be aware of them in the distance—as if they belonged to someone else.

Someone who could park her car behind Rafe's, take her suitcase out of the back hatch, follow him up the three steps that led to the front door of her childhood home and wait for him to find the key and let her inside. Someone who only blinked when the door was opened and it was obvious that something was very wrong.

'What on earth is that horrible smell? Oh, my God...' Rafe had stepped inside. 'This carpet's sodden. There's an inch of water in here. No wonder it smells like a swamp.'

Isobel could hear the squelch of his shoes as he walked down the hall. She put her suitcase down on the doorstep and followed him. Her feet were cold and wet anyway and she felt so miserable that it really couldn't get much worse, could it?

'There's water coming down the stairs. There must be a burst pipe in the bathroom.' Rafe shook his head. 'It could have been leaking for the last couple of weeks. I don't suppose anybody has been in here since the accident.'

It felt as if he was glaring at Isobel. As if this too was somehow her fault.

'I came as quickly as I could,' she said defensively. 'I only got the solicitor's letter a few days ago. It would have helped if it hadn't been sent to an old work address.'

'It would have helped if someone had known your current address,' Rafe snapped back. 'I had no other way of tracing you except to go through the police in New Zealand and I didn't think you would appreciate them turning up on your doorstep.'

The hall led into the living room that was directly beneath the upstairs bathroom. Dark smudges of mould were clearly visible on the walls and curtains. The huge bulging area of the ceiling was even more alarming, especially with water still trickling in a fast drip through the light fitting in the centre of the bulge.

Rafe stepped back. 'I didn't actually think you'd come back at all,' he added. 'Or that you'd even give a damn that your mother and sister were dead.'

*Oh...* Things could get worse, couldn't they?

Those words stung. Isobel could feel a wave of grief—not dissimilar to that bulge in the ceiling—ready to burst at any moment and release a torrent of painful tears. This was so unfair.

'You know why I left.' Her voice had broken edges. 'I'm sure you wanted me to leave as much as they did, to make it easier for everyone.'

'Easier for everyone or just easier for you?' Rafe had moved to peer into the kitchen. There was a lake on the linoleum and food on the bench that was covered with mould. The smell was more than simply dankness in here. 'You've been gone for more than six years, Belle. Not a word from you. Not. One. Word.'

She could deny that but what was the point? Maybe he didn't know that trying to stay in contact with her mother had only made things harder and it was hard enough to try and start a completely new life. He wouldn't want to hear about how she'd finally thrown herself into studying for a new degree and new career and how the months and then years had slipped by and how it had just become easier to put everything behind her.

'Maybe I wasn't ready to rake up the past,' she said quietly. 'Maybe I thought I had more time.'

Rafe was shaking his head again. Unimpressed. 'Well, you were wrong, weren't you? And you were wrong about something else too.' He waved his hand to encompass the destruction around them. 'You won't be staying here. It's uninhabitable.' He looked up at the bulge in the living room ceiling. 'It's dangerous, that's what it is. There's a bathtub up there that could come through the ceiling at any moment. We need to get out of here.'

He walked past Isobel into the hallway. 'I'll make some calls so that we can get the plumbing fixed and then the damage assessed. In the meantime, you'd better come home with me.'

'*What?*' Isobel almost gave an audible huff of laughter. 'Why would I do that?'

Rafe stopped in front of the obstacle her suitcase was creating, turning so quickly that Isobel almost bumped into him. She could see that the drizzle had turned into heavy rain outside now. She could also see that Rafe was angry. Or was he disappointed in her? Or hurting? Or all of the above? It twisted something inside her chest, at any rate. Another disturbing twinge that was pulling her somewhere she didn't want to go.

'To meet your nephews?' Rafe suggested, his tone impassive. 'Two little boys that have lost the mother they don't remember but that their grandmother was always telling them would come back one day because she loved them. Only she never did. They know they've got an aunty who's part of our family, but I don't suppose they believe that *she* loves them either.' He turned away to walk down the steps. 'She's never even wanted to meet them, has she?'

Isobel said nothing as she pulled the door closed behind her to lock it. That wasn't true either. She actually had a photo of the twins, when they were just a few weeks old, tucked into a pocket in her wallet. The picture that had come in the last letter she'd ever received from her mother. The one that said how blessed they all were that Rafe and Lauren had found each other.

Rafe pressed his remote and his car beeped as he looked over his shoulder. 'You might want to consider meeting your niece too,' he said.

Isobel's jaw dropped. 'So there *is* another baby? But you said you hadn't seen Lauren in years...'

Rafe had his driver's door open by the time Isobel got to the footpath. 'Oh, it's not *my* baby.' He raised his eyebrows. 'Come to think of it, I guess that, legally, *you're* her only known family.'

This was incomprehensible.

Shocking.

And Rafe must have seen that on her face because he took a deep breath.

'Look...we can't stand out here in the rain talking

about this. You need to get into some dry clothes. We both do. Come home with me and I'll explain everything. If you still want to go to a hotel after that, fine, I'll help you find one.'

He was offering her a smile. Okay, half a smile but he was definitely making an attempt to be kind. Because she was his sons' aunt? Because it was the right thing to do?

Isobel swallowed hard. Her fingers were aching with cold and she could feel rain trickling down the back of her neck. Perhaps this wasn't the right thing for her to do but it felt as if she had no choice. Her world had already been spinning out of control and the new information Rafe had just delivered meant that none of it was even making sense now. She couldn't even tell if they were tears on her face or whether it was the rain. She couldn't say anything because there was a massive lump in her throat. It felt as if she couldn't even make her legs move to carry her to her car.

Rafe walked around his car to the footpath. He took the suitcase out of Isobel's hand and put it in the back of the car with an authority she couldn't begin to resist. It was, in fact, an enormous relief that somebody else was making decisions for her so that she didn't have to try and make her brain work.

Rafe opened his passenger door and met Isobel's gaze.

'Hop in, Belle,' he said quietly. 'You're in no fit state to be driving, are you? We can come back and get your car later.'

Isobel was being looked after. Being spoken to as if how she felt mattered. Being taken to a warm, dry house, shown to a bathroom and given soft, fluffy towels. Rafe put her suitcase on top of a chair and turned on the shower.

'It'll need a minute or two to get hot. The plumbing's not the best in old houses like this.'

The impressions of Rafe's house so far were a bit blurred. A huge old house in a leafy suburb. A big garden. Central heating and a nice savoury sort of smell that had to be coming from a kitchen. The house was full of comfortably worn furniture and a bit messy with toys scattered about. There was a dog too. A golden retriever that had obediently gone off to find its bed when it had been told to. It felt like a home, this house. A real family home.

Rafe pulled a string that turned on a fan heater on the wall. 'Help yourself to anything you need, like shampoo.'

Isobel nodded. 'Thanks.'

Her voice was barely more than a whisper. This was worse than that disturbing moment at the funeral when she'd realised she still cared about Rafe far more than she would have believed possible. This was more like the beginning of those dreams she used to have so long ago. Dreams when she was so much in love and knew without a shadow of doubt that she'd found the person she wanted to be with for the rest of her life. When she'd been so sure that he felt the same way and it was only a matter of time before he changed his mind about marriage. Dreams that had her cocooned in bliss only to morph into broken-hearted nightmares that she would wake from with her pillow wet with tears.

'Come and find me when you're finished. And bring

your wet clothes. There's a rack over the Aga which will have them dry in no time. I think I smelt some of Helen's vegetable soup on the go too, and it must be lunchtime by now.'

*Helen?*

Who the heck was Helen? A new wife? That would hardly be a surprise, would it? A man like Dr Raphael Tanner wasn't likely to stay single long. Certainly not for five years. Did that have something to do with the estrangement with her mother—his ex-mother-in-law?

Isobel had to try hard to make her stiff fingers open the zips on her long black boots. She peeled off wet tights and the rest of her clothes and stepped under water that stung her skin with the heat until she got used to it. Then she stood there for goodness knew how long, letting it rain on her head and flow over her entire body, as if it could start to wash away some of the overflow of emotion that had done her head in.

It definitely helped. By the time she got out of the shower her skin was pink and she felt warm for the first time in many hours. Her suitcase provided the comfort of well-worn jeans and an oversized oatmeal-coloured jumper that was a favourite. She towel-dried her hair but didn't bother trying to straighten the sun-streaked blonde curls that reached her shoulders. She didn't bother putting any make-up on either. Perhaps she still felt too raw to think there was any point in trying to disguise it. Or in trying to impress Rafe—which begged the question of why it would even occur to her at all.

Isobel picked up her wet clothing and set off to find the kitchen. She could still cope with everything she had come here to do. She just needed to swallow her pride

and accept any help that she was offered from Rafe—
the man who, as far as her heart was concerned, had
cheated on her...with her own sister.

How was it that someone could have been gone from
your life for more than six years but look younger than
the last time you'd seen them?

Was it her bare feet? Or that huge jumper that made
her look like a kid who was wearing their dad's clothing? Maybe it was just that Isobel was looking so pale.
So...vulnerable...

Oh, help...was he really going to have to fight the
urge to take her into his arms and hug her? This was
twisting his gut even more than seeing her standing outside her mother's house with tears streaming down her
face had. He could make sure he wasn't going to give
in to the urge, anyway, by using his arms to lower the
clothing rack on its pulleys but a physical distraction
wasn't enough to stop what was going on in his head. It
would seem that he was also going to have to fight insistent memories that wanted to escape from the place
they'd been banished to when he'd promised to be the
husband and father that Lauren and their boys deserved.

'Here... I'll hang those clothes up.' He took the damp
bundle from Isobel's arms. 'Have a seat. There's freshly
made tea in the pot. I'm just heating the soup up again.'

It felt weird handling her clothes. Especially those
tights. There were memories trying to surface that he
hadn't allowed to see the light of day for what felt like
for ever. Those intimate memories. How on earth had
he ever convinced himself that that marriage was going

to work? Isobel had been the one he'd been in love with, not her sister.

That was all in the past, of course, but there was nothing like the finality of a funeral to bring things back. To make you remember things that you wished you could go back and do differently. This was a very emotional time for them both, but it had to be far harder for Isobel than for himself.

He sat at one end of the old wooden table, at right angles to Isobel because it seemed less formal than sitting opposite her. He poured himself a mug of tea. Isobel was stirring a spoonful of sugar into hers.

'This is a very nice house,' she said. 'I love kitchens like this.'

She was looking over her shoulder at the length of the room, with this old work table at the same end as the Aga and a comfortable old couch where the dog was blissfully stretched out sound asleep. There was a bench and double sink in the middle, a massive dresser stuffed with crockery beside the door leading to the pantry and a dining area at the other end of the room in front of French windows that led to the garden.

Rafe sipped his tea. 'It works well,' he said. 'I chose it because it would be walking distance to the boys' school when the time came and not far from the medical centre in Harrison Street where I work.'

That surprised her. 'Are you not working in ED now?'

Maybe it was because she widened her eyes that Rafe realised he'd forgotten just how blue they were. He hadn't forgotten it had been the emergency department where they'd first met, however. He looked away.

'Being a GP was far more practical as a single father.' Rafe wasn't about to tell Isobel how hard it had been to give up the high-pressure responsibility of running an emergency department and trauma centre that had been everything to him before his world had been tipped upside down. Instead, he let his breath out in a sigh. 'It's been a long time, Belle. Lots of things have changed.'

She was nodding. 'Of course. You're married again?'

'*What?* No...' As if he'd had the time, or the inclination for that matter, to go looking for another wife. 'What on earth makes you say that?'

Isobel seemed to be finding the colour of her tea interesting. 'I thought that's who Helen is.'

Rafe gave a huff of laughter. 'Helen is my housekeeper and she's old enough to be my mother. She's also a treasure that I couldn't do without. She comes for a couple of hours in the morning and then again after school. She also makes the best soup in the world. Are you hungry?'

Isobel shook her head. 'There's too much I need to know,' she said. 'My stomach feels like it's in too much of a knot to eat anything. But please don't let that stop you having some lunch.'

'I'm okay for a bit.' Rafe took a deep breath. 'Where shall I start? What do you need to know first?'

Isobel shrugged. 'Maybe what actually happened? All I got told was that there was a car accident.'

'There was. On the M25. It was late, dark and in filthy weather which had created surface flooding. I was told that your mother's car was overtaking a lorry. The lorry driver said they just cut back in front of him, too close. There was nothing he could do.'

'I don't understand.' Isobel was shaking her head. 'Mum hated driving on the motorway, especially in the dark. Why was she there?'

'Apparently Lauren had flown into Heathrow from Spain that evening. I guess your mother went to pick her up.'

'*Spain?*'

'That's where she's been living for the last few years.'

'Oh… I didn't know that.'

'No…'

In the silence that followed, he could sense the way Isobel was gathering her courage. She had her hands wrapped around her mug of tea as though the warmth was comforting and she didn't meet his gaze when she spoke again, questions tumbling out.

'But why did she leave in the first place, Rafe? How could she have left her kids? How old is this new baby and who's the father? I don't understand any of this.'

Oddly, seeing the brave set to Isobel's shoulders and the way she pressed her lips together so hard after asking her questions made her seem even more vulnerable. She was preparing to face whatever was coming and he had the power to make that a whole lot harder if he wanted to. To hurt her, perhaps, by telling her that he wished he'd never met any member of her disastrous family?

Except that wasn't entirely true, was it? And hurting her was actually the last thing that Rafe wanted to do. It felt like the urge to protect this woman was resurfacing from where it had been hiding somewhere very deep. It seemed like it hadn't lost any of its strength either.

'You told me something about Lauren once,' he said

quietly. 'That she always got bored when she got what she wanted and then she needed to find something else. She got bored being a wife and mother. She ran off to Spain with her Pilates instructor. That didn't last but she loved the lifestyle there. Maybe she decided to come home because of the baby.' Rafe shrugged. 'I guess she knew her mother would help, no matter how much trouble she was in.'

Isobel's half smile was wry. 'Yeah…that was the way it always worked.'

'So that was when the accident happened. Your mother had gone to the airport to collect Lauren and they never made it home. Your mother died instantly.' Rafe swallowed. 'I'm so sorry, Belle. I know it was never an easy relationship, but that can make things harder in some ways.'

Her head was dipped but it didn't hide the single tear that trickled down the side of her nose. Rafe put his hand over hers and she didn't move away.

'Lauren was badly injured but still alive when the paramedics got there. They airlifted her to the ED at St Luke's but there was no chance of saving her. She had a traumatic injury to her aorta that ended up rupturing. They did everything they could but, in the end, they made the call to try and save her baby and performed a post-mortem Caesarean in the ED.'

'Oh, my God…' Isobel probably didn't realise how hard she was gripping his hand. 'She was *pregnant*? I assumed she'd already had the baby. How far along was she? And was she, I mean, is she…?'

Rafe knew exactly what those unfinished questions were about. Was the baby even likely to survive?

'She seems to be doing well,' Rafe told her. 'She's tiny, of course. They estimated the gestation to be twenty-eight weeks. She weighed one and a half kilos at birth—three and a half pounds—but she's dropped a bit since, which is normal. She was on a ventilator for a few days and is on CPAP now but being weaned off. She'll probably be in the Neonatal ICU until close to what would have been her original birth date, which will be another eight or nine weeks now.'

Isobel seemed to be hanging on every word he was saying, her eyes full of the same conflicting emotions that Rafe had experienced himself ever since he'd learned about the birth of this baby. Horror due to the tragedy surrounding the birth and the risk of it not being successful. Sadness for the tiny, helpless creature who was arriving in the world and having to fight for survival totally alone. But there was hope to be felt as well, because this baby girl *was* fighting and surviving and it was a bit of a miracle.

'There's no sign of any brain bleed, which is always a risk with preemies,' he added. 'She had a scan at seven days which was clear. And the paramedics and ED staff knew they were dealing with a pregnant woman so made keeping her oxygen levels up an absolute priority.'

Isobel was still staring at him. 'What's going to happen to her?'

It was easy to let go of her hand now. All he needed to do was reach for his mug of tea. 'There's plenty of time for decisions to be made. In the meantime, I've taken guardianship because I'm the father of her only known relatives—her half-brothers.'

'So that's why you know so much about her?'

'Yeah. Plus, I'm visiting her every day.'

Isobel was silent for a long moment. He could hear her taking a deep breath. He could almost feel the hesitation, as if she really wanted to know more but didn't want to be involved?

'Does…does she have a name?'

'Not yet. Maybe you'd like to think of one, what with her being your niece?'

Rafe stood up and turned away before he could see her reaction that could well make him feel guilty for reminding her that she *was* involved, whether she liked it or not. Besides, Isobel might not feel like eating but it had been too long since breakfast for him. He went to the Aga and ladled some of the soup into a bowl. Then he cut a thick slice of the sourdough loaf beneath a tea towel on the bread board. He had torn a chunk of bread off to dip into his soup as he turned back to the table.

'Are you sure you wouldn't like to try some? It's really good.'

But Isobel had her face in her hands and she simply shook her head. Rafe could see a faint shudder run through her body which couldn't be due to cold because this room was overheated, if anything, thanks to the stove. It was more likely to be that Isobel was crying. Or trying not to, as she processed a tsunami of highly emotional information.

He put his bowl and slice of bread down on the table, letting his breath out in another sigh. He didn't want to feel this sorry for Isobel. He certainly didn't want to have to grapple with the urge to comfort or protect her. If he was totally honest, he didn't actually want her here, in his home, either.

But there it was. She was here and he was feeling it all, spiced up by being peppered with unavoidable memories.

'Did you sleep on the plane?'

She shook her head again.

'And you've been travelling how long?'

'About sixty hours, give or take, thanks to a big delay at Singapore Airport.'

And she'd had to walk straight into the aftermath of the funeral. It didn't matter how much distance there'd been between Isobel and her mother and sister in the end, they were her family and she had to be devastated at this loss.

Rafe touched her shoulder, waiting for her to look up and confirm what he was thinking.

'You have to sleep,' he told her. 'Doctor's orders. Before you fall over completely. As soon as I've had some lunch, I'm going to go into the hospital to see how our patient is doing and to visit the baby. I'm picking the boys up from school after that but I'll make sure they're not rowdy. You can sleep as long as you need to.'

He could see the irresistible pull that Isobel was feeling towards the prospect of a temporary reprieve. Escape from something so big, she had no idea how to start dealing with it.

Rafe held her gaze. He couldn't summon a smile but perhaps he could make his tone gentle enough to have a similar effect?

'Come on. I'll show you your room.'

# CHAPTER THREE

Isobel slept the clock around. And then she slept some more. Such a deep sleep that she couldn't have roused herself if she'd tried but not deep enough to keep dreams at bay.

Dreams that had no basis in reality, like one in which she was holding a newborn baby, with its umbilical cord trailing, as she ran through a vast house with increasing desperation, trying to find the room where the baby belonged—where it needed to be to survive. And dreams that were too close to reality, where she was back at that fateful hospital Christmas party searching the crowd to find Rafe, who'd promised to be there but he wasn't. Going to his apartment and letting herself in because he'd just given her a key. Finding empty champagne bottles in the living room and finding Rafe in his bedroom...with her sister...

There'd been snatches of that horrible final conversation days after she'd fled that scene.

*'She told me you were with Michael.'*

*'I was with Michael—in Resus—I couldn't leave work on time.'*

*'But I'd seen him yesterday...kissing you.'*

'He had mistletoe. He was kissing everybody.'

'Lauren said you'd moved on. That you were happy we'd broken up.'

'And you believed her?'

'You know why...'

'I'm not your ex-wife, Rafe. What I can't get my head around is that you not only believed her—you went to bed with her!'

'I don't even remember how that happened. It's never going to happen again, that's for sure. I know how stupid it was.'

'It was unforgivable. That's what it was. It's really over now, Rafe. I just wish it had never begun. You know what? You and Lauren deserve each other. Good luck with that...'

Perhaps it was the dream that combined everything—where she was holding newborn twins as she confronted the betrayal of her boyfriend and her own sister—that finally made it possible for Isobel to escape into wakefulness. Even then, she had to lie there for a long time, waiting for her heart rate to settle and the dark cloud of the dream to evaporate completely.

The betrayal had been undeniably crushing but it was all in the past and she'd realised many years ago that looking back was never going to help her move forward, it would probably only trip her up. Yesterday's exhaustion, both emotional and physical, on top of actually being in Rafe's company had made it impossible not to look back, which explained the disturbing dreams, but Isobel *had* moved on and being here was only temporary. She could find a hotel today and get on with sorting the disaster her mother's house had become.

More urgently, she needed to use the en suite bathroom this bedroom provided. Then she had to stare at the screen of her phone for ages, making a considerable mental effort to remember time zones and why it was still completely dark outside, to get her head around the fact that she'd slept for such an unbelievably long time and it was now just after six o'clock in the morning, local time.

Too wide awake now to lie in bed any longer, Isobel got dressed in the same clothes she'd been wearing yesterday afternoon. It was also too long since she'd had a hot drink and the thought of coffee was irresistible. If she was quiet enough, perhaps she could use the kitchen without disturbing anyone else in the house?

The dog was in the kitchen, but he just thumped his tail on the cushions of the couch and went back to sleep. Isobel had never used an Aga but there was an electric jug to boil some water, a jar of instant coffee on the bench and milk in an enormous refrigerator that was stacked with an impressive amount of food. It was the two clear boxes with snap-lock lids that caught her eye on the shelves first, though, because she could see the sandwiches inside them, along with an apple and carrot sticks and what looked like a home-baked biscuit.

School lunches.

Two identical school lunches that belonged to her two identical nephews. Rafe and Lauren's children, Oscar and Josh.

Oh, boy…she needed coffee to stop that mental fog rolling back in to cushion things that she had to face, preferably sooner rather than later. Isobel spooned a generous amount of coffee into a mug she took from a

hook under the first shelf of an old hutch dresser. She
added water and milk and some brown sugar from a
bowl on the table. She intended to add the sugar anyway, but the loaded spoon shook and then emptied itself
onto the table when she heard a small voice behind her,
speaking in a stage whisper.

'That's *her*, isn't it? Belle?'

Oh, help…she wasn't ready for this. Isobel put the
spoon down and started trying to sweep up the sugar
granules in front of her with her hand, pretending not
to have heard anything.

But then there was another voice.

'We know it is, Josh. She's our *aunty*.'

'I know that. Daddy told us. She's Aunty Belle.'

Aunty Belle. Did it sound so natural because it was
so similar to Isobel? It made her smile at any rate, as
she looked towards the door.

'Hey…you must be Oscar and Josh.'

The boys gave up hiding in the hallway and seemed
to explode into the kitchen. The dog leapt off the couch
to greet them.

'But which of us is which?' one of the boys demanded. 'Bet you can't tell.'

Of course she couldn't tell. Not only did they look
identical, she'd never met them before. What she could
tell, instantly, was that these children, in their matching
dinosaur pyjamas, were just gorgeous. They had curly
dark hair and brown eyes like their father but, unlike
Rafe, they had big, welcoming smiles that held no hint
of any reason not to like her.

'You're Josh,' Isobel said confidently.

He looked crestfallen. 'But how did you know?'

'I just guessed,' Isobel confessed. 'I had a fifty per cent chance of being right.'

'You've made a mess.' It was Oscar who was pointing to the table.

'I know.'

'When we make a mess, we're s'posed to clean it up by ourselves.'

Isobel nodded. 'That's a great rule. I was just about to do that.'

The dog was sitting in front of the boys, wagging his tail. And then he barked.

'Cheddar wants his breakfast.'

'Cheddar?'

'He's yellow,' Josh explained kindly. 'Like cheese.'

This time, Isobel didn't only smile, she actually laughed. 'That's a brilliant name. I love it.'

'Will you give him his breakfast?'

'Um… I don't know what he has for breakfast.'

'Biscuits. And a bit of our porridge. Are you going to make our porridge?'

'Um…'

'I have golden syrup on mine,' Oscar told her.

'And I have sprinkles,' Josh added. 'Hundreds and millions. Because they're pretty when you stir them with your spoon.'

'I'm not sure I know where the porridge is,' Isobel said cautiously.

'I'll show you.' Oscar took hold of Isobel's hand.

'No… I'll show her.' Josh took hold of her other hand. 'It was *my* idea that she can make the porridge.'

Cheddar barked again, turning a circle or two before heading towards the pantry, but Isobel wasn't aware of the dog's excitement. The only thing she was aware of was the feeling of those two small hands tugging hers. There seemed to be a direct line between her hands and her heart because she could feel *that* being tugged on too. This was more than simply being charmed by a couple of adorable kids. A whole lot more. Isobel could feel the connection and, as soon as she truly acknowledged it, these boys would be hers. *Her* nephews. Her *family*.

The enormity of the thought was enough to make Isobel freeze and, because Oscar and Josh were still tugging her hands, they lost their grip and turned back in surprise to see what had gone wrong with their plan. Cheddar was also looking back from the door of the pantry, clearly wondering what was taking so long and, for what seemed like a long, long moment, everything stopped—as if the universe was asking Isobel what she was going to do. Take the plunge and invite the twins into her life or take a step back and then flee, like she'd done in the past?

'What on earth is going on in there?' It sounded as if Rafe had only emerged from sleep a few seconds ago. They could all hear the slightly muffled voice coming from the hallway. 'What happened to quiet time until seven o'clock?'

'But Aunty Belle's here, Daddy. She's going to make our porridge,' Josh said.

'She doesn't know about the seven o'clock rule,' Oscar added. 'We only told her about the cleaning up a mess rule.'

Isobel turned her head cautiously as Rafe came into the kitchen, very much hoping he wouldn't be in pyjamas like his sons. He wasn't, but he was still pulling a woollen jersey on and the button on his jeans hadn't been fastened. His hair was rumpled as well and his jaw heavily shadowed.

And, dear Lord…the only thing Isobel could think of was how that overnight stubble used to feel against her skin first thing in the morning…

She looked away instantly. 'I'm sorry if you got woken up,' she said. 'And I do know about the cleaning up rule so I'm about to fix that mess on the table.'

Rafe rubbed his eyes and then moved towards the table. 'Is that instant coffee?' He shook his head. 'I'm guessing you'll be in need of the real stuff this morning. I'll make a pot.' He veered towards the Aga. 'Boys, you can go and get dressed. I'll make your porridge when you come back.'

'But…'

'No "but"s.'

'But, *Daddy*…this "but" is important.'

'Okay.' Rafe put the coffee pot down and crouched, holding his arms out in what looked like a well-rehearsed routine, as one boy nestled within each arm and they both put an arm around Rafe's neck and peered into his face at very close quarters. Isobel had no idea which of the twins was whispering.

'But what if Aunty Belle goes away while we're getting dressed?'

Oh…the anxiety in that question didn't just tug at her heart, it was wrapping itself right round it. There was a new guilt to be found as well. These children were prepared to welcome her into their lives without hesitation and she was suddenly aware of everything she'd missed in the last six years. Those milestones of these babies learning to walk and talk and start school. Rafe looked up to catch her gaze in that instant and she knew that *he* knew exactly what she was thinking. She could guess that he also thought it was no more than she deserved.

'I won't go away, Josh,' she said quietly. 'I promise.'

'I'm Oscar.' The correction was gleeful. 'You got it wrong.'

'Sorry. It might take me a while to make sure I don't get you mixed up.'

'That's okay.' Josh nodded. 'Our grandma used to get it wrong *all* the time.'

'But she's dead now,' Oscar said sadly. 'Like Mummy.'

'And Whistle.' Josh was watching Isobel closely. 'Do you know who Whistle was?'

'No...' Isobel bit her lip. Should she say something about their mother and grandmother? Or go with the flow? 'Um...who *was* Whistle?'

'He was our guinea pig. He whistled. Like—'

'Right...' Rafe's tone was a decisive move to close the conversation. He ruffled the dark curls on both boys' heads. 'Off you go, both of you, and get your school uniforms on.'

The boys went, making odd whistling noises. Isobel bit her lip again but then caught Rafe's gaze and couldn't help a smile emerging, which felt inappropriate given the enormous family loss that had just been mentioned. But Rafe smiled back at her as he straightened and reached for the coffee pot again.

'Never a dull moment round here,' he said. 'And,

to be fair, that was a very good imitation of guinea pig noises.'

Isobel watched for a moment as he measured ground coffee beans into the pot and put it on the Aga. A moment later he had a damp dishcloth in his hands and was deftly wiping up the spilt sugar on the table.

'That's my job,' she said. 'I made the mess.'

'I suspect I've had more practice at this than you,' he countered. 'And this is nothing. Sit down. By the time I've fed Cheddar and got the porridge on, that coffee should be about ready.'

Isobel did what she was told and sat down. 'You do it well,' she told Rafe.

'What? Cleaning up?' He'd scooped the last of the granules into the cloth and was heading towards the sink.

She smiled. 'No. I meant the whole "dad" thing.'

That made Rafe pause. He didn't turn around and his voice was quiet but there could be no mistaking his sincerity. 'Those boys,' he said, 'are the best thing that's ever happened to me.'

He held the cloth under the tap to rinse it and then he squeezed it dry and put it down on the bench. It was only then that he turned and looked directly at Isobel.

'That's why I'm prepared to take on raising their half-sister,' he added, even more quietly. 'If no one else that's part of her family can be found to take it on.'

'Meaning me?'

Rafe simply held her gaze for another heartbeat. Then he stooped to pick up a dog bowl and headed for the pantry with Cheddar on his heels.

'The boys are very excited that you're here. I haven't told them that you might want to go to a hotel today.'

Isobel closed her eyes as she took a breath. She could hear the rattle of kibble being poured into the dog bowl. She could smell the coffee that was coming to the boil on the stove. And, if she thought about it, she could still feel the imprint of those small hands tugging on hers only minutes ago. She could also still sense the crossroads she was standing at, where one direction would let her escape but the other would make those little boys a permanent part of her life—and her heart.

Could Rafe sense her hesitation as he came back out of the pantry?

'You did promise that you wouldn't go away.'

He knew as well as she did that she'd only been reassuring the twins that she wouldn't disappear in the time it took them to get dressed but it seemed that he was also offering her a way to say she'd stay longer without them needing to discuss why either of them might not want that. Maybe it was more than that, in fact. This felt as if Rafe was focusing on the future rather than the past. That he was offering her a second chance? A way to make up for at least part of what she'd missed already?

Isobel swallowed hard. 'I won't go away,' she said softly. 'Not yet, anyway. If…you're really okay with that?'

The dog bowl clattered as Cheddar stuck his nose in and moved it across the wooden floor in his enthusiasm to eat his breakfast but Rafe must have heard her tentative query because he gave a single nod.

'I am okay with that,' he said. 'And the boys will be delighted. This is where you should be. Now, let me get the porridge on and this coffee sorted and then I need to fill you in on what got sorted yesterday with your mother's house. You've got an appointment to meet an insurance assessor later this morning. I'd come with you, but I doubt that I can get away. Our practice nurse got taken to hospital last night with what appears to have been a stroke. Until we can get a replacement, it's going to be a bit chaotic at work.'

'It's not a problem,' Isobel assured him. 'The house is my problem. Thank you very much for getting the ball rolling but I'll take it from here.'

Rafe had arranged for the utilities of water, gas and electricity to be turned off yesterday and he'd contacted Sharon Matthews' solicitor, who'd provided the name of the insurance company.

'You could get a taxi to Barrington Street. Or I could ask Helen to drop you off?'

'It's not that far,' Isobel said. 'A bit of fresh air will be good for me and I should make the most of it not raining. I'll have my car after that. I might drive around and get my bearings again.'

'You could drop into St Luke's if you're in that part of town,' Rafe suggested. 'There are personal things of your mother and Lauren that got collected in ED and it hasn't felt right for me to be the one to pick them up.'

Isobel could understand his reluctance. She found herself thinking that she didn't want to pick them up herself, as she walked towards her mother's house later that morning. Collecting random personal things, like handbags or the last clothes that had been worn, felt like it could well be a lot more challenging than attending the formal ceremony of a funeral. She was still think-ing about the funeral when she saw the curtain twitch on the house next door as she stood on the step finding the key and remembered that Louise had been the only person to acknowledge her presence there, other than Rafe. It was no surprise that her mother's friend was coming up the path by the time she had the door open.

'I saw all the comings and goings yesterday,' Lou-ise said. 'And the plumber's van here so I asked him what he was doing. It's awful, isn't it? As if you don't have enough on your plate as it is. I'm very sorry, love.'

'It's not your fault, Louise. It was a burst pipe.'

'But I didn't notice anything wrong and I'm right next door.'

'I'm glad the water didn't get into your house. It's made an awful mess here. I'm afraid there's going to be a bit of disruption for you when they start fixing it.' Isobel looked into the hallway. 'I'm not even going to go inside until the insurance assessor gets here. It's quite dangerous. The whole living room ceiling is on the point of collapsing.'

'Oh, my goodness… Do you want to come and wait at my place? It's a bit warmer inside.'

'I'm okay. The assessor's due here in a few minutes.'

Louise nodded. She opened her mouth and then closed it again, as if she'd thought better of what she intended to say. And then she tried again. 'I never liked it,' she told Isobel. 'I knew that things weren't going so well for you and your boyfriend, but Lauren had no right to jump in like that and steal him. And when I heard she was pregnant, I knew it was no accident. Not that I could say that to Sharon. Not without ruining our friendship. I didn't blame you, though…for not talking to either of them after that.'

'I don't think boyfriends get stolen unless they want to be,' Isobel said evasively. She really didn't want to get into a blame apportioning discussion. 'But we can't change the past.'

'Aye…true enough. And the future's a mystery. Goodness me, who would have thought that this would happen?'

'Mmm…' Isobel tilted her head to look up the street. Was the insurance assessor running late?

'Your mum was planning to sell this place,' Louise said. 'She was going to go and live in Spain with Lauren. She was right miffed when Lauren said she was coming back here to have her baby. It was the first Sharon knew that she was even pregnant again.'

'Oh?' Isobel wasn't sure she wanted to discuss this with Louise either.

'Well, we all knew she hadn't been able to handle motherhood the first time round with the twins, so why on earth was she doing it again? Your mother didn't enjoy helping with the twins either. Said she "couldn't be bothered with babies at her stage in life".'

Isobel was watching someone park a car further up the street but she was thinking about the twins. About how adorable they were. About that picture of them she'd carried in her wallet for so long. How could anyone have not wanted to 'be bothered'? Rafe had been bothered. He'd said that the twins were the best thing that had ever happened to him. And the palpable bond between them had been striking. The way they'd wrapped their arms around their dad's neck to discuss the important 'but'. Did her mother ever think about what she might have been missing out on?

'Why didn't Mum want to have anything to do with her grandsons?' she asked Louise. 'After Lauren had left?'

Louise seemed to be watching the man who was now getting out of his car. He had a clipboard in his hands.

'It was all very awkward. And Sharon really couldn't cope with trying to help with two babies at the same time. And then they got old enough to talk and would ask her when their mummy was coming back or if she still loved them and that made her feel guilty, I suppose. She saw them sometimes. For their birthdays. She usually went to Spain for Christmas. She loved the sunshine in winter.'

'She would have known Lauren's partner, then? The baby's father?'

'Oh, no…' Louise made a tutting sound. 'I don't think even Lauren knew who that was. Or, if she did, she never told her mother. She worked as a barmaid and loved living the high life. There was a new boyfriend every few weeks as far as I heard.'

*She got bored…and then she needed to find something else…*

But her sister had decided to keep her baby. Had she finally realised how lonely her lifestyle was? Had she wanted to come back to England to be part of a family? To be with her sons again, even?

'Hi. Are you Isobel?' The man had reached the gate.

'Yes.'

'I'm Colin. From Sure Shield Insurance? I'm here to assess the damage from the flooding.'

'I'd better leave you to it.' Louise patted Isobel's arm. 'Just knock if you want a chat any time, dear. I'm always at home.'

And probably lonely. She was going to miss having her friend next door. Isobel smiled at the older woman. 'I'll let you know what's happening with the house as soon as I know myself.'

With the first shock of having seen the damage in her mother's house over, Isobel found she was noticing far more personal items today as she went through with Colin, the insurance assessor, and her reaction only confirmed that it might be confronting to go and collect those personal items from the hospital.

Just seeing a pair of reading glasses and a novel on a cluttered bedside table brought a wave of sadness that was unbelievably deep. Her mum had loved getting lost in a romantic fantasy. The small photograph beside the lamp, of her mother and Lauren, looked like it had been taken in Spain and it hammered home how little Isobel had known of their lives in recent years. Had this been taken at Christmastime? She could imagine them both having such a good time, eating tapas and flirting outrageously with any man willing to play. Had she been more jealous than she'd ever admitted of the close relationship her sister had had with their mother? And could that have been as damaging to the fabric of family as Lauren's jealousy of everything Isobel had had in her life? Like her career? Like Rafe?

She could throw some confusion in with the guilt and grief now. She turned away from the photograph to follow the assessor out of the room.

'Not so bad up here,' he was saying. 'The main damage is downstairs, of course. Bit of mould happening, though. Nasty stuff. It'll all have to be thrown out. Carpets, wallpaper, curtains. Probably the mattresses in these bedrooms as well.'

Isobel followed him into the smaller upstairs bedrooms that had been hers and Lauren's. Her old room was completely bare of any childhood memories but there was a shelf in Lauren's that held a few old toys, including a small, soft hand-knitted teddy bear that had originally been Isobel's. A slightly misshaped bear that had oddly short limbs and one ear much larger than the other, but Lauren had wanted it and Isobel, at about the age that Josh and Oscar were now, had only hesitated for a heartbeat before giving it to the baby sister she'd adored. Without thinking, grownup Isobel took the bear from the shelf and tucked it into her shoulder bag as she followed the assessor downstairs.

'I've done a few of these jobs,' he told her. 'There's a process to go through. First up, we'll get the rest of the water pumped out and then one of our specialist cleaning contractors will come through. Everything water-damaged will get thrown out and they can clear anything else you don't want. This is an estate clearance as well, yes? You're planning to sell the place?'

'Yes.'

'You'll need to come and get anything you want to keep before the cleaners get started then.'

'Okay.'

'The next step is stripping the house—downstairs, for sure and the bathroom upstairs. The floorboards will have to be replaced—maybe the subfloor as well.

The wall coverings have to come off too, so that the studs get a chance to dry out, otherwise you'll end up having big problems down the track. And that living room ceiling's got to go pronto, if it hasn't fallen down by itself before the builders get in.'

'How long is it going to take?'

'Weeks. Especially at this time of year. You can't leave damp anywhere because it's just a health hazard. Nobody would want to buy the house if it's not done properly. And drying it out is just the start. After that, it has to get rebuilt and that can take even longer, depending on how busy our building contractors happen to be. Sorry, it's not going to be a quick fix. This is going to take months.'

Isobel was thinking about the complications this was going to cause. She'd taken a single month's leave from her job in New Zealand, thinking that would be more than enough time to clean out the house and put it on the market, but it felt as if the walls of a trap were closing around her now. How could she leave before things were sorted here? But how could she stay for that long? Even Rafe, with his firm ideals about supporting an extended family member, would be justifiably daunted by that prospect but she couldn't afford a hotel on top of keeping up the rent on her apartment in New Zealand.

'At least it's covered by the insurance,' the assessor said. 'It would cost a fortune otherwise. I'll keep you posted, yes? Might be best to leave it a few days before coming to get what you want out of the place.'

Isobel could feel the lump of the teddy bear in her bag under her arm. 'I don't think I want anything,' she said quietly. 'It might be better if the cleaning company just sorts it out.'

The assessor gave her a curious glance. 'I'll get in touch anyway. You might change your mind.'

Isobel did change her mind once she was in her rental car and turning onto one of Balclutha's main roads. Not about searching the house for keepsakes but about picking up her mother's and sister's Patient's Property bags from St Luke's Hospital. She decided she might as well get the worst things out of the way on the same day. It wasn't as if she had to open the bags straight away, after all.

The route to the hospital was easy to remember and brought other memories along with it. How excited had she been, after graduating from her nursing degree to get a job at Balclutha's most prestigious hospital? And then to end up working in the emergency department, which was a dream come true, especially after she'd moved into her own tiny apartment in the nurses' accommodation block near the hospital.

Lauren had been so envious of her independence, although not enough to move away from being waited on hand and foot by a doting mother. She'd envied the exciting job Isobel had too, but her attempt to follow her sister's career choice became unstuck when she failed her first set of Health Science exams at university. She'd never been able to stand the sight of blood anyway. Becoming a receptionist at the hospital's main entrance had been a much better fit for someone who was happy to talk to anyone and could charm them all.

They'd been so very different, but Isobel had truly

loved her sister and made allowances for any shortcomings. Until that last, unforgivable incident. She'd never intended the estrangement to become permanent, however. She'd gone away for Christmas that year and then arranged a transfer to a London hospital, a few hours' drive away. It was the news that Lauren was pregnant that rubbed salt into an unhealed wound. And then, much later, after the twins had been born, that wedding invitation had been enough to send her as far away as she could get—without leaving a forwarding address.

But the blame couldn't be laid purely on one side of the equation, could it? Lauren had been at least partially justified in her denial that she'd broken up Isobel and Rafe's relationship because they'd broken up weeks ago, hadn't they? Maybe she'd also been correct in suggesting that it was just wishful thinking on Isobel's part that Rafe was going to realise how much he was missing her and change his mind about the breakup. She needed to get over it and move on, her mother had chipped in. All Lauren had done was to help her see that Rafe wasn't the man for her.

And, while Isobel might have done what she felt she had to do to protect herself at the time, had she gone too far, for too long? The love that had once been there for her mother and her sister hadn't disappeared, it had just been buried beneath layers of hurt and anger. The finality of knowing she could never do anything to even try to put things right was making the waves of grief unbearable and Isobel found herself in the hospital car park, with her head resting on her hands on the steering wheel, sobbing uncontrollably for a long time.

No wonder Rafe was less than impressed with her,

she decided, when emotional exhaustion began muting any grief and her tears finally began to dry up. She didn't much like the person she seemed to have become herself. Things had always seemed so black and white, and she'd considered herself to have been the only one who'd been betrayed, but it wasn't really that simple, was it? Rafe had been betrayed by his ex-wife before his time with Isobel and he'd made it very clear he wasn't looking for a permanent, committed relationship with her but she hadn't been able to keep hiding how much in love with him she was so it shouldn't have come as a shock that he'd backed off.

He'd been betrayed again when Lauren had walked out with another man, from not only their marriage but her own children. He'd done the 'right thing' all along though, hadn't he? He'd ended the relationship as gently as possible with the woman who'd wanted more than he was able to give. He'd married the woman who'd accidentally become pregnant by him. He was raising his sons alone—and doing a damn good job of that, from what Isobel had seen. He was even prepared to raise the boys' half-sister.

A baby who was here—in this hospital's Neonatal Intensive Care Unit—without any family around her. Without even a name.

Isobel wiped the last tears from her face and gathered her coat and bag to get out of the car. A new thought was gaining traction in both her head and her heart. Maybe it wasn't too late to try and put something right, after all. As she reached the main entrance of the hospital it almost felt as if Rafe was watching her and Isobel knew he would approve of what she was planning to do. There was a tiny gleam of warmth to be found there. Not because it had once been so important to win his approval. This was more to do with how Isobel felt about herself. About her own need to do the 'right thing'.

Because she'd changed her mind again. She wasn't going to go and find the bags of personal property that would be in safe keeping somewhere in the basement of St Luke's. She was going to go to the NICU.

To meet her niece.

# CHAPTER FOUR

*Baby Tanner*

THAT WAS THE name above the incubator Isobel was led to in the NICU, having introduced herself to the staff on duty.

'You're her aunt? Oh…that's fabulous.' They had welcomed her appearance. 'We were starting to wonder if we'd ever discover a family member for our wee Button.'

'Not that Dr Tanner hasn't been amazing,' another nurse put in. 'But it's a big ask for him to take centre stage. Nobody's been able to track down even a hint of who the father might be and we knew that you were the only relative on Mum's side. We weren't sure you even knew about the birth, though.'

'I didn't,' Isobel admitted. 'Not until yesterday.'

'You're here now, that's what matters. Let's get you a gown and mask and some hand sanitiser and you can come and meet your niece. She's a little miracle as far as we're concerned—the only baby we've ever had who's been born after…'

Her voice trailed away and Isobel could feel the wave

of sympathy from everyone in this central desk area of the Neonatal Intensive Care Unit.

'We're so sorry for your loss,' someone said quietly.

A pager bleeped and one of the doctors moved away swiftly. A nurse responded to the quiet but insistent sound of a nearby monitoring alarm going off and a parent came to ask for assistance from another staff member. It was an older nurse, Brenda, who took Isobel to one of the closest positions to the central desk, where Baby Tanner's incubator was in direct sight at all times.

'We all try to spend as much time as possible with her,' Brenda said, 'but it gets too busy so she still has too much time alone. She's touched everyone's hearts here, that's for sure.'

Isobel nodded, her gaze fixed on the tiny baby in front of her. There were heart-shaped patches sticking heart monitoring electrodes in place, nasal cannula taped to her face delivering oxygen and IV lines under bandages. The baby seemed to be awake and, distressingly, seemed to be less than happy. A tiny hand waved in the air, sticklike little legs were trying to kick and her mouth was open although no sound was being made. The squeeze in Isobel's chest made it hard to take a breath.

'She's not in pain, is she?' Isobel asked.

Brenda was checking all the screens surrounding the incubator. 'I don't think so. Nothing's changed in the last hour and if she was in pain I'd expect her heart rate and blood pressure to have gone up. We have all been too rushed to have anyone sitting with her for a while though. Maybe she's lonely, which means you've timed your visit perfectly.' She smiled at Isobel and gestured towards the comfortable recliner chair that was beside the incubator. 'Take a seat. I'll have a word with her consultant and see if it's okay for her to come out of the incubator for you to hold her for a bit.'

Someone was pushing a trolley past them. 'Brenda, have you got a minute? I could do with some help.'

'Will you be okay?' Brenda asked. 'I'll come back as soon as I can,' she added as Isobel nodded. 'In the meantime, you can put your hand through one of the holes and hold hers, if you like.'

Isobel sank onto the edge of the chair. She hadn't expected to be allowed anything more than a peep at this fragile newborn baby and to perhaps be allowed to leave the little teddy bear she had in her bag somewhere nearby, if not at the foot of the incubator's mattress. She certainly wouldn't have asked to touch the baby, let alone hold her, and she hesitated now, even though she'd been given permission. Maybe part of her knew that touching this infant would make it all more real somehow. That she would be stepping forward to play her part in this tiny human's future. To take responsibility even?

After the emotional release of her heartbroken crying in the car, Isobel was too drained to think about something so huge and maybe, if it hadn't looked as if the baby was trying, and failing, to cry, Isobel might have resisted the urge to touch her for more than a minute or two. But, with everyone so busy around her, it felt as if she was the only one who could offer comfort. More than that, she wanted to be able to comfort this baby who had, as far as anyone could ever know, been born an orphan.

Isobel put her hand in through the access port, reaching out gently with a single fingertip to touch the miniature hand lying palm up on the mattress. Almost instantly, those impossibly tiny fingers closed and Isobel could feel the warmth and a surprising strength in the grip. What was even more surprising and just as instantaneous was the feeling that it wasn't just her finger being held. Her heart was also well and truly caught.

This was more than the invitation to be part of their lives that the twins had unknowingly given her this morning when they'd been tugging on her hands. This was…just there. And this wasn't going to be a case of choosing whether or not she took responsibility for this baby, because that was just there as well. The logistics might prove to be complicated and overturn her life completely but there was no way Isobel could walk away from this—something that the grip of those tiny fingers was telling her was the most important thing that had ever happened in her life.

When the neonatal specialist came to talk to her a short time later, Isobel had only one urgent question about the care of her niece.

'What can I do to help?'

Rafe Tanner checked his watch as he left the cardiology ward and then took the stairs up instead of down. If he was quick, he could pop in to see the baby before heading home at the end of an overly busy day.

Seeing the screens around the incubator was alarming because that usually meant some kind of potentially serious intervention was going on but, as he paused to rub sanitiser gel onto his hands, he caught the eye of

a nurse who was busy with another baby and was re-
assured. Brenda's smile, in fact, suggested that things
were better than simply good. She even gave him a
quick 'thumbs up' signal.

And what he found behind the screens a moment
later was nothing like he had expected. There were no
medical staff in this space and no procedures happening. There was also no baby in the incubator. There was,
however, someone sitting in the reclining chair with her
feet up, a blanket draped around her body and a look on
her face that made Rafe catch his breath.

'I'm doing kangaroo care,' Isobel whispered.

*Wow…*

Just…wow…

Rafe couldn't say anything yet. He moved to the side
of the big chair and crouched down, resting his elbows
on its padded arms, and then he stayed there, completely
still for the longest time, just getting his head around
so many unexpected things.

Isobel was wearing a hospital gown, opened at the
front, and the baby was nestled between her breasts,
on her bare skin, the soft blanket covering them both
for warmth. It was the first time Rafe had seen this
tiny baby out of the incubator and she seemed smaller
but somehow less fragile. She was asleep and the soft,
steady beeping of the monitors was evidence that her
heart and respiration rates, blood pressure and the oxygen saturation in her blood were well within desired
parameters. Even without any of that technology, however, Rafe would have known that this baby was calm
and contented.

So was Isobel. Perhaps it was because she was wearing a mask that her eyes seemed so much more expressive. Or maybe it was what he was seeing in them. Catching and holding her gaze over the tiny head in its little woollen hat, he could almost feel the connection she had found with the baby and it reminded him of the kind of overwhelming feelings he'd had when he'd held his newborn twins for the first time.

It also reminded him of the way he'd begun to feel within such a short time of becoming very close to Isobel Matthews. When he'd begun to wonder how sure he really was that he could never truly trust another woman. Or that there was no such thing as love at first sight…

It had been a new kind of love in his life when the boys arrived, however. One that gave him so much joy and kept him busy enough that he could ignore any disturbing reminders that he might be missing out on something else that was just as important. The thing he'd lost when Isobel walked out of his life?

It was Isobel who finally broke that eye contact and it felt as if she'd been reluctant to do so. Her breath hitched as she drew it in.

'I asked what I could to help,' she said softly. 'And the doctor told me that this was the best thing I could do. It can stabilise heart rate and breathing and improve oxygen saturation. Research is suggesting that it can even have a positive effect on brain development that shows up when they're older.'

Rafe nodded. 'I've read about it. It didn't occur to me to offer though. I guess I thought it was too early for her to be held yet.'

'I'm just doing it for an hour today, but it can be more

than that. I could do several hours a day by next week, if she's well. And if I want to.'

Rafe swallowed what felt like a lump in his throat. 'Do you? Want to?'

Isobel was looking down at the baby's head and she was blinking rapidly as if trying to prevent tears gathering but she was nodding at the same time. 'Looks like I'm stuck here for a while. The insurance assessor told me it will take weeks to even dry out the house before any repair work can start.'

'Oh…'

Rafe watched the exquisite gentleness with which Isobel was cupping the baby's head with her hand and he could feel an odd sensation in his gut, as if a knot the same size as that head was forming—and being held. He wasn't sure whether it was a pleasant sensation or something to be concerned about. A warning, even? When Isobel glanced up, he could see a question in her eyes as well and he realised that this was new ground for both of them.

Maybe it could be a completely new start?

'That's good,' he added. 'I mean, it will be wonderful for this little one.' He dropped his gaze to the baby. 'And it will be great for Oscar and Josh.' Again, he had to swallow hard. He didn't know what to say about how he felt about it himself and he suspected that Isobel had the same kind of internal conflict going on. But he needed to say something. 'It's good,' he repeated. 'It's…good to see you again, Belle.'

And it was, now that the first shock had worn off. It would be good to be able to put the past behind them, if that was possible. To forgive, if not exactly forget.

She didn't look up. They were both keeping their gazes firmly on the baby and Isobel said nothing for a long moment. Then she cleared her throat quietly.

'I've thought of a name,' she said.

'What's that?'

The baby moved her head when Isobel lifted her hand. Her tiny arm stretched out towards Rafe and he touched her hand as he'd done many times through the access port on the incubator. As always, her tiny fingers curled around his and gave him that overpowering wave of connection. Maybe it was because she was lying on Isobel's skin that made it feel as if the connection was travelling via that tiny body to include Isobel as well. She was always going to be a part of his life, wasn't she?

'She's so small and delicate,' Isobel said. 'It made me think of holding a flower and being careful not to bruise a petal or stem. And my favourite flower has always been a daisy. What do you think? Could we call her Daisy?'

What did he think?

He could see that Isobel was smiling behind her mask by the way those crinkles appeared by her eyes. His first thought, however, was a memory of a picnic on a lazy late-summer Sunday afternoon when he was lying on a grassy hill with her. When he was becoming aware that he was falling in love with her but hadn't defined what that feeling was. In that delicious space of time before the alarm bells began ringing loudly enough to be impossible to ignore. He'd idly started picking daisies from the grass that day, making a chain to rest on Isobel's sunshine-coloured curls.

*'Daisies are absolutely my favourite flowers. I love them so much...'*

Her eyes had told him that she loved him even more than daisies and the sun had been shining and, for just a few wonderful minutes, he'd never been so happy in his life. He'd kissed her. So slowly it had made time stand still. And when the world had started turning again, before he remembered what it was like to have your heart broken and convinced himself that he had to get away before it could happen to him again, he'd kissed her a second time, even more slowly...

His voice was raw when he found some words.

'I think that's a great name.'

Oscar and Josh also thought it was a great name when Rafe told them as they were eating dinner that evening.

'She's our sister, isn't she?'

'Half-sister.'

'What's a half-sister?'

'It means that Daisy has the same mummy but a different daddy.'

'Why aren't *you* her daddy? You're our daddy.'

Isobel caught the long blink that suggested Rafe was finding this line of questioning from his sons difficult.

'Because Mummy hasn't lived with us for a long, long time. So I couldn't be Daisy's daddy, could I?'

Surprisingly, it didn't seem to cause the children any distress to be reminded that their mother had abandoned them years ago. It was simply a fact of life. Was that because it had happened when they were so young they had no memories of Lauren? While it was an acceptable answer, however, it wasn't the end of the questions.

'Where's she going to sleep?'

'She has to stay in the hospital for a while, Josh. She was born too early so she's very, very little.'

'But when she comes home, where's she going to sleep?'

'She can be in our room,' Oscar suggested.

'That's very kind,' Rafe said. 'But I think your room is quite full with both you boys in it and all those toys.'

'She can be in Aunty Belle's room then.'

Was Rafe deliberately avoiding catching Isobel's gaze?

'Eat your beans up,' he said. 'Green things are good for you.'

'I don't like beans.'

'I don't like anything green.' Josh was backing his brother up. 'Do you like green things, Aunty Belle?'

'Green things are my favourite,' she told them. This was good. They had moved away from the subject of where Daisy was going to sleep, which was too big to even think about today. Especially now, only hours after she'd had that tiny baby sleeping right on top of her heart—and when jetlag was hitting all over again and Isobel knew she would probably need to go to bed at the same time these six-year-old boys did.

'Beans, broccoli, spinach,' she added. 'They're all my favourites.' She picked up a bean with her fingers and ate it with a smile to demonstrate how much she liked green things. The boys shared an open-mouthed glance and then grinned at their father.

'Aunty Belle didn't use her fork.'

'Mmm…' Rafe seemed just as relieved that the subject had been changed. 'I guess she knows that eating beans is more important than the way you put them in your mouth.'

The twins shared another glance and grin. And then they both picked up a bean with their fingers and ate it. Rafe shared a glance with Isobel and the corner of his mouth twitched as he suppressed a smile.

'When you've finished your beans, you can have half an hour of television while I clean up and then I'm going to hear your reading homework, okay?'

'Can't Aunty Belle hear our reading homework?'

'Not tonight,' Rafe said firmly. 'She's tired, aren't you, Belle?'

Had he been aware of how much effort it had been to stay awake enough to eat the delicious dinner that Helen the housekeeper had left keeping warm in the Aga? Or was he hoping she'd go to her room early so that he could relax with his sons like any normal evening?

She wasn't about to rush off, however, because she'd remembered something she should probably have told Rafe earlier, but she needed to wait until two small boys were out of earshot.

'I spoke to Mum's neighbour today, when I was at the house,' she told him as she carried plates to where he was stacking the dishwasher. 'They've been friends ever since I was a kid and told each other everything. She said that Lauren never said anything about Daisy's father. That she might not have actually known who it was herself.'

The implication that there could be a choice of men in his ex-wife's life didn't seem to surprise Rafe.

'Yeah... The police made some enquiries at the bar where Lauren was working. Nobody could remember

who she was with around the time she would have become pregnant and there were more than a few one-
night stands.' He was bent over, fitting cutlery into the
tray on the bottom shelf of the dishwasher. 'I guess she
never found what she was looking for, which is kind of
a sad way to go through life, isn't it?'

He straightened and took a plate from Isobel's hands.

'I would never have chosen to marry Lauren,' he said
quietly. 'I was being completely honest with you when I
said I never wanted to get married again. Or have kids.
But she told me that if I didn't marry her, I'd never see
the twins. That my name wouldn't even be on the birth
certificate. I grew up without a father in my own life.
My mother told me he was dead but when I was about
ten I found out she'd lied to me—he just hadn't wanted
me.' Rafe put the plate in the rack and then met Isobel's
gaze as he reached for another one. 'I've never forgotten that first taste of feeling rejected. Betrayed, even,
and the thought of that happening to my own children
was unacceptable. It was just after they were born. Just
after I'd held them for the first time...'

Oh... Isobel knew what that was like. How a newborn baby could capture you, heart and soul, with a
connection that would be there until you took your last
breath. Daisy had done that to her today and she wasn't
even this infant's mother. Imagine how much more powerful it could be if it was your own children, even if
you'd believed you never wanted them? How you could
not fall instantly in love and be prepared to do whatever
it took not to lose them?

Rafe was holding the plate in her hands now, but Isobel hadn't let go of it. It almost felt as if Rafe was holding her hands—the way he was also holding her gaze.

'I never wanted to marry your sister.' The words were no more than a murmur. 'You were the one I loved, Belle.'

# CHAPTER FIVE

WORDS.

That was all they were.

Only a very few of them, in fact, so how was it that they could have the effect of a bomb going off in your life?

*We need to stop seeing each other...*

*You slept with my sister...*

*She's pregnant. It's twins...*

*You were the one I loved, Belle...*

They'd never actually used the 'L' word in the time they'd been together but Isobel had been convinced it had been hanging in the air between them for days. Ever since that gorgeous picnic on the hill when he'd crowned her with a daisy chain. She had to wait for Rafe to say it first, though. And even then she'd known she would have to give him all the time and space he needed to be able to trust the idea of a future together. To change his mind, even, about the commitment that marriage could bestow? She'd been happy to wait. She'd wanted to be sure it was safe, herself, before opening that portal to a future that was glowing with the potential for life to be everything she could have dreamed of.

Would it have made a difference if Isobel had managed to get to that fateful Christmas party and had said something to Rafe that night? If she'd told him how desperately she was missing him? That he was the person she wanted to be with for the rest of her life?

Would it make a difference now?

Yes.

Isobel's body clearly thought so as she lay, sleepless, in her bed later that night, aware of the tingling sensation that was coming from somewhere in her gut and spreading into her limbs—almost like the first hint of the 'pins and needles' that signalled a compressed nerve starting to function again to bring a foot or hand back to life—only this was surely far more emotional than physical. Was it excitement coming back to life?

Hope…?

How she'd escaped the kitchen without responding to Rafe's extraordinary confession was a bit of a blur but she could remember jetlag being mentioned despite her head spinning so much she couldn't think straight. The twins' competition to be first for a goodnight cuddle was easy to remember too, because it had almost knocked her off her feet, made Cheddar bark with loud approval of this new game and earned a reprimand for everyone from Rafe.

The house was quiet now. She could imagine Cheddar asleep on the old couch in the kitchen. Perhaps the twins were also asleep, or was Rafe in their bedroom reading them a story with a son snuggled in on each side of his body? She could imagine peeping through a bedroom door to see that as well. Maybe some of that tingling had reached her brain now as well, because it was more than willing to run with that image and let her imagine that she was the mother of those children. That Rafe would finish the story, tuck sleepy boys into their beds and then come to find *her*. It then deftly skipped the mundane part of any evening parental chores that might have needed doing after that and got straight to the part where he took her to *their* bed.

It wasn't even fantasy after that. There were buried but unforgotten memories of exactly what it had been like to be in Raphael Tanner's bed. How he could look at you as if no other woman had ever existed. How he could touch—and taste—your skin as if it was the most delicate and delicious thing ever created. How he could take you to the brink of ecstasy and just hold you there to build the anticipation to a point where the climax took you to a place where time and location had no meaning. All that there was in that timeless space was how close you were to this man you loved so much.

How perfect it felt…

Oh, *help*… Isobel rolled onto her side, seeking a softer patch on her pillow and hoping that her brain might realise how badly her body needed sleep and switch off so that it could happen some time very soon.

Why had he said that?

Did he still have feelings for her?

Did she *want* him to still have feelings for her?

Yes.

No.

He'd betrayed her. With her *sister*. It would have been quite bad enough knowing that he'd made love to any other woman but for it to have been Lauren…well, there was no coming back from that because it had touched something so deep it felt as if it had been there for ever. Lauren had always been the favourite. More special because she had been born after their father had died. So much prettier with her platinum shade of shiny, straight blonde hair rather than the messy, dark gold riot of curls that Isobel had and eyes that were a much paler shade of blue. That smile could get her anything she wanted and that ability to capture and hold the attention of those around her and simply…bring joy, that was what it had been. Isobel had loved her butterfly of a sister as much as anyone, until she'd taken something she knew she would never be able to find again.

The ability to believe that she wasn't second best. That the man she'd fallen so completely and utterly in love with had wanted to be with her because *she* was the special one. Because he loved *her*. And she'd known he had loved her. She'd seen it in his eyes when he'd put that crown of daisies on her head. Just before he'd kissed her senseless. And, okay, he'd backed off but she'd been so sure that he was missing her as much as she was missing him. He'd looked so miserable at work, despite the anticipation of Christmas festivities. When he'd asked if she was going to the party, she'd been sure that there was every chance they would be together again by the end of the evening.

Now she knew that Rafe had never been in love with Lauren. He wouldn't have chosen to marry her if he hadn't been blackmailed. That the marriage to protect his right to be a father to his newborn children had only lasted a matter of months.

That *she* was the woman he'd loved.

And a part of Isobel knew—a big part that was currently the obstacle to her falling asleep—that everything was shifting. Changing. Puzzle pieces had been thrown into the air and she could see them floating.

Maybe it was a combination of jetlag and the trauma of major loss in her life. Or perhaps it was a form of procrastination because she wasn't ready to seriously consider the daunting responsibility she would be taking on if she stepped up to raise Daisy. It could even be that this was a process of finally dealing with things she had avoided confronting for far too long, like the complex family dynamics she had grown up with but, whatever the emotional alchemy that was going on, Isobel could see the possibility that, if she allowed it to happen, those puzzle pieces could settle and form an image that might be eerily similar to the future she'd dreamed about long ago.

He shouldn't have said that.

Things were already complicated enough without dredging up something from the past that was best left buried. How much more awkward was it going to be to have Isobel in his house now?

At least she seemed to be sleeping later this morning and Rafe avoided any awkwardness by leaving the house the moment Helen arrived to look after the boys and get them to school. He was well on the way to Harrison Street Medical Centre by the time he realised he'd left his phone on the kitchen bench but he didn't turn around. The phone had been on the bench because he'd received a text to let him know that the temporary practice nurse who'd worked with them yesterday was not coming back for a second day and, unless the agency could find someone else in a hurry, it meant they would all be under enough extra pressure to make things potentially chaotic. Even a small head start on his working day was too valuable to sacrifice.

It should have also meant that Rafe would have no head space to consider that ill-advised confession he'd made to Isobel when they'd been clearing the table last night. As soon as he stepped into his consulting room, he got on with the urgent admin tasks that were already piling up. There were blood and pathology test results coming in, discharge summaries and specialists' reports to read and prescriptions to sign that would be being collected from reception as soon as the doors opened at nine o'clock for morning surgeries. He only had half an hour before he needed to take telephone triage for calls requesting same-day appointments so this was quite likely to be the least stressful time of his day. Perhaps that was why errant thoughts were able to sneak into the back of his mind in between his focus on a report or when he was waiting for the printer to spit out a new batch of prescriptions to sign.

He really shouldn't have told Isobel that he'd loved her but not her sister. He *wouldn't* have said it, if he hadn't been on what felt like an uncontrollable emotional rollercoaster ever since he'd seen her with that tiny premature baby nestled between her breasts. The baby she'd chosen to call Daisy. And the kind of expression on her face that he knew meant that she was in love.

The way she had once been in love with him…

He'd known that, even if she hadn't said anything, by the way she'd looked at him. By the way she'd touched him. But it had been vital for it to remain unspoken because he'd needed to be able to trust it. To let his own barriers down enough to not only accept that he felt the same way but to find the courage to take the risk of a commitment that could shape the rest of his life.

It would have been a daunting prospect for any man, let alone someone who'd already done it once only to have been betrayed in such a devastating fashion. That blow had come completely out of left field many years ago now. His wife had not only been having an affair with a colleague for the entirety of their marriage, she was leaving him because the baby she was carrying was not his.

He had found that courage, though. Just pushing Isobel away had been enough to make him realise how much he did want her in his life and he'd been going to tell her that at the Christmas party.

Did Lauren telling him that he was too late—that Belle had already moved on to a colleague—excuse what had happened after that?

No. Of course it didn't.

He hadn't blamed Isobel for hating him for what had happened but he had largely managed to bury it, the way he'd chosen to leave behind the total failure of both his marriages. It was hardly surprising that the shocking events of the last few weeks, with the tragic accident, Daisy's birth, the funeral and seeing Isobel again was stirring up everything he'd thought he'd left behind.

What Rafe wanted, more than anything else right now, was to simply go back to what had become his life as a hard-working GP and a devoted dad to his two boys. He could at least try to make that happen for the next several hours, as he focused on the patients who needed his help.

Like Susan Sugden, the young mother who was on the other end of the first telephone triage call he picked up. He could hear her productive cough over the phone and her symptoms, that included uncontrollable shivering and an episode of coughing up blood, sounded worrying.

'It sounds like this has become more than just the cold that's going around,' he told her. 'Can you come into the surgery or do you need a home visit?'

'I can come in. I've got to get the older kids to school, anyway, so it's on my way home.' Susan sounded exhausted. 'Mum's got her yoga class this morning so she's not helping with the school run today.'

By the time Susan arrived for her urgent appointment, it was clear that the potential for chaos had become reality. It was only half past nine but every chair in the waiting room was occupied and there was a small queue waiting for the attention of their receptionist. Rafe's colleagues were all busy with consultations already and Susan was looking pale and unwell enough for alarm bells to ring. On top of that, the toddler in the stroller she was pushing had flushed cheeks and a runny nose and could well end up being an unexpected extra patient. This wasn't the time to think about the inevitable tension that would ramp up with increased waiting times for everyone else, however.

'Come this way, Susan. And…is it Dylan?'

'Yes. He's got this horrible cold as well… It's been through…the whole family now… I just can't seem to shake it…'

His patient's broken sentences were an indication of how short of breath she was and Rafe's rapid assessment of other vital signs had him heading back to the reception desk only minutes later. The queue had been dealt with but there was another person coming through the door. Rafe stepped close enough to keep his conversation with the receptionist as private as possible.

'Deb, could you please call for an ambulance? I need to send Susan Sugden through to hospital. Get hold of her mum too—the number will be her emergency contact on her file. We'll need her to come and look after Dylan.'

'Sure.' As Rafe turned away Deb was opening a window on her computer that would give her the information she needed. 'I'll be with you in just a moment,' he heard her say to the new arrival.

'No problem. I just need to leave this for Dr Tanner.'

Rafe swung back. 'Isobel...what on earth are you doing here?'

'You forgot your phone.' She held it out. 'I thought you might need it.'

'Thanks...' He reached out to take it. This was disconcerting enough to add a new level to the tension in this crowded space. There was a baby howling in its mother's arms, an elderly gentleman talking very loudly on his phone, a pre-school child throwing toys out of the playpen in the corner and someone holding a plastic bag in front of their face as though they were about to be sick. Isobel didn't seem fazed by the chaos but her eyes did widen as someone rushed towards the reception desk from the direction of the consulting rooms, her baby in her arms.

'Dr Tanner? It's Dylan…he woke up coughing and… and now he can't breathe…'

The toddler was in Isobel's arms by the time Rafe got to the other side of the desk. He could hear the harsh sounds of stridor and wheezing which were warning signs that an airway was getting dangerously obstructed. He could also see the way Isobel was holding the child upright in a cuddle and calming him by her soothing tone and he was instantly reminded of how good she'd been with paediatric patients in the emergency department when they'd worked together. Always calm and capable and caring and the kids had seemed to recognise that. She'd been the nurse everyone wanted for their youngest patients.

'Hey, Dylan…let's get you feeling better, sweetheart…' She looked up as Rafe got closer. 'Where's your treatment room?'

'This way…' Rafe didn't try and take Dylan from her arms. Creating any more anxiety would only add to his respiratory distress and could potentially turn a serious situation into a life-or-death emergency.

'Is there any chance of this being a foreign body obstruction?'

'No.' Rafe followed Isobel into the treatment room, a hand on Susan's arm to support her. 'He's been asleep in his stroller while I was checking his mum.' He guided Susan to the chair at the end of the examination couch. 'Try and focus on your own breathing right now,' he told her. 'And let us do our job and look after Dylan.'

Isobel started to put Dylan onto the bed, but he clung to her neck.

'Stay like that,' Rafe said. 'I'll listen to his chest first and then we'll try and get some oxygen on.'

Isobel was looking over Dylan's shoulder at his mother. 'Tripod position,' she murmured.

He nodded, fitting his stethoscope into his ears. He knew that Susan was demonstrating a classic indication of respiratory distress by leaning forward as she sat, propping herself up with her hands on her knees.

'Bilateral pneumonia,' he told her. 'The whole family's been sick with a respiratory virus so it's likely to be a secondary infection. She's got haemoptysis, tachypnoea and tachycardia. Fever and rigors. I've got an ambulance on the way to take her into hospital, but we should get some oxygen on her as well.'

*We.* It felt oddly normal to be working with Isobel, even if she wasn't in any kind of uniform. It was also reassuring. Judging by the way she'd dealt with the cardiac arrest at the funeral, she hadn't lost any of her medical skills.

'Dylan's running a temperature too,' she said now. 'And I can feel the respiratory effort he's making.'

'I knew he was looking flushed.' Rafe was silent for a moment as he listened to the amplified chest sounds of a small body struggling to breathe well. 'I was going to check him as soon as we'd made the arrangements to get Susan looked after.'

'Croup?' Isobel suggested quietly. 'Bronchiolitis? Epiglottitis?' She was still rocking Dylan gently.

Epiglottitis was the most serious diagnosis to consider here and it was definitely a possibility, given that it could be caused by the same bacteria that could cause the pneumonia that Dylan's mother had. It was also a condition that could rapidly deteriorate and cause a respiratory arrest that might need a major intervention like an emergency cricothyroidotomy to open an airway via a surgical incision in the neck.

'I don't think it's epiglottitis,' Rafe said. 'He's not drooling and, if anything, he's less distressed than he was a minute ago. Being upright is obviously helping.'

He was, in fact, looking as if he was almost falling asleep again.

'Is he going…to be okay?' Susan was the one sounding distressed now. 'I should have…brought him in before…'

'He's better than I thought he might be,' Rafe told her. 'But I think he needs to go to hospital with you, so that the paediatric team can keep an eye on him for a while. The airways in young children like Dylan are so much smaller than ours so they can start having difficulty breathing quite suddenly when they have a chest infection.' He turned back to Isobel. 'His lung sounds are more in the lower fields and not exactly what I'd expect with croup.'

Isobel nodded. 'So just oxygen for now then, if his saturation is below ninety two percent? No nebuliser, adrenaline or corticosteroids.'

'No…' Rafe handed her the finger clip attached to the small oxygen saturation meter, his eyebrows raised. 'Have you become a paediatric specialist nurse in the last few years?'

'No.' Isobel cuddled Dylan closer. 'Can I put this on your finger, darling? It doesn't hurt, I promise.' She glanced up at Rafe. 'I retrained,' she told him. 'I've kept my nursing registration up to date and pick up occasional shifts in ED or as a flight care nurse but I'm also a critical care paramedic now.' She glanced down at the screen on the meter. 'Saturation's ninety four percent,' she said.

Rafe continued attaching a mask to an oxygen cylinder. He held it over Susan's mouth and nose as he slipped the elastic band over her head and then tightened it to fit.

'This should help with your breathing,' he told her.

Deb put her head around the door of the treatment room. 'The ambulance is on its way,' she informed them. 'And I've spoken to your mum, Susan. She's on her way here as well.'

Deb sounded anxious and the glance in Rafe's direction was a plea for help, although she kept her voice calm. 'We've got some less than happy people in the waiting room,' she told him. 'Perhaps I should start cancelling appointments?'

Rafe could see that Susan was less short of breath already. And Dylan was sound asleep in Isobel's arms.

'Could you stay here and monitor Dylan and his mum until the ambulance arrives?' he asked. 'I'd better go and see if there's anything urgent in our waiting room.'

'Of course.' She looked down at the sleeping child in her arms. 'I wasn't planning on disturbing this little guy before I had to.'

Rafe crouched in front of Susan's chair, holding her gaze so that she could see how confident he was that, although she needed extra help right now, both she and Dylan were going to be fine. He held her wrist to check her heart rate and could actually feel her pulse slowing a little with the reassurance.

'I'm not far away,' he told her. 'And Belle's more than qualified to look after you both.'

'I can see that.' Susan was managing a smile beneath the mask. 'We'll be fine, Dr Tanner. I'm sure there are people out there who need you more than we do at the moment.'

Oh, wow…

The way Rafe had been looking at his patient as if her wellbeing and that of her baby were the most important things on his mind. That aura of caring had been as palpable as the warmth of a snuggly blanket and his confidence would inspire trust in anyone. He was the kind of general practitioner that everybody wanted, wasn't he? No wonder this medical practice was obviously so popular and that waiting room so incredibly crowded.

With the ambulance pulling out from the rear of the clinic buildings, Susan and Dylan safely tucked up inside, Isobel headed towards the reception area where she'd dropped her bag when she'd first reached to take Dylan from his panicked mother's arms.

Deb, the receptionist, was dealing with an angry man.

'I took time off work to come here. I'm losing money with every minute I'm hanging around in here and it's just a routine blood test that I had an *appointment* for. I've been waiting for nearly an hour and it's not bloody good enough.'

'I know, I'm so sorry, Mr Jamieson. We've had a bit of an emergency here.'

'That's not my fault.' The man's voice rose. 'It's not

as if I even need to see a doctor, it's only the nurse I had an appointment with.'

A woman with a baby was also standing at the counter. 'I've got an appointment with the nurse too, to get my blood pressure checked. I can't wait that long. I've got another appointment to get to.'

'Don't try jumping the queue,' someone seated in the waiting room called out. 'We're all in the same boat. I'm waiting for an ECG.'

Someone else laughed. 'Reckon we'll all have blood pressure problems before too long.'

'I'm sorry,' Deb repeated. 'Our practice nurse is unavailable and we're having trouble replacing her. You *will* be seen as soon as possible. One of the doctors will do your blood test, Mr Jamieson. And check your blood pressure, Mrs Allsop.'

'It won't be soon enough.' The man had his fists clenched. 'I'm leaving. And I'll be making a complaint about this.'

Rafe had come from the corridor leading to the consulting rooms and picked up a file from the basket on the end of the reception desk, clearly about to call for his next patient, but he'd heard what was being said.

'Mr Jamieson? What's the problem?'

'This place is a circus, that's the problem. No wonder it's called a "practice". Maybe one day you'll actually get good at doing the job properly.'

'Waiting time is getting longer,' Deb told Rafe. 'Especially for the appointments like routine blood pressure checks that need to be slotted in with the doctors, with no nurse available.'

Isobel watched as Rafe glanced over his shoulder

at the crowded waiting area before looking back at the man in front of him. It wasn't just the concerned frown creasing his face that caught Isobel, it was the way he unconsciously lifted his hand to rub the back of his neck. A sure sign that he was thinking fast in order to deal with a difficult situation.

She knew that because she'd seen it many times before, often in the context of an emergency department that was experiencing the same kind of chaos that this medical centre had been plunged into this morning. It felt like a step back in time. It also felt impossible not to offer to help.

'I could do Mr Jamieson's blood test,' she told Rafe. 'And take blood pressures and do twelve lead ECGs.'

'Are you sure? Don't you have other things you were planning to do?'

'I've got an appointment with Mum's solicitor but that's not until four o'clock this afternoon. I said I'd go to NICU and spend time with Daisy, but I could do that afterwards. And I can ring the insurance company any time.' It actually felt good to be making a plan for her day and not simply responding to events or emotions. 'So, yes... I'm sure.'

The receptionist's eyebrows had been rising as she listened to their rapid exchange.

'It's okay, Deb,' Rafe said. 'I've worked with Isobel before at St Luke's. She's a well-qualified nurse. And a paramedic.' He turned back to Isobel. 'Are you still registered with the Nursing and Midwifery Council in the UK?'

Isobel nodded. 'I just kept it going,' she told him. 'In case I ever needed to come home.'

Except it wasn't home any longer. So why did she feel so comfortable in this place, with the accents of her childhood around her and a medical environment that she was perfectly confident she could cope with?

'You could check online with the NMC,' Rafe told Deb, 'if you want to check Isobel's credentials, but I'd be more than happy to accept her offer to help this morning.'

'Oh, stop faffing around.' Mr Jamieson was glaring at Isobel. 'If you're capable of taking a blood test, let's just get on with it, shall we? I'm about ready to stick the needle in my own arm.'

Isobel caught Rafe's glance.

'Come with me,' he said. 'I'll show you the nurse's room and give you a quick orientation.'

There was a gleam in his eyes as he opened a door next to the treatment room a moment later. 'You might want to check Mr Jamieson's blood pressure as well,' he murmured. 'Good luck. And thank you.' A corner of his mouth had a wry curve to it. 'I'm rather glad I forgot my phone this morning.'

# CHAPTER SIX

'I WAS STARTING to get worried about you.'

Yes… Isobel could see the concern on Rafe's face as he turned to see her entering the kitchen that evening. How long was it, she wondered, since she'd seen someone genuinely concerned, on a personal level, about her welfare? It gave her a glow of something warm. Something rather nice. Something that instantly tapped back into that dream she'd once had, of having someone to care about her like this for the rest of her life. Someone that she cared about just as much in return.

The someone that she thought she'd found in Raphael Tanner that night when he'd sat down to talk to her and check that she was okay after they'd been unable to save the patient they'd worked on so hard together. Clearing her throat was also an attempt to clear that ghost of a memory that needed to be avoided. Rafe might have said that she'd been the one he'd loved but that was it in a nutshell, wasn't it?

The past tense.

*Don't look back*, she reminded herself. *It's not the direction you're going in now.*

'Sorry, Rafe.' Isobel needed a quick breath to steady

her voice. 'I should have let you know. I didn't think I'd be this late back but I actually fell asleep doing the kangaroo care with Daisy and the nurses didn't want to disturb either of us. Apparently that's the longest she's been off CPAP with all her vital signs staying within normal parameters. Even her oxygen saturation levels didn't drop enough to set off any alarms.'

'That's great news.' Rafe clicked shut the lunchboxes he'd been filling. 'She's getting stronger.'

'She's even put on a tiny bit of weight. That's another reason they didn't want to wake me up. Apparently the calories saved by being asleep and contented can contribute to weight gain.'

'Speaking of calories, I saved you some dinner. It's in the oven. Nothing very exciting, sorry—just bangers and mash, because I was cooking and it's the boys' favourite.'

'Oh...thank you, but I grabbed a sandwich as I went past the hospital cafeteria. I'd love a cup of tea, but I can make that. Are the boys asleep already?'

'I certainly hope so.' Rafe stored the lunchboxes in the fridge. 'I put them to bed an hour ago. And you sit down. I'll make the tea. I'm still in your debt from this morning.'

Isobel sank onto a chair at the old table at the working end of the kitchen near the Aga. Not only was someone concerned about her wellbeing, he wanted to take care of her on a physical level as well. She'd lived on her own for so long that this felt like a new experience to come home to and that warm glow, deep in her gut, got a little brighter.

Because it was Rafe who was doing the caring?

She put her shoulder bag on the floor beside her, the patch of brown wool beneath the open zip catching her eye as she did so. She pulled out the little teddy bear, putting it on the table in front of her.

'I was going to leave this with Daisy, but I decided I'd better give it a good wash first. It's really old and probably full of things like dust mites.'

Rafe looked towards her from where he was filling the kettle. 'What is it? A dog?'

'My first teddy bear. I think it might have been Louise from next door who knitted it, and the pattern obviously went a bit wrong, but I still loved it. I gave it to Lauren when she was a baby so I thought Daisy should have it now.'

Rafe sounded surprised. 'And it's something you usually carry around with you in your bag?'

'No…' Isobel let out a huff of laughter. 'I picked it up from the house when I went through with the insurance assessor yesterday. It was about the only thing that looked worth saving.'

The beat of silence between them acknowledged that there were many things Isobel would not want to save from her family home, including the memories of how it had all fallen apart. How her own sister had broken a fundamental rule inherent in family loyalty. How her own mother had failed to defend her. And how her dream of being with the man she loved so much had blown up in her face, along with any conviction that she could ever get any support she needed from her family.

Rafe had a box of milk in his hand but was now staring into the fridge with a thoughtful expression on his face. 'How 'bout a glass of wine instead of that cup of tea? I happen to have a rather nice New Zealand Pinot Gris in here.'

'Oh…'

A bit of time out to really unwind before going to bed and an excuse to linger in this warm, comforting room that was the heart of such a real family home was irresistible. No…it was the thought of turning back time and sharing a glass of wine with just Rafe for company that was really irresistible, wasn't it?

This was probably not the best idea, but Isobel wasn't about to summon the common sense to think about it. Instead, she closed her eyes as she spoke, letting go of any doubts. 'That sounds perfect. It has been rather an eventful day.'

He handed her a glass moments later. He was holding one for himself as well, and he sat down at the end of the table and raised his glass to touch against hers in a toast.

'Thanks again for your help this morning. We would have sunk completely if it hadn't been for you seeing so many people. Your ability to triage and provide us with an initial assessment of vital signs was especially valuable for saving time and clearing the backlog.'

'I really enjoyed it,' Isobel admitted. 'Even having to hunt for so many things, like more ECG dots and where the flu vaccines were stored in the fridge, was good. Oh, you're very low on specimen jars and I used the last urine dipstick this afternoon, but I mentioned it to Deb and she's ordered some more. Hopefully you won't get any more UTIs coming through the door before they arrive.'

Rafe seemed to be listening carefully. 'I did wonder

how well Linnda was keeping up with some aspects of her work,' he said, 'but she loved her job so much she wouldn't hear of retiring. I saw her today and she should make a good recovery from the stroke but there's no way she'll be coming back—which could be a blessing in disguise once we've found the right person to fill the gap. You've reminded me of just how many balls need to be juggled and kept in the air at the same time. It takes a particular kind of person to thrive in a stressful job like that.'

'It was exactly what I needed today,' Isobel said. 'I've got so many things that I can't control to worry about at the moment so it was kind of nice to focus on stuff that I know exactly how to manage.' She took an appreciative sip of her wine. 'Stuff that doesn't… I don't know…mess with your head, I guess.'

Rafe didn't say anything but she knew he was still listening. His silence made her think he was waiting for her to say something more. That he *wanted* to hear more? Having someone genuinely interested in what was going on in her life was adding another layer to that feeling of being cared for.

She let her breath out in a sigh this time. 'Everything seems to be getting more complicated. Mum's estate is a bit of a mess to say the least. She didn't leave a will, which means that it would have been divided equally between her children, but Lauren died straight after her and she didn't leave a will either, so that means her half gets divided between her children. All three of them. The solicitor says it'll take quite some time to get sorted and it may have to wait until the house is repaired and valued. Or sold, even.' She took another, longer, sip of her wine. 'And that's another huge question mark. Goodness only knows how long it will be before the house can be valued, let alone go on the market.'

If seemed more and more likely that this process was going to take months. That meant she would definitely have to find somewhere else to stay, but Isobel bit her lip to stop herself saying anything about moving out. Because her heart was sinking at the thought of doing that?

She might have believed she'd never wanted to see Rafe again but it was nowhere near as disturbing as she had expected. It was unsettling, sure, but not in an entirely unpleasant way. And she loved this house. This kitchen. The feeling of life that came with two small boys and quite a large dog sharing the space. She had to admit that a large part of her didn't want to move out any time soon. Especially when Rafe was looking at her as if he really cared about whatever was messing with her head.

It was a bit like being in some strange hall of mirrors where reality got twisted. This was like a glimpse into the life she could have had, if that Christmas party had worked out the way she'd hoped it would. If she and Rafe had both realised that they couldn't see their future without sharing it with each other and had reignited their romance that night.

'Is there anything I can do to help?'

Oh…that was a question and a half, wasn't it? Could he turn back time, perhaps, and make all that devastation disappear? Make the family feel of this house and kitchen and children and dog the real heart of her current life? No… Of course he couldn't.

Isobel shook her head. 'You've done enough. It's me who should be thanking you for everything you've done already, like organising the funeral. That can't have been easy given how badly my sister—and my mother, by the sound of it—treated you.'

Rafe's shrug suggested that it wasn't something he intended dwelling on. That it had only been the right thing to do, perhaps, but another thought had suddenly occurred to Isobel.

'I must owe you a small fortune for the funeral costs. There's no reason you should have to foot that bill for your ex-wife.'

Rafe shook his head. 'Forget it. It was something I needed to do for my own conscience,' he said quietly. 'A token apology?' He rubbed the back of his neck, his gaze dropping. 'I didn't try hard enough to make things work. When I wasn't at the hospital, I was look-ing after the babies. I knew Lauren wasn't happy so I didn't blame her for leaving—I was just grateful she hadn't taken my boys. It was never a real marriage. We never even shared a bedroom…'

Oh, dear Lord… Isobel studied the last few drops of liquid in her wine glass. She didn't need that kind of intimate detail of what had gone on in his marriage to her sister. It was doing something odd to her body, like the way hearing him say that he had once loved her had done. She drained the last drops of her wine from the glass, carefully avoiding catching Rafe's gaze. She didn't want him to see what might be showing in her own eyes. Not when it could be something that could scare herself as much as him.

He got to his feet and, thankfully, it felt like a signal that the subject was closed.

'I could help with keeping an eye on the house repairs,' he offered as he came back from the fridge with the wine bottle in his hand. 'If you need to go back to New Zealand for a while.'

'I've told people I'm unavailable for any shifts for a month or so. And someone's keeping an eye on my apartment. I'll have to make other arrangements if I'm staying longer than that, but there's bigger things than my job to think about.'

This time the silence between them felt even more loaded. Rafe sat down again, caught her gaze and then held it, nodding slowly. That concern for her was there in his face again, along with a sincere empathy in those dark eyes.

'Daisy,' he said quietly.

Isobel could feel the prickle of tears gathering behind her eyes. That he understood that bond with a baby that could come from nowhere and hit with such strength gave them a new connection. It gave her the impression that he was on her side and wasn't about to make any judgements on whatever she was feeling. The kind of support that a family could provide but something she'd never been able to rely on.

'Maybe it was a mistake giving her a name,' she confessed. 'It felt so different today. As if…as if…'

'As if she's yours?'

The suggestion was just as quiet but carried all the understanding in the world and Isobel nodded just as slowly as he just had. She could feel a tear escaping at the same time and brushed it away with her fingers.

'It's too big,' she whispered. 'And I don't know what I'm going to do.'

'You don't have to know yet. Or do anything other than take one day at a time right now,' Rafe told her. 'You'll know when you know. What you *are* doing is being there for her and helping her to get stronger and… and that's a very special thing to be able to do.' He nudged the little brown teddy bear on the table between them. 'This is special too, in its own unique way.' He smiled. 'I'll bet it becomes something very precious for Daisy. A family heirloom.'

Isobel smiled through her tears. 'A rather wonky one.'

Rafe's smile widened. 'Perfection is overrated.'

He refilled her wine glass. 'New Zealand makes some great wine,' he said. 'I'd love to visit the place one day. Maybe a campervan trip with the boys when they're old enough to appreciate it. I'd better pick your brains while you're here and make a list of all the "must-see" places.'

'It'll be a long list,' Isobel said. 'I've been there for years and feel like I've barely scratched the surface, even working on helicopters for a while and being able to fly into some of the top tourist spots, like the national parks.'

Rafe's phone beeped as she finished speaking and she watched the frown line appear between his eyes. He glanced up a heartbeat later, as if he'd been able to feel the touch of her concerned gaze.

'It's the locum agency,' he told her. 'They're working late, obviously, but they haven't been able to find a practice nurse for us that can start immediately. End of the week at the earliest.' He shook his head and put his phone back in his shirt pocket. 'Dealing with that can wait till the morning.' He took a mouthful of his wine. 'It sounds like you have an exciting job. Where are you based at the moment?'

'My apartment's in Queenstown. I have casual employment with both the ambulance service and the local hospital, which is great because I get to pick my hours but it may be a while before a permanent position anywhere gets advertised. It's a popular place to live.'

'I can imagine. That's *Lord of the Rings* country, isn't it? Spectacular mountains and lakes and forests and lots of snow in winter?'

'It's gorgeous. I love it.'

'And have you got family there?'

Isobel blinked at him. He knew perfectly well that she'd just lost her only family members.

The expression on Rafe's face suggested embarrassment. Or an apology? 'I meant, you know…a husband. Or kids, even.'

'Oh…' Fair enough. She'd thought that Helen was Rafe's new wife, hadn't she? And that he had added a couple of kids to his own brood in the time she'd been out of the country.

She took a much larger sip of her wine. 'No. On both counts.'

It felt as if she was admitting to some kind of failure. It wasn't that she hadn't tried to find a special person to share her life with. She'd dated quite a few men over the years, but it never seemed to go anywhere. She changed jobs, or spent too much time on shift work, or…there just hadn't been enough to build on.

Or, maybe, she'd been trying to find someone that made her feel exactly the same way that Raphael Tanner had and there would only ever be one man who could do that. That, perhaps, it was preferable to live with the loneliness than in a relationship where it was so obvious that something important was missing.

'I'm footloose and fancy free, really.' She could hear the unnaturally bright tone to her voice. She needed to change the subject so she added the first thing she could think of. 'Apart from keeping up rental payments in one of the priciest real estate areas in the country.' She bit her lip as she remembered worrying about finances earlier today, when she was talking to the solicitor dealing with her mother's estate. 'There'll be costs I have to keep up on Mum's house until it gets sold too. I might need to find a budget hotel when you've had enough of your life being disrupted by an uninvited visitor.' She managed a wry smile. 'Maybe it's just as well I still have current nursing registration. You never know, I might end up looking for a job while I'm here.'

'Well, what do you know? I happen to know about a job you'd be perfect for. At the Harrison Street Medical Centre.'

The words had come out of Rafe's mouth before he'd really thought about them. Maybe it was some kind of protective mechanism to cover up what he was *really* thinking about. That Isobel was single. That there was nothing to anchor her on the other side of the world, other than a job.

There would be many, many jobs available for someone with her abilities right here in Balclutha. And that would mean he could see more of her. There could be other occasions when he could sit and share a glass of wine with her and talk about life and…

And be reminded, yet again, of how he'd stuffed up the best thing that had ever happened to him? That surprised expression currently on Isobel's face could quickly morph into wariness, couldn't it? What was he thinking? And after he'd suggested the wine instead of a cup of tea to try and soften the unpleasantness of their shared memories.

He pasted a grin onto his face. 'Just kidding… I know you've got more than enough demands on your time right now. But you were brilliant this morning. You even picked up what was probably a silent myocardial infarction on old Mrs Maloney when you spotted the changes on her routine ECG. No wonder she's been so short of breath lately.'

Isobel didn't seem to register the praise. She was looking thoughtful rather than pleased.

'Are you looking for a full-time practice nurse?' she asked. 'Because if it was part-time I'd have time to spend with Daisy every day and there'll be other things I have to do, I expect. Like decisions for the house and legal stuff.'

Rafe stared at her. 'Would you really consider it?'

Was this a step in the wrong direction? It would mean spending even more time in Isobel's company. Working with her, in fact, which was how they'd met in the first place. Did he want to do that?

No.

*Yes…*

'The hours you worked today were great,' Rafe said.

'I know everybody would be thrilled if you could do that Monday to Friday. And I'm in charge of employing someone so we can figure out what would work best for you. But…are you sure?'

'I meant it when I said how good it had been today to be able to focus on stuff that's easy to handle. It almost felt like I had a bit of control over my life which has been rather lacking lately. Having a routine would probably be even better. But are *you* sure? Was today typical for what your practice nurse needs to be able to do?'

Was he sure?

Not exactly. He was confused, to be honest. There were feelings being stirred that he'd successfully kept buried for a very long time. He'd said too much already too, not just telling Isobel that she'd been the one he'd loved but admitting that he'd only ever slept with her sister that one time. He'd thought he'd lost everything he'd ever had with Isobel Matthews. He hadn't even expected her to turn up to the funeral, let alone that she would be staying in his house but, now that she was here, he was remembering just how much he *had* lost.

Was it remotely possible that some of the good things he remembered from their relationship were still there?

It had felt like that when he'd seen her sitting with Daisy on her bare skin. When he'd remembered with such bittersweet clarity what it had been like when he'd fallen in love with this woman. And it had felt like it this evening, when he'd wanted to take care of her. To reassure and support her.

They couldn't go back, he knew that. He didn't expect to be forgiven, if they could ever get to the point of talking honestly about what had happened, but a step towards understanding would surely be worthwhile. It could bring some sort of peace, perhaps, and create a foundation for friendship, even? What if something important was still alive between them, even if it was only there because of the bond they had by their relationships with and through Oscar and Josh and Daisy? It could be deeper than friendship. The kind of caring that would make them part of the same family and… yes…that was worth nurturing.

He *was* sure about that.

'Absolutely.' He nodded to emphasise his response. 'The job description includes the ability to assist with emergencies like resuscitation and stabilisation, which we both know you're more than qualified for with your experience in ED and as a paramedic.'

Isobel echoed his nod. 'I've done advanced resuscitation training.'

'There's admin stuff like following up test results and communicating with patients, acting as a chaperone if needed, assisting with minor surgery and what you were doing today with taking vital signs, doing blood tests and vaccinations et cetera. Oh, and home visits too, if they're required. We're one of a dying breed of medical centres that provides home visits from both doctors and the practice nurse. The doctors are on a roster to cover each day and I do mine on Tuesdays and Fridays between lunch and afternoon surgery.' His smile was wry. 'Sometimes instead of lunch. I eat my sandwiches while I'm driving.'

'I'm used to that too. I've done twelve-hour shifts on ambulance where it felt like a luxury to be able to go to the loo.'

He could imagine that. He knew how dedicated Isobel could be to her work. To everything she chose to include in her life, for that matter. If she chose to do it, she would give it everything she had. And then a bit more.

'The main attribute we'd be looking for, aside from medical qualifications, is the ability to troubleshoot. To make intelligent decisions and be able to recognise who needs urgent additional care. You're overqualified in all respects, of course, but it would be a godsend for us, even if it's only temporary.'

A flush of pink was colouring Isobel's cheeks and the look in her eyes touched something deep in his gut. She was looking as if his praise really meant something. As if she was proud of herself because he was the one telling her how good she was?

'How 'bout you try it for a few days and see how it goes?' Rafe suggested. 'If it doesn't look like it's going to work, we can try someone else from the locum agency next week.'

But, if it did work, it would keep Isobel close. It could build a new foundation for the unusual family group they were both part of.

'Forget about finding a hotel,' he added, trying to sound as if it was no big deal. 'Budget or otherwise. If it does work, you could consider room and board a part of the job package if that helps. Oscar and Josh are so thrilled to have their new aunty here. They think you're the best thing since sliced bread. Especially since I told them you can drive an ambulance. Giving them the chance to get to know you is an unexpected bonus to come out of a very unfortunate situation.'

'It's a bonus for me too,' Isobel said. 'They're gorgeous kids, Rafe. A real credit to you. I'm just sorry I haven't been part of their lives so far. I've got a bit of making up to do, haven't I?'

'Kids can be astonishingly forgiving.' Rafe shared the last of the wine between their glasses. 'We can probably learn something from them in that regard.'

Maybe it was the mention of forgiveness that did it. Or the idea that Isobel was prepared to make an effort to repair damage on his side of the equation. Whatever it was, he could feel a prickle of what had to be tears at the back of his eyes.

He raised his glass. 'It's been a long time, Belle.' He blinked back any embryonic tears but that didn't make the feeling that went with them disappear.

Relief? Hope…?

His voice softened. 'If we wanted it to be, this could be a fresh start for us as well.'

Isobel's heart skipped a beat and then accelerated as she touched his glass again and then took what turned out to be more of a gulp than a sip of the wine. Was he talking about a fresh start that involved them being together again? In the wake of his ex-wife's funeral? Her *sister's* funeral? *No*…she already had far too much to deal with emotionally. This was just another reflection in those weird reality-distorting mirrors. She might be having some confusing memories and glimpses of what could have been—possibly could still be—but she couldn't afford to give them any real head space because they held an undercurrent of very real fear.

The fear of feeling that depth of love for someone and the hopes and dreams of a future together because she knew the flip side—the devastation when it was ripped away, leaving a heart, and life, torn and bleeding. She couldn't willingly volunteer to go through that again and, if she thought that Rafe was issuing an invitation, she would most likely run for the hills. She could actually feel her muscles tensing, ready to act on a flight or fight reflex.

But she knew Rafe would never be that insensitive. He probably had no idea how much of what he felt showed on his face and in his actions. Like how much he adored his sons. The way he cared about his patients. That genuine understanding about the life-changing bombshell addition to her life that a small, fragile baby in NICU was presenting.

And what she could see on his face right now was an expression that was reassuring rather than inviting. For a moment, when he'd made the suggestion of a fresh start, she'd thought she'd seen the glimmer of tears in his eyes—as if it meant something very significant—but that had gone now.

And he might have admitted that he'd loved her rather than Lauren, but he'd also just reminded her that it had been a very long time ago. It was part of a past that no longer existed and perhaps what he was really suggesting was that they both put it behind them and start again with simply a clean slate. That was fine with Isobel. A relief, in fact. She could feel the tension in her muscles subsiding.

This was a professional proposal. One that happened to also offer a way to turn back time on an emotional level. To return to a time when they had worked to-gether and had formed a genuine friendship before becoming lovers. A chance to push a 'reset' button and, yes…have a fresh start.

And it was purely professional, which made it feel… safe.

It was a job tailored to suit both her qualifications and her available hours. Free accommodation thrown in. Staying here could provide a solid base—along with the company of someone who had just demonstrated that he cared about her wellbeing—that would undoubtably make it much easier to deal with difficult times in the weeks to come.

Yes. The whole package felt solid and safe. The kind of rock that Isobel desperately needed to cling to right now, given that the familiar foundation of her life had just been whipped out from beneath her feet. Her family was gone and her future hung in the balance, given that if she chose to raise Daisy, going back to the life she had created for herself in the last few years would be totally impossible.

But she didn't need to think about that in this moment. As Rafe had said, all she needed to do for now was what she was doing. One day at a time. Today had made it very clear that being able to plan her days to include using her medical skills in a job she loved could only be a good thing for everyone concerned. Those few hours of being totally focused on patients had provided her with a means to help silence the overload of personal emotional stuff she was having to process as well as a chance to escape the draining thought spirals of the biggest things, like the future for herself and Daisy or the past for herself and Rafe. Having had that break had enabled her to simply be in the moment with Daisy, which could well have been why they'd both ended up in a contented nap. Building a break like that into almost every day would be better for everyone concerned.

Especially herself.

With how long the house repairs were going to take, she actually had plenty of time to consider what was going to be the best option for herself and Daisy going forward. And she could banish her past history with Rafe back into that secure part of her brain because this was a fresh start and it was all about the present. About the children who linked them. And a new professional relationship.

The relief was becoming so palpable Isobel found herself smiling at Rafe, in fact. 'I'd better get to bed,' she said. 'It seems like I've got work in the morning.'

# CHAPTER SEVEN

'Rafe?'

Rafe didn't need to glance at his dashboard to confirm that it was Isobel calling. Somehow, in the last couple of weeks, he had become familiar enough again with her voice to know that this was her professional tone. Which was entirely appropriate, given that it was the middle of a working day. What wasn't quite so appropriate, perhaps, was how much of a pleasure it was to hear her voice.

It might only have been a short time since Isobel had joined the staff at Harrison Street Medical Centre, but it had worked remarkably well right from day one and there'd been no question of getting the locum agency to find them another contender. Rafe had known she would be good at doing this job, but he hadn't realised quite *how* good, and he was proud of her. He also liked the feeling that, at least on one level, they were managing to turn back time to a point where they'd been colleagues. Friends. And it still felt safe enough.

'What's up, Belle?'

'Are you at work at the moment?'

'No, I'm on the road. I've got a home visit to do.'

'Is it urgent?'

'Not particularly. A potential bedsore to assess. Why?'

'I'm on a home visit. With Albert Morris.'

Rafe frowned. 'Type Two diabetic?'

'That's him. He didn't sound too bad when he rang to ask for an appointment this morning. He's been off colour for quite a few days, very thirsty, frequent urination and a bit "fuzzy", he called it. Said he'd run out of test strips for his glucometer, but he sounded a bit confused and I'm not happy about his condition. I think I should call an ambulance.'

Rafe had pulled to the side of the road to focus on what Isobel was telling him.

'Signs and symptoms?'

'Airway's clear but resps are up at thirty. He's tachycardic at one thirty and his blood pressure's one-oh-five over sixty-five. He's very dehydrated. Skin tenting and his eyes look sunken. Blood glucose level is too high to record. His temperature's thirty-eight point two and I found blood in his urine when I did a dipstick.'

'Ketones?'

'No.'

'Not diabetic ketoacidosis then, which I wouldn't expect, anyway, unless he's a Type One diabetic.'

'No. I can't smell any ketones on his breath and he hasn't complained about abdominal pain or vomiting but I'm wondering about HHS. I've noticed a few ectopic beats but I can't do an ECG here. A urinary tract infection could be the cause and he's obviously confused. He couldn't tell me what day it was or how old he is.'

Hyperosmolar Hyperglycaemic Syndrome. Just as

dangerous as DKA in that it could lead to coma or death due to cardiac complications from electrolyte imbalances.

'Where are you?' Rafe asked.

The address Isobel gave him wasn't that far from where Rafe was himself. 'I've got a life pack with me,' he told her. 'Call an ambulance but it probably doesn't need to be a Priority One response. I'll drop in and we'll get an ECG. We can upgrade the request if we need to but he should be monitored for hyperkalaemic arrhythmias that could develop.'

It took Rafe less than ten minutes to reach the address where Albert Morris lived but it had been enough time for the condition of the seventy-two-year-old man to deteriorate.

''Bout time you got here,' Albert mumbled. He was sitting slumped on his couch. 'But you can leave your dog outside. I don't want hair all over my furniture.'

'No problem.' Rafe raised an eyebrow at Isobel. Hallucinations? His query was silent but Isobel nodded.

'I had to shoo the invisible cats out a few minutes ago,' she whispered.

'I'll get an IV in,' Rafe said. 'Fluid replacement is going to be a priority for treatment here. Can you do an ECG?'

'Sure.' Isobel uncoiled the leads from the side pocket of the life pack but spoke to their patient before opening his pyjama jacket to attach the electrodes.

'I need to put some sticky patches on your chest, Albert, so we can see what your heart's up to. Is that okay with you?'

'You can do whatever you like to me, darling.' Albert

closed his eyes. 'I'm thirsty… I think there's a beer in my fridge. Could you get it for me?'

'In a minute,' Isobel murmured. 'I'm just going to do this first, okay?'

Rafe slipped a tourniquet around Albert's arm, having unrolled his IV kit. 'Keep your arm as still as you can,' he warned their patient. 'Sharp scratch coming up.'

He kept well out of Isobel's way as she opened Albert's pyjama jacket and stuck electrodes for the limb leads below his collarbones and above the hipbones. Then she quickly placed the precordial leads around his heart, counting intercostal spaces by feeling for the ribs and gauging the vertical lines by sight. As Rafe slid the cannula into a vein and secured it, Isobel was attaching the leads to the electrodes and watching the screen of the life pack to make sure the connections were good.

'Keep nice and still for me, Albert,' she said, putting her hand on his shoulder too. 'I'm going to take a picture of what that ticker of yours is up to.'

She was smiling at the older man, who might well be confused and even hallucinating at times but he was clearly captured enough by Isobel's smile to lie very still and simply smile back for as long as it took the machine to record the electrical activity going on and print out a graph for them to see. And that didn't surprise Rafe one little bit. He could remember being just as entranced with smiles that Isobel Matthews had bestowed on him, long ago. Smiles that could light up the world and make it a better place. The best place…

He pushed the spike of a giving set into the port on the bag of saline he was holding with slightly more force than necessary but it was a deliberate action to stop his mind spending any more than a nanosecond on that train of thought. Because he knew it would lead into an out-of-bounds space—the space where he could remember, with more and more ease, what it had been like to be falling in love with Isobel—when he'd known she was already in love with him, even though nothing had been said out loud.

Was it because it felt safe to be working together again and making that fresh start, that it was becoming a little too easy to step into that unwise space? Ironically, because they were working together, it was equally easy to step out of that space and push the thought firmly away. As he attached the tubing of the IV fluid to the line in Albert's arm and adjusted the rate of infusion, Rafe was keeping an eye on the screen on the life pack, completely focused again. The rhythm trace was somewhat irregular and was being interrupted quite frequently by the bizarre shape of premature beats—a warning sign that things weren't stable and could potentially deteriorate into a fatal rhythm and cardiac arrest.

Isobel handed him the recorded trace. 'Peaked T waves, wide QRS and diminished P waves. All consistent with a high potassium level.'

Rafe nodded. 'And there's no ST elevation so we can rule out a heart attack.'

'Shall I upgrade the urgency of the ambulance call?'

'Let's see if we can get that rhythm a bit more settled first.' Rafe turned back to his kit to take out the drug roll. 'How would you treat this as a critical care paramedic?' he asked.

'IV calcium chloride to stabilise cardiac membrane potential,' Isobel responded. 'It lasts thirty to sixty minutes, which is usually plenty of time to get to an ED where treatment with insulin and glucose can happen. Nebulised albuterol is also useful to shift potassium into the intracellular space.'

'Sodium bicarbonate?' Rafe was drawing up fluid from an ampoule into a syringe but he glanced up to catch the gleam in Isobel's eyes. She knew he was testing her but she didn't mind.

'Not unless the patient's in known acidosis,' she said. 'As I'm sure you're aware, Dr Tanner.'

She turned away, hiding a smile. 'You're doing well, Albert. You're going to feel a lot better soon, I promise.'

The calcium chloride had an almost immediate effect on the rhythm of Albert's heart, with the ectopic beats starting to get less frequent. Minutes later, the ambulance arrived and Albert was soon on a stretcher and ready for transport.

'But I haven't had my beer,' he complained. 'I'm still thirsty.'

'It'll be here for you when you get home,' Isobel told him. 'And I'll be back to check on you.'

'Any time, darling.' Albert lay back on his pillow and closed his eyes as the stretcher was rolled away. 'Any time…'

There was no time to waste packing up the life pack and kit and Isobel was onto it.

'Sorry to have held you up but I'm so glad you were here. I'd hate to have had to deal with an arrest on my own without any gear.'

Rafe was going to be pushed to visit his patient with the bedsore before he needed to be back at Harrison

Street for the afternoon surgery hours, but he was just as glad he'd been able to be here.

'I think we should make sure you've got a full resuscitation kit available, given that your skill level is well above the average practice nurse. But let's talk about that tonight. I've really got to get going.'

Rafe was perfectly confident that they would talk about it tonight because it was becoming a familiar—and increasingly pleasant—end to most of their evenings to share a cup of tea or sometimes a glass of wine and talk about their days, which often led to talking about snippets of their lives in recent years. Josh couldn't get enough of hearing about cases where Isobel had been winched out of a helicopter or had to drive on precarious mountain roads to reach a patient. Rafe wasn't sure if it was a need to fill in the gaps of what had been happening in her life since she'd left or whether he was searching for things that had changed and made her different or trying to rediscover the things that hadn't changed—the things he'd loved about her right from the start, but it wasn't a problem because it felt safe.

An even bigger question might be whether that was what Isobel was also doing when she asked questions about what it had been like being a single father and his rather dramatic change of career from the fast pace of a busy emergency department to the far more predictable routine of a general practice. Perhaps they both needed this time to get to know each other again. Laying foundations that could provide a base for something important, like a genuine friendship and an extended family for Oscar and Josh. It felt as if they were building trust that clearly hadn't been there enough in the first place because it had been too easily broken—on both sides.

It was a time alone together that was feeling that bit safer with every day that passed, despite those unexpected steps into the forbidden space. Not safe enough yet to step onto ground that had been shelved by mutual consent, but it wasn't unthinkable that they might close some of that distance between them one of these days by talking about their shared past.

But not just yet. They needed this safe space to get to know each other again. To build trust. And Rafe wanted to remember what it had been like when they'd first met. When they'd been colleagues. Friends. Before things had spiralled into something intense enough to be overwhelming for him. Before he'd pulled the plug on something that he wasn't ready to trust enough. Before he'd messed things up to the point where he'd lost the chance of the relationship he later knew he'd wanted far more than he'd realised.

It wasn't just Rafe and Isobel that needed that safe space either. Even more, there were two small boys who needed to be protected.

Isobel hadn't been wrong in thinking that a routine, including a job, would help her navigate what was probably the most difficult period she had faced in her life so far. Okay, *definitely* the most difficult, but it took some doing to knock the memory of how hard it had been to travel as far away as she could get on earth and start a completely new life, when it had felt like her broken heart was unlikely to ever heal, from its top position on that scale.

It had only taken a matter of days for her new routine to become familiar enough to reveal that it was going to be beneficial on more levels than simply providing a structure to her days. Things were chaotic enough to block any personal thought spirals that threatened to create emotional overload and, by the end of each day, Isobel was tired enough to fall into a dreamless sleep.

The chaos began each day in the company of the twins and Cheddar, there was the surprisingly satisfying work as a practice nurse that kept her focused from nine o'clock till three o'clock—with her lunch break being used to keep up with what was happening with the structural work to repair her mother's house and the plans that needed to be made for renovations. Then there was the time with Daisy, between work and getting home to Rafe's house for dinner, that was falling into its own routine of feeding and doing the kangaroo care and it was going to be extended soon to include a bath as her tiny niece continued to grow and get bigger and stronger.

Isobel was sure that Daisy was coming to recognise her as a special person in her life. She didn't fall asleep so often during their time of snuggling skin-to-skin and Isobel would find dark eyes locked on her face. It felt almost like a secret language they were communicating in as that eye contact remained unbroken for such long periods of time.

Sometimes she was too late to share dinner with Rafe and the boys, but she was always back by seven o'clock because it had also become an important part of her routine to hear Oscar and Josh's reading homework, admire any new artwork and maybe play a game if there was time before the bedtime story with their dad.

And then came the part of Isobel's day that she was starting to look forward to the most. The quiet half hour or so where she and Rafe shared a drink and chatted about the day.

'The insurance company is covering new furniture and curtains after all the mouldy stuff had to be thrown out,' she told him one day. 'Look what I found online today—I just love these reproduction brass beds. You can get patchwork quilts to go with them.'

'Nice.'

'The better the house looks when it's finished, the quicker it will sell. Any furniture can be sold with it, I expect.'

On another day, Rafe had been in to see Daisy.

'I'm sure she's smiling. Look, I took a photo.'

'Could be wind.' Had Isobel been jealous that Rafe might have been given Daisy's first smile?

'Oscar and Josh reckon she's smiling. They're dead keen to meet their sister but I've told them they'll have to wait a bit longer. There's a few bugs going around at school at the moment and we can't risk taking them into NICU.'

Sometimes it was a purely professional discussion, like going over the details of their management of Albert Morris the other day and sharing any follow up. Albert's infection had been brought under control, along with his blood sugar and electrolyte levels, and Isobel would be able to do another home visit very soon and make sure he was managing his new glucometer. The benefits of her having a life pack in her own vehicle for home visits was already on the agenda for the next medical centre staff meeting.

And, every time, there was the sheer pleasure of simply being in Rafe's company. Listening to his voice and waiting to see that smile she'd always loved. And okay…if she let herself drift off to stand in front of one of those mirrors, that wasn't a problem, was it? It wasn't as if Rafe had any idea that she might be watching his hand lift a mug of tea and remembering what it had been like to have those fingers touching her own skin.

If that memory happened to give her that delicious spear of sensation deep in her belly that went with a level of physical attraction that had been missing from her life for so long, that was okay too, wasn't it? Maybe she needed the reminder of how important something like desire could be? How it could add a colour and vibrancy to the most ordinary things, like sharing a cup of tea? And it was hidden well enough for Rafe to have no idea that those mirrors existed and that made it safe.

Weekends brought more time with Daisy and more time with the boys and Rafe and it had only taken a couple of outings for walks on the nearest beach to become another new favourite for Isobel. Cheddar would chase seagulls and the boys would fly their kites on windy days or compete with each other to add to their collection of stones with holes in them.

'I believe they're called hag stones,' Rafe told Isobel one Saturday afternoon.

'No…really? That's a horrible name for them. I've always called them bead stones. I collected them when I was kid and threaded them onto a string to hang from a branch in a tree. They might still be there—I'll have a look next time I go to the house.'

'Can we do that, Aunty Belle?' Oscar begged. 'I want to make a string of bead stones.'

'Me too,' Josh added.

'You'll have to find lots more stones, then.'

The boys ran off and it was when Isobel heard the first shriek of glee at a successful find that it happened. So suddenly that Isobel stopped in her tracks and Rafe turned back to look at her.

'What is it? Is something wrong?'

'You were right,' Isobel said slowly.

Rafe grinned. 'Of course I was. What about, exactly?'

'That I would know when I know. About what I want to do?'

Rafe was watching her intently but he wasn't saying anything. Because he knew how big this moment was? It wasn't just what Isobel wanted to *do*. It was what she wanted in her life.

She wanted this.

Family.

Not exactly this one, of course. This was Rafe's. But she did want a family of her own—more than anything she'd ever wanted in her life.

'I'm going to adopt Daisy,' she said, slowly enough to make each word crystal clear.

The boys were well away from them now, scrabbling about amongst the millions of stones on this beach, with Cheddar helpfully trying to dig a hole. Rafe was keeping an eye on them but his gaze returned to Isobel's face and she was startled to see something that looked like disappointment in his eyes. Fear, almost...?

'You'll take her to New Zealand?' he asked quietly.

Isobel shook her head. She also tried to shake off the wild thought that it might be herself that Rafe didn't want to lose from his life, rather than Daisy. This decision was entirely separate to anything to do with any ghosts from the past or possibilities for the future. This was the present and Isobel was about to change the entire shape of her life.

'How could I do that? Daisy has her brothers here. My nephews. She has an uncle. We're part of the same family.' Isobel swallowed hard. She couldn't read the expression in Rafe's eyes any longer. Did he need reassurance that she wasn't expecting something he wasn't able to give?

'I'm the one choosing what Mum's house is going to be like so it's already feeling like it could be my house,' she added. 'I could live there. I mean, New Zealand is a wonderful place but this...this is home...'

Rafe had her in his arms before she'd finished speaking so she was wrapped in his hug as she said those last words.

And, heaven help her, but *this* felt like home as well.

Rafe's voice, right in her ear, sounded raw.

'I'm so happy that you're back,' he said softly. He pulled back just far enough to see her face. 'I've missed you, Belle.'

This time, it was Isobel who couldn't find anything to say. She was totally caught by what she could see in Rafe's eyes. Joy? Relief? *Tears...?*

Whatever it was, she couldn't look away. Neither

could Rafe, it seemed. And then something else—possibly as momentous as Isobel's decision had been—happened. Rafe bent his head. Isobel went up on her tiptoes and she closed her eyes as Rafe's lips touched hers.

A kiss that was seasoned with the salt of tears. Rafe's? Or her own? Not that it mattered. This might have only been a brief kiss, but it was the most intense that Isobel had ever experienced. It had all the bittersweet memories of past kisses they'd shared but it had something that was celebrating new beginnings as well.

A huge decision had been made.

Maybe more than one?

# CHAPTER EIGHT

IT WAS STILL THERE.

The sea breeze should have been enough to disperse it, given that both Rafe and Isobel could see that it was making the boys' cheeks very pink as Oscar and Josh ran back across the beach towards them, but it was still there.

Hanging in the air between them.

That kiss…

A kiss that had been hidden by Rafe's back and brief enough to have gone unnoticed by the two small boys. A kiss that had simply been a natural extension of a hug to celebrate what was, to Rafe, the amazingly good news that Daisy was going to be raised by the closest family she had. That she wasn't going to end up a world away from her brothers. A kiss that could—and should—have been no big deal.

Except that he had kissed Isobel's lips, not her cheek.

And the touch had not only unlocked that forbidden space full of memories and broken dreams again, it felt as if the key had also been taken out and possibly thrown away. They might be carefully avoiding catching each other's gaze right now but it was inevitable that they were going to have to talk about what had just happened. Rafe was, in fact, almost desperate to know what Isobel was thinking. How she was feeling. Whether she, too, had a space locked away in her heart that was significant enough to make it risky to visit.

Was it possible that she was without a life partner for the same reason as himself? That she'd never found something as good as that, albeit fragile, promise they'd found with each other?

'Your face is all red,' Oscar told Isobel.

'So is yours, darling.' Isobel ducked her head, clearly aware of what might have *really* made her cheeks quite that pink. 'That's what a cold wind can do.'

A heartbeat later, however, Isobel's gaze flicked up to Rafe's face as if she couldn't help herself and there was a sparkle in those blue eyes that he hadn't seen before. No...that wasn't entirely true. He *had* seen it before. Before things had fallen apart. Before he'd made the biggest mistake of his life. The eye contact was even more brief than that kiss had been but it was enough to suggest she wasn't unhappy with what had just happened. The thought that it could be quite the opposite was enough to make Rafe's heart skip a beat and it was his turn to try and hide what he was thinking. This was dangerous ground to be merely looking at, let alone stepping onto.

'Show me what you've found.' Rafe crouched to look at the stones the boys were clutching in their hands.

'Mine are the best,' Josh declared. 'Look at this one.' But it was to Isobel that he handed the smooth oval white stone with a hole just off centre.

'I'm sure I found one just like this,' she said. 'And it

was my favourite too. Along with one of those grey ones that's like a little bit of a pipe that you've found, Oscar.'

'Can you show us?'

'I don't know if they'll still be there.' Isobel shook her head and the breeze helped another curl escape her short puff of a ponytail. Rafe watched as she brushed it away from getting tangled in her eyelashes and, heaven help him, if his boys weren't standing right here, he would probably be brushing her hair back himself. And kissing her again…

'It was a long, long time ago,' Isobel added. 'I wasn't much older than you boys are now.'

The twins looked suitably impressed. 'But you're really old. Like Daddy.'

Rafe laughed. 'I'm not that old,' he protested. 'But I am getting *cold*. Are you guys ready to go home?'

They both shook their heads.

'We need more stones. To make a string. Aunty Belle's going to show us how.'

'We do need a couple of sticks of driftwood,' Isobel said. 'To hang the strings from. But we could find them next time, yes?'

*Next time*… That had a ring to it that was a promise. Because Isobel would be part of that 'next time'? That bubble of what felt like hope should be more than enough to be a warning. Especially given the expression on his boys' faces as they hung onto every word she was saying. Could he trust Isobel enough to even try and find out how she felt about him? What if they got closer—as close as he was yearning for right now—and then she changed her mind and simply vanished from his life again? Because it wouldn't be just his life she was leaving. Oscar and Josh would be asking where she was every day. Their little hearts would be aching from missing her.

He had to protect his boys. Rafe was an adult and he could handle the fallout when a relationship of any kind failed. His sons had been too young to have been visibly traumatised by their mother's departure, but if Isobel did anything to hurt them when they were already showering her with the kind of unconditional love children were so able to give, it would be unforgivable.

'What about if we get hamburgers on the way home?' The tone of his voice was overly enthusiastic as he tried to push away an unwanted level of...what was it...*yearning*? The twins shifted their gazes for a moment and the head shakes were noticeably less emphatic this time.

'What about if we go past my old house on the way,' Isobel said, 'I can show you the tree in the garden and you can see if my bead stone string is still there?'

'*Yes*...'

Stones were being stuffed into pockets and each of Isobel's hands were firmly grasped by each twin.

'Come on...let's *go*...'

Isobel was laughing as she was dragged up the slope of the stone-covered beach. Cheddar was bouncing after the trio, barking happily, but Rafe stood still for a moment. Just watching. Feeling something squeeze so tightly in his chest that it was enough to bring that prickling sensation to the back of his eyes again.

Good grief...was the emotional rollercoaster he'd been on for weeks now ever going to slow down enough for him to get off?

Did he want to get off?

Yes. He needed solid ground beneath his feet. Time to think about the implications of what was happening. To protect his boys from any fallout.

*No…* The swoops of that rollercoaster might be far more uncomfortable than anything in his life had been in recent years, but the climbing sensation was…well, it was exciting, that was what it was. And he had the feeling he hadn't actually reached the highest point yet.

Rafe turned into the chilly breeze as he followed his sons back to the car. Feeling emotions this intensely was a bit like being buffeted by the fresh sea air, he decided. It might not be the most pleasant sensation, but it had an extraordinary effect of making you feel so much more alive.

Time and weather had long since eroded the integrity of the string Isobel had used but the stones were going to last for ever and all that had changed was that they were lying, half buried under plants and earth, in the garden beneath the old silver birch tree.

'Keep looking,' Isobel encouraged the twins. 'I'm sure there were more of them.' She bit her lip as she glanced up. 'Sorry—they're getting a bit dirty.'

Rafe smiled at her. 'They're six-year-old boys. Getting dirty is part of their job description.'

Oh…there was something different about that smile.

Did that have something to do with that kiss?

Isobel knew she needed to stop thinking about it because it was only making it seem more significant and she was fairly sure that that significance was very likely to be purely one-sided. She had to stop herself looking into those distorting mirrors, especially if she was going to be back in Raphael Tanner's life long-term. Not as in them getting back together. She only had to remember the expression on Rafe's face when he'd seen her arrive at the funeral to be reminded how much had changed between them. It would be a new kind of relationship, with her being an aunt to Oscar and Josh and a mother to the sister of his sons.

Now, that decision she'd made with such conviction *was* something really significant.

Totally life-changing.

Saying it out loud had made it real but hadn't diminished how right the decision felt. Rafe's approval had only made it shine a little more—brightly enough to see it as the new sun her world was going to revolve around. Instead of being scared by the prospect, however, Isobel couldn't wait to get the ball rolling to make it happen.

'I'll go and see Mum's solicitor on Monday. I have no idea how to go about starting an adoption process.'

'It'll be much easier for you than it would have been for me,' Rafe said. 'I doubt that we're ever going to find out who her father is so you're the closest relative she's got.'

'It could be possible to find him,' Isobel suggested. 'They can do astonishing things by tracing biological family through DNA now.'

'Would you want to go down that track?'

Isobel shook her head. 'If it's possible that Lauren didn't even know who the father was, it's very unlikely that he would welcome the news but it could open a whole can of worms if his relatives got involved.'

The choice to keep Daisy safe from a tug-of-war,

not only between strangers but between countries, felt as right as the decision to raise her as her own child.

'If it was something that Daisy wanted to do when she's old enough, I'd support that,' Isobel added, 'but all she needs for now is to be safe. And loved. She'll have a mother. And an uncle…' Isobel had to swallow a lump that suddenly appeared in her throat. 'You're such a great dad, Rafe,' she said quietly. 'I know you'll be the best uncle.' She cleared her throat. 'And she has brothers. That pretty much adds up to a whole family, doesn't it?'

'More than I grew up with, that's for sure. And I've never been tempted to go looking for the man who fathered me. He obviously didn't want me enough to hang around.' Rafe looked as though he had a lump to swallow as well. He cleared his throat a moment later, looking away from her towards the back of the house. 'You even have a home almost ready for her, judging by the building work I could see through the windows. I'm sure that will count in your favour as well, as far as the adoption process goes.' He looked back to catch her gaze. 'I meant what I said, Belle. I'm really happy that you're so sure about this. And that you're not going to disappear again.'

And there it was again. The whisper of this being about more than adopting Daisy. It was right in front of them. That kiss…

But Isobel didn't want to talk about it. Maybe she didn't want Rafe to make the magic of those mirrors vanish for ever by admitting that he didn't quite trust her not to flee to the other side of the world again. It might not be such a good idea to keep looking into those mirrors either, but it felt like it needed to be her choice to stop and she needed a bit more time to get her head into the right space, given the emotional overload of the past weeks. Maybe she'd never really processed the heartbreak of losing the future she'd wanted so much?

Yes… She needed time. And a bit of space. Rather urgently, in fact.

'Would you mind dropping me at St Luke's before you take the boys for hamburgers? I need to visit Daisy. I can get a taxi home.'

'No problem. They'll be hanging out to get you to help make the strings, though.'

'I'll be back in time to start that before bedtime. If you've got string, that is?'

'I think there's garden twine in the shed. That natural brown sort?'

'That's perfect. Rustic is good. We can make the strings and then find driftwood later to give them something to hang from.'

'They love fossicking around in the shed so that should keep them out of mischief for a while. They'll need a good long bath to get rid of all that dirt too, so that's the rest of our afternoon sorted.'

'They can put the stones in the bath with them. And you can supervise sharing them out so I don't have to be the referee.'

Rafe laughed. 'You're not silly, are you? A visit to Daisy will save you all that angst over who gets which stones. I promise they'll be in their PJs and guarding their personal stone piles by the time you get home.'

The sense of being given a reprieve made Isobel smile. Okay, they were going to have to talk about that kiss some time but not immediately. Maybe never, in fact, if she was right that it didn't mean anything significant to Rafe, so it would be wise to leave it up to him to broach the subject. Maybe he'd meant to kiss her cheek but she'd just moved her head or something. Whatever. If it meant nothing, they could both pretend it hadn't happened and, eventually, she could just forget about it.

Yeah…right…

# CHAPTER NINE

IT FELT DIFFERENT.

From the moment Isobel walked back into the house that evening, Rafe could sense the difference.

'How's Daisy?'

'Hmm…' Isobel was taking off her coat. 'She seems okay but she didn't want her bottle. And she wouldn't settle to sleep in kangaroo care. It was like something wasn't quite right.'

Rafe was feeling that way himself. He couldn't quite put his finger on what it was, but it was definitely a hint of something awkward. Confusing, anyway.

Like the echoes of that kiss? Or was it the glimmer of something being uncovered enough to be seen again—like the shimmer of an unexpectedly different future? Judging by the way Isobel avoided direct eye contact by heading to where the twins were sitting in front of the fire playing with their stones, she was feeling it too. Talking about it wasn't likely to be easy but Rafe knew it would only get harder the longer it was left. And if they left it too long it might get shoved into a 'too hard' box and become another part of the past that they couldn't talk about. He didn't want that to happen.

He wanted something new between himself and Isobel. Something real and honest, even if the prospect was daunting. He needed to know where he stood so that he could be confident that his boys were safe.

'Fancy a glass of wine?'

'Yes…please.' Isobel had discarded her coat and bag and was already on the rug beside the twins.

'Daddy's been telling us stories. About the stones,' Josh told her.

'Ledges.' Oscar nodded.

'Legends.' Rafe handed Isobel the glass of wine and then sat on the couch. 'Turns out there's quite a lot to find out about hag stones. Also known as adder stones, apparently. Or witch stones. Held in high regard by the Druids.'

Josh handed Isobel a ball of twine. 'We found the string. In the shed.'

'And spiders. There were lots of spiders.' Oscar's eyes were wide. 'I don't like spiders.'

'Don't tell anyone…' Isobel leaned close to him and spoke in a stage whisper that made Oscar giggle. 'But I don't like spiders either. They're really scary.'

'Not as scary as snakes,' Josh said. 'Daddy says the snakes all got together and used their poison to make the holes in the stones.'

'We did look at some natural causes,' Rafe put in. 'Like the holes being created by small shellfish, or water movement. Not quite as exciting as snake venom, I guess.'

'I guess not.'

'And one legend has it that if you close one eye and look through the hole in the stone, you can see a magical world.'

'Oh… I like that one.' Isobel picked up a stone and held it to her eye.

'What can you see, Aunty Belle?'

'Ooh…' Isobel turned her head, scanning the room and then her smile widened. 'I can see Daddy.'

The boys laughed. 'That's not magic,' Josh declared.

It kind of was, as far as Rafe was concerned. He could actually *feel* that smile rather than simply seeing it. He might be on the wrong side of that hole, but he could feel a bit of magic going on, himself. He took a long sip of his wine. Yep. They were going to have to talk about this. Preferably as soon as the boys were in bed. He had to know how Isobel felt about it because…she didn't look as if she was upset about anything. Quite the opposite…

Being a Saturday, with extra time allowed up, getting the children to bed took long enough for Rafe to finish his glass of wine and pour another one. Isobel helped them thread twine through the holes in the stones and tie knots to hold them in place.

'Bedtime in five minutes,' Rafe finally warned.

'No…we're not finished.'

'But it's a good time to stop,' Isobel said. 'Because you can have a think about whether you want one long string or a few short strings. When we find a nice piece of driftwood we can tie the strings onto it and then hang them somewhere. In your room, maybe? Or outside, on a tree?'

'When can we find the driftwood?'

'You'll have to ask Daddy.'

'Daddy? Can we go to the beach again tomorrow? *Please?*'

'How 'bout you see how fast you can get yourselves

into bed and asleep and if it's really, really fast then I reckon we could go to the beach again tomorrow.'

'Will you come too, Aunty Belle?'

'Not this time, sweetheart. I'm going to spend tomorrow with Daisy. She wasn't so happy today and I think she might need more cuddles.'

Oscar put his arms around Isobel's neck. 'I need a cuddle.'

Josh was on her other side. 'Me too. Will you come and tuck us in, Aunty Belle?'

'Only if you guys stop strangling me.' But Isobel was laughing. 'I can't move.'

Isobel could feel it the moment she walked back into the living room, having left two very sleepy boys snuggled under their matching duvets.

It was still there, as if it had only happened a heartbeat ago.

That kiss…

And it felt as if she was standing at a crossroads where she had to choose the direction she would take towards her future, but that was something she had already done today when she knew that she had to adopt her baby niece. It was too much to have to make another huge decision so soon but it couldn't simply be left to evaporate—or not—on its own because it had changed something.

It had opened a door to the past that was not going to quietly swing shut again.

Rafe had topped up her glass of wine while she'd been tucking the boys in to bed.

'Just a nightcap,' he said. 'It's been quite a day, hasn't it?'

'Mmm.' It still was. Isobel sat in the armchair at right angles to the couch, which put her close to Rafe but with a gap between them. A safety barrier?

He raised his glass. 'You're going to be the best mum,' he said quietly. 'My boys absolutely adore you.'

'The feeling's mutual.' Isobel touched her glass against his. 'I'm just sad about how much of their lives I've missed already.'

'Yeah…' She heard the slow breath that Rafe pulled in. 'But at least you were a mysterious person who lived on the other side of the world. It was worse that their own mother didn't want to be part of their lives. Or their grandmother. It was well beyond sad. I've been angry about it for the longest time and…and when I saw you arrive at the funeral it felt like that anger was never going to go away. It actually went up a notch or two.'

Isobel nodded slowly. 'I know. I knew how angry you were and you had every right to be. I'm…sorry…'

'No. I'm the one who should apologise. It was all my fault, after all.'

Isobel couldn't meet his gaze. She'd always believed that herself, hadn't she? So why did it feel more and more as if Rafe shouldn't be taking all the blame? She opened her mouth to tell him how her perspective had changed but he was talking again.

'How much do you know about my marriage?' His breath came out in a huff of unamused laughter. 'My *first* marriage, that is. We never really talked about it, did we?'

'Apart from you saying you were never, ever going to

do it again?' Isobel shrugged. 'It didn't seem relevant. It was in the past. I figured you'd talk about it one day if you wanted to but it didn't matter if you didn't. I'm not one to base my opinions of people on gossip.'

'I didn't talk about it to anyone,' Rafe said. 'Because I didn't want to. And probably because it made me look like an idiot. When the marriage finally imploded it turned out that everybody knew about the affair except me. My wife's lover was in and out of the ED all the time on cardiology consults and I had no idea at all.' Rafe paused long enough to swallow, looking down at his hands. 'We probably got married far too young,' he added quietly. 'But I was in love with her. I trusted her. I thought we had a lifetime to be together and raise a family and I could be the kind of dad that I'd never had and always wanted so much. All those dreams and that trust got shattered in fairly spectacular fashion and it was painful enough to make sure I was never going to let it happen again. There was never any chance of it happening again.' He raised his gaze to catch Isobel's. 'Until I met you.'

Isobel caught her breath. So he had been thinking that he might want to marry her and raise a family with her? Had they been on the cusp of sharing the same dreams? Had she messed it up by revealing too much of how she felt, too soon?

'I was too obvious, wasn't I?' she said aloud. 'You must have known how much I was in love with you. And how much I was hoping you'd change your mind about getting married again. I scared you off...'

'I scared myself off,' Rafe said. 'As soon as I realised that I was falling in love with *you*. And then, when I broke it off, I realised how much I was missing you. I only went to that Christmas party because I thought you'd be there. The only thing I wanted was for us to be together again. But you weren't there. And someone came up and introduced herself as your sister and she told me where you were and…and I should have known she was lying but…she made it sound like everybody except me knew about you and Michael and…'

'And it was history repeating itself,' Isobel finished for him. 'It was a perfect storm really, because it was history repeating itself for me as well.'

The frown lines on Rafe's forehead were puzzled.

'I'd been competing with Lauren ever since she was born,' Isobel told him. 'And I always came second. Always… When I met you, I think it was the first time I ever felt like I was being chosen. That I wasn't second best.' Isobel let her breath out in a sigh. 'That's why I'd never introduced you to my family. I didn't really want you to meet Lauren.'

There was a long beat of silence.

'I'm sorry.' Rafe closed his eyes as if his thoughts hurt. 'Like I said…my fault.'

'Nothing's that black and white,' Isobel said. 'Like any disaster, there are links in the chain and taking any one of them out could have changed everything. Technically, we weren't together so I shouldn't have reacted as if you were cheating on me. That kind of makes it Lauren's fault because she knew how devastated I was. I suspect she knew I was only going to that party to see you again.'

'And, even if it had been true that you and Michael *had* hooked up, I had no right to feel like *you* were cheating on *me*. Especially seeing as I was the one who broke us up.' He offered her a wry smile. 'The grapevine at St Luke's was on your side, if it's any comfort. Especially after Lauren left me. Two wives had run off with other men. "No smoke without fire" was the general impression—I was clearly bad husband material.'

Isobel shook her head. 'I hope you don't actually believe that.'

'But it's true.' Rafe drank the last of his wine. 'I was too young the first time round, and my career was the most important thing in my life. With the long shifts and extra study, we barely saw each other. She needed something I wasn't giving her. And I was never in love with Lauren, but the boys became the most important thing ever. They still are.'

Isobel met his gaze. 'I get that,' she said softly. She picked up her glass to finish her own wine because this felt like a punctuation point. A pause, because a decision was about to be made. 'Daisy has to be the most important thing in my life from now on. What she needs feels more important than what I want.'

And there it was. The choice of direction. One road had Isobel's life—her heart and soul—firmly focused on the tiny baby she'd fallen so totally in love with. The other made Rafe just as important. Possibly more important because it was still there.

It wasn't that kiss that was still there this time, however.

It was that feeling. The one Isobel had been aware of when she'd first met Rafe. The knowing that Rafe had been the person she had found without realising that she'd been searching for him. The person that she'd wanted to spend her life with. The man she loved.

She took a deep breath. This was the most honest conversation they'd ever had and, way more than living in the same house or starting to work together, this felt like a completely fresh start.

She smiled at Rafe. 'It doesn't mean we can't be… you know…'

What had she been going to say before something stopped her? That what she wanted the most might be exactly what Daisy needed the most? That she and Rafe could be together? Be open to falling in love all over again? Be a real family?

'Be friends…?' Rafe supplied. 'The best of friends?'

'Mmm…' The sound was somewhat strangled.

Putting the children first didn't mean that Isobel didn't want him to kiss her again. *Really* kiss her this time, even knowing where it was highly likely to lead. But how could she suggest that they could be physically close and still protect the children? Or admit to how much she'd been thinking about how amazing the sex had always been with Rafe. How badly she wanted to do more than simply relive the echoes?

It wasn't so much the thought of scaring him off again. It was more that there was nothing needy or desperate about Isobel Matthews these days. She wasn't likely to run away and hide if something went wrong either, but Rafe might need time to trust that history wasn't going to repeat itself yet again. She hadn't given him enough time at the beginning, but it was something she could do now.

She stopped herself saying anything at all.

It turned out that it was a bit harder to be the one to end that eye contact, though.

Dear Lord… The way Isobel was *looking* at him.

He'd seen that look before. That invitation. He knew the steps to this dance too. The kissing. The touches. The way everything else became so totally irrelevant because every single one of his senses was drowning in overwhelming pleasure. The sight and scents of her body, the tiny sounds of both desire and satisfaction that she would make, the way it felt to touch her and *be* touched by her. The *taste* of her…

He couldn't look away. The part of his brain that was sounding an alarm was being instantaneously silenced by another part. An entire argument in the space of only a few heartbeats.

*The boys are in the house.*

*They're asleep. I'll hear them if they wake up. If they come looking for me, they'll go to my room, not the guest suite. They won't know…*

*You've just said that they're the most important thing in your life.*

*They are! But that doesn't mean I can never do something for myself. Something that I want. Something I think I might desperately need.*

*But…*

*It doesn't mean that I'm putting the boys at risk. We're both adults. We're both going to put our children first. I know I can trust Belle. I should have always trusted her. And she wants this as much as I do…*

That did it. Stifled the sound of the alarm enough for Rafe to reach out and take the wine glass from Isobel's unresisting fingers and put it down on the coffee table without breaking the gaze that was still locked on her eyes. He could even remember the very first step of that dance, when the invitation was accepted and he steadied her chin with the pad of his thumb. As if he needed to know exactly where to find her lips as he closed his eyes, tilting his head as he bent towards her.

Isobel automatically closed her eyes as she felt the touch of his thumb under her chin, as if her body knew exactly what she needed to do to make the most of this moment. This way, she could really feel the warmth of Rafe's skin and breath as he moved closer. She could smell the wine and another, deliciously masculine scent that she had forgotten until it filled her nostrils again—the scent that was purely Rafe's and was only noticeable when you were *this* close. When it wasn't going to be swept away by a sea breeze or so brief it almost didn't happen.

Isobel could delight in the sensation that rocked her all the way to her toes at the first touch of his lips. She felt her head tipping back as her lips parted to beg for this kiss to be deepened. This would have been unthinkable for a first kiss in a new relationship but this sensation was also deep in her cell memory and she wanted the magic she knew he'd make with both his lips and his tongue. She knew that, in another heartbeat, he would be sliding his fingers into her hair…like *that*…and the press of his fingertips would be as arousing as this kiss.

It would be incredibly hard to turn off the desire that was rapidly escalating out of control but Isobel had to give Rafe that option when they finally ended this kiss.

What if he'd just been responding to what he must have seen in her eyes? She'd know for sure, as soon as she caught his gaze again, whether he wanted this as much as she did. She'd also know whether it was pushing boundaries too far for anything to happen in the house his sons were sleeping in.

She did know—the moment his gaze caught hers again—because that intense focus of those dark, dark eyes unlocked another memory. The one where *she* was the most important person on earth to Rafe and she felt exactly the same way about him. Where, for the length of time it took for a physical conversation to celebrate that, the rest of the world was irrelevant.

'Come with me.' His voice was almost a growl.

They couldn't get down the hallway fast enough but Rafe paused for as long as it took to peep into the boys' room and check that they were sound asleep. He closed the door of their room quietly. Moments later, he closed the door of Isobel's room behind them just as quietly.

It felt like another tiny pause. It could have been long enough for either one of them to change their mind but it did the complete opposite. Isobel could feel the flames of desire become white hot and the heat seemed to be contagious because Rafe was unbuttoning his shirt to pull it off and then reaching to help Isobel take off her jersey and the tee shirt she was wearing beneath it. The garments puddled on the floor beside them and then there was another pause. A moment of palpable stillness as they stood there, simply looking at each other.

Had Isobel forgotten how beautiful Rafe's body was, or was the real thing simply so much more intense than a memory? His gorgeous olive brown skin and the irresistible copper disks of his nipples. Oh…and that soft arrow of dark hair that dragged her gaze down to the waistband of his jeans. She *had* forgotten what it felt like to release the stud button on his jeans. And the way the rasp of a zip opening could make it unbearable to wait any longer, but she remembered how Rafe would make her wait, teasing her with his hands and lips and tongue until she was begging him to give her what she needed the most.

And that wait would end up being the best part because it made her feel as if *she* was worth waiting for.

She hoped he would still whisper her name when he reached his own peak. It was on his lips now as his hands reached to trace the shape of her breasts before undoing her bra.

'Belle…'

# CHAPTER TEN

THIS FELT LIKE a genuinely clean slate.

Okay, you could see old writing that could never be completely wiped clean, but that was all it was. Something that had happened that couldn't be changed. Ghosts from the past that would always be there if you went looking for them. Unfortunate things had happened, like the aftermath of that Christmas party and the lack of loyalty from Isobel's family that had led to its disintegration, but there had been unknown, complicating factors on both sides that had played a big part and knowledge could lead to both understanding and forgiveness.

Tragic things had more recently been layered on top of what had happened so long ago, with the deaths of Lauren and Sharon Matthews and the birth of orphaned Daisy but, with everything out in the open between herself and Rafe, and the benefit of distance in time, Isobel could clearly see that it was not the total fault of any particular person involved. They were all to blame in some ways but the tragic finality that had brought her back into Rafe's life meant that everything that had come before was now irrelevant.

That first stolen night together was not only the start of something new and wonderful. It was the beginning of something even better than it had ever been. Life itself seemed better than it had ever been as the busy days slipped past, full of work and children and hospital visits, a house that was dry enough for the rebuilding to be well underway, wheels in motion for Daisy's adoption and steps in place to break the lease on Isobel's apartment in New Zealand and ship her personal items back to England.

Everything was perfect.

Except that Daisy wasn't well again.

The tiny baby had been a little out of sorts the day of the bead stone collecting and she had been running a slight temperature the next day, when Rafe took the twins back to the beach to hunt for some driftwood branches, but every parent in NICU knew to expect that their time in the intensive care unit was unlikely to progress completely smoothly. Most described it as a rollercoaster where it felt as if you were taking three steps forwards and then two backwards. There were always setbacks, sometimes small, sometimes large and, sadly, sometimes life-threatening.

That first setback for Daisy had only been small and she had recovered within a couple of days so Isobel was hopeful that whatever was causing Daisy to be irritable and unhappy again only a week later would be resolved just as easily. Isobel spent the entire day in the NICU that Sunday and managed to coax Daisy into drinking a little milk and she had been more than happy to remain in the armchair with skin-to-skin contact with the fragile infant for as long as Daisy was content.

Isobel talked to her softly as she fell asleep and didn't move after those dark eyes stopped staring into her own and drifted shut as one hour ticked over into another. Private words that were no more than whispered promises.

'Tomorrow, I'm going to talk to the solicitor about the next steps in adopting you, little one. There'll be lots of other people to talk to as well, I expect, and hundreds of pieces of paper to sign but, by the time you're big and strong enough to come home, you'll be my little girl. It'll be you and me in our own house.'

Daisy's head was still so small it fitted too easily into the cradle of Isobel's cupped hand.

'There's a tree in the back yard and we'll put a swing out there. We'll go to the beach too, when you're a bit bigger, and find the stones with the holes in them to make a string that's just for you. I'll tell you how you can close one eye and look through the hole and see a magical place.'

Isobel had looked through the hole in one of the bead stones and she'd seen Rafe…

It might be more complicated to find a way to steal more of those magic nights together, but it might also be a good thing. Rafe had said that it wasn't until he'd broken off their initial relationship that he'd realised how much he was missing her. Living in a different house might make him realise how much they all needed to be together. And, if real magic happened and he found himself falling in love with her all over again, they could all be together. As a real family.

'You've got the best uncle anyone could ever have,

my love. And two big brothers. They'll all be there to look after you whenever you need them.'

Isobel certainly wasn't going to jump the gun in any way because this new honesty and deeper level of trust between herself and Rafe was something too precious to risk breaking so it didn't matter how long it took. Even if it never changed from what it was right now, it was a broken dream that was, amazingly, being glued back to almost its original shape. And there was so much to look forward to.

'I'm going to choose the colours for your bedroom this week, darling. Not pink, though, and no unicorns. Shall we go for yellow and blue? Like a summer sky and sunshine? Maybe some soft green somewhere, like grass, and I could paint daisies everywhere. Daisies for Daisy...'

An alarm began to sound and a nurse was swiftly by Isobel's side.

'Did you forget to breathe for a second, button?' The nurse tapped Daisy's foot gently to stimulate a response and they could both see the tiny chest expand. 'What's going on? You haven't had one of those for a long time.' Her tone, as she gathered the baby into her hands, was a lot calmer than Isobel felt. 'Let's put her back in her incubator. Just to make sure we've got everything monitored properly.'

Isobel could still sit with her and help with her care, like changing her nappy, but Daisy was still miserable and by late that afternoon, after another apnoeic episode, a NICU consultant and her team were called in to assess her.

'It looks like it might be the first signs of an infection,' she told Isobel. 'But try not to worry too much. We're going to get on top of this as fast as we can.'

The specialist turned to the group of staff around her and, despite being a medical professional herself—or perhaps because she understood too much of what was being left unsaid, Isobel found her head spinning as she listened to a discussion around her that was full of potential dangers to this tiny baby beside her.

*Her* baby.

It was impossible not to worry too much. Antibiotics were being charted. Blood tests ordered. Forms for blood cultures being signed. Urine cultures and chest X-rays were discussed. A lumbar puncture was also mentioned and it was at that point that worry tipped into fear for Isobel. She knew why a lumbar puncture might be required and she knew all too well how dangerous an infection like meningitis could be to any baby, let alone one that still hadn't reached the weight and stage of development of an average newborn.

There was nothing Isobel could do for Daisy. She couldn't even be close enough to the incubator now, to talk to Daisy or put her hand through an access port and touch a tiny foot or cradle her head. All too soon there were doctors, nurses and technicians crowded into the space, more medical equipment with monitors and trolleys going in and out, and sometimes Isobel could only catch a glimpse of a small brown bear that had become wedged between the mattress inside the incubator and the plastic wall at the end.

Some of the specialist staff hadn't met Isobel before and maybe they didn't know her story.

'The best thing you can do, Mum, is to go home for

a while and get some rest yourself. We'll have a better idea of what we're dealing with tomorrow and, in the meantime, if anything changes we'll call you straight away.'

It didn't feel at all weird for someone to assume she was Daisy's mother because, in the space of just a few short weeks, that was how Isobel was feeling about this baby. Looking back, that rush of overwhelming love and the need to protect this child had probably come, without any warning, with that first touch. When she'd reached into the incubator to put her fingertip on Daisy's palm and felt those teeny, tiny fingers closing around it.

She *was* Daisy's mother.

But there was nothing she could do to protect her and walking away that evening was the hardest thing Isobel had ever done. As the double doors into the NICU suite swung shut behind her, however, Isobel realised that she was walking in the right direction. She knew perfectly well that, in order to be strong for Daisy, she needed to try and take care of herself. She needed to go home, not just to sleep but for something she needed even more urgently.

She needed to be with Rafe.

She knew he would talk to her and offer reassurance and support on both a medical and personal level, but all she really needed in this moment was simply to be *with* him.

One look at Isobel's face when she came through the door that evening and Rafe forgot about sorting the boys' lunchboxes and backpacks for school tomorrow.

He dropped homework books on the kitchen table and had Isobel in his arms before she had time to take her coat off.

'What's happened?'

'Daisy's sick… They think she's got an infection and…and maybe it's something I did? But I washed that little bear so carefully, and I always wear a gown and a mask, and I've never sanitised my hands so often in my life and…and…'

Apart from the day of the funeral, when it was only to be expected, the last time Rafe had seen Isobel really fighting tears had been in this kitchen, that night she'd arrived home late with the odd little brown bear in her bag, although she'd come close that first day of doing kangaroo care with Daisy, judging by the sparkle in her eyes. And Rafe was pretty sure he'd tasted tears when he'd kissed her on the beach that day but he hadn't been entirely sure that those tears weren't his own. This time was very different. These weren't tears that had any element of happiness or poignancy or even grief mixed into their cause. This was deep misery.

Fear…

'And…oh, Rafe… I don't know what to do and I'm really, really scared.'

Isobel buried her face against his chest as she burst into tears and Rafe could swear he felt something crack in his own heart at the sound of her sobbing. As he tightened his hold and bent his head to press his cheek against her hair, all he could think was how much he wished he could take this pain and fear away from her and shoulder it himself.

And then he realised that you only ever felt like that

about someone you truly loved and that stole his breath away completely.

He'd been *in* love with this woman long ago, with all the overwhelming emotions that went with that—and all the pain that came from losing it. He'd been so badly hurt by her and angry with her for such a long time but more recently he'd been impressed by her all over again and…yeah…attracted to her all over again as well. He hadn't forgotten how astonishingly good the sex had always been between them but he had been amazed to discover it seemed to be even better the second time around.

He understood her far better than he ever had too—how had he not known that she'd lived in her sister's shadow all her life? And they had a new bond in the way they felt as parents, because there was no doubt that Isobel had become Daisy's parent and he knew only too well how huge that was.

But the way he was feeling right now, as he held Isobel until she'd released enough of her own emotions to be able to talk to him, was something different. Something that was a combination of everything else and more. Something deeper than anything else.

Soul deep.

The kind of love that had actually been there all along, possibly from the moment he'd met Isobel.

The kind of love that could last a lifetime.

'Come and sit down,' he said gently, guiding her towards a chair with his hands on her shoulders. 'And tell me everything that's happening.'

Rafe had been able to offer real comfort when Isobel had been overwhelmed by the new direction her life was taking, by telling her that she didn't need to know what to do, she just needed to keep doing what she *was* doing and take one day at a time.

What was happening now, with this crisis for Daisy, meant that there was no way she *could* do anything, but the underlying message of taking one day at a time was still helpful. And this time there was more that Rafe could do to support Isobel when it became apparent by the next day that the worst was yet to come. Baby Daisy had pneumonia.

Rafe could—and did—take away any obligation for Isobel to be anywhere other than in NICU during the day by finding a new agency who were able to provide a locum practice nurse. He could—and did—make time to be there at St Luke's with her as often as possible. Helen was more than happy to spend more hours looking after the house and the twins. The staff at the Harrison Street Medical Centre knew Isobel now and were only too willing to offer whatever assistance they could and when Oscar and Josh told their friends that their baby sister was very sick, other parents began to step in to help as well.

It felt, to Isobel, as if she'd not only found the closest thing to a real family by coming back to Balclutha. She'd found an entire village. She drew strength from that support as she watched Daisy become even more unwell over the next few days. There was no kangaroo care now. She was back on CPAP, which meant her button of a nose was covered by a snugly fitting mask on the end of a tube, attached to equipment which delivered air at a constant pressure to keep air sacs open and prevent apnoeic episodes. The function of every major organ in that tiny body was being carefully watched, by monitors and electrodes and blood tests amongst the battery of technology and expertise that was available.

Rafe was in NICU with Isobel the afternoon that Daisy's team decided they needed to gain peripheral arterial access to monitor both her blood pressure levels as accurately as possible and her blood gas levels to see how much oxygen was circulating and how much carbon dioxide was being removed by her lungs. She knew this was an invasive enough procedure to be a warning that they were still a long way from getting on top of this crisis. And it was terrifying.

It felt as if it could be the beginning of the end.

And Isobel's heart was breaking. Because she knew she had found what she wanted most in her life—a family of her own—and she was in very real danger of having it simply ripped away from her if this baby she loved so much couldn't survive this. She didn't want to go back to her old life. She couldn't. What she had found here with Daisy and Oscar and Josh and Rafe was so different she could look back on her life in New Zealand and realise that, while it might have been professionally the best it could have been, it had been missing something far more important.

Love. People to care about and *be* cared about by. She couldn't go back to the loneliness that she'd sadly become so used to. She *wouldn't* go back but, if she lost Daisy, she would lose the foundation stone of the new life she wanted more than anything.

In this moment, she knew that Rafe was another foundation stone. He was probably losing all feeling in his hand with her clutching it so tightly, but he wasn't showing any sign of discomfort. He stood by her side when Isobel refused to leave Daisy alone with her medical team—a solid human rock rather than a simple stone, that she could cling to as tightly as necessary. Far enough away for any whispered conversation not to disturb what was happening.

Isobel watched as Daisy's wrist was pressed by fingers that looked large enough to be hurting her and squeezed Rafe's hand even more tightly. 'What are they doing?'

'It's called an Allen's test,' Rafe told her. 'You block both the radial and ulnar arteries in the wrist and then release the ulnar. If normal colour returns fast enough then the collateral circulation is okay and the radial artery can be cannulated.'

Maybe it would be easier to focus on something clinical, Isobel decided. But looking at what was being arranged on the sterile drape didn't help. There was antiseptic, and a cannula with its hollow needle that might be the smallest size available but it still looked far too big for Daisy's arm. She could see syringes and an infusion bag for flushing the lines, a three-way tap that would be used to withdraw blood for testing and transducers and cables that would be monitoring blood pressure. And there was more tubing and wires to add to what Daisy had already collected in the last few days.

Isobel closed her eyes tightly. Best not to look. Best just to hold Rafe's hand.

'It's not hurting her.' Rafe had bent his head so that he could whisper right beside her ear. 'She's fast asleep with the sedation she's been given.' His lips were close enough to tickle. 'Deep breath, hon. Daisy might know that you're here and she needs her mum to be strong.'

Isobel leaned into the warmth of his voice and the feel of his hand enclosing her own. She kept her eyes closed and just held on physically and let go mentally, deliberately not thinking about what was happening here. In the next few minutes, until the procedure was over, thoughts bubbled to the surface and then drifted away to allow others to take their place. There was grief there for her sister and mother. Fear for Daisy but also a wash of love that was so powerful Isobel knew it had changed her for ever. And there was also the realisation that her love for this man, standing beside her and holding her up, was just as powerful.

This wasn't a dream of what a perfect future could look like. Or a peek into a distorted mirror. This had no connection to the future. Or the past, for that matter—even the most recent past that included their love-making—because, in this moment, both the future and past were irrelevant. This awareness was so all-encompassing that her mind, and heart, could only soak in this moment. Her love for Raphael Tanner was simply there. A fact of life, as much as the way her heart was beating without needing any conscious direction. As solid as the man himself and as real as the grip of his hand around her own.

Isobel opened her eyes and took in a slow, deep breath. She could do this. She could be strong for Daisy and cope with whatever was going to come, as long as she had Rafe by her side.

# CHAPTER ELEVEN

RAFE'S HEART WAS BREAKING. Both for baby Daisy and for Isobel. The procedure to insert an arterial line had been so hard to watch that it was probably just as well that Isobel wasn't there in the middle of the night a couple of days later when the team made the decision to intubate this tiny baby because the levels of carbon dioxide still in her blood were dangerously high and she needed more help to breathe. Isobel had finally been persuaded to come home for a few hours to get the kind of sleep that was impossible when she was in the armchair beside Daisy's incubator.

The chair where Rafe had first seen her holding Daisy with that oh, so small head nestled between her breasts and he'd seen—and remembered—exactly why he'd fallen in love with this woman. It was nearly a week since Daisy had become so sick and days since she'd even opened her eyes. There was talk about multi-organ failure, so antibiotics and other drugs were being carefully juggled.

They needed a miracle, but when it began to happen it seemed too rapid to be trustworthy. How could blood gas levels return to being within normal parameters so quickly after the addition of extra assistance from a ventilator? Vital signs like blood pressure and heart rate were stabilising and the function of organs like her kidneys were heading towards acceptable levels. One by one, the tubes and wires and monitoring equipment were being taken away.

The next time Rafe stole some time from work to visit, he had fully expected to find Isobel sitting in that familiar armchair in NCIU but the last thing he'd expected to find was that she had the baby—*her* baby— snuggled against her skin again.

'It's just for a short time today.' Isobel's voice wobbled. 'But she's doing so well, they thought she deserved a cuddle. She's lost weight but it really looks like she's finally beaten this infection.'

Rafe didn't care that he had tears rolling down his face as he crouched beside the chair to gaze at Daisy's little face, fast asleep and utterly content.

'She's a wee fighter,' he said softly. 'She wants to be here, that's for sure.'

'I want her to be here,' Isobel whispered. 'More than I could ever have imagined. It's weird, isn't it?'

'What?'

'That she's only been in my life for such a short time but I can't imagine my life without her.'

'That's how fast it can happen.' Rafe smiled as he nodded his complete understanding. 'I felt like that the first moment I held Oscar and Josh.'

Isobel wiped away a tear. 'How are the boys? I feel like I've barely seen them for far too long.'

'They're good. They'll be so happy to know that their little sister is getting better. Even happier, though,

I have to admit, that they're going to their friend Simon's birthday party and sleepover tonight. It's a pirate party and there's even going to be a boat that arrives on a trailer and there's some mechanism that means it can be rocked like they're sailing through a stormy sea.' He glanced up at a large clock on the wall. 'I can't stay too long because I promised I'd be back in time after school to help them get dressed up. We've got costumes with eye patches and hats and swords and everything.'

'I'm sorry I won't see them.'

'I'll take lots of photos,' Rafe promised. 'And I'm going to cook something special for us too. We can have our own party to celebrate this little miracle...' He used the tip of his forefinger to stroke Daisy's cheek. A featherlike touch that was intended not to wake her up but she felt it. Her face scrunched up and then relaxed again, except for one side of her mouth that was still curled up.

'Oh, my God...' Rafe breathed. 'Is she *smiling*?'

'She heard you calling her a little miracle,' Isobel whispered. 'I think she liked that.'

It might have only been a small curl of Daisy's lips but it had wrapped itself entirely around Rafe's heart. He was feeling a bond with this baby that was right up there with how he felt about his own boys and the ripple of that bone-deep emotion was including the woman who was holding this precious infant.

It was not the first time he'd felt the need to care for and protect Isobel, but it was getting stronger every time. And, man, she needed a bit of pampering after the rough week she'd just been through. It looked as if it hadn't been only Daisy who'd lost weight and those dark shadows under Isobel's eyes were all too obvious against her paler than usual skin. He found himself trying to remember something that he knew would make her happy.

'Is Mexican food still your most favourite thing in the world to eat?'

Isobel blinked. 'I can't believe you remembered that. Yes, I still love it.'

'Tacos?'

'And nachos. And quesadillas.' Isobel was smiling. 'I'm hungry already.'

'I'm not sure I'm up to cooking them, but I'll give it a go.'

'Don't cook.' Isobel shook her head. 'You've missed nearly as much sleep as I have in the last few days and I know how tired you must be. I'll pick up takeout on my way home.'

*Home…*

He knew perfectly well that Isobel and Daisy would be moving to their own home in the not-too-distant future, but life at the moment, especially while Daisy had been so sick, had become just a day at a time so it didn't matter that it felt so right to hear her say that. She *was* going to be coming home.

And the idea of her moving out to a home of her own was giving Rafe an odd empty feeling in his gut—as if he was missing her already.

The way he had when he'd backed out of their relationship all those years ago and pushed her out of his life? He didn't want to feel like that again. He wanted what they had so unexpectedly found together again and this time he wasn't about to panic. He knew he could trust this. And trust Isobel.

He'd never told her he loved her. Not directly, anyway. He'd only said that she'd been the one he'd loved rather than her sister. Past tense. Isobel had never said it to him either, even back when it was so obvious she was in love with him. Had she just been waiting for him to say the 'L' word first? Confident that it would happen, despite him telling her that he would never go there again, because what they had together was so amazing?

It *had* been amazing.

But this second time around it was even more amazing, wasn't it? More real, perhaps, because they knew each other so much more intimately. And because there were children and a baby involved who all needed their protection and love. More trustworthy, because they'd both been battered by life but what was holding them so close seemed to be growing steadily stronger.

Rafe had really given up on even the idea of marriage after Lauren had left him. He'd given up on ever trying to find love again but, just like the first time he'd had his convictions challenged, things were changing because he'd met Isobel.

Because she'd come back into his life.

It felt like time to tell her that.

But not here. There was a much better place for something so personal and private.

'Compromise,' he said, his voice slightly raw. 'You're even more exhausted than I am. Just come home and we'll get it delivered.'

It was a Mexican feast, covering the table in Isobel's favourite room of Rafe's house. They weren't sitting at the dining table because it was the old wooden work table that had become *their* place to be together, sitting at right angles to each other at the end of the table, sharing food or wine under the watchful eye of Cheddar, usually lying in *his* special place on the old couch.

This was where Isobel and Rafe had talked properly for the first time since their relationship had broken up. Where she'd learned that he'd given up a career in Emergency that he'd been so passionate about to become a GP and raise his sons. She'd learned that, shockingly, Lauren had been well advanced in a pregnancy when she'd died and that, miraculously, that baby—*her* niece—had survived.

It had been in this room that she'd first met her nephews and felt those first powerful connections that could come from the kind of unconditional acceptance and love a true family could provide. And it had also been in this room that Rafe had told her that he hadn't wanted to marry her sister. That Isobel had been the one he'd loved.

She'd found employment in a new job sitting at this table, along with the fresh start that a professional relationship promised to offer them both and that had been worthy of celebrating but this was the first time it felt as if they were having a party in this kitchen that was the heart of Rafe's house.

There were all of Isobel's favourite Mexican dishes here. A nachos platter with a nest of corn chips holding a delicious dip of refried beans, guacamole and sour cream. Crunchy fried tortillas filled with melted cheese that were the best kind of quesadillas and tacos with melt-in-the-mouth pulled beef, spicy salsa and crisp lettuce. The restaurant had also supplied the icy cold lager they were drinking with a wedge of lime stuffed into the neck of the bottles.

'There's no way we can ever eat all this food, Rafe.'

'Just as well our boys love Mexican food almost as much as you do, then.'

*Our* boys?

Isobel needed a moment to absorb that. Or maybe it was more that she wanted to tuck away the fact that it didn't feel odd to hear Rafe say that. That she really did feel like part of this family.

'It feels different without them here.'

'Mmm…' Rafe was smiling as he loaded another corn chip with dip. 'Quieter.'

'You know what I mean. Even when they're in bed, you know they're in the house and…and you can feel it.'

Rafe ate his chip, nodding as he swallowed. 'There speaks a true parent.' He lifted his bottle of lager, his voice softening. 'Here's to Daisy's mum for coping with a rough stretch. And here's to Daisy for being the fighter she is. May she grow up to love Mexican food as much as the rest of her family.'

'I wonder what the pirates are eating?'

'Fish fingers, I reckon.'

'Or meatballs for cannonballs?'

'Crackers. For Polly the parrot.'

'And gold coins for treasure.'

They were both laughing but not enough to account for the tears that suddenly sprang into Isobel's eyes. Rafe's smile evaporated instantly.

'What is it?' he asked quietly.

'I hope Daisy wants a pirate party one day.' Her

breath hitched in a kind of hiccup. 'I was so scared she might never actually get a birthday party.'

'I know…'

Rafe took hold of Isobel's hand. His skin was chilled from where he'd been holding the cold bottle of lager and, without thinking, Isobel put her other hand on top of his.

'I've never been so scared in my life.'

'I know,' he said again.

He had put his other hand on top of Isobel's and then, in a silence that stretched on and on, their hands did a kind of slow dance—moving in and around each other, interlacing fingers with a touch that was so gentle it was astonishing that it could be felt in every cell of Isobel's body.

When she lifted her gaze it felt as if Rafe had been waiting to catch it with his own. So that she would know he was feeling it as well? The connection—and the silent communication—was so powerful there was no need for either of them to say anything out loud.

Except…there *was* a need, wasn't there?

Isobel needed to hear Rafe say it out loud. That he loved her. She needed to tell him how much she loved him out loud, not through this poignant kind of touch, however meaningful it was. She needed to tell him that she trusted him absolutely now. That she would trust him with her life in a heartbeat, because she couldn't imagine a future without him in it, any more than she could imagine one without Daisy. And she desperately needed to hear him tell her that he felt the same way.

She watched his lips part and knew he was about to say something. Given how much love she could see in his eyes, Isobel knew that it was going to be exactly what she wanted to hear and her heart skipped a beat as she held her breath.

She was still holding her breath when Rafe's phone buzzed.

And while she watched the colour drain from his face as he listened to what sounded like a frantic female voice.

'I'm on my way,' he said, standing up as he abruptly ended the call. His eyes were so dark they looked black when he caught Isobel's gaze. 'It's Oscar,' he said. 'There's been an accident.'

It was Isobel's turn to give Rafe the kind of support he'd been giving her ever since she had crash-landed back into his life. Her training enabled her to stay calm, despite her own personal connection to this victim, in the face of what could possibly be a time-critical incident, judging by how ashen Rafe was looking.

'I'll drive.'

'I can do it.'

'I know what I'm doing, Rafe. Trust me.' She took the keys from his hand. 'Where are we heading? Simon's house?'

'No. They called an ambulance. They're already on their way to St Luke's. Simon's mother's gone with him and she had to take Josh. I could hear him in the background.' Rafe's voice caught. 'I've never heard him sound that distraught.'

Isobel checked that Rafe had done up his safety belt and then put her foot down on the accelerator. She knew she could drive fast and keep them safe. If she got a speeding ticket, she'd deal with it later.

'What's happened to Oscar?'

'He fell from that damned boat when it was rocking. He was holding his plastic sword and it went straight into his leg on impact. It sounds like it might have hit an artery before it snapped off.'

Under Rafe's direction, Isobel parked his car in the doctors' space of the ambulance bay and when they ran into the emergency department of St Luke's Hospital they could see the stretcher holding Oscar being wheeled into one of the resuscitation rooms. A woman, presumably Simon's mother, was holding Josh, who appeared to be desperate to follow his brother and was screaming with frustration at being held back.

For a few moments, at the doors to the resuscitation room, it was fraught.

Isobel could see Oscar being transferred to the bed. A pale ghost of a little boy in a pirate's costume and face paint of a moustache and goatee beard who looked barely conscious.

She could hear the paramedics giving a swift handover.

'Heart rate of one twenty. Blood pressure seventy-six over forty.'

Isobel's heart dropped like a stone. Oscar must have lost so much blood he was in haemorrhagic shock and that was, indeed, a time-critical injury.

'Estimated blood loss approximately a litre,' the paramedic continued. 'There's no pedal pulse in the left foot.'

She could also hear Josh's sobbing as he clung to his father.

'I've got to go and look after Oscar, Josh. I'm sorry but you can't go in there.'

'*No*...don't go, Daddy. Please don't go...'

'Aunty Belle's here. She's going to look after you.' Rafe was staring into Resus, clearly needing to see and hear what was going on.

'We couldn't get venous access,' Isobel heard a paramedic say. 'He's too shut down.'

'We'll go for central venous access for fluid resuscitation.' It looked like every ED doctor was in there with Josh and it was a senior consultant who was taking the lead. 'Type and cross-match in case we need a whole blood transfusion and get Theatre on standby.'

Rafe caught Isobel's gaze over the top of Josh's head and there was a desperate plea in his eyes.

'Come with me, sweetheart.' Isobel prised Josh away from his father and, much to her relief, he wrapped his arms around her neck and burrowed his head against her shoulder as he continued sobbing. 'Daddy's going to help look after Oscar and he'll come and tell us what's happening really soon.'

The relatives' room had a television and a DVD player. It had books and toys and snacks but there was nothing that Josh was remotely interested in. Isobel did everything she could to soothe him, holding him in her arms and rocking him as they sat on a small couch. Telling him over and over again that Oscar was being looked after by very clever doctors and nurses and they were doing everything they could to make him better. She stopped short of telling him that everything was going to be all right. She didn't know that herself so she couldn't promise something that might turn out to not be true.

It was the longest hour of her life as she waited for news. Josh eventually exhausted himself crying and fell asleep in her arms and Isobel just kept on holding him and counting every minute that ticked past. When Rafe finally came to find her, it felt as if she had frozen to the spot. She couldn't even find any words to break an awful silence as Rafe sat down on another couch and buried his face in his hands.

'He's in Theatre.' His words were muffled. 'They've repaired the artery and stopped the bleeding. They're just closing up now but he's going to be okay.'

'Oh…' Isobel had to bite her lip hard to stop herself bursting into tears which would scare Josh if he woke up. 'Thank goodness… Did he need a blood transfusion?'

'No. He responded very well to the fluid resuscitation and was stabilised enough to have a CT scan before going to Theatre, so the surgeons knew exactly what they were dealing with. I don't think the blood loss was as bad as they initially thought.'

'It's a hard thing to estimate. It can look far more than it is, especially if it's a hard surface or there's no thick clothing to soak it up.'

Rafe tipped his head back, rubbing his eyes. 'Simon's parents panicked. They knew to put pressure on a wound to stop bleeding, but they also knew not to pull out an impaled object. It wasn't till the paramedics got there and put a doughnut dressing and pressure bandage on that it was controlled at all.' He sat up. 'How's Josh been?'

'Frightened. I did my best to reassure him but I couldn't make promises that I might not have been able to keep. And… I was scared too. As scared as I was when I thought I might lose Daisy.'

Had it only been an hour or two ago that she'd been telling Rafe how terrifying that had been? When he'd held her hands and she'd been so sure he was about to tell her that he loved her? There was certainly nothing on either of their minds now other than the wellbeing of two very much-loved small boys.

'Could you take him home, Belle? So that you can both get some sleep?'

'Of course.'

'I'll carry him out to the car.'

Josh woke up as his father lifted him. 'Daddy?'

'It's okay, Josh. Everything's okay. Oscar's had an operation on his leg and it's fine. It's not bleeding any more. He needs to stay here tonight but he might be allowed to come home tomorrow.'

'Can I stay here too?'

'No. Aunty Belle is going to take you home to your own bed. I'm coming down to the car with you so I can say goodnight and then I'll stay with Oscar so he's not lonely.'

Isobel followed as he carried Josh into the corridor.

'Aunty Belle can bring you back in the morning,' Rafe told Josh as they went through ED towards the ambulance bay. 'Maybe you could bring Oscar something to wear so he doesn't need to be a pirate when we go home? You could bring him a treat for breakfast too, if you like.'

'Like a hamburger?'

Rafe chuckled. 'Sure. Why not?'

Josh was almost asleep again as he buckled him into the back seat. Rafe closed the door gently and then turned to Isobel, drawing her into his arms for a brief but fierce hug.

'I'll text you as soon as he's out of Theatre.'

Isobel hugged him back just as tightly. 'I'm with Josh. I don't want to leave you.'

'It's going to be all right.' Rafe's voice was against her ear. 'Go and get some rest, Belle.' His lips were on her temple. 'Everything's going to be all right.'

Except it wasn't.

It took only one look at Rafe's face when Isobel arrived at St Luke's with Josh the next morning to know that something was very wrong. He almost looked worse than he had last evening when he'd been about to join Oscar in the resuscitation area.

And Isobel was terrified all over again. She froze while Josh, carrying the fast-food paper bag full of treats, ran past her towards the bed he could see Oscar sitting in.

'What is it, Rafe? What's wrong?'

She took another glance towards Oscar, but he was looking far better than she'd expected this soon after his surgery. Josh was sitting on the end of the bed now and the bag was being delved into. Not for the food yet. It was the toys that had come with it that had the boys' attention first.

Rafe had followed her gaze. 'Oscar's fine,' he told

her. 'He'll be discharged to go home later today after he's been seen by his surgeon.'

There was something odd about Rafe's tone. Because it lacked the joy she would have expected to hear with that news?

'I don't understand,' she said quietly. 'It's obvious that there's something wrong.'

Rafe wasn't meeting her gaze and, for some reason, that sent a chill down Isobel's spine. He'd done this once before, hadn't he? When he'd been finding the words to tell her that it was over. That he didn't want them to be together any longer. That he needed…space…

He was pulling something out of his shirt pocket. A small folded piece of paper. A test result? Isobel caught her breath. Had something shown up that was wrong with Oscar? Something serious, like leukaemia? But, if that was the case, why would Rafe have said that his son was fine?

The information on the paper made no sense either.

'This is a blood type and cross-match result,' she said. 'It's just Oscar's blood group and rhesus factor.'

Rafe's breath came out in a huff that sounded broken. 'Yeah…*just* his blood group,' he echoed.

Isobel glanced over her shoulder but the twins weren't looking at their father so they wouldn't see an expression that might have alarmed them. They were showing their toys to a nurse and eating French fries at the same time.

'Come with me,' she said to Rafe, 'and tell me what the hell's going on. Somewhere that you're not going to upset the boys.'

Rafe hesitated but then followed her, the grim ex-

pression on his face a warning that Isobel wasn't going
to like what she was about to hear.

'So… Oscar's blood group is A. I don't understand
what the problem is.'

'Lauren's blood was cross-matched when she came
here after the accident because she *did* need a transfusion. That's how I know that her blood group was O.'

'And…?'

'So's mine. I'm an O.' Rafe shook his head at her obvious lack of comprehension. 'It's not possible for two
O parents to have an A baby,' he said slowly. 'And that
means that I'm not Oscar's father. Or Josh's, obviously.'

Isobel could feel the shockwave start at the level of
her ears as she heard his words but then it pulsed down,
right to her feet, like a lightning bolt finding the earth.

'But that means…'

'That Lauren was already pregnant before the night
of the Christmas party.' Rafe gave another one of those
broken-sounding huffs of breath. 'We all thought the
twins were in great shape when they were born. With
better-than-expected weights. Now I know why.'

'Oh, my God…' Isobel's head was spinning. 'I had no
idea. She lied to me as well. Unless…she didn't know
herself? Like with Daisy?'

'She must have known there was a chance that I
wasn't the father. And she definitely knew how much I
loved those babies.' Rafe's voice was dangerously quiet.
'Enough to let myself get blackmailed into a marriage
I never intended to have. I wasn't going to let history
repeat itself and not be a father to my boys, but that
wasn't difficult because I loved them.'

'I know,' Isobel whispered. She'd seen that love. That

amazing bond Rafe had with the twins. He couldn't *be* a better father.

'And now it turns out that I'm not even related to them. How am I supposed to explain that? How do I tell them that their Aunty Belle is the only *real* family they've actually got? How ironic is that?' Rafe was shaking his head. 'I was worried at first that they might get hurt if they got too close to you, but the idea that our family might get destroyed never occurred to me.'

'Are you saying that this is somehow *my* fault?' The shockwave had been replaced by a numbness that was spreading just as rapidly.

Rafe turned away. 'No, I'm not saying that,' he said. 'I just wish I'd never met your sister.'

His voice was as raw as Isobel had ever heard it. So was the unspoken message. If Rafe had never met Isobel and they had never fallen in love with each other, he wouldn't have met Lauren and none of this heartbreak would have ever happened.

He might as well have said that he wished he'd never met *her*.

'Daddy?' Josh had come to the door of the paediatric surgical ward. 'Why are you out here? We've got a hamburger for you too.' He took hold of Rafe's hand and was pulling him away. He looked over his shoulder as he did so. 'There's one for you, Aunty Belle, remember?'

'Save it for me, sweetheart.' It was astonishing that Isobel could keep her tone this cheerful and completely hide the fact that the world felt as if it was falling away from beneath her feet. 'I'm not very hungry just at the moment.'

Food was the last thing she wanted right now. It was

hard enough to even pull in a new breath with this curious numbness seeping through her body. It was a bit like that feeling when she'd first arrived back and there'd simply been too many huge emotions to try and process. The loss of her mother and sister. Seeing Rafe again. The flooded house. The news of another baby. Jetlag and exhaustion.

She needed to escape. To find somewhere she could breathe more easily. And think. If she could just clear the foggy feeling in her head then perhaps she would be able to make some sense out of what felt like a complete disaster that she hadn't seen coming.

# CHAPTER TWELVE

ISOBEL WENT HOME.

The moment she arrived outside the house, however, it hit her that this wasn't her home at all. It was the home of Rafe and his boys. And that, despite everything that had happened since she'd first walked through this door, in this moment she felt about as welcome as she'd been the day of the funeral, when she'd shocked Rafe by turning up in his life again. For a long time Isobel stayed in her car, her thoughts swirling.

The shock of her reappearance seemed insignificant now, in comparison to the blow he'd just received. Isobel was feeling so torn in two herself that she buried her face in her hands. She wanted to be with Rafe. A large part of her desperately wanted to be as much of a rock for him in this rough patch as he'd been for her when Daisy had been hovering on the edge of survival. Surely he knew, deep down, that it made no difference to the relationship he had with his sons whether or not he was their biological father—in the same way that she couldn't love Daisy any more, whether or not she'd given birth to her?

But a larger part of Isobel knew that, as heartbreaking as it was, the last thing Rafe needed right now was to be in the company of Lauren Matthews' sister when it must seem as if she had managed to deliver an ultimate betrayal. This wasn't Isobel's fault and maybe Lauren had convinced herself that Rafe had fathered her twins, but it certainly wasn't Rafe's fault in any way, and it was totally unfair that he had to deal with this. He'd had one betrayal after another in his life, hadn't he? A father who'd rejected him as a baby, a wife who'd cheated on him, a woman who'd blackmailed him into marriage...

Had he now somehow linked letting Isobel back into his life with a worst-case scenario that his family was going to disintegrate?

Surely he'd see how wrong that was as soon as the initial shock of this news wore off?

But what was Isobel going to do in the meantime?

She couldn't stay out here in the car any longer. With a sigh that was almost a groan she went and let herself into the house.

Should she stay out of Rafe's way until he was ready to talk to her? Give him some time to feel safe with his boys in their own home? Until he could see her and not be reminded of the appalling secret her sister might have used to trap him and change his life for ever? Isobel could pack a bag and go to a hotel. She could even make the move into her childhood home in Barrington Street. The work on the house was by no means finished but it had been stripped and dried out enough to not be a health hazard. Lots of people managed to live in houses while renovations were happening around them.

But would her absence make things worse rather than better between her and Rafe? And she couldn't pack up and leave before explaining things to Oscar and Josh, could she? Had Rafe really been worried about the effect on his children of letting her back into his life? She would never intentionally do anything to hurt his boys. Or him, for that matter. You didn't do that to people you loved.

Absorbed in her thoughts, Isobel had walked into her favourite room of this wonderful old home. She let Cheddar out into the garden and then put the kettle on, thinking that maybe a cup of strong coffee would help with the dark, foggy feeling in her head that made it impossible to know what the best thing to do was. Did Rafe need time alone with his boys to realise that nothing had really changed?

Or would it break any trust that had formed that she wasn't about to run away at the first sign of trouble?

There was no question of running away from this.

Because… Daisy… And Oscar. And Josh…

And because… Rafe…

Isobel wasn't about to let her sister take away—for the second time—that dream of a future with the man she loved. It was more than worth fighting for. The only problem was that she had no idea how to begin that fight.

The kitchen was spotless, because she'd used the first anxious hours of waiting for news on Oscar last night to clean up the leftovers of the Mexican feast. Instead of opening a cupboard to find a clean mug for her coffee, Isobel opened the dishwasher. She could put these dishes away and use one of the clean mugs in there.

But when she pulled out a plate from the bottom

rack, the feel of it in her hands made her head spin all over again.

It really felt as if someone was holding the other side of this plate.

No. Not someone. Rafe.

She could hear his voice.

*'You were the one I loved, Belle. You were the one...'*

Oh, help...

This wasn't helping clear her head at all. A scratch on the back door when Cheddar wanted to come back inside made Isobel wonder if being out in the garden would be better. And then she realised that she'd known the best place to go for some fresh air all along.

She'd just needed Cheddar to remind her.

It was early afternoon by the time Rafe got home with the boys.

He carried Oscar into the living room and found pillows and blankets to make him a bed on the couch.

'Just movies and games this afternoon, okay? On the couch. You're going to need to be careful of your leg until it's all healed up.'

'Can I go to school?'

'Not until your leg's better. Josh will have to go back tomorrow but he can stay home with you this afternoon.'

'Will you stay home with me too?'

'Today I will, buddy. I'll get Helen to come and look after you tomorrow while I'm at work.'

'Aunty Belle could look after me.' Oscar's eyes were already drifting shut as he lay back against the pillows. Rafe tucked a blanket over him.

Josh looked up from where he was searching for a favourite movie on the shelf below the television. 'Where *is* Aunty Belle?'

'I don't know.'

'And where's Cheddar?' Oscar opened his eyes. 'I want him to come and sleep on the couch with me.'

'I don't know that either, buddy. Maybe he's out in the garden. I'll go and have a look for him.'

What Rafe *did* know was he needed to talk to Isobel. He'd had to focus on Oscar and being sure it was safe to take him home while he'd still been blindsided by the shocking discovery that he couldn't possibly be the twins' father but, in the back of his mind, waiting to surface, was the memory of how shocked Isobel had also been. The look in her eyes when words were leaking from what felt like a broken heart and he'd said that he wished he'd never met her sister.

A look that suggested she was hearing that he wished he'd never met *her*.

He didn't blame her for leaving the hospital. If he hadn't had his boys to care for, he might have done the same thing and gone to find a private place to think about what had happened and what it could mean but, in a way, having to keep them entertained and out of trouble, reassure Josh that his brother was going to be absolutely fine and pretend that hamburgers and French fries for a late breakfast was the best ever had been exactly what he'd needed to do in that initially stunned period.

Because it had allayed any fear that what he'd just found out could hurt his family in some way. It made it crystal clear that these boys were his. He'd taken responsibility for them before they were born, had loved them from the moment they'd taken their first breaths and would protect and support them in any way he could until *he* took his last breath. Whether or not he'd actually fathered them didn't matter a damn. Any more than it mattered that Isobel hadn't given birth to Daisy. She *was* that baby's mother. Rafe had known that since he'd seen her that first time, with the precious infant against her bare skin. When he'd seen the love in her eyes when she'd made the decision to adopt Daisy and the courage with which she'd stepped up to take on that enormous responsibility.

The kitchen and the garden felt empty enough to let him know instantly that Cheddar wasn't anywhere to be found in or around the house. That Isobel wasn't either. And it felt as if Rafe had actually swallowed that empty feeling because it was lodged in his gut. In a Belle-shaped kind of hole. It wasn't until he came back inside that Rafe saw the note on the table, near the school books that weren't going to be needed today. He took it back to the living room.

'Aunty Belle's taken Cheddar for a walk. She's left you guys a note.'

'What does it say?'

'Um…' Rafe cleared his throat. 'It says…um…' The words on the note were blurring slightly and he had to blink.

Josh took the slip of paper from his hand. 'Let *me* read it, Daddy. I'm good at reading now.'

'Me too.' Oscar was pushing himself upright on his pillows and Josh wriggled onto the couch so they could both look at Isobel's clear printing.

'Dear Oscar and Josh. I'm taking Cheddar for a walk... because I want to find a... What's that word, Daddy?'

'Special.'

'And that one?'

'Bead.'

'A *special* bead stone for Oscar because he's got a sore leg.'

The boys were taking turns to read each line.

'And one for Josh because I know how scary it is to have something bad happen to someone you love. You're both very...what's that word, Daddy?'

'Brave.'

'Lots of love from Aunty Belle.'

Oscar and Josh looked at each other.

'I love Aunty Belle,' Josh said.

'Me too.' Oscar nodded.

'Daddy?' Josh was looking very serious. 'Do you love Aunty Belle?'

Rafe had to try and swallow the huge lump in his throat. 'Yeah...' He had to blink again too. 'I really do.'

Cheddar had given up chasing seagulls.

Isobel had found what she'd been searching for. The two special stones but, more importantly, a clear head and a calmness that came with certainty. It was probably past time she went home but she hadn't wanted to move. The sunshine was warm enough today for the sea breeze to be a delight and the wash of gentle waves on the pebbles was a balm to her soul. But she was ready now and she pushed herself to her feet.

She'd been sitting just below the point where the

stony shore started sloping towards the sea so it wasn't until she stood up that she saw another person on the beach. The figure was too far away for her to recognise but she knew who it was.

Rafe…

Pebbles crunched and slid beneath her feet as she tried to walk faster. Cheddar bounded ahead and then ran in figures-of-eight between them as they got closer. And closer. Close enough to both reach out at exactly the same time to hold each other tightly enough to suggest that neither of them ever wanted to let the other go. Except they did, of course. Just far enough to kiss each other. And then kiss each other again.

And then they both sat on the stones and held hands just as tightly as they'd held each other and Cheddar lay down with a resigned sigh because no one was paying him the slightest attention.

'I *was* coming home,' Isobel told Rafe.

'I know. But I couldn't wait. And there are two little boys who want to see you.' Rafe was smiling. 'Helen told me to take as long as it took, though. I think she knew how important this was.'

'You coming to find me?'

'No.' Rafe leaned in to kiss her again. 'I've already done that. I found you and I fell in love with you. Again. Or maybe I still was even after all these years. This was about not losing you.'

'Not possible.' Isobel caught her bottom lip between her teeth. 'I could go to the other side of the world again but I'd be leaving most of me here. With you. Important bits—like my heart. I know that because I've already done it and I don't want to do it again.'

'I don't want you to do it again. I want all of you here. I'm happy to share, with Oscar and Josh and Daisy but…you know what?'

Isobel's smile felt misty. 'What?'

'The house felt so empty when we got home and you weren't there. My life would feel even emptier without you.'

Isobel was blinking back tears now. 'I love you. It's only ever been you, Rafe. Like someone wise once told me, when you know, you know.'

Rafe was blinking too. 'Very wise, that person. When I stopped being scared this morning I realised that I know I'm a father. Nothing can change that. And I know how much I need *you*. How much I love you. Nothing's going to change that either.'

There was only the sound of the wash of waves on pebbles for a long, long moment as Isobel let herself fall into the love she could see in Rafe's eyes. It really was time to go home now. Because it really *was* home she would be going to. She remembered to pick up the stones she'd spent so long searching for.

'Can I see?' Rafe reached for one of the stones—an especially smooth, flat, round white stone with a perfect hole right in the centre. 'Wow…this is a beauty.'

'I like this one too.' Isobel held onto the hollow tube of grey stone that was lined with white.

They both held their stones up to their eyes.

'What can you see?' Isobel asked softly, even though she knew perfectly well that Rafe could only see her.

'A magic place,' Rafe told her. 'I can see into the future.'

Isobel could see his smile through the hole in her stone. 'How 'bout that?' she murmured. 'I can see exactly the same thing.'

# EPILOGUE

*Nearly three years later...*

'I'VE GOT SOMETHING to tell you.'

'I think I already know.' Rafe was standing beneath the biggest tree in the garden, a magnificent old oak that had a branch strong enough for a swing made out of rope and an old tractor tyre.

'Really? But I only just found out myself. Like, a minute ago.'

Isobel kept walking until she was so close to Rafe her body was touching his. And then she leaned a little closer, pushing him back against the trunk of the tree, and tilted her head up in an invitation to be kissed.

'Daisy told me.' Rafe accepted the invitation and kissed her with a thoroughness that made her toes curl.

'Oh… Really? I wonder how she knows?'

Isobel turned her head at the sound of barking. Their new puppy, Brie, was trying to entice Cheddar to play but the older dog was simply sitting there like a golden rock, wagging his tail. Brie gave up and bounced towards where Oscar and Josh were kicking a football around on the lawn, knocking Daisy off her feet as she went past her. Daisy shrieked with laughter, got up and also joined the game of football.

'She's about to turn three, that girl of ours. She knows everything.'

Isobel laughed. 'And she's so bossy.'

'Yep.' Rafe was grinning. 'I'd tell you what she said but I think it's supposed to be a secret.'

He lifted a hand to touch one of the strings hanging from another branch of this old tree. A string with stones knotted down its length. There were three of them now. Daisy had been helping to find bead stones since she began walking. Before that even, when they sat on the beach for a picnic and she would sit there, having invented the game of holding up every stone she could fit into her little hand to find out if it had a hole in it or not.

Isobel merely raised her eyebrows and Rafe's grin widened. 'Okay, okay…she told me that she was going to have a pirate party for her birthday.'

'I wonder whose idea that really was?'

'I know. Oscar's still telling everyone he's a real pirate and he's got the scar to prove it.'

'I don't mind doing a pirate party, if that's what she wants. And it probably is, because she loves everything her big brothers love. We won't do the boat, though.'

'No.' Rafe's agreement was heartfelt. 'Or plastic swords.'

'That wasn't what I came out here to tell you, though.'

'Oh?' Rafe was watching Isobel's face and maybe there was something in her expression that gave him a clue. 'Oh, my God…' he breathed. 'You're not…?'

'Mmm. I am. I just did the test.'

Rafe pulled her into his arms, a bead stone string still tangled in his fingers. He was hugging her as tightly as he had that day he'd come to find her on the beach. The day they'd seen exactly this future through the holes in their stones.

'Okay, that does it,' Rafe finally said, his voice catching. 'We need to get married.'

Isobel laughed. 'I thought you'd never ask.'

'You mean you *want* to get married?'

Her smile faded. 'I've always wanted to marry you, Rafe. From the moment I met you.' Isobel stood on tiptoes to kiss him. 'But I knew you didn't want to do it again.'

'I want to now. When you know, you know.' He untangled the string from his fingers but, instead of letting it go, he caught one of the stones and held it up between them, so they could both see through the hole.

'What can you see?' he asked softly.

Isobel could see the man she loved through the frame of that hole. And behind him she could see three happy, healthy children and a couple of dogs playing in the evening sunshine. She could see the life she loved with all her heart. The family she loved so much that sometimes it hurt—in a very good way. And this family was growing in both size and strength. Isobel had to blink because the picture in that frame was getting a bit blurry now.

'Magic,' she whispered. 'That's what I can see.'

Rafe's voice was a whisper as well. 'Me too...'

* * * * *

# A GP
# TO STEAL HIS HEART

KARIN BAINE

**MILLS & BOON**

For Paddy,
who never let the truth get in the way of a good story. xx

# CHAPTER ONE

THE FRESH SEA air smelled like freedom. Daisy got out of her car and inhaled a lungful as she stretched out her limbs. She had expected to reach her destination three days ago but her replacement at the clinic had taken ill and Daisy had agreed to stay on to share the workload until another could be found. As a result, the leisurely break before she began her new job had not happened and she would be throwing herself in at the deep end today.

It had been a long drive from London and, exhausted, she had made an overnight stop in a motel to break up the journey rather than risk falling asleep at the wheel. Her last-minute decision meant she had not been able to inform the clinic of her later arrival, but she would still make it on time for her first day.

It would be worth all the trouble to get her own space. Not only was she taking up her new position as a GP in the village of Little Morton on the south coast of England but also she was moving into her own cottage, complete with country garden. A whole world away from the cramped and stifling city where she had been working since qualifying. However, before she could enjoy this new country life she literally had to check in at the medical practice for a pass into the village.

Little Morton was privately owned by the same Earl who had awarded her the scholarship which got her through medical school and away from her controlling ex at the time.

Since training as a GP she had worked hard to keep her independence. Though they had never met in person, she had kept in touch with the Earl of Morton through emails and video calls. Through her brief, unsatisfactory relationships, he had been her one constant. Her most recent partner, Ed, had called her a workaholic, accused her of not enjoying life. Although she had not mourned his loss when their relationship had ended, his words had stayed with her.

Her abusive past had left her afraid to trust anyone enough to get serious, but she wondered if she had let that influence other aspects of her life too. Gradually, she had begun to see the truth in Ed's words and realised she made very little time for herself. The fast pace of city life had made it acceptable but, when she had taken a good look, it was obvious she had no real friends or roots. Not 'belonging' anywhere made her worried that one day she would come to regret the decisions she had made and begin to yearn for something new.

When the Earl had told her he was retiring and that his medical practice was in need of someone like her, Daisy thought it the perfect opportunity to start over, as well as finally getting to thank him in person. Yet her arrival was tinged with sadness, with news of the Earl's death coming only weeks before completing her move here. They would never get to meet after all.

The village was every bit as beautiful as she had imagined. Higgledy-piggledy old houses marched down the cobbled street to meet the sea, history evident in every whitewashed wall and timber frame. The vibrant splash of pink and purple dahlias and violet agapanthus bursting from hanging baskets and window boxes welcomed her.

She locked her car and began her walk down the rocky street. In order to maintain the village's original features, only residents were apparently permitted to drive past the town sign. Yet to obtain her status as a local she had to get a parking permit from the medical centre.

The quirkiness of the crowded Elizabethan buildings made her smile, and she could see why traffic was more than an aesthetic issue. Any more than two cars at once here would block the whole road. Yes, Daisy thought, Little Morton was exactly where she needed to be to start her new life.

The medical centre was easy enough to find, a converted old school house which was signposted at the bottom of the hill overlooking the harbour. She thought of the lucky children who had once attended and the fun they must have had down on the shore during sunny days such as today.

As a child she had missed out on simple things like visits to the beach because her stepfather didn't include her in any family outings. Although she'd taken part in swimming lessons provided by the school, an incident in the pool when she had taken cramp in her leg and nearly drowned left her fearful around water.

Something which had not been helped by Aaron, her

abusive ex, who found her phobia funny and had pushed her into a pool on a rare holiday together. That panicky feeling of gasping for air while he watched her, laughing, was always at the back of her mind. Along with the notion that if she got into difficulty in the water no one would come to help her.

However, as part of her new life here she thought about working through those fears. If she was brave enough perhaps she could learn to swim here with some support. It would be a shame to live in such a picturesque seascape and not enjoy something as simple as paddling in the shallows.

When she reached the clinic, she ducked under the half-opened shutter and approached the affable-looking lady on the reception desk. 'Eunice? It's me, Daisy. I just need to get the keys for my cottage and a pass so I can get my car in and out of the village before I start work.'

Daisy had spoken to the practice manager on the phone lots of times, but this was their first meeting in person. From everything she had gathered, Eunice had been the Earl's right-hand woman at the clinic. She had even set up video calls between Daisy and her benefactor so they could see each other while they chatted about everything from complicated medical cases they had worked on to their favourite TV shows. It was Eunice who had suggested the online interview which had sealed her position here in Little Morton and Daisy was thankful to know at least one person in the village.

'Daisy? We were expecting you yesterday.' Eunice rushed around from behind her desk and wrapped her in a friendly hug.

'Yes, sorry. I got stuck in traffic and I was so tired

I decided it would be safer to check myself into a hotel for the night.'

'No problem. You're here now and I'm sure we have time for a cuppa and a catch-up before we start the clinic.' She took Daisy by the arm and began to guide her towards the back of the building.

'I still have to unpack my stuff at the cottage...' Daisy began to protest but was manoeuvred into a chair in the staffroom, where Eunice set about making that cup of tea.

'That can wait. I'm sure you are dying for a cuppa and I want to hear all about you. I know about the scholarship, of course. Daniel mentioned you'd had a bit of trouble in the past and that was what had set you on the path to medical school.' Eunice had her back to Daisy as she poured water into two cups, unable to see her raised eyebrows.

She was not prepared for someone to be so openly curious about her personal life after living in the city, where most people kept themselves to themselves. But this was the country and Daisy supposed she would have to get used to people in this close-knit community being interested in her background. Even if it was not the most comfortable subject for her to discuss with anyone.

'Er...yes. I was in a difficult relationship. Aaron was...controlling. The Earl's scholarship enabled me to strike out on my own.' It was disconcerting talking about her painful past with a virtual stranger when she did not tend to open up to anyone, but she could already tell Eunice was a kind soul who simply wanted to make her feel at home. Perhaps it was that empathy which drove her to spill more about her troubles.

'You must have been a good student before that though to even get into medical school.' Eunice handed Daisy one of the cups and sat down in the chair next to her, ready to hear the rest of her story.

'I was when I was younger.' School had been her source of stability and the one place she could earn praise for all of her hard work. As a result she had become one of the top students but that had only earned sneering from her stepfamily, who did not like her to get 'above her station'. Despite her detractors Daisy had planned to go to medical school to make something of herself. Then she had met Aaron.

It was not surprising that she had found herself in the thrall of a domineering, manipulative man after the upbringing she'd had. Once her mother had run out and left her with her stepfather and stepbrothers, she had bent over backwards to keep them happy lest she got kicked out of the house.

They had taken advantage, treating her more like a servant than family. Her days had been taken up with chores and looking after them, leaving her no time for a life of her own. She'd swapped that prison for one with a partner who thought a woman's place was in the home, and who was she to disagree when he was the sole breadwinner?

'My partner didn't want me to further my education because he preferred to have me at home in a more "traditional" role.' Which invariably meant tied to the house and not allowed out unaccompanied because he was so paranoid she would cheat on him. It was that stifling behaviour which had made her question her life with Aaron and realise the way he was treating her had nothing to do with love.

When control had turned to violence, that was when she had known it was time to get out.

'Uh huh. I can guess the type. I have daughters of my own and not every boyfriend I have met has been ideal. Thankfully, they're both happily married now so I don't have to worry about them any more in that respect.'

'That's good. It's not easy to meet the right man. Unknown to Aaron, I joined an online support group for women in a similar position to me. That's where I learned about the Earl's scholarship and the rest is history.' Once they had got to know each other better, Daisy had shared some of the details about her background with the Earl. She had no idea if he had told Eunice any of her story, but it was helping them to bond now as they got to know one another. With the Earl gone, Daisy needed as many friends as she could get.

'He was very fond of you. I think he saw you as the daughter he never had.' Eunice's blue eyes filled with tears and Daisy could see theirs had been a special relationship too.

'He was certainly very kind. A real role model for me.' There had not been a supportive male presence in her life until Daisy had received his financial assistance and she liked to think of him as her surrogate father. The one she would have liked to have growing up, instead of the emotionally abusive stepfather she'd had throughout her childhood.

'You and Thomas should get on well. He's very like his father: good with his patients and always puts the job first. I'm sure the two of you have a lot in common. He has been through a lot too and I'm sure he will enjoy having some company around the place.'

'I'm looking forward to meeting him.' It would be a connection to the Earl again and Daisy hoped they might bring each other some comfort when they were both grieving the recent loss of a wonderful man.

'Of course, Thomas inherited his father's title along with the medical practice and the village. He's our new Earl now.'

Daisy could not help thinking those were some big shoes to fill.

'Thanks for the tea and chat, Eunice, but I should really get moving. I've got a busy day ahead of me.' Daisy got up and poured what was left of her tea down the sink. She did not want to get used to lazing around before a shift. Especially when she had so much to do now she was three days behind schedule.

Eunice took an envelope out of her trouser pocket. 'Okay, there are your keys and your pass. Just wave it in front of the barrier and you can come and go as you please. Soon you'll feel like you've always been here.' She gave Daisy a wink.

'Hopefully it won't be too long before I'm considered a local.' Daisy laughed a little too loudly, suddenly wondering if she would be accepted at all.

At that unfortunate moment a man dressed in a navy three-piece suit walked into the room. Well over six feet, it was easy for him to look down on her five feet four inches, one eyebrow raised as he caught the end of the conversation. The new Earl, she presumed, as she stuck her hand out.

'Daisy Swift. The new GP. Pleased to meet you.'

The tall, unsmiling man looked at her outstretched hand for several moments before shaking it, as though he was worried he might catch something from her. It was difficult not to compare the two Ryan men when on first impressions they appeared to be complete opposites. He did not have the same smiling, ruddy-cheeked face as his father, who had always put her in mind of a Father Christmas figure. Junior had more of a Grinch vibe going on.

'Thomas Ryan. Dr Thomas Ryan, senior partner.' He had that air of superiority and dismissive tone that meant Daisy would have guessed he was the heir apparent even if she had not been told. The Earl never had any airs or graces when they had spoken but Daisy would not have been surprised if Thomas had insisted that everyone addressed him as 'Sir' and decreed no one should make direct eye contact with him.

Nevertheless, Daisy owed a lot to his family and she reminded herself that this was a man in mourning for his father. Dr Ryan Senior had been nothing but sweet to her and she held onto that last ember of hope that Thomas had inherited some of his father's warm nature along with his estate.

'I was very sorry to hear about your father.'

Thomas gave a curt, unemotional nod. 'Your office is next to mine. You'll want to get yourself acquainted with your patient list before your first appointment.' He glanced at his expensive watch as he began to walk away.

Daisy assumed he meant her to follow, but he had not actually welcomed her or acknowledged he knew anything about her arrival. It was such a hefty blow, realising the cheery offspring of her saviour she had dreamed she would be working with in her perfect new job was, in reality, as unwelcoming as the closed barrier to the village. Everything about him shouted, *Stay away. You're not wanted here.*

'I didn't think we opened for another hour or so and I've just arrived. I have my pass now; I'll head to the cottage, throw my belongings inside and come straight back.' She got the distinct impression she had already screwed up before actually doing any work.

He stopped and spun around so suddenly she almost ran into him. 'You mean you haven't even moved in yet? Anyone with an ounce of sense would have come here at least a day early to get settled in. Not try to do it when they're about to start their first day of work.'

'It's not as though I have very far to travel.' Daisy bristled at his tone and criticism. It wakened that need to defend herself hedgehog-style, where her prickles were deployed to repel any potential predators. She could have told him the reason for her delayed arrival, as she had done with Eunice, but since he had not given her the opportunity to explain before chastising her she was entitled to bite back. Besides, she had still made it here on time ready to work so it shouldn't be a big deal. He didn't know her duty to her patients was always at the forefront of her mind, but she would certainly let him know. Along with the fact she did not take orders from anyone.

Dr Ryan checked his watch again and huffed out an exasperated breath. All this exchange was missing was an eye roll and she would feel about two foot high.

'Dr Swift, I'm not sure about the way you're used to working but our patients, the residents of Little Morton, have certain standards.' The way he looked her up and down suggested her appearance alone did not meet acceptable requirements. By starting off on the wrong foot, it seemed he was going to pick over every aspect of her appointment here.

Daisy would have been apologetic over her less than satisfactory timing if it wasn't for his haughty attitude. As it was, she felt the need to give him a taste of his own medicine so he would realise she was no pushover. Those days were long gone.

'I'm used to working in a very busy city surgery, above and beyond normal hours, with people from all walks of life, and I've never had any complaints. If Little Morton's high standards entail starting work earlier than I've been contracted for, I will take note for future reference. Now, in order for me to get back in suitable time for the patients, it might be provident if I have an extra pair of hands.' Daisy folded her arms and waited for his response to her frankly brazen request. It was a risky move, but she had dealt with domineering men her whole life and had finally figured out the best way to deal with them was to stand her ground. To stay strong and not cave in to demands. That did not mean her heart wasn't pounding as she waited for his response.

With another long breath, he began to stalk back the way they'd come, leaving an open-mouthed Eunice behind. It was difficult to tell if her shock at the exchange was because of Thomas's rudeness, after she had sung his praises, or because of Daisy's sharp retort. Either way, their personality clash did not bode well for their future working environment.

She wondered what it was about her that had apparently brought out the worst in Dr Ryan when Eunice had been extolling the virtues of the new Earl to her. This was not the kindly man Daisy had been expecting to meet. Okay, so she was a little later than expected but she was here. There was something in his attitude towards her that made her think his problem with her was about more than her delayed arrival. Perhaps he did not appreciate women who stood up for themselves and refused to be browbeaten. Whatever it was, it irked her until she could not resist one last jibe.

'You might want to leave the jacket and waistcoat behind. It wouldn't do for you to get them dirty before clinic starts. How on earth would that look to your discerning patients?'

He unbuttoned his waistcoat and stripped off his outer layers. Hopefully Dr Ryan had got the memo she was not going to be bossed around as though she were a second-class citizen. She might have relied on his father's generosity to get her to this point in her life but she had earned the right to be treated as an equal in their place of work. If he continued to forget that she would simply have to keep reminding him.

Daisy Swift was everything Thomas had feared she would be—loud, obnoxious and unwilling to adapt. The village deserved better in their GP. This was his father's doing but now he was gone Thomas had no one to voice his reservations to any more.

There had been dozens of scholarship recipients over

the years who had received his father's help to further their education and career prospects. Most of whom had expressed their gratitude at the time by way of phone calls or gifts, the occasional update in a Christmas card. Daisy was the only one who had become a seemingly permanent feature in his father's life. It had made Thomas question her motives for remaining in contact with an elderly man she had never met. Especially recently, when she had decided to come and live in Little Morton to be closer to him.

There had to be more to her interest in his father than his witty repartee for a young, attractive woman to come all this way, giving up her life in London to do so. Was it his money? Did she think there was something for her in the will? Now his father had passed away, was Thomas her latest target? Too bad for her if she thought he could be sweet-talked when he was still in mourning for a father who had been taken from him by the last duplicitous woman to cross their paths. It was only natural for Thomas to be wary of another stranger in the village, given past events.

His own mother had been a city girl here on holiday when she had caught his father's eye. From what he'd gathered, they had been madly in love for a while, at least on his father's part. When Thomas had been about six years old it seemed his mother had grown tired of life in the village and her family. In typical cliché fashion, she had run off with the gardener after emptying their joint bank account. Thank goodness his father had kept money from his investments in a separate account of his own or she might have cleaned him out entirely. Thomas had not seen or heard from her since and had few memories of her to be over-emotional about the loss.

It was testament to his father's strength of character that the betrayal had not stopped him reaching out to strangers less fortunate than himself. He had offered Thomas's mother a lifeline when he had come along, their union giving her the financial means to escape poverty and the rundown council estate she had been living in. Thomas suspected he had carried on the tradition through his charity work because he had seen the difference money could make in someone else's life. He had tried to get his father to rein in the amount of money he gave away to good causes, through fear that people were taking advantage of him, but helping others had seemed to make the old man happy.

In an effort to recreate that for himself, Thomas had set up his own charitable arm providing monetary assistance to local single parent families who were finding things tough. It was there that he had met Jade, a confident, attractive volunteer whose company he had enjoyed. Unfortunately, their short relationship had apparently provided her criminal associates with the necessary information to burgle the family home when Thomas had been out of town.

The betrayal had been painful, but not as much as watching his parent's health decline after the robbery. Tied up and beaten, he had been left a shell of a man who no longer felt safe in his own home. It was the guilt of being the one who had brought these people into the village which Thomas had struggled with, on top of his grief. Now he was expected to work alongside someone else he knew nothing about. Of course he was wary.

Especially when she did not appear to respect him or his station. He wanted this village to be the safe community his father had always intended and that was hard to achieve with a stranger moving in. It was probably Thomas's own fault he knew very little about Daisy; he'd tended to switch off when his father waxed lyrical about her. There might have been some jealousy at work on his part that she had so much of his father's attention, and now he was stuck with her.

Far from letting her know who was in charge here, he was about to roll up his sleeves and do her heavy lifting. Apparently the 'mug' tattoo on his forehead was still visible.

'You have got to be kidding me,' he said as they approached a very compact pastel blue Volkswagen. Which, judging by the boxes visible through the rear window, was already jam-packed.

Daisy shrugged. 'It gets me from A to B. I don't usually carry passengers of extraordinary height.'

Thomas contemplated walking to the cottage, but the extra time taken to get there would only impact further on his day. The sooner they completed this task, the quicker they could actually start work.

'So I see.' The passenger seat was pushed so far forward he had to duck to get in and fold himself over until his knees were up near his chin so he could close the door. He did not miss the smirk on Dr Swift's bright red lips as they drove away.

'Do you live close by?' she asked as she drove much faster than he liked, taking the corner without even shifting down a gear.

Thomas held onto the dashboard before he ended

up sitting on her knee in the driving seat. That would probably amuse her no end, at further expense to his dignity. At least the speed with which they had accelerated away from the village meant few would have seen him hunched up in her dinky car.

Thankfully, because of her driving and the short distance they had to travel, they arrived at the cottage before his knees seized up altogether.

'Home sweet home.' Daisy was out of the vehicle carrying an armful of boxes to the door of the white-washed building before Thomas managed to extricate himself from his pretzel position.

'I don't live in the village itself. The family home is up on the hill there.' He pointed up to the grey stone mansion isolated from the rest of the community. Thomas could not help but think they should have kept it that way, then his father would never have been hurt. It was his safe haven now. Nobody else came in and only he went out. His sanctuary and sanity when it was the one place on earth he could control. Even if it came too late to help his father.

'Very imposing and it looks down on the rest of the village. I'm sure you enjoy that.' She nudged the front door open with her hip, leaving him to follow. He did not rise to the bait when she was right, though for a different reason than she thought. It was not a feeling of superiority he got from his position up on the hill, but of safety. The distance between him and everyone else was a welcome barrier. Goodness knew what Daisy was hoping to gain from her continued quips but Thomas was not going to lose his temper over it. He supposed this life was different to the one she knew in the city.

Hopefully she would either get used to it or decide it was not for her and move on quickly. Thomas knew which option he would prefer.

Although he and his father had shared the patients between them, when he had decided to retire, Thomas had tried to convince him he could manage on his own. Generations of Ryans had always staffed the local clinic and Thomas did not need a stranger moving in on his territory now. Work was all he had in his life and he needed to stay as busy as possible so he did not have time to dwell on mistakes and regret.

'I think this will do nicely.' Once she had set her boxes down, Daisy stood back to take a look around the property.

'I'm sure it's not what you're used to in London.' There wasn't a lot of space in these old places but the Ryans had always done their best to maintain the authentic feel of the village. All owned by the family, which now only consisted of himself, none of the listed buildings were for sale; they were rented by the inhabitants. At least that was one way he could keep track of who was staying. If they had allowed the cottages to be used as second homes for holidaymakers, the heart would have gone out of Little Morton a long time ago.

'No, but that's not a bad thing. At least I have more than two rooms and, bonus, no noisy neighbours on either side. Not to mention the lovely wild garden. This would cost an arm and a leg in central London and would never be half as cosy.' She plopped down on the floral sofa which came as part of the furnishings and fittings. The twee country cottage décor did not suit her. Dr Daisy Swift was a sophisticated, glamorous woman who would only ever be at home in a cityscape, he was sure.

Her white-blonde curls, piercing blue eyes and pale skin were striking. The corporate black skirt, tailored grey silk blouse and impossibly high stilettos would never fit in here, but she would find that out for herself after a few ankle-breaking days on the cobbles.

Thomas dumped his share of her belongings on the floor, sending a dust cloud up into the air, making him sneeze.

'Sorry, I think I brought that with me. A souvenir from London. These boxes haven't been unpacked since my last move. Housekeeping isn't really my thing any more.' She wore a look of pride on her face as though it was a badge of honour to be so busy there was no time for something as mundane as cleaning. Yet her voice suggested something else. A past which kept her on the move.

All the more reason to be wary of her. He should have paid more attention and asked more questions about this woman who had become a big part of his father's life. As far as Daniel Ryan had been concerned, Daisy's character and qualifications were all the verification needed to hire her. That was his father all over— too trusting for his own good. They had both learned that the hard way, too late. Eunice had at least suggested an interview, which had taken place on the internet to keep things above board. Although his father had pulled rank and insisted on conducting it on his own, waiting until Thomas was away at a conference to arrange it, to ensure he could not interfere. Making her appointment a foregone conclusion, no matter what Thomas had to say on the matter.

This woman had certainly had a hold on his father that unnerved him and made him suspicious about the nature of their relationship.

'If you're finished, could we get back to work please?' He was already more involved in her personal life than he wanted to be, by helping her move in when things between them should be kept strictly professional. That way he was not likely to compromise himself outside of the workplace, as he had done with Jade. What Daisy did away from the clinic had nothing to do with him and vice versa.

'There are just a few more bits and pieces. Oh, and my shoes.'

They had both traipsed out to the car where she had begun to load him up with more boxes. She had black bin bags in both hands and under her arms, which he presumed contained her now wrinkled clothes.

'Can you manage a pair of shoes?' She dangled a pair of strappy silver sandals from his finger before he could protest. His humiliation was complete when she hooked a handbag over his shoulder too.

Thomas was definitely going to have his work cut out for him, getting Dr Swift to toe the line.

'What do you do around here for fun?' Daisy cradled her well-earned cup of tea in her hands as she leaned against Thomas's desk.

The day's surgery was over at last, having run well past their official surgery hours. Judging by the minor nature of most of her patients' ailments, a lot of them had simply wanted a glimpse of the new GP. She had no idea what the verdict was, but she had felt like a mannequin in a shop window with everyone gawping at her. Only time would tell if the novelty would wear off and she would ever be considered anything other than an outsider. If she wanted to be part of the community, and she did, she would have to embrace everything they had to offer here.

It was a completely different way of life compared to the city, where she had been able to live anonymously, but she welcomed the change. She could not hide away for ever behind her workload. It meant people like her ex were still controlling her, preventing her from living her life freely and without fear.

Romantic relationships were not something she formed easily, given her lack of trust and fierce need for independence, but it shouldn't mean she couldn't have friends and neighbours to socialise with. She had forgotten that somewhere along the way, shutting everyone out, letting no one closer than on the periphery of her life. It was time to be part of something, belong somewhere, instead of merely existing.

Until now, the only people she had had a conversation with were Eunice and Thomas. Unfortunately, the friendly face around here had rushed off to babysit her grandchildren, leaving only the hard-working doctor to answer her questions. If only sighing and refusing to look up from his computer screen could be counted as a sign he was willing to accept her company.

At least he had shown her earlier he was not completely unbearable, by helping her move into the cottage. She'd had a little fun at his expense and, though his expression was priceless at having to carry her hand-bag and shoes, he had done so without a tantrum. There was hope he was not the stuck-up so-and-so he had projected himself as so far.

It was a shame when he was such a beautiful-looking man with his grey-blue eyes and dark blond hair. Not that Daisy was searching for a man and even if she was it would not be another one who thought he could boss her around. At least she had made it clear that was never going to happen.

'Fun?' Eventually he glanced up at her, his forehead creased into a frown.

Daisy sighed. Removing the stick from his backside was going to be harder than she'd thought. 'Yeah. Fun. The thing you do outside of work.'

'I don't really do anything.'

That didn't surprise her. He probably polished the family silver or counted his millions when he wasn't here. 'What do people do around here to socialise?'

He had to think about it. 'There's the pub or the coffee shop. We have a few festivals during the year where everyone gets together.'

Now they were getting somewhere. Daisy would be content exploring the countryside or enjoying a cup of tea in the café, but she knew she had to find some way of integrating into the village if she was to be accepted.

She wondered if their quaint festivals were like the ones she had seen on TV. Where the whole village came out to support each other, having fun at the coconut shy and kissing booths. Thomas would make a fortune if he volunteered those soft lips of his for a pound a smooch.

She sniggered, imagining some of the old dears she'd

had in this morning emptying their purses for some quality time with 'that lovely Dr Ryan'.

'That sounds more like it. Do I need a pass to get into that too?' It was a tongue-in-cheek comment, but Thomas didn't appear to get the joke.

'No. Everyone is welcome to attend.'

*Even you*, she was sure he was silently adding.

'We have the Crab Festival next week, if you want to go to that.'

'Of course. How could I turn down a personal invitation from the Earl himself? I'd love to attend the Little Morton Crab Festival with you. I'd be honoured.'

'But that's not—'

'Thank you for making me feel so welcome on my first day, Thomas.' Daisy gave him her biggest smile and succeeded in making him shift uncomfortably in his chair.

He sighed and appeared to resign himself to the fact she was staying.

'I'm sure you will be an asset to the clinic,' he said through clenched teeth.

Once she made sure Dr Ryan knew she was no pushover, her life in Little Morton could be just the place for her to start living.

# CHAPTER TWO

THOMAS HAD NO idea how he had been roped into this.
Wait…yes, he did. Daisy. She had the knack of getting
her own way without giving anyone the chance to say
no to her. He'd also felt guilty about how he had treated
her on her arrival and was now trying to build some
bridges. Okay, he had his suspicions about her motives
in coming here, but his father would have berated him
for the way he had spoken to her on her first day. Eunice
had also reminded him that they had to work together,
and she had done nothing except take up the post which
his father had given her. Since then, Thomas had done
his best to be civil at least.

Now, not only was he down at the harbour with the
rest of the village at a festival he had no interest in,
but he was also sitting on a ducking stool about to be
dropped into ice-cold water.

'It's for charity,' Daisy had coaxed when they had
arrived and found the dunk tank was short of volunteers. He was not entirely convinced by her altruistic
display, and with good reason.

'They're raising money for the lifeboat station. I'd do
it myself but I'm not sure I'd get many takers.' Thomas

was sure he had seen a rare flicker of fear in her eyes at the prospect, which she'd quickly blinked away, taking his arm and steering him towards the crew manning the station.

Although he would have paid good money to drop her into the tank he was currently staring down into, he could tell it was not something she would have been comfortable doing herself. The usually confident Daisy clearly had found her kryptonite and it would not have been chivalrous of him to expect her to be dunked underwater in the name of charity.

Even if she had turned his life upside down in the space of a week. Not only was she making her presence known at work, walking into his office and using his desk as a seat when drinking her countless cups of tea, but she was sneaking her way into his personal life too. He didn't usually come to these things; they were more for tourists and kids. As she was part of his medical practice he had felt obliged to help introduce her into the community so she would become familiar to the patients. His father would have wanted him to make the effort. That was uppermost in his mind when she was driving him to distraction. Thomas had to respect his father's wishes. He just didn't have to like it.

Another ball hit the canvas target beside him, completely missing the bull's-eye. So far only a few children had stepped up but he knew, come the afternoon when the dads had the chance to sample the homemade cider on Billy Jackson's stall, things could change.

With his bare feet dangling in the water and his trousers rolled up to his knees, Thomas was simply waiting for the inevitable. Especially when Daisy moved to the top of the queue, casually tossing one of the red rubber balls in her hand.

'I hope you've made your donation first, Dr Swift,' he shouted from the cage housing him and the tank of water.

Daisy waggled a ten-pound note before handing it over to the member of the lifeboat crew holding a charity box. 'I'm sure this will be worth every penny.'

She took a step back and launched the ball with more force than one would have expected from her small frame. Thomas let out a long breath as the ball smacked loudly just to the right of the target.

'So close,' he teased, and immediately regretted it when he saw the look of determination on her face as her bright red lips tightened into a thin line.

'Just getting my bearings.' She closed one eye and took aim with as much force as her first attempt. He was regretting treating her so harshly a lot right now.

Thomas barely had enough time to register the 'ding' as she hit her target before he was dropped unceremoniously into the tank. The cold water stole the oxygen from his lungs so he was gasping for air when he stood up again. He wiped his eyes and shook his head like a wet dog trying to dislodge the water from his ears. This was not the image he usually projected to the community and he couldn't say he was loving it. However, it would not have been very charitable if he'd declined to help.

'Good shot,' he spluttered as she came to high-five him, enjoying this way too much.

Thomas caught her blue eyes sweeping over his body,

where his clothes were sticking to his skin, and it was then he realised he did not have a change of clothes.

Daisy had been having fun with Thomas at the dunk tank. Until now. She could not tear her eyes away from the sodden clothes clinging to his body. The wet fabric of his white shirt had turned transparent, giving her an eyeful of his muscular torso and flat stomach. Even his trousers were moulded around those thigh muscles and everything else south.

The joke had definitely backfired when she was the one who had been left blushing Although she had volunteered Thomas as one of the 'dunkees' today, it had not been a plot to humiliate him. When she had been approached to take part she had panicked at the thought of being dropped into the water. Instead, she had pushed Thomas forward to detract from any idea she should take part.

To his credit, he had agreed and saved her from making a spectacle of herself. Since their first terse exchange he had seemed to mellow a little towards her, though that could possibly have been at Eunice's urging. She had insisted Daisy had caught him on a bad day and he was not usually as abrasive as he had been with her. In fact, if Eunice was to be believed, Thomas Ryan was an absolute sweetheart of the highest order. The woman was apparently prepared to lie to make the atmosphere in the clinic more harmonious.

Daisy did get the impression he needed to integrate here as much as she did. He seemed to go between home and work with very little interaction with anyone in between. With his father gone too, he must be lonely up in that house on the hill and she knew from experience that was not fun. It was the whole reason she had moved here, to get out of that rut herself. She might not have anyone controlling her, but she was not fully living when she was afraid to let anyone get close in case she got hurt.

It was not her intention to manipulate Thomas into doing what she wanted or what she thought he needed; she would never do that to another person. He had surprised her by agreeing to accompany her here and helping out at the dunk tank. By spending the day together and seeing this co-operative side of him, it would help dispel any preconceived ideas they had of each other. She could put today down as a bonding exercise, nothing else. Certainly not an excuse to ogle her handsome work colleague.

'You're all wet,' she managed to mumble.

'I thought that was the intention when you threw the ball?' He ruffled his wet hair with his hand, making it look as though he'd just stepped out of the shower fully clothed.

Her imagination began to run rampant. Clearly her life of singledom was missing something as base as sex or she would not be fantasising about a man with whom she had absolutely nothing in common except work.

'Well, I've had my fun. I suppose I should get you a towel to dry off.'

'I'm sure I'm going to get much wetter as the day goes on. You're not the only one who apparently wants to drop me into a tank of water.' He nodded over at the queue of villagers which had formed, likely attracted by the cheering which had sounded when Daisy had dunked him in the water.

She didn't think the rush to dunk Thomas was malicious, more a novelty to see the Earl participating in such an event. To his credit, Thomas was still smiling as he climbed back onto the stool. Daisy didn't think it would do her any favours to stick around and watch the scene on repeat, or she would end up being the one who needed dunking in some cold water.

'I could take a run up to your house if you'd like and get you some dry clothes.' It was the least she could do when it was her fault he was in this predicament.

'No.' His response was short and sharp, as if the idea was completely out of the question.

'Really, it's no bother. If you give me your keys I can drive up and be back in ten minutes.'

'I said no. I'm not in the habit of letting people wander around my property unsupervised.' The gruff, unyielding doctor she had encountered on her first day was back, treating her as though she was about to single-handedly destroy life in the village as he knew it. All because she had offered to do him a favour.

Was it really so unheard of for someone to help him or did he merely have a problem accepting it from her? She wondered if she would ever know what went on in his head when he was so changeable around her. It would become exhausting trying to figure him out and Daisy hadn't moved across the country to have another man cause her stress.

'I'm not about to steal the family silver, if that's what you're worried about.' It was a throwaway comment to highlight the absurdity of his behaviour. Except the guilty look on his face told her she had hit the nail right on the head.

'It's nothing personal,' he added, only adding more heat to the burn.

'How can it be anything but personal?' She was trying not to get too animated and draw the attention of the people milling around; as a result she hissed out the words like an angry cat.

'I just don't want anyone snooping around my house.' He shrugged, unperturbed by accusing his co-worker of intending to steal from him.

Daisy had been accused of being many things over the years, but a thief was a new and unwarranted descriptor. If that was how he saw her—someone who would take advantage of him like that without her conscience pricking her—he didn't know her at all. Worse, it showed a major lack of trust and respect from someone she was supposed to be working alongside. Eunice would have to go a long way to convince her now he was a nice guy at heart and not some uppity toff who thought everyone was out to get him. She wondered who had hurt him in the past to cause this level of paranoia.

'Fine. Freeze to death. I was only trying to help, not casing the joint.' She flounced off, so angry with him that she was ready to spend the rest of the afternoon dropping him into that cold water. Her sole consolation was hearing a splash behind her as someone else did the job for her. She made her way around the rest of the fair with a smug smile.

The whole harbour was lined with stalls, colourful bunting hung from the streetlights and the noise of laughter was a glorious sound on the hot summer day.

It was essentially a street party, a real community coming together for the day to have fun. There were tourists of course, keen to spend their money to join in, but Daisy recognised the majority of faces around her now.

Those who were not her patients worked in or frequented the local coffee shop and pubs, others she knew in passing. The layout of the village meant it was easy to get around on foot and there were some beautiful scenic views to be had during these promenades. She had yet to have a walk without exchanging pleasantries with others taking a stroll. So far she had not encountered any real opposition to her presence at the clinic but she did sense wariness. Especially from Thomas.

It would take time, she supposed, but she had hoped today would have gone some way towards her and Thomas bonding, as well as making their presence known more around the village. Now she felt more unwanted than ever.

'Hi, Dr Swift. Would you care to try some of our homemade fudge?' The woman behind the sweet stall was one of Daisy's new patients, Marie Talbot. She had brought a basket of chocolate chip muffins in on Daisy's first day, so she would always be one of her favourite people. Today her warm smile and sugary treats were especially welcomed.

'I would love some, Marie. Thank you.' Daisy took one of the small samples laid out for potential customers to taste and let the sugary sweetness dissolve on her tongue.

'What's the verdict?' The pretty mum of two waited for her review even though she had other customers lining up.

'I think my waistline is in trouble.' She handed over her money in exchange for the bag of fudge tied with curled pink ribbon which she would comfort eat later when she replayed her conversation with Thomas alone in the cottage.

By the time she circled back to the dunk tank, Thomas, having finished his stint as a merman, was there waiting for her. He had changed into dry clothes which someone had apparently donated. The tight white T-shirt with *Little Morton Crab Festival* emblazoned in bright pink and colourful board shorts were not quite his style but still managed to catch her attention.

Daisy was trying not to stare at the water dripping from his hair down the front of his shirt or the drops sitting on the ends of his long eyelashes like early morning dew on the grass when she was still mad at him.

'I'll see you on Monday at work,' she said, turning away, having seen and heard enough of him for more than one day.

'Wait. I'm sorry about what I said earlier. I've had plenty of time to think it over in between dunkings. I didn't mean to offend you. I just don't let anyone into my house.'

'No one?' Daisy was not a party girl who invited all and sundry back to her house, and she understood the need for privacy, but Thomas's attitude was a tad over-the-top in her opinion.

'No one. So you see—it's not you, it's me.' The big warm smile he sent her was equally unsettling, as though she had watched him change right in front of her. It was Thomas, naked, no longer hiding behind that stern façade she had first encountered.

'Uh huh. Well, perhaps you should remember that next time you're about to snap at me.' She should have dug deeper to find out the reason behind his fierce protection of his personal space, but she might regret chipping away at that hard exterior when Thomas's soft inner core was even more terrifying. She didn't want to like him, given his propensity to make her feel small, no matter how unintentionally. It was important she started expanding her social pool here so Thomas Ryan wasn't the only person in the village she was getting to know on a personal level.

'Sorry. I'm not used to sharing any aspect of my personal space since my father died. I will do my best to think before I speak in future. Can I buy you some lunch by way of apology?'

'I suppose so.' Although she should let him sweat a bit longer, it wouldn't help their situation by refusing his olive branch or, in this case, the smell of salt and vinegar emanating from the catering vans.

They ordered some fish and chips to share and sat down on the harbour wall to eat it.

Thomas plonked the bag containing his wet clothes on the ground and helped himself to some of the golden chips fresh out of the fryer. 'I'm starving.'

'How come you don't usually go to these things? It's been fun today and I think everyone is glad to see you.'

He shrugged his shoulders. 'I used to come when I was little but school and work soon took up most of my time. I don't know... I suppose I thought it could diminish my reputation here. My father was a well-respected man and I felt the pressure to be like him. I'm doing my best to honour him wherever I can.'

'Is that why you don't want me working at the clinic with you?'

He blinked, the chip he was holding hovering on its way to his mouth. 'That's not—'

'There's no need to deny it. I think it was obvious to me and poor Eunice that you weren't happy about my arrival from day one.'

Thomas hung his head before glancing up at her from below those lovely long lashes. 'I apologise if I didn't make you feel welcome. I've been wary of outsiders since my father's death and, well, I don't know anything about you beyond your CV. He was the one who hired you, who considered you a friend, but you're a stranger to me. You could have been coming out here to stake a claim on his money for all I knew.'

There was so much information there to make Daisy uncomfortable, but it was just the truth and she should be thankful for that at least.

However, he was still talking about her as though she was a threat to him, when she'd thought they'd been making progress up until today. He didn't say he'd changed his opinion about her or that he realised she was not here because she was interested in his father's money and that was difficult to accept. She would have to double her efforts for him to appreciate she was good at her job and work was the only reason she was here.

'Why would your father's death affect your trust in people who come from outside the village? I don't understand.' If she did, it might go some way to explaining his attitude towards her.

Thomas launched his chip into the sea for the hungry

seagulls to dive upon, his appetite apparently deserting him as she touched on the subject of his father's passing.

Obviously his grief was raw, when Dr Ryan senior had died only months ago, but Daisy suspected there was more going on here than mourning.

'As you know, he was a great believer in helping others and was involved in a number of good causes.'

Daisy nodded. If it hadn't been for the Earl's scholarship programme she would never have escaped that prison her ex had kept her in through sheer fear alone.

'He was a very generous man. I owe him a lot.'

Thomas huffed out a breath, suggesting he wasn't in complete agreement with some of his father's practices.

'What does that mean?' Her hackles were rising now at the suggestion that she might have been taking advantage of his father's kind nature in some way.

Although the scholarship had been arranged through a third party, Daisy had written to the Earl to express her gratitude and explain what it meant to her. Freedom. She liked to think they had struck up a real friendship, keeping in touch about her progression through medical school and beyond. The Earl, in turn, had told her about village life, sufficient to make her fall in love with the place without ever having seen it. In his letters he had told of his pride in his son and she'd hoped he'd passed on some kind words about her to his heir. However, it seemed Thomas thought of her as no more than a gold-digger. That hurt. Part of the reason she had come here was to repay the Earl's kindness by filling in the gap in his medical practice, but she got the impression Thomas saw her as someone who had wormed her way into his father's affections and his wallet. Now her motives for being here were in question it tainted the new start she had hoped to have here.

Once more she was forced to justify her presence here, but she wouldn't do it at any cost. If they couldn't get past their differences she would have to move on. She was not going to spend any more of her life believing she wasn't worthy of her place.

'It means he thought with his heart instead of his head and acted accordingly.'

Something Thomas would never be accused of doing.

Before Daisy drew herself up to her full height with the offence she had taken at that comment, Thomas carried on with his explanation.

'He trusted too easily and apparently so did I.'

She snorted at that, but he ignored her derision.

'When I was away at a medical conference, some people broke into the house. They tied him up and beat him before stealing whatever they could find.' Thomas picked some small stones up from the ground and fired them into the water one by one. Perhaps in an attempt to rid himself of all the things which were bothering him.

'I'm sorry you both had to deal with that. Your father was such a lovely, generous man. He did not deserve that.' Daisy's stomach lurched violently at the thought of the Earl being subjected to such brutality when he had been kindness personified. It was understandable that Thomas should be bitter about what had happened, but she was having trouble putting the pieces together. 'Forgive me for saying, but I thought your father died from heart failure?'

As the date for her start date had grown near and she hadn't heard from the Earl, Daisy had phoned the clinic.

That was when Eunice had broken the news to her that he had passed away in hospital. There hadn't been any mention of a robbery or an assault. It would have compounded her grief, as it apparently had with Thomas. Gradually, she was beginning to see why Thomas acted the way he did around her.

'Ultimately, that's what killed him, but his health took a sharp decline after the incident. In the year after it happened he became very stressed about his personal security, to the point of paranoia. Understandably so, but I don't think he ever felt safe again in his own home. That was down to me. I should have been there to protect him.'

'I can see why you would feel that way, but the only people to blame are those who carried out that heinous act.' She could only imagine the Earl's terror and Thomas's shock when he had heard what had happened to his father in his absence. It would have been traumatic for both of them.

Even now, picturing the horrific scene herself made her want to weep for the sweet man who had given her a second chance at life. The Earl had only deserved good things to happen to him and hearing what he had gone through, how he had suffered as a result, was devastating. She had come to Little Morton partly to try and repay his kindness, but she would never get to do that because of the evil act of greedy, unscrupulous people. He hadn't told her about the robbery but she suspected his pride had prevented him from sharing the traumatic events with her. Another layer of sadness was added to her loss that she never had the opportunity to comfort the man who had done so much for her. It would have destroyed the Earl to realise they had gone to his home with no compunction about hurting him when he'd only ever done good. Daisy would have found it equally as hard as Thomas to forgive or trust again.

'They were caught, judged and given pitiful sentences for their act. It gives me no comfort to know they're in jail. Their incarceration makes no difference. It won't bring my father back.'

It was easy to see how a grieving son would blame himself for his father's untimely death and it explained why he had been so against the idea of a stranger joining the practice or being in his home. If they had exercised that same caution before now, perhaps the Earl would not have suffered as much as he had.

Although Thomas seemed to be getting used to her, Daisy was certain trust wasn't something he would give easily again. That was something they had in common. Her experiences in the past meant she was always waiting for people to reveal a darker side. Like her stepfamily and her ex. Unfortunately she was usually proved right in her need to be cautious. When people didn't get what they wanted their true colours would appear, warning her to back away.

These days she didn't hang around when someone proved untrustworthy. It could be that Thomas was waiting for her to slip up too and give him a reason to get rid of her in case someone else got hurt. It was lucky for both of them that she had no hidden agenda. She was honest and forthright and appreciated people who were the same. As long as they didn't try to tell her what to do or how to behave…

'Anyway, I should get going. I think I've done

enough socialising for one day.' Just like that, Thomas ended their lunch and the conversation, apparently coming to the conclusion that they should keep their relationship strictly professional and within the walls of the clinic too.

There was nothing Daisy could say or do to change his mind over the burden of guilt he was carrying, but hopefully he would see she had no ulterior motive in moving out to Little Morton other than to start her life anew. She would prove to him that his father had known best by bringing her here, simply by doing her job.

# CHAPTER THREE

COME MONDAY MORNING, Daisy was on board with the idea that her relationship with Thomas should be strictly professional. She had no right to know the ins and outs of his personal life and vice versa. It would keep things simpler. As long as he could do the same and remember she was here as a GP and not some con woman who had come to squeeze money out of him now his father had gone.

She still respected his position as the senior partner and when she wanted a second opinion concerning one of her patients she didn't think twice about seeking his opinion.

'I'm going to go and talk to my colleague for a moment. It's nothing to worry about. I just want to consult him on this,' she told her young patient as she left the room. He had presented to her with an itchy red rash on and around his thighs. Normally she would have put it down to prickly heat or an allergy but the intense itching he was describing, along with a recent trip to Florida, made her think it might be something else, especially when she did some quick online research into the area where he had been staying.

The door to Thomas's room was slightly ajar but she knocked out of courtesy and waited for a response.

'Yes?'

'Sorry to disturb you, Thomas, but I was wondering if I could get a second pair of eyes on a patient next door.'

'Sure. What's up?' He set down the pen he had been writing with and gave her his complete attention.

'I have a young surfer in his twenties who has just returned from Florida. He has a red bumpy rash in his groin/inner thigh area which is causing him severe itching. Something tells me it's not the usual summer allergies we're dealing with here. I've found there's something called Seabather's Eruption which can occur and wondered if you had ever come across this before.'

Thomas got up from behind the desk, ready to see the patient's predicament for himself. 'Is he experiencing any vomiting, headaches or fatigue?'

'Not so far. It's the itching which is mainly bothering him, apart from the unsightliness of the rash, of course.'

'I'll take a look,' he said, following her back into her own room.

'Thanks.' Although Daisy could happily have prescribed treatment which would cover most allergic reactions or skin rashes, she preferred to find out exactly what she was dealing with for future reference. If that meant asking someone with more experience for his opinion, so be it. The patient was more important than her pride.

'Hi, I'm Dr Ryan. Dr Swift tells me you have come home from Florida with a nasty rash. Would you mind if I took a look?' Thomas washed his hands before pull-ing back the curtain around the bed in the corner.

Justin the surfer joined him in the cubicle for the consultation while Daisy waited.

'I think you're right, Dr Swift. It's not something we would commonly deal with in the UK, but I have seen this before when I did a placement in dermatology. A chap came back from his honeymoon in Mexico with the same unfortunate problem.' Thomas washed and dried his hands again as Justin emerged from behind the curtain.

'Is it serious?'

'Not at all. There are a lot of names for it—Seabath-er's Eruption, pica-pica, marine dermatitis—but it's all the same thing. Basically, it's caused by stings from cer-tain sea anemones or thimble jellyfish. The rash is con-centrated on your bottom half as it's believed the tiny organisms get trapped under the bathing suit, against the skin there.'

Justin turned up his nose at the thought. 'Does that mean these things are still living on me?'

'No. This is simply an allergic response to the stings. Just make sure you thoroughly wash whatever you were wearing in the water at the time. Dr Swift will prescribe you some steroids and some antihistamines to reduce the severity of the itching. If you experience any other symptoms such as a fever or nausea, do come back and see us.' Thomas made his way out of the room and Daisy offered her thanks as she saw him out.

'Good call. Not many would have gone the extra mile to look into that beyond the initial symptoms.' Thomas's praise warmed her and she hoped he was beginning to see she took her job and her patients seriously. It would make things easier for her here, as well as improving relations between them.

'What a day.' Daisy bumped open the door into Thomas's office with her hip and walked in carrying two mugs of tea.

'What's this in aid of?' he asked a little suspiciously. At the start of the day she'd seemed distant with him and he'd wondered if he had upset her at the festival with his honesty. Normally he wouldn't have given away so much personal information, but he thought he owed her some explanation for the way he'd behaved towards her. When he'd realised he had perhaps overshared, he had tried to put some distance between them. It seemed to have stuck but at least Daisy had felt able to come to him earlier about her patient. Hopefully he hadn't ruined the rapport they had managed to build and they'd be able to work together as a team here at the clinic.

'I thought it would be good for us to debrief at the end of the day. You know, talk over our cases, see if there is anything that warrants both our attention. The best way to do that is over a cup of tea.' She set a cup in front of him, then slid his files to one side so she could lean back against his desk.

'Generally, we do that during our morning staff meetings.' In the company of their other colleagues and in the staffroom.

'I know, but I thought we could start our own routine with things still fresh in our minds. It will give us a chance to catch up and swap notes.' Daisy kicked off her heels so she was barefoot as she lounged against the desk.

'There is another seat, you know.' He indicated the empty seat next to her. There was something unnerving about having her hover in his office, making herself at home like this. Even though this was within the boundaries of their professional relationship, it still felt intimate, too familiar for his liking.

'I've spent most of the day sitting down. I want to stretch my legs,' she said, ignoring his discomfort.

'So…is there anything you need to urgently discuss about today's patients?' If she insisted on doing this then he wanted to get it over with as quickly as possible and send her on her way.

'The only thing that really stands out is our surfer with the rash, Justin. That's one I will have to remember in case I come across anything like it again.' She seemed pleased to have discovered the cause of the young patient's problem and rightly so. It wasn't every day that they successfully diagnosed a tropical illness without the intervention of a specialist. That was down to her determination to diagnose on sight. It was lucky that he had seen that particular rash before to confirm her suspicions, so it had been a successful collaboration he hoped they would see more of together.

'That was well spotted. I was impressed.'

'Not as much as I was to learn you had treated the condition before. Remind me to come to you for all the rare and unusual cases which come through the door.' She was teasing him, but Thomas appreciated the respect she was showing him and his experience rather than insisting she knew best in all cases. It was better for their patients to have two doctors who worked well together to provide the best treatment for all.

'We're on the coast so we get a lot of surfers and divers. It's only to be expected that we'll get the odd rarity from someone who has taken their hobby abroad. It's not just all hip replacements and hearing aids in Little Morton, you know.' He couldn't resist a little joke of his own and it was nice to know there were still some surprises to be had in their sleepy village. It might prevent the city girl from getting bored and seeking some excitement outside the clinic.

'Do you need a lift home? The rain is pouring down out there.' Thomas poked his head around Daisy's office door.

'No, thanks. I've a lot of paperwork to catch up on here.' Her fingers were flying over the keyboard much quicker than he had ever managed. Although it wouldn't surprise him if she was simply pretending to have a heavy workload so they didn't break their unspoken 'no fraternising away from work' rule.

Thomas hoped he hadn't offended her by talking about his distrust of 'outsiders' after the festival. Whilst he didn't know a lot about her background, she was fitting in well with everyone at the clinic after her first couple of weeks. It would be a while before he could fully trust her, if ever, but he had to think about the welfare of their patients and Daisy was a good doctor. He no longer had the urge to run her out of town. If anything, it was the opposite. They worked well as a team here and she was fun to be around.

It was probably for the best that they didn't spend

their personal time together. Seeing each other too much could be a bad thing when they were together all day at work too. Over-familiarity could turn out to be detrimental when he had so much going on. Not only was he the lead in the clinic but he'd had to take on his father's other projects too. He didn't have time for anyone, or anything, else.

However, he'd got used to her popping into his office uninvited for a chat or bringing him a cup of tea every time she made herself one. That was one of her quirks. He had never seen someone drink so much tea and he had added a decaf option in the staffroom for the sake of her health, and his. So far, she had not seemed to avail herself of the alternative.

Now Daisy was here he no longer had to deal with everything on his own. He had been prepared to do that on a work basis when his father had talked of retiring, but Thomas had not expected to lose him altogether. Without his presence at home or work, life had become *too* quiet. At least with Daisy he had someone to talk to about patients or the day he'd had.

'I can wait. I'll make us a cuppa and hopefully the rain will have died down by then.' He headed off to the staffroom without giving her the chance to refuse again.

There was no way he was going to let her walk home in torrential rain simply to avoid spending time with him outside of work. They could make an exception in this sort of circumstance.

It was a while before she conceded and finally left her office with her coat and bag in hand. Thomas would have been willing to sit it out all night if he'd had to.

It was not as though he had anyone waiting at home for him.

'I'm ready to go,' she said on her way to wash her cup in the sink.

Thomas would have been in danger of dozing off in the armchair waiting for her if it had not been for the rain thudding on the roof and pelting against the staff-room windows.

'Then what are we waiting for?' He bounced up out of the chair with more enthusiasm than was called for, but he wanted her to know he was happy to give her a lift.

She walked most days but, as he lived further away and had his own parking space, Thomas usually drove to work. It wouldn't have been very chivalrous of him to leave her to walk home in this weather while he stayed warm and dry in his car.

It was so overcast outside when they did leave the clinic he wondered if he had fallen asleep after all and had slept half the night away. The wind was whipping up a frenzy, with bits of branches and other debris spiralling up into the sky. However, it was the amount of rain which had apparently fallen which was causing him most concern.

The drains were bubbling up and there was a deluge of water running down the length and breadth of the main street.

'I think we should check on the river out by your place, just in case there is a danger of it bursting its banks.' He didn't want to worry her unnecessarily but the cottage was the closest building and there was a chance that it could be in danger. Historically, there had been one or two incidents of flooding from the river, but not for a long time. There had been some rain forecast but not to this extent or they would have taken precautions earlier.

As the owner, any damage would have to be repaired by him, so it was in his best interest to prevent it if possible. Okay, he was concerned about Daisy's safety too. With the boundaries they appeared to have created, he couldn't be certain she would come to him if she needed any help.

'I'm sure it will be fine. Isn't the river under your jurisdiction too? I doubt it would risk your wrath by going against any of your rules.' Although he could see her slight grin in his rear-view mirror, he wondered if the distance between them was about more than maintaining a professional relationship. Perhaps she had a problem with the fact he pretty much ran the village. He didn't want to use the word 'dictated' but Daisy might if she was too stifled by the way things worked around here. Thomas wanted her to feel comfortable, part of the community, but for his father's sake and everyone else in Little Morton he had to be careful.

'Well, if it hasn't got a pass, it's not getting in.' He attempted some humour but as they pulled up outside the cottage the joke was forgotten when they saw how dangerous the situation outside was becoming.

Even in the early evening gloom the flooded fields surrounding the house were apparent, the water obliterating everything but the highest ground. Thankfully, the cottage was not submerged, but that could be just a matter of time. Sitting away from the main street, it was hidden from view or one of the other residents would have noticed and forewarned them.

They stepped out of the car and found themselves ankle-deep in water. He saw the wide-eyed look of panic on Daisy's face.

'How are we going to stop it getting into the house?'

Despite the gravity of the situation and the costly implications for him, Thomas was glad she was including him in resolving this problem with her. The way things had been, she might have insisted she could deal with everything herself. It left an opening for him to do something, hopefully without being accused of being too domineering.

'There are some sandbags out in the shed. We can stack those up against the doors and keep our fingers crossed that does the job. I'll phone the council and the water company and anyone else who can come and help.' He let Daisy lead the way to one of the outbuildings behind the house. She didn't hesitate in shifting the heavy sandbags, unperturbed by her ruined shoes or waterlogged trousers.

Thomas continued to be impressed by her work ethic, even though he had seen it in abundance at the clinic. Patients loved her sympathetic nature, along with that same determination he could see now as she got to the root of people's ailments and sought suitable treatment. She was certainly earning her place and he silently thanked his father for knowing best in this instance. If Thomas had been forced to fill the vacancy at the practice he would have wanted a local replacement and could have struggled with double the workload if Daisy hadn't been so persistent in the face of his reticence.

Once Thomas had notified all the relevant authorities, emergency services and as many residents as he had in his phone book that there could be a risk of flooding, he loaded up with sandbags to shore up the back of the cottage. Although the village was experiencing the effects of the strong winds and the road was slick with rain, there was no indication down there of the possible catastrophe heading their way.

'What about the rest of the village? Should we start warning people?' Daisy, like him, was soaked through but undeterred as the wind and rain battered her. Her hair was plastered to her face, the rain dripping off her chin as she shivered with cold.

'I've phoned ahead and I'm going there next. If you're coming, put something warm and dry on. I don't suppose you've got a pair of wellies?'

She took time to give him a dirty look. 'You've seen my shoe collection.'

'Not to worry. I think I have some in the boot of my car. I'll finish here; you go and get changed.'

'What about you? You're soaked too.'

'I'll manage. I'm going to get a whole lot wetter soon anyway. You don't have to come if you want to stay and get your things out of harm's way. Just in case.'

She didn't take time to consider it. 'No. I want to help.'

'Okay then, go and get changed. You'll be no use to me with pneumonia.' He shooed her away and carried on heaving the sandbags between the buildings until he had utilised all of them.

Thomas hoped for Daisy's sake they did the job they

were supposed to do when she didn't have a lot of belongings she could afford to lose, never mind her home.

As soon as she appeared again in suitable layers of warm clothing and a waterproof jacket, they jumped into the car. Other than to continue warning people of the potential flood risk, he didn't know what else they could do but they would damn well try to prevent a tragedy befalling the village. It would be his worst fear come true to see the place destroyed with no way of him preventing it. For the second time in his life he felt completely powerless.

Daisy's heart was in her throat as they drove towards the village. Thomas's forehead was almost touching the windscreen trying to see where he was going. The rain was coming so fast and heavy now the wipers couldn't keep up, making visibility next to impossible. Despite their impatience to get through, the conditions meant they were moving at a slower pace than either of them wanted. The roads were already treacherous, the water swirling around the car, detritus hitting the roof and blocking their path.

'I'm going to park at the top of the village at the barrier.' He didn't have to say any more. It was obvious why he wasn't risking driving any further when Daisy was worried too that they might get washed down the road and into the harbour. It didn't bear thinking about.

For one thing, she couldn't swim. Even if she had faced her fear of water to learn, that level of independence hadn't been encouraged by either her stepfather or her ex, and hobbies weren't something she'd had time for in London. If she survived this, it was something she would look into, in case near-drowning was a common occurrence in these parts.

She shuddered, but this time through fear rather than from the cold. Thanks to Thomas she was at least warm and better prepared to go back out into the storm.

A glance across at him told her his suit and shoes were ruined. Goodness knew how he or his clothes would ever dry out when he was saturated. Guilt clawed at her, knowing he had stood out in that rain working to protect her home whilst she'd had a chance to change. He had even been prepared to sacrifice his wellies for her but she had found an old pair of boots in her wardrobe which she had worn once to a festival and were more practical than heels at least.

'Don't forget your wellies,' she called to him as he got out of the car. Not that they would make much difference to him now, but he did stop at the rear of the car to retrieve them.

When Daisy stepped out she nearly lost her footing altogether, the water was rushing down past them so fast. She had to take a few deep breaths to regulate her heartbeat after the shock.

'This is bad. Are you sure you want to do this? I'd prefer to get you to safety. You could take the keys to the clinic if you want.'

She was touched by his concern, and tempted to get out of harm's way, but Thomas couldn't rouse the whole village alone.

'Don't worry. I'm made of tough stuff.' Although she was projecting a bravado she did not feel when she was so frightened of losing her footing and somehow ending up underwater, fighting to breathe, her lungs filling up…

'I never doubted that.' He smiled and took her hand as they waded down the street. Daisy knew it was only to keep them both anchored, but it was nice to feel the warm security of his large hand in hers. She kept a tight hold and not only because she needed him to keep her upright. It had been a long time since anyone had wanted to hold her hand. Longer still since she had allowed it.

'For the record, you need to know in case I get swept out to sea or something, I can't swim. I hate the water. So if you see me bobbing about in the harbour you'll have to throw me a lifebelt.' She didn't wish to feel too comfortable with him and the prospect of death by drowning was a subject guaranteed to keep her mind occupied elsewhere.

'I think I'd try harder than that to save you, Daisy. I'd be straight in there after you.' He squeezed her hand to reassure her and though she stopped believing he would let her drown, it did the opposite when it came to her growing feelings towards him and made her feel as though she was in too deep already. Thankfully, Thomas couldn't tell what was going on in her head and kept hold of her hand the rest of the way down the street.

The residents Thomas had sent urgent text messages to were already out, trying to block the fronts of their houses. Nevertheless, they went door to door knocking frantically and shouting out for everyone to hear. By the time they reached the bottom of the hill there was a torrent of water carrying all sorts of debris down the main street.

'Watch out!' She tugged Thomas back as someone's garden bench came rushing down past them.

'We should wait this out indoors. I don't think there's much else we can do until the emergency services get here.' It was he who made the call to put their safety first, just as a loud roar sounded somewhere behind them.

He unlocked the shutters on the medical centre, pulling Daisy inside the door just as a tidal wave appeared to engulf the street outside. Cars, trees and anything else shaken loose by the storm were being washed away down the road.

Daisy could only watch in horror as Little Morton disappeared under water. She rested her head on Thomas's broad shoulder, knowing he must be devastated too when this was his village and his buildings being destroyed before his eyes. Even now the water was pouring in under the door and invading their refuge.

'We need to get to higher ground, but I don't want to risk going out there again. There's an old attic we use for storage if you don't mind the dark?' Thomas grabbed a long wooden pole from behind Reception and hooked a hidden hatch up in the hallway ceiling.

'I'll take it over dirty water,' she muttered as it was now swirling around her ankles.

'We can sit it out up here until it's safe to come down. There's no way of knowing how high the water levels will get. You go on up and I'll try to move as much equipment as I can out of harm's way.' He brought a

stepladder down for her but there was no way she was
letting him do all the hard graft on his own again.

'You know that's not going to work for me, right?'

Daisy saw a flicker of a smile on his lips as he nodded and stopped waiting for her to climb the ladder.

Between them they unplugged the electrical equipment, including the computers, and moved them and the
patient files out of imminent danger. Once the water
was close to waist-deep, Thomas grabbed his medical
bag and insisted they made a move to safety.

From the safety of the loft they watched in despair
as the water continued to rise below.

'I hope everyone else is safe,' he said, watching his
own property being destroyed.

'We gave everyone as much warning as we could.
With any luck they'll all be waiting this out like us.
However long that may be.' If this lasted all night they
were not going to have the best night's sleep in their wet
clothes on these hard floorboards lining the attic space.

Thomas had used the light on his phone to show the
way since the electricity had cut out and all she could
see up here were boxes of old files and Christmas deco-
rations. Nothing that was going to provide any comfort
during the storm.

'I did manage to salvage something…'

Daisy could see the glint in his eye as he reached
around for something behind him. She wondered if he
had a practical radio or something more personal and
sentimental. When he produced a flask of tea and biscuits from his medical bag she laughed out loud.

'Tea? At a time like this?'

'Essential emergency supplies for a rural GP who

might find himself stranded, miles away from the nearest kettle. Anyway, it's the best thing for shock. Tell me you're not dying for a cup.'

She could have kissed him as he poured the comforting beverage into two tin mugs and handed one to her. Instead, she let her mouth savour the chocolate biscuit she had taken from the packet.

'There's nothing we can do yet. We're best up here out of the way. Safe. I can't see the water reaching us here, but in the worst-case scenario we can get out onto the roof from here.' Thomas reminded her that if not for him she could have been washed away like one of the cars being carried down towards the harbour as though they were nothing. If he hadn't convinced her to accept a lift home she would have been caught by the storm and the flood. All because she was dodging being with him.

She took another bite of her biscuit. That plan had worked out well. Not. She had to face it, there was no escaping him when their lives were so closely entwined.

'Thank you for everything tonight. You've been very kind. Amazingly so.' When she had first arrived she would never have expected the stuck-up Dr Ryan to turn out to be the local hero. He had literally waded into the middle of this crisis in his expensive suit without a thought for himself, only for others in the village, including her. It was not in keeping with the plan to keep things strictly professional.

'It's nothing anybody else wouldn't have done.'

Daisy didn't want to like him as much as she did right now, but damn it if he wasn't making that impossible as he shrugged off the compliment.

She finished her biscuit and washed it down with some tea and began to think about everything which had brought her to this moment.

'I broke up with someone recently; that's why I decided to move here and start again.'

Thomas set his cup down and fixed her with those incredible blue eyes. 'I ended a relationship recently too. I know I've been difficult to work with at times, but I enjoy your company. You're not afraid of hard work or telling me if you think I'm out of order.'

'You do need coaxing down out of your ivory tower sometimes. Speaking of which, what about your place? You've been so busy helping everyone else you haven't checked there for possible damage.'

'It should be okay with the house being on higher ground. There's no one there to get hurt. Not any more.' Daisy wouldn't have been human if she hadn't reached out when he was clearly still in pain over his loss. Vulnerable.

A hug was the sort of comfort people gave each other every day. Not Daisy. She held hands, consoled people who might have had bad news, but hugs were too intimate for her to casually give away. It was different with Thomas. She could sense he needed one as much as she did. This human contact, compassion and sheer need to be held.

He buried his nose in her hair. Daisy breathed in the scent of him, so reassuring during this chaos. She was grateful for his support, for not giving up on her even when she had pushed him away. Most of all, he was a reminder that she didn't have to be alone. In times like this it was comforting to have someone to lean on.

However, her relationship status was a conscious decision she had made and with good reason. Those feel-good hormones that came with a hug or a kiss didn't last long and they certainly weren't worth the long-term consequences of being stuck with another controlling man. They didn't come much more controlling than the Earl who owned the whole village. These days Daisy didn't do serious romantic entanglements and getting involved with her co-worker/boss/landlord had major flashing warning lights. She would be a fool to ignore them.

# CHAPTER FOUR

'The rain sounds as though it's dying down.' Daisy released Thomas from her embrace and moved away to reclaim some personal space.

'Yeah, and I think the water's beginning to subside down there.'

Daisy couldn't tell if it had or if he was making an excuse to escape this sudden awkwardness between them too.

'Be careful.' She didn't want him in danger simply because they'd had a moment and were both regretting it.

'I'm just going to take a look outside.' Thomas jumped down out of the loft with a splash. He cleared the obstacles swimming in his path and gently eased the door open.

Daisy held her breath, worried another wave might suddenly sweep in and overwhelm him. Thankfully, the water swishing around him didn't rise any more than knee height, so she could breathe again.

'How does it look out there?' she shouted, keen to abandon their hiding place to explore with him.

'I think it's safe enough for you to come down.'

That was all the encouragement she needed to wade out into the street after him. The rain was easing off and though there was a river flowing down the street, the immediate danger appeared to have passed. Some of the other residents had ventured out to inspect the carnage too. Most were dressed in waterproofs and she could even see others using inflatable dinghies as their mode of transport.

'We should check everyone's okay.' Typically, he wasn't thinking of himself or his own losses first. Daisy respected him so much on a personal and professional level it made her wish even more she had met his father to thank him for his amazing son along with all of his other good work.

'I'll get some supplies in case we need them.' Daisy trudged through the clinic to retrieve her medical bag. Hopefully everyone had been given time to get to safety but, until the emergency services got through, she and Thomas would be the only medics on scene.

He was already banging on doors and talking to neighbours by the time she joined him outside. 'Is everyone inside all right?'

'I'll check the other side of the street.' Daisy left him so they could move quickly from house to house doing their welfare checks.

Most people were generally upset and in shock but without any serious injuries to report. She put that down to Thomas's quick thinking in warning them, getting everyone to safety as soon as possible.

Once they reached the bottom of the hill they met up to compare notes.

'A few people are shaken up, but all accounted for here,' he reported back.

'Pretty much the same on this side. A lot of people took refuge up in the function room at the bar. There might be a few sore heads in the morning but nothing to warrant serious concern. The only place I didn't get any answer from was the cottage on the corner. I don't think I've ever seen who lives there. Is it empty?' She had knocked on the door and the windows but had not seen any sign of life about the place.

Thomas's frown immediately rang warning bells. 'Hmm. That's old Jimmy's place. He doesn't usually go too far from the house so he should be there. I'll try him again in case he didn't hear you.'

They hot-footed it over to the cottage and Thomas hammered on the front door. 'Jimmy? It's Thomas Ryan. I want to make sure you're all right in there.'

When there was no answer Daisy peered in the window, but couldn't see anyone inside. 'He's not in the front room.'

Some more hammering and shouting followed but they received only silence in response.

'Wait. Can you hear that?' Thomas stilled, listening, on alert for any noise.

Daisy was about to tell him he must have imagined it when she thought she heard a faint voice. 'I think it's coming from around the back.'

'Jimmy likes to tinker with old cars out there.' Thomas started off around the side of the house and Daisy went after him. The place looked as though it was being used as a junkyard and it was surprising Thomas let him get away with hoarding so many unsightly car parts and engines when the rest of the village was picture postcard perfect. At least it had been, until the flood had wreaked havoc.

He must have seen her expression as they squeezed past an old washing machine jammed up against the wall beside a broken Welsh dresser. 'It seems as though he's collecting more than car parts these days. He's an old friend of the family so he gets special dispensation, but I think I'll have to have a word with him about health and safety matters.'

That went some way to explaining why this had been allowed to get so out of control, but Daisy thought it was also partly due to Thomas knowing it would make the old man happy to let him get on with it. It had become a death-trap though now the water had shifted some of the heavy white goods into precarious positions. As proved when they heard another faint cry for help coming from somewhere behind all the chaos.

'Jimmy? It's Thomas Ryan.'

Another pained sound and what she thought was splashing sent them running to find the source of the noise. The back garden was a veritable swimming pool with the old cars and stacked household appliances around the perimeter.

'Help!' A silver head was bobbing up out of the water beside one clapped-out old vehicle.

They both rushed over to give assistance in the waist-deep water. Jimmy was spluttering, clinging to the body of the car in an upright position, trying to keep his head above the surface.

'My leg's stuck… I think it's broken. I jacked the car up so I could take a look underneath at the chassis but the whole thing collapsed on me. Next thing I knew a river of water had flooded the yard and nearly drowned me.' The old man was clearly in pain and gasping for air. It seemed as though he hadn't secured the vehicle properly. Given the state of the place, she didn't think he took his health and safety seriously and was now suffering the consequences.

'We might need the fire brigade to move this off you, but we'll do our best, Jimmy. Daisy, can you make sure his head stays above water and keep him talking? I'll get down and take a look at the leg.' Thomas stripped off his sodden outer layer and with one deep breath dipped below the water. There was no thought given to the dirty water he was immersing himself in, he was so focused on helping. They would all need to be hosed down after this and perhaps have to take antibiotics as a preventative measure against any nasty bacteria lurking in there.

'It's going to be all right, Jimmy. Help is on the way.' She was using all her body weight to prop him up, his head leaning back against her chest. He was tiring, his body weak. They'd got here in the nick of time. Thanks to Thomas.

Thomas had to feel around the leg to see where Jimmy was injured and how he was trapped. It was not going to be easy to get him out, and it would be painful, but it was also necessary. Not only could an open wound get infected from the dirty water, but they couldn't keep him afloat indefinitely. At the moment Jimmy was able to co-operate but if he lost consciousness or went into shock they would struggle to save him.

Thomas resurfaced to take a breath, gasping greedily for air. 'On initial examination I think we're dealing with a compound fracture to the tibia. I can feel the bone poking through the skin. I need to free the leg before we can treat it. This isn't going to be pleasant, Jimmy. Honestly, it will hurt like hell but I'll be as quick as I can.'

Ideally they would align the bones and immobilise the leg so it could heal properly but, given the situation, their priority was to get Jimmy out from under the car and out of the water. Until then, there could be all sorts of complications, such as infection setting into the open wound from the dirty water or hypothermia or shock setting in because of the cold. It was likely he was going to need surgery to align the bone properly and a cast to help stabilise it, but they could do all that at the hospital. For now, the important thing was to get him somewhere dry and keep him conscious.

'Do what you have to, Doc. I don't know how much longer I can hang on.'

'Daisy, if I can brace my weight against the car, I need you to pull the leg free.' It meant she would have to go underwater but it was the only way they could get Jimmy out.

She nodded. 'Jimmy, you'll have to support yourself until we get this done, okay?'

'Whatever it takes,' the old man replied.

'Okay then, let's do this.' Thomas was looking at Daisy as he said it, doing his best to express his support when he knew that she was not comfortable in the water.

She helped manoeuvre Jimmy so he could hold on to the car door to keep him upright before she moved away from him. Thomas positioned himself under the car chassis and prayed for superhuman strength to shift it enough to free him.

'One, two, three…' He braced himself against the heavy weight, pushing with everything he had while Daisy ducked under the water. It was difficult to see what she was doing but guessed the moment she pulled the leg free when he heard Jimmy cry out. He knew Daisy would do her best not to jolt his injury any more than she had to and cause him unnecessary pain, but the circumstances were making that a difficult task.

Thomas was doubled over, his hands on his knees, legs shaking with the effort it was taking to keep the weight off Jimmy and Daisy.

Eventually she came back up. Knowing her lack of swimming ability made her endeavour all the more re-markable.

'Pull him as far away from here as possible. I can't hold this up much longer.' His body was spent, fuelled on pure adrenaline to keep them safe.

As soon as they were a suitable distance away he let the car down and dodged out of the way himself.

'Are you okay, Thomas?' Daisy called to him as she helped Jimmy to the back of the house.

Thomas waved, too physically exhausted to speak. Although he couldn't rest when they had a broken leg to tend to.

'We…we have to get him somewhere dry.'

'Where?'

They both looked around the swamped garden and saw the impossible task, with the scrap metal causing obstructions everywhere. He tried the back door and was relieved to find it unlocked, though the kitchen floor was flooded too. The surface of the wooden dining table was dry even if the legs were surrounded by water. He cleared the dirty dishes onto the nearest worktop before going back to fetch the others.

'Do you think you can help me lift him in there?' Thankfully, Jimmy was of slight build, but it was still a big ask, taking into account his injury and how long Daisy had been submerged in the water too.

'I'll do my best, but we should stabilise that leg. Can you reach the medical supplies?' She pointed to the bag she had set on the roof of one of the cars. Thomas retrieved it but he was sure there was nothing in there capable of holding the leg in place to prevent further injury. However, he did have painkillers. After popping a couple out for Jimmy he spotted an old wooden packing crate, bobbing about over by the shed, and grabbed it. With some brute force using his hands and feet, he was able to pull it apart. They hauled Jimmy up the back steps and tied two wooden slats around his leg with bandages to hold it steady. Once they had done their best to limit movement of the injured limb, Thomas grabbed him under the shoulders.

'Okay, Daisy, if you can take the legs we can try and get him inside and up onto the table. Brace yourself, Jimmy.' He tried to take the bulk of the weight and staggered back inside. Jimmy winced but he was a trooper, as was Daisy, managing to lift their patient's lower half.

It was a struggle to get him up onto the table and involved a lot of manoeuvring, pushing, panting and swearing from all three of them.

'Do you have any dry clothes or towels, Jimmy?

Those wet things are going to have to come off so we can keep you warm.' Daisy voiced their other concern over him getting pneumonia or going into shock.

'There's stuff upstairs in the airing cupboard.'

While Daisy went in search, Thomas hunted in the drawers for scissors. 'I'll have to cut these clothes off you, Jim. It's important we do this quickly and don't jolt you about too much.'

'Okay.' The weariness was beginning to tell but they had to keep him conscious until they could get him to hospital.

Thomas removed the torn, bloodied trousers quickly. Once Daisy came back, they were able to prop Jimmy's head up on a folded towel and cover him in a warm thick blanket.

'I'll go and see if there's an ambulance on the way.' Thomas left the room to chase up the ambulance on the phone and to see if there were any emergency services in the vicinity.

Firemen were going door to door to evacuate anyone still trapped in their houses and transporting the very young and elderly by dinghy to safety. The paramedics were taking any of those seriously injured or in shock away by ambulance. Thomas managed to flag someone down to explain their predicament. With a lot of expert help, Jimmy was finally stretchered out.

'How are things looking back there?' Thomas asked one of the paramedics, keen for news about any other residents they might have missed.

'There don't seem to be any other serious injuries but obviously the flooding has left a lot of people with nowhere to sleep tonight. The pub has offered rooms, but they're overrun at the minute.'

'What about your place, Thomas? You could put a lot of the residents up until tomorrow, when we find out for sure how bad the damage is. The house should be high enough up on the hill to be unaffected and there's sufficient room.' Daisy was biting her lip as if she knew what she was asking was out of order when he had made it clear how he felt about sharing his space.

His initial reaction was to say no and shoot down the idea before the guilt began to weigh on his mind. It wasn't fair of Daisy to burden him with the responsibility of leaving these people spending the night wet and cold in homes that probably were not fit for habitation in their current state. Yet she had put her fears aside tonight to help Jimmy because her strength was needed in that moment to save the man. Now he had to dig deep in order to help those in need of support. It wasn't going to be easy, but he was sure Daisy would be there for him when they'd been working as a team all night.

'You're right. Tell anyone in need of somewhere to stay to go to Dr Ryan's house. It's the grey one up on the hill.' Thomas gave his permission to the emergency services to direct people to his place, but his stomach was already rolling at the thought of so many traipsing into the family home.

Even though it had been her suggestion, the look of concern on Daisy's face told him she understood what a big deal this was for him. 'Are you sure?'

He nodded. 'These are my friends and neighbours and I'll do whatever I can to help them.'

'After tonight, I doubt anyone would think otherwise.' Her smile was as warm and welcome as a hug, although not as enjoyable as the one they had shared earlier. When he'd been content to hold her, to breathe her in as long as she would let him.

That comfort, that strength and heart that only came with a connection from another person was something he hadn't had since Jade. A feeling he hadn't realised he was missing until she was gone from his arms again. Thomas didn't know what it was about Daisy that had made him come alive again, but he knew it didn't come around every day.

The problem was that he didn't know what to do about it.

# CHAPTER FIVE

DAISY WAS TIRED, her very bones ached, she was soaked through and more than a little bit emotional but, with Thomas still ploughing on, she knew she had to do the same. He had insisted on stopping off at her place before driving back to his house. Thankfully his car had survived the storm, even if it was a little battered.

'Are you positive you're okay to do this?' He was checking on her emotional state again, as he had been doing continually since they'd left the village, regardless that he was the one about to be tested so far out of his comfort zone with the influx of strangers in his house.

She wasn't used to anyone caring about her enough to ask and the question alone made her well up. To have someone with her during a difficult time meant all the difference after years of coping on her own and trying to stay strong. Thomas's support let her express how she was actually feeling and was healthier than holding everything back for fear of appearing weak. He wouldn't try to take advantage of that vulnerability when he was leaving himself so exposed too and it made her less afraid to let her guard down a little.

Tonight, all he had shown was compassion and generosity, thinking of everyone but himself, when she knew the personal demons he was fighting at the same time.

'There are others who have lost a lot more than I have.'

'That doesn't diminish your loss or make your upset any less important. I can manage alone if you want to take some time out.'

Daisy appreciated his concern but wouldn't have been comfortable sitting doing nothing while he ran around the village in his superhero cape and tights. Besides, she needed to keep busy to take her mind off whatever mess was awaiting her at the cottage.

'I told you, I'm fine.' She gave him a smile she hoped was convincing enough to stop him worrying.

As anticipated, the floodwater had covered the entire ground floor of the cottage, ruining everything in its path. It was a lot to take in, seeing the devastation when she hadn't long moved in.

The rug she'd bought to provide some warmth underfoot when walking on the wooden floors was floating in a sea of dirty water, the once vibrant colours now a muddy brown. Even the dachshund-shaped draught excluder she'd bought from a local craft store, and nicknamed Dex, had doggy-paddled away from his prime spot along the bottom of the door. Now he was buried, only his back end visible, apparently having suffered from some sort of mummification from the pile of sodden magazines which had been swept off her coffee table.

It seemed absurd to have a lump in her throat over such trivial things, but she'd been trying to make this a home. These small purchases and additions to the cottage represented her setting down some roots and tonight that had been taken away from her. Her efforts to fit in, to make a life for herself had been wiped out in a flash. She felt as though she was back in that limbo, with nowhere to really call home.

Not that she would let anyone see her cry over something as pathetic as some ruined soft furnishings. She was stronger than that now. At least on the outside.

'No offence, but I didn't like the choice of décor anyway. It will give me a chance to redecorate to my own taste.'

'I can see you've tried to put your own stamp on the place already. I'm so sorry about everything you've lost.' Thomas put an arm around her shoulders in sympathy and it was all she could do not to bury her head in his chest and sob when he was offering her some much-needed emotional support.

'The insurance should replace anything you need to get the place back to how you want it, Daisy. Obviously we'll have to wait until we get the place dried out first.'

For Daisy, it wasn't about the monetary value of the items destroyed; it was the time and joy that had gone into choosing those things, in trying to make a home for herself. Little Morton was the first place she'd put any effort into that kind of thing. As though this was the one place where she could see herself settling down. Belonging. This was a reminder that nothing for her was certain, and she didn't have family to help her pick up the pieces.

'There's not much we can do about it in the meantime so we should probably go and see to your house guests,' she said, keen to get away from the sight of her life here in ruins. Thomas's house was about to become her welcome refuge for the night too.

Thomas had ferried as many people as he could to his house in his car and had instructed the emergency services to send anyone else there who needed a place to stay. The fire brigade was working hard to move any large obstructions in the area and pumping water away as best they could. The paramedics were on hand giving hygiene advice to those who might not have been seriously injured but had come into contact with the dirty water. Everything would have been contaminated by the bacteria present in the floodwater and needed to be cleaned thoroughly. The electricity supplier had sent out engineers to make sure the power lines were safe and running after the storm. Everyone was rallying around to repair the significant damage done to the village.

Goodness knew how long it would take to get back to normal. Especially if they had any more rainfall like they had experienced earlier. The clear-up was going to be tough, but at least for now those most affected would have somewhere safe and warm to stay.

As a result, Daisy and Thomas had become the hosts, welcoming people in and providing hot food and beverages. They were in the kitchen now, making tea and coffee with bottled water for the people currently huddled in the living room.

'Where is everyone going to sleep tonight?' Though the house was four times the size of hers, there were more people than bedrooms. She hadn't thought things through properly before volunteering his home as a hotel for the night. Likely because she'd never expected him to agree so willingly. They had only known each other for a short time but Thomas was an inspiration to anyone struggling with their demons when he faced his so heroically. Daisy wished she had the same strength. Then she might not be facing spending the rest of her days alone, afraid of history repeating itself and burning her in the process.

'I'll put the young families in the bedrooms and hopefully the rest will bed down where they are. There should be enough blankets and pillows for everyone to have a makeshift bed at least.' If he was indeed fazed by having his home invaded by so many at once, he wasn't showing any visible sign of discomfort. Probably for her benefit and those who'd been invited to stay. Daisy was impressed that he was capable of setting aside his personal issues for the sake of others, when not so long ago he'd been stressing over one stranger arriving in his village.

He had mellowed from the man who had 'greeted' her on her arrival to the village. That barrier protecting him from people like those who had hurt his father was gradually lowering and Thomas was doing his best to make everyone feel at ease instead of pushing them away.

Daisy distributed the drinks and whatever snacks she could find in the kitchen to the house guests dispersed throughout the reception rooms on the ground floor of the family home. It was a huge, imposing building filled with the history of previous generations. The wooden panelling on the walls made the house seem even more dark and imposing. Thick rich red carpeting underfoot gave the place a regal air, along with the gold-plated fixtures and fittings. It was no wonder Thomas was paranoid about letting people in when the place felt like a museum. So many precious heirlooms were dotted about which probably should have been behind glass for protection. It would only take one errant child or a clumsy visitor to shatter the Chinese vases or porcelain figures and a piece of history could be lost for ever.

Despite the portraits of his ancestors frowning at any intruders from the walls, Daisy could see how lonely Thomas could be here, miles away from village life. There were no neighbours, no noise outside and he likely only inhabited a fraction of the large dwelling. It reminded her of her London apartment, only on a much larger scale.

Hopefully he could take something positive away from tonight's events too, seeing the house come alive with people, laughter and chat. With any luck it wouldn't be for the last time. He was clearly a much loved, well-respected member of the community and Daisy knew if Thomas would let people in they would gladly include him in the whole of village life. She could only dream of the same. Perhaps then they wouldn't seem to be each other's only lifeline.

There were lots of pats on the back and words of gratitude uttered to Daisy and Thomas as they did their best to make everyone comfortable. He came to her empty-handed after handing out bedding to their exhausted neighbours.

'Is there anything left for me or should I curl up in the bath for the night?' She was only half joking. As much as she was longing for a bed, she would sleep anywhere right now.

'I thought you could sleep in my room.'

Her eyebrows shot up at the presumption. 'Excuse me?'

Thomas at least looked embarrassed when she queried his proposition. 'I mean, you can take the bed. I'll take the floor. I know I should give up my room for someone else but I'm not ready to leave strangers alone with my personal items.'

There was a warm glow inside her at the thought that he was happy for her to have entry into his inner sanctum. He no longer saw her as an unwanted stranger.

'In that case, take me to your bed, Your Grace.' She couldn't help but tease him when he looked so adorably ruffled. Up until now she hadn't seen him as anything other than confident and cool in his actions. Perhaps she wasn't a totally safe option after all if she could manage to get him a tad flustered before bedtime.

They walked up the stairs in silence to his bedroom, as though they were expecting something major to happen. Daisy knew that wasn't a possibility, not just because there was so much else going on here tonight, but also because neither of them was ready for any romantic entanglement. They were two broken souls who had simply found some comfort together. Now they had to be careful they didn't mistake that for anything more dangerous.

Thomas opened his bedroom door and let her walk in first. It was such a stark contrast to the rest of the house, Daisy could see why he was reluctant to share it with strangers. Gone were the stern faces of previous Earls, replaced with sunny images of the harbour. The furniture was modern but looked comfortable, unlike the expensive pieces she had seen downstairs but had been too afraid to sit on in case she broke something priceless. Thick luxurious carpet cushioned her feet with every step she took into Thomas's domain. It felt homely.

'This is such a lovely room. Why don't you redecorate the rest of the house like this?' She plonked herself on the edge of the super-king-size bed in the middle of the room.

Thomas smiled and closed the door behind him, locking them into their own world away from everyone else for a while. 'I guess I haven't got used to being the owner yet. It feels almost as though I'm merely the caretaker here, looking after someone else's stuff. I wouldn't even know what to do with everything or where to put it.'

'The opposite of my problem.' Her mind drifted back to the devastation at the cottage and whether or not she would be able to salvage anything.

'We can deal with that tomorrow. It's been a long tiring day and we should both get some sleep. There's bottled water in the bathroom if you'd like to get washed?' Until they could be sure the water was safe to use again, the water company had provided bottles of water for washing and drinking to everyone in the village.

Thomas rummaged in a nearby chest of drawers and pulled out some grey tracksuit bottoms and a T-shirt. 'I know they're not your size or style, but they are dry.'

'Thanks,' she said as he tossed them over to her and she hurried into the bathroom before she embarrassed herself by crying or, worse, by making an unwanted advance.

It would be easy to give in to that urge to hug him, to kiss him when he had been her strength tonight. He had been everyone's strength, yet she knew he wouldn't expect anything from anyone in return. It wasn't something she was used to. In her experience when people, men in particular, provided her with security she was expected to hand over her independence in gratitude. Tonight she would have gladly done so, uncaring of the consequences, if it meant she could let go of that tight control of her emotions and let Thomas look after her for a while.

She washed sparingly with the cold water from the bottle provided. They had left enough downstairs for their guests to do the same.

By the time she had dried off and dressed in his too big, comfy clothes, he had bedded down on the floor with the array of cushions which had been decorating the bed.

'I'll just go and brush my teeth then I'll turn the light off.' He disappeared into the bathroom, but not before Daisy had a peek at his half-naked form.

It was just as well she was climbing into bed before she swooned at the flash of toned torso and tight buttocks encased in jersey fabric as he left the room. She lay down and attempted to force herself to sleep. Impossible now she had seen that body, which had been teasing her ever since the festival. Okay, so she was attracted to him. Big deal. Most people in the village likely had a crush on the rich, handsome doctor who had come to the rescue tonight. It didn't mean anyone was going to act on it, including her. Even if it was torture lying in his bed, knowing he was so close.

As promised, he turned the light off once he had finished brushing his teeth and she heard the rustle of cushions as he tried to get comfortable.

'Night,' she said into the darkness.

'Night, Daisy.'

It was impossible to say how long she lay there, wide awake, replaying the events of the evening in her mind. As exhausted as she was, sleep was elusive because of the drama and the personal loss she had suffered. Not to mention the awareness that Thomas was lying in his boxers on the floor beside her. The intermittent sound of him plumping the cushions and tossing and turning finally became too much for her.

'You know this bed is big enough for the two of us to sleep in without being in the same postcode. We're both adults, Thomas. I think we can manage to share without making a huge deal about it.' She didn't want him to think she was making a move on him. It was simply the guilt from having this huge bed to herself which had prompted the suggestion.

'Are you sure? I can't seem to get comfortable here.'

'I noticed,' Daisy grumbled as the mattress dipped and Thomas slid in beside her.

'You can't sleep either?'

'Nope. Too much going on in my head to switch off, unfortunately.' A matter which was not going to be helped now he was lying next to her. If she turned onto her side there was a possibility of coming into contact with his warm, partially naked body and that temptation alone was enough to keep her awake.

'It's been a weird day all right.'

'In the hope I don't sound too condescending, I want to say I'm proud of you for letting everyone stay here tonight. I know that was a huge leap of faith for you.' She saw the glint of his smile through the darkness.

'Thanks. Although I'm not sure there was much choice. I couldn't leave everyone else to fend for themselves.'

'No, but considering everything that's happened in the past, I know it can't have been easy.'

'It wasn't and not simply because I've opened up the house to people.'

Daisy heard a movement and a tilt of her head found him staring into her eyes.

'Oh.' She held her breath, afraid to interrupt his train of thought, and waited for him to open up some more.

'The men who broke into the house and assaulted my father were strangers to us but not to my girlfriend at the time. Jade was a volunteer at a charity I started. I thought I should take a leaf out of my father's book and commit my time and money to a worthy cause. I was doing it for all the right reasons, I thought. I wanted to make a difference to those who, through no fault of their own, didn't have the same opportunities in life I had.'

That was a leaf straight out of his father's book, helping the less fortunate for no other reward than knowing he was doing the right thing, and Daisy had to commend him for that.

'What happened?'

'Jade became a big part of my life. Of course that meant taking her home, introducing her to my father and sharing my life with her. It never occurred to me that I was being played. That it was all a scam, a set-up to find out as much about my family and our finances as possible. She waited until I was away from home before making her move. Unknown to me, she was sharing all those details about my life with her nefarious friends. She stopped by the house, my father invited her in, unaware she had brought a criminal gang with her. I was so wrapped up in myself, in Jade and in getting my project off the ground, I was blind to the danger waiting out there. I brought it home with me.' The pain and guilt in Thomas's voice was difficult to listen to. It was raw, without self-pity, only regret.

'That's terrible. Such a betrayal on so many levels.'

'It's not your fault. If anything, I should be apologising to you for taking out my issues on you when you first arrived.'

'I survived, didn't I? As it happens, I was trying to lay some ghosts of my past to rest too.' She had never shared the details of those troubled years with anyone except Thomas's father but here, under the cover of darkness, having a heart-to-heart with Thomas, it felt safe to share.

Another deep breath. 'Where to start? I never knew my dad. I think he and my mum were passing ships in the night. She married when I was nine but took off a year or so later, leaving me with my stepfather and stepbrothers, who treated me like their personal servant.'

'A real-life Cinderella?'

'I never thought of it that way, but in some ways I suppose so.'

'Didn't social services get involved?'

'I was too terrified to tell anyone what was going on

at home. I'd been threatened not to open my mouth or I would end up in a children's home, which sounded scary to a young girl who already felt alone in the world. Besides, my stepfather could have charmed anyone. From the outside he seemed like a respectable family man, because that was what he wanted people to think. No one would have believed the monster he was at home. His sons were no better. They were teenagers who should have been capable of looking after themselves or standing up for me, but they were carbon copies of him and enjoyed making my life hell. Your father was a little like my Fairy Godfather. At the time of applying for his scholarship I was living with my boyfriend, Aaron, which wasn't much better than the house I'd left. He was controlling, didn't like me going out and didn't want me working. I was completely dependent on him and I thought I had to be grateful for it. Then I saw an article about the scholarship your father was offering and I knew it was my way out. Since then I've worked hard to keep that independence he helped me achieve. I owe him so much and I'm truly sorry I'll never get to tell him that in person.' It choked her up that he had been so cruelly taken away from both of them. Of course it was a huge loss to Thomas not having his father, but Daisy felt it too when he had helped her take back her power.

'He was one of a kind all right. Too soft-hearted for his own good. I was afraid you were taking advantage of him.'

'I got that. You didn't know me and I suppose you were just looking out for your father. I like to think we were friends at the end and that's why he told me about the position at the medical centre. I had recently split up with someone and was keen for a new start. He always seemed to appear when I needed him most.'

'He talked about you a lot and how proud he was of everything you'd achieved. Bringing you here was his way of telling me "I told you so" when I became cynical about these strangers he was helping.' Thomas laughed. It was a warm comforting sound Daisy wanted to snuggle into.

'He'd be proud of everything you've done in the village.' It was plain to see Thomas's devotion to his family's legacy went far beyond his title and property. The people of Little Morton were his family now, but he just couldn't see it.

'He deserved better than he got. You don't know the half of what he went through and still put everyone else's needs first. Even my mother treated him badly. She cheated on him with the gardener—so cliché— then cleaned out their joint bank account. Thankfully, the majority of his money was tied up in investments and was too difficult for her to get at, otherwise she would probably have left him destitute. We never saw her again. Anyone else would have tightened their hold on their wallet, but not my father. He poured all of his love and money into his charitable projects after that.'

'Am I one of his charitable projects?' she asked with her tongue firmly in her cheek.

'You are his greatest success.'

Daisy turned onto her side so they were mere centimetres away from each other. 'I think that honour goes to his high-achieving, caring son.'

Although it sounded cheesy as they formed their mutual appreciation society, Daisy meant every word of it.

The Earl might be gone, but he had raised this beautiful man who had come along just when she'd needed him. Her life had not been lonely since she'd set foot in the clinic and crossed paths with Dr Ryan.

All of a sudden the room seemed more intimate, the space between them minute, and the air filled with crackling anticipation. Daisy knew she should turn away from him and temptation, but she didn't want to. Every second since she'd met Thomas had been leading to this moment. Although she hadn't expected to be sharing his bed tonight.

They were smiling at each other, knowing what was coming next but both wary of making that crucial move. Then Thomas moved across until his head was resting on her pillow and pressed his lips against hers.

Daisy shut her eyes to fully let go of her inhibitions, closed her ears to those voices of doubt trying to spoil it and kissed him back. That first soft pressure appeared to be Thomas seeking permission for more and she willingly granted it. They parted for a mere second before reconnecting, this time with more force and increasing passion.

Daisy's heart was pounding somewhere in her throat as he cupped her cheek with his hand whilst his mouth sought hers again and again. He teased his tongue along her bottom lip before dipping inside.

This was definitely not the buttoned-up Earl she had thought she would be working with.

Arousal was flooding her body the same way the river had crashed through the village, causing just as much devastation. She hadn't come here to get involved with anyone, let alone her work colleague. Yet they had a connection she couldn't ignore, or apparently walk away from.

Thomas slid his hand up under her loose top and palmed her breast, taking a possessive hold which left her gasping at the bold move. It turned her on so much she was a writhing mass of hormones restless for more. She wanted him, wanted his hands all over her body, making her forget everything except how he was making her feel in that moment. Alive, sexy and, most of all, wanted.

Impatience saw her reach for him, being as daring as he had been. She took hold of his hardness through his boxers, enjoying the hiss of air through his teeth as she tested his resolve. The feel of him in her hand was a powerful aphrodisiac, knowing she'd been the one to get him in this state.

'Daisy—' His strained plea only spurred her on to want to please him and make him feel the way she did.

'Hmm?'

'Daisy. Stop.' He grabbed her hand and moved it away.

'What—what's wrong?' She scooted back, giving him some space and trying to distance herself from the humiliation threatening to engulf her.

'Do we really want to go here?' His tone had changed from rampant and ready to regretful, suggesting that he didn't.

'I thought—' Well, she hadn't been thinking or she would have realised what a big mistake they were about to embark on too.

He was right. Events had completely overtaken them tonight, forcing them together. They were tired, emotional and seeking comfort and that would never be a good reason to sleep together. They would only come to regret it once everything went back to normal. Their lives had been turned upside down and now they were clinging to something familiar and comforting like sex to save them from drowning.

'Tonight has shaken us both up and we're not thinking clearly. Are we really ready to start something, Daisy?'

'When you put it like that…' His words were enough to throw cold water over the previously sizzling sheets. To Daisy, a relationship of any kind entailed giving up who she was to please someone else, compromising her life to accommodate a partner's wishes. She hadn't come all this way to repeat those mistakes.

'I didn't think so. Should I move back onto the floor?' Thomas kicked off the covers, ready to scramble away from her.

She didn't want him to think she couldn't control herself around him. 'There's no need. Honestly. Point made, loud and clear.' Doing her best not to take offence or let him think she would attempt to seduce him in the night, Daisy punched one of her pillows into a makeshift barrier between them. There would be no inadvertent touching or straying into temptation now. It was unlikely there would be any sleeping either, now she knew exactly what Thomas could arouse in her. Just one look, one word from him and her mind would bring her straight back into his bed. Where lips were clashing, bodies were writhing and that thrill of anticipation made her feel more alive than she had in years.

It would have been easier to keep working alongside

each other if she had let him keep resenting her instead of lusting after him, yearning for the release they had just denied each other.

Whether they had slept together or not, they would never look at each other the same way again. Damn it if Daisy didn't want him to feel the same way she did and to hell with the consequences. In that moment she would have quit her job if it meant one hot night together. Then there would be no relationship worth worrying about. Except she would still be giving up her life for a man. She simply couldn't win.

# CHAPTER SIX

THOMAS ROSE IN the early hours of the morning. He had to before the last of his restraint gave way with Daisy lying next to him in bed. Last night had been a close call and he wondered if he regretted not giving in to the desire to make love to her more than if he had.

Goodness knew he wanted nothing more than to have her completely naked in his arms, but damned common sense had just about managed to override his natural instinct. The moment she had touched him back he'd realised the implications of taking that next step.

Never mind that they still had to work together, but they had just opened up to one another about why they were so unsuited as a couple. Neither were ready to trust again or share their lives with anyone. That would never be a good basis for a relationship and, being in such close proximity, a fling was not a possibility. Nor was it likely they could have one night together and then he would simply walk away and forget about it. It was going to be difficult enough putting their passionate encounter behind them and carrying on as though nothing had happened.

With so many house guests, he thought it prudent

to make a start on breakfast or at least set out enough food for people to help themselves. Whatever it took to kill time before they were able to survey last night's damage in the daylight.

He pulled on his shirt and trousers in case he offended any ladies from the village he might run into. It was also his way of calling time on sleeping next to Daisy.

She was fast asleep, looking very much at home in his bed. The room must have become too hot for her in the night; now she was lying on top of the covers, his joggers discarded on the floor. Her T-shirt-cum-nightdress was riding high on her thighs and corrupting his thoughts.

Ignoring his horny inner demon, he left the room and the delectable sight of Daisy sprawled across the pillows to deal with the needs of the others who had stayed the night. Those who were easier taken care of and didn't leave him worrying about the aftermath. At most, the only trouble there would be downstairs was a lack of food and extra housework when everyone had gone.

Neither he nor Daisy had eaten last night, too busy making sure their friends and neighbours had enough to keep them comfortable for the night. As a result he was ravenous and in need of a caffeine fix. He briefly contemplated making some breakfast for Daisy, but walking back into that room and seeing her in his bed again would be asking for more trouble. It would be better to leave her until daylight and let her help herself. To breakfast and nothing else.

Despite trying to be as quiet as possible so he didn't disturb anyone, Thomas thought he heard someone moving about upstairs. He prayed Daisy hadn't wakened and decided to follow him down. It would defeat the whole purpose of him escaping the sexual tension between them.

He waited, listening for the sound of footsteps on the stairs but none came. Then a shrill cry pierced the silence and Thomas was bounding up the stairs in his bare feet, taking as many as he could at once.

His thoughts were only of Daisy, concerned she might have hurt herself in the dark, and he cursed himself for leaving her alone. When he reached the communal landing, the commotion seemed to be coming from the opposite end of the hallway to his bedroom, in one of the spare rooms. Daisy appeared in the doorway of his room, hair flattened on one side, wiping sleep from her eyes.

'Thomas? What's wrong?'

'I don't know. I thought you'd hurt yourself.'

She shook her head. 'Whoever that was woke me up. I was fast asleep. I didn't even hear you get out of bed.'

The pointed look accusing him of taking the coward's way out didn't go unnoticed by Thomas but that was a discussion which could wait. Another anguished cry sent them both rushing towards the source. One of the guest bedroom doors was wide open, a man he recognised as one of his patients frantically pacing the room with his phone clamped to his ear.

Thomas gave a polite knock on the door to make him aware of their presence. 'Is everything all right, Neil? We thought we heard someone in pain.'

The man threw up his hands. 'I was just about to

come and find you, Doc. Janine is in labour and no one can tell me when an ambulance can get here.'

A lowing sound came from the en suite bathroom and Daisy rushed in first to give assistance.

'How far apart are the contractions?' Thomas asked as she gained admittance to the bathroom.

'They're coming fast. Too fast.' There were already dark shadows beneath the father-to-be's eyes. Clad only in his underwear and white as a sheet, his wife's labour seemed to have come as big a shock to him as everyone else.

'She's almost full-term, isn't she?' It wouldn't be surprising if the ordeal the couple had been through, with the flood and the potential loss of their home, had started labour prematurely. Something which would have ideally been dealt with in a hospital environment but here, with no real idea of when help would arrive, they wouldn't be equipped to deal with any possible complications.

'Thirty-six weeks. We don't even have her bag here or anything for the baby.' The anxious father dropped down onto the mattress, apparently overwhelmed by the occasion and it was little wonder.

Thomas wondered how much of their baby's belongings had even survived the water damage. Although he was sure the community would rally around to make sure the family had all they needed. The most important thing now was to make sure this baby arrived safely.

As another contraction made itself known to the mother and the rest of the household, Thomas knew that job was going to be down to him and Daisy. Even in these difficult circumstances, he was sure their working partnership would prove more successful than their personal one.

'Thomas? You need to get in here.' Daisy's urgent tone drew him into the bathroom straight away. She was kneeling on the floor beside Janine, who was holding her hand so tightly it looked as though she had cut off the circulation.

'Can't you give her something?' Neil, unable to bear his wife being in distress, was practically begging them to do something for her.

'I'm sorry, it's too late to give her any pain relief,' Daisy added.

'Can she hold on until the paramedics get here?' Thomas kept his voice low so as not to startle the couple.

Daisy shook her head. 'This baby is coming now.'

'Do you have any experience assisting a birth?' he asked, prepared to let her take the lead if she had more expertise in this area. The last time he had assisted in a birth had been during his first year at the clinic. A patient had gone into labour during a snowstorm and he and his father had been able to reach her before an ambulance could. He'd had his father to guide him then, the man who had been present at most of the births of the locals over the years.

'Not since medical school,' Daisy said, a faint flicker of uncertainty in her eyes before she returned her attention to Janine, who was crying out as another contraction hit. Thomas knew Daisy would step up and do what needed to be done for her patients, just as he would. They worked well together, so he had no doubt they could do this between them.

'In that case, we'd better get organised.' He rolled up his sleeves before grabbing all the fresh towels he could find from the cupboard.

'You can't deliver our baby here. Can't you at least get her over to the bed?' The worried partner was hovering in the doorway, the compact bathroom too small to house them all.

Thomas understood the need to make her comfortable, to make the birth special, but circumstances had overtaken them. 'I'm sorry but we can't move her now. It's too late.'

'The baby's head is crowning.' Daisy moved into a prime position so she could see what was happening, with Janine panting hard and apparently ready to push.

Thomas knelt down on the floor. 'Okay, Janine, big deep breaths and when the next contraction hits I want you to push as hard as you can.'

The frightened woman nodded back at him, trusting that he knew what he was doing. In truth, he hadn't delivered a baby in a very long time, but it looked as though Janine had done most of the hard work already.

Daisy poured some cold water from one of the bottles the water company had distributed onto a flannel and laid it on the woman's forehead to try and cool her down. 'That's it, big deep breaths. You're doing so well, Janine.'

The expectant father was pacing up and down the room but keeping an eye on the proceedings. Janine's breathing suddenly became quicker, panting through another contraction.

'With this one I need you to bear down, and I'll be here to catch Baby, okay?' He gave what he hoped was a reassuring smile even though his heart was pounding hard and he was beginning to perspire.

Everyone needed to have confidence in him to deliver this baby safely, and he had to push away his own fears to believe it himself.

Janine cried out as she squeezed Daisy's hand when the next contraction hit hard.

'Good girl. You can do this.' Although Daisy was talking to their mother-to-be, Thomas took the positive statement for himself. He could do this too.

With the towels covering the cold tiled floor, he got ready for the baby to slither out. Except when the head emerged, panic began to set in that perhaps he was out of his depth after all.

'Janine, I need you to stop pushing for a while and take long deep breaths.'

Daisy immediately turned to see what was wrong. 'The umbilical cord is wrapped around baby's neck so we need you to slow things down until the doctor can release it.'

The matter-of-fact way Daisy delivered the news kept Janine calm during a time which could have been potentially life-threatening for the baby. It was up to Thomas to unwrap the cord from the baby's neck before it cut off the blood flow and oxygen supply, causing long-term brain damage or worse.

He was breathing more heavily too as he deftly worked to undo the thick cord. As soon as he was sure the baby was out of danger, he gave Janine the go-ahead to continue pushing. He caught the baby quickly and wrapped him in a clean towel to keep him warm. With his little finger Thomas made sure the airway was clear and gave him a quick check-over to make sure everything was okay.

'Congratulations. You have a lovely, healthy baby boy.' He laid the infant on his mother's chest, welling up himself as she sobbed happy, exhausted tears.

'A boy?' Neil, looking relieved it was all over, appeared beside them.

'Come on in, Dad, so you can get a cuddle too.' Daisy scooted aside so the parents could coo over the baby together.

When she caught Thomas's eye he could see she was teary too, understandable when things could have turned out so differently. She probably felt as he did— relieved that everything was okay and happy for the couple about to embark on the new chapter of their life together as a family.

Although he had no doubt that if further complications had arisen Daisy would have assisted him in their improvised delivery suite. She was every bit as confident and capable as him, and great at keeping people calm in a crisis, including him.

Despite running out on her in the early hours, he was glad she had been there with him. Getting involved romantically would be a complication they could both do without, but Daisy was becoming quite a fixture in his life these days and he wasn't complaining. It felt good to be in company again, to share the wonderful and difficult events with someone who understood the importance of his work. Where most women he had been with inevitably got tired of coming second to his job, Daisy lived her life the same way he did. If a relationship had been something he would ever think about again, she would have been his perfect woman.

It was a touching scene, Janine's head lying on her husband's shoulder as they marvelled at the new life they had created, and Daisy couldn't help but think of the family she would never have. If she couldn't trust another man she wouldn't bring a child into the world and into an unstable environment.

Thoughts of Thomas automatically flitted into her head when he was the only man she had let close in a long time, but recreating this happy little scene was merely a fantasy. Both she and Thomas had been left too scarred by their pasts to entertain the idea of sharing their lives again.

It was a pity. She loved children and could tell by Thomas's kind heart and generous nature he would make a good dad some day. He'd certainly had the right role model in his own father. Maybe Thomas would go on to have a family with someone, but it wouldn't be her. Not when he wasn't even willing to share a bed with her for one night.

When she'd woken up, she'd expected to find him still in bed beside her. Although he'd rejected any idea of sleeping with her, she'd liked the thought of waking up next to him, so she wasn't alone on a night like this. Even that had apparently been too much for him to contemplate. She was going to have to accept he wasn't interested in anything other than a working relationship. No matter how much of a slap to the ego that was to her.

The coloured lights flashing in through the window

and onto the ceiling signalled the arrival of the ambulance. 'Looks like the cavalry has arrived.'

'I'll go and direct them up to the room.' A relieved-looking Thomas went to meet the paramedics. She was grateful to have them here too so they could monitor Janine while delivering the placenta.

Daisy and Thomas hovered nearby as the crew carried out their checks on mother and baby. Once they were stretchered out, wrapped up in blankets to protect them from the cold, the tension finally left Daisy's body. They had handed over responsibility to the local hospital now, who would carry out further precautionary measures to ensure all was well before discharging the family back home.

'Well, it's been an eventful day and night, hasn't it?' Daisy made Thomas chuckle as they waved the ambulance off at the front door.

'That's one way of putting it. I wonder if it's safe to try and go back to sleep for a few hours?'

'I'm too wired to sleep now. Though I should probably go back inside where it's warm.' She was still dressed in his oversized shirt and little else.

'Yes, go and put some clothes on. I can't afford to have a staff member down with the cold when the clinic will be chaos after the flooding.' He shooed her away but not before she turned back with one last thing to say.

'Congratulations, by the way, Dr Ryan. It's reassuring to me and everyone else that you're confident in a crisis. It could've been a bit hairy back there so, in case no one else says it, well done.'

Daisy was shivering as she went back into the house, but she had thought it important for Thomas to know he was appreciated and not on his own. Being a doctor could be a lonely profession at times, but she suspected more so for him now his father wasn't around to share the workload or the experiences.

They had just witnessed one of life's miracles together. Thanks to Thomas. Given the conditions, the birth could have been more traumatic, but he had proved yet again he was someone who could be relied upon. That was more important to her than a meaningless fling or giving in to temptation for one night and jeopardising her career and her new life here in Little Morton.

With that in mind, she went back upstairs to put on the pair of baggy joggers he had given her. From now on she was going to remain professional around him and set aside whatever attraction she felt towards him. It was the only way she could move forward and stop driving herself crazy.

'You're just in time. Tea's ready.' Daisy poured two cups of hot, sweet tea. They needed it after the morning they had already had.

'Thanks.' He took a long sip and sighed.

Thomas was bound to be exhausted when he hadn't slept at all. At least she had managed forty winks before their extra guest's premature arrival.

'I'll call later and see how mother and baby are doing, but they both seemed in good health all things considered.'

'I hope there are no more surprises. I don't think I can take much more.' He pulled a chair out from the kitchen table and sat down with his cup of tea.

'Judging by tonight's performance, I would say you can deal with anything thrown at you.' Daisy took her cup and joined him at the table, trying to keep her voice low so as not to wake anyone else. Although all the commotion had stirred a few of the visitors, the house remained reasonably quiet.

'You were with me through everything, Daisy. I didn't do it on my own.' He wouldn't accept her praise without a fight.

'Yay us.' She clinked her cup to his in celebration, bringing a smile to his lips.

They sat in silence for a few moments drinking their tea before Daisy blurted out what had been bugging her since she had woken up.

'Why did you leave the bedroom? And your bed, with me in it?'

Thomas set his cup down, taking his time to formulate an answer. He could have lied to her and say he had heard Janine long before they had known what was happening.

Instead, he said, 'Because I knew it was the only way I'd be able to keep my hands off you.'

His voice was gravelly, as though he was struggling with the inner turmoil of that decision. She knew because she felt the same. Everything in her body had said to give in to the chemistry but her head kept telling her it would be a bad idea. That didn't stop the wanting.

The thought of what could have happened if he had not listened to his inner voice gave Daisy that fluttery feeling she thought she had long since grown out of.

'Would it be such a terrible thing?' Her own voice was husky, full of desire and what-ifs.

'Probably not. Which is exactly why I need to keep my distance.' He was grinning and she was sure he was just as frustrated as her, even if common sense was winning out for now.

He had made his position clear, and Daisy wasn't going to resort to begging simply to scratch that itch when she knew he was right. It didn't mean she would let the subject lie altogether.

'Didn't the sight of the new family tonight make you think about marriage and children at all?' A person would have to be made of stone not to have been moved by bringing a new life into the world and she was sure it had at least made him think about what it would be like. Just as she had.

'I let you share my bed for one night and you're already talking about marriage and babies? Wow. You're a fast mover.'

She rolled her eyes at his teasing, knowing he was avoiding the subject. 'I'm being serious, Thomas.'

'It's very special being part of something like that but, personally, it doesn't change anything for me. Bringing home people I've known and lived beside for years was a huge step for me tonight. I can't see how I'll ever get over the betrayal and hurt my father and I both suffered. Call it self-preservation if you like, but I don't think it's worth jeopardising everything I have to risk my heart on someone else. I simply can't see myself getting past that to settle down with someone.' His half-smile said it wasn't a decision he had made lightly or easily and he was aware of what he was sacrificing to protect himself. Daisy understood when she was guilty of the same.

However, she believed in Thomas's case it was the burden of unnecessary guilt which was preventing him from living his life to the fullest.

'Does this mean you're considering putting an ad out there for a significant other, with a view to having babies in the future?' He turned the question back on her when she'd been trying to work out what was going on in his head. Daisy hadn't been prepared to share the contents of hers.

'I'm not really in a position to think about that, but you've got this big house, the medical practice and the whole village. Wouldn't you like to share that with someone? To have an heir to carry on the family's good work?' She wasn't volunteering for the position, but she was certain his father wouldn't have been happy that Thomas was using his death as an excuse to stop him getting close to anyone else.

Although the picture of the perfect family was fresh in her memory, it seemed little more than a fantasy to someone who was currently homeless and intentionally single. She had never considered things like marriage and motherhood a possibility when she had shut herself off from the rest of the world as an act of self-preservation. It wasn't as though she had parents who had shown her either were a good idea. Now she couldn't help but wonder what it would be like to have those things with someone like Thomas, who had a loving father to emulate. Who had shown her what it was to have support and work together as a team. Things she was sure were essential in a marriage. If it was ever a notion she would have been willing to give up her independence for, Thomas would have made the ideal husband and father.

He shrugged. 'Of course I would like it. In an ideal world I'm sure you would want that too. I'm simply saying I can't see it happening now. I'm too busy with work and keeping the village on its feet. The clear-up after the flood is going to take some work. I've more than enough to keep me from being lonely, don't worry. Anyway, I wouldn't inflict the upkeep of this place on you or anyone else. When I'm gone, there will be a board appointed to make all the decisions about the house and the village.'

So he had at least thought about it. More than she had, if she was honest. It had been easier to block out things like marriage and babies rather than face up to the fact that those things might not be compatible with her solitary lifestyle. She didn't want to compromise who she was for anyone after fighting so hard to establish a life where she wasn't indebted to anyone. Her Cinderella role wasn't one she intended to return to, ever. Regardless of Prince Charming living all alone in his castle.

It would take more than a glass slipper and the promise of a happy ever after to convince Daisy that fairy tales could come true.

# CHAPTER SEVEN

THOMAS WOKE ALONE in bed some hours later, after Daisy had convinced him to get some sleep while she oversaw breakfast for the masses. He would have protested except for the weariness which had overtaken his body and the prospect of the busy day ahead. The needs of the village and its residents would require all the strength he could muster in the aftermath of the flood.

There was a soft knock on the bedroom door. 'Thomas? Are you awake?' It was Daisy calling him softly.

'Yes. Come on in.' He sat up in bed and raked his hand through his hair in an attempt to make himself more presentable.

Daisy emerged, carrying a tray of tea things and what smelled like a cooked breakfast. His stomach rumbled and he realised it had been an age since he'd eaten anything. Even if he had drunk his weight in tea over the past twenty-four hours.

'I brought you some breakfast. Everyone else has been fed and is heading back into the village to see what can be done.'

'You didn't have to do that. Although I am starving.'

He took the tray with gratitude and set to work filling his belly with bacon and eggs.

As he tucked in, he was aware of Daisy's lingering glance at his bare chest, which only increased his hunger for more than breakfast. It wasn't easy putting last night behind him when she kept staring at him as though she was ready to jump into bed beside him again.

'Was there enough food for everyone? Did you manage to get anything to eat yourself?' he asked, attempting to distract them both from the half-empty bed where she had lain only hours earlier.

'I did. Queenie brought some more supplies from the corner shop and helped me cook for everyone.'

'That's very kind of her. I'll pay for it all, of course, and thank you, Daisy, for covering for me. I should get up and do my own inspection of the village.' He took another bite of toast and gulp of tea before throwing the covers back.

Daisy's eyes flitted everywhere, as though she didn't know where to look. He wasn't naked, but he might as well have been by the way she was reacting. It amused him that she was acting so coyly when she had been anything but shy in bed with him before he'd had an attack of conscience and called a halt to their fun. He got out of bed and stretched, enjoying the lustful look it drew from his audience.

Yes, he had been the one to put an end to things last night before they went too far, but that didn't mean his ego didn't enjoy a little boost every now and then.

'I…er… I'll let you get dressed, then I'll go with you to see what's needed in the village.' She scurried

back out of the door, pretending she hadn't done more
than just look last night. He could still feel where she
had touched him, the memory growing stronger by the
second.

Even without laying a finger on one another they
were still able to drive each other crazy. However, he
wasn't helping himself get over his wayward fantasies about Daisy. It seemed, no matter his good inten-
tions or his determination to remain unaffected by her,
his thoughts, feelings and very actions were driven by
Daisy. He was a lost cause but simply too afraid of getting hurt to admit it.

No one would ever have guessed Thomas had been up
at dawn that morning delivering a baby by the way he
had taken charge of the clean-up operation. He had contacted the insurers to have the damage assessed, then
set to work repairing it.

'I have a professional crew coming to help clear the
debris, along with those the council has appointed, and
I've hired skips to dump whatever rubbish has been
accumulated in the street. Hopefully, with everyone
working together, we can get the job done twice as fast.'

Along with the people he had hired, Thomas had
done his own share of the heavy lifting of broken tree
branches and dislodged street furniture. While the rain
had stopped long ago and the streets had been dried
out by the sun, the devastation left behind was clear
for all to see. Everything was covered in a layer of silt
and mud. There were cars stranded down by the harbour and though they luckily hadn't been completely
submerged it was doubtful they would ever start again.

Daisy had joined the householders doing their best to clear the dirty water from their houses using brooms to push it out as best they could. They were all wearing protective clothing, as advised by the authorities, to prevent any further contamination or infection.

'We should get down to the medical centre and see what the damage is there too.' She caught Thomas as he passed down the street, directing the volunteers who had arrived from the nearby area to help.

'Yes, I suppose so. Are you free to come down and do an inventory with me?'

'Sure.' She handed her broom over to one of the volunteers and steeled herself for whatever they were about to face behind the clinic door.

'You can't put off going home again for ever either,' Thomas reminded her as they dodged the waves of water being cleared out from the doorways.

'Next stop. I promise.' So far she had managed to keep some emotional detachment from everything going on, but she was worried seeing the cottage again would prove too much. In her exhaustion the sight of her new life in ruins might just break the dam.

Thomas was used to seeing the strong Daisy. She didn't want him to witness the fragile version she kept hidden in case anyone tried to take advantage of her again.

'Okay…here goes.' Thomas rolled up the battered shutters and unlocked the door.

Daisy held her breath, waiting for the heartbreak. Once the water had rushed out over their feet and down the hill, she was able to breathe again.

Of course the carpeting was ruined, the walls damp

and dirty, but it seemed to be mostly superficial damage so far. They made their way further inside to find the waiting room chairs blocking their way.

'They'll have to be replaced, but that should be easy enough. Once everything is dried out, we'll check the floor is intact, then get the carpet-fitters and decorators in.' He was being practical and logical and it made dealing with the mess that bit easier.

'At least we managed to save the important stuff but it's going to be a while before we can open up again.' It was disheartening to think she had lost her new job as well as her new home, just when she was beginning to feel like one of the locals.

'I'm sure we could set up a temporary clinic up at my house. If it comes to it, you can stay too until your place is ready to move back into.'

'That's a very generous offer—' It showed how far he had come already from the man who hadn't wanted her setting foot in his village only weeks ago. Not to mention inviting patients into his home, which had been his sole sanctuary until last night.

He held up a hand to stop her offering any more thanks. 'Purely selfish on my part. It means you'll be on site whenever you're needed. I would rather you were there than holed up in some hotel miles away from the clinic. It makes sense.'

It did, practically speaking, but, as they'd discovered, they couldn't always rely on common sense to keep them out of trouble. They'd come close to doing something they would have come to regret and if they were working and living together under the same roof there would be no escape from the sexual tension which had a tendency to flare between them.

Once they had cleaned the surgery as much as was possible, they returned to Daisy's cottage to see what could be done there. As they worked to clear out the water and any furniture that was beyond salvaging, Daisy felt the tears she'd managed to hold back the first time stinging her eyes again.

The lack of sleep, manual labour and trauma from the last couple of days finally caught up with her and Daisy burst into loud, messy tears.

'Oh, Daisy, come here.' Thomas clutched her to his chest and she let herself be comforted. She was allowed to be upset and Thomas had already proved he wasn't someone to take advantage of her weakness. Otherwise the two of them would never have left his bed.

The tears stopped long before the embrace ended. She was drawing so much warmth from him she didn't want to let go. It had been a lifetime since she'd been held like this, with someone lovingly stroking her hair and telling her things would be all right. If ever. She had forgotten how it felt to let go of the stress and share her troubles without fear of reprisals. If this had been her ex, he would have used the moment to tell her she was better off with him, that she couldn't cope on her own, reinforcing the idea that she wouldn't be able to manage without someone else's help, leaving her indebted for ever.

Thankfully, those days were behind her and Thomas was nothing like her controlling, manipulative ex. Just as she was no longer the clingy girl with low self-esteem.

Daisy took a step back and wiped her eyes. 'Okay,

hysterics over. We've done all we can here. If you don't mind, I'd like to get back to take a shower at your place.' Until she had an expert out to check the electrics, she wasn't sure how safe it was to use her own.

'You'll need to pack some things too.'

'The water doesn't seem to have reached far up the stairs. There's probably no need for me to inconvenience you long-term, Thomas.'

'Don't be silly, Daisy. You can't live upstairs indefinitely, and you could never be an inconvenience. That house of mine is so big I'll hardly notice you're there.' He was doing his best to make this less traumatic for her and she wished it were true.

However, she knew they could be living at opposite sides of his house and her thoughts would still be of him. They managed to disrupt each other's lives without even trying.

'I doubt that… I'll eat all of your food, use all your hot water…'

'And I'll be grateful to have someone share it again. Now, do you want me to come upstairs with you?'

Daisy raised her eyebrows.

'I mean to check things over.' He narrowed his eyes at her, although there was a smile playing on his lips.

She wondered what he would do if she said yes, she wanted him to come upstairs and check her out…

Although he had made it clear he was able to resist everything she had to offer.

'No need. I'm sure it's all fine. I won't be too long. I'd tell you to sit down and make yourself at home but—' She looked around her sodden living room, bare except for the paintings hung high enough on the walls to have avoided the flooding, and another wave of melancholy crashed over her. It seemed she was more invested in this life she had begun in Little Morton than she had anticipated.

Thomas saw the flicker of despair cross her face as she surveyed what was left of her home. While part of him was glad she had become emotionally attached to the place already, he hated to see her upset. After all she had done to help him and everyone else in the village, she deserved a little kindness and happiness herself.

It was said that money couldn't buy happiness, but it could cheer people's spirits when it was used in the right way. He pulled out his phone, aware that cash could also bypass waiting times for deliveries. In fact, on this occasion, he was going to take advantage of his wealth and status for once to get what he wanted. It was for a good cause, and if it made Daisy smile again it would be worth every penny and favour he called in.

Daisy was relieved to have left the cottage, and the dank smell permeating the air within, to go back to Thomas's house, which seemed more welcoming in the daylight. It was set back off a winding driveway, surrounded by flat green lawns and a protective barrier of leafy spruces. Plenty of space and privacy for a young Thomas to play outdoors and have all the adventures and fun she'd never got to experience, trapped in a childhood of servitude and fear. Despite their different upbringings, she was happy he'd had all of this space to explore as a child and hoped his early years had been relatively normal and happy. She wanted him to have had some joy in life, when the last few years appeared to have ground him down.

'I have a few things to sort out. You know where the bathroom is, and the water is back on so just help yourself to anything you need.'

'Thanks.' Daisy was almost relieved to have some space to herself for a while. Dealing with the carnage at the cottage had been emotionally exhausting and she was still processing her reaction to it and the way she had let Thomas comfort her. It had been nice to be held and supported when it felt as if her whole life had just floated away downstream. His presence reminded her there was still something left for her here.

She was glad to have some physical distance from the devastation too, so she didn't have to constantly think about it. At least Thomas's house was warm and dry and free from the havoc which was in evidence everywhere in the village. It was a little oasis of calm and she could see the benefits of hiding away up here, avoiding real life down below. Even if it couldn't be healthy to sustain that detachment on a long-term basis.

She let Thomas go off and do whatever good deeds he had planned to avail herself of his amenities upstairs. It should have felt intrusive letting herself back into his bedroom, using his private bathroom instead of the many she was sure were dotted around the building, but it wasn't. He had invited her into his bedroom and she had found herself enjoying sharing his personal space, getting to know the man behind the family loyalties.

She took her time washing off the trauma of the flood under the hot water before wrapping herself from head to toe in fluffy towels. Her skin was flushed from the heat of the shower, along with her fantasies about Thomas inadvertently offering himself to her earlier. Left alone with her thoughts and frustrations which lingered from the night before, she had imagined what it would have been like to have him share the shower with her. It was difficult not to think of him in anything other than a romantic light when he had been a hero to the whole village and to her personally.

Not only was he assisting her in the clear-up at her home, he had offered her a place in his house for as long as she needed it. A privilege when she knew how greatly he valued his privacy. It was also further proof that he no longer saw her as an outsider. He trusted her not to betray him and she felt embarrassment that she had been sexually objectifying him in response.

It took her some time to unpack her essentials and to pick out a suitable outfit. Although she wanted something practical for whatever physical work was required, Daisy still wanted to look good. After the day she had had it was important to her self-esteem, though she did forgo blow-drying her hair and applying her make-up, which she deemed too frivolous for the current collective mood in the village. She opted for a stylish all-in-one, olive-green boiler-suit, belted at the waist, which still hinted at her curves despite its function as a cover-all.

When she moved to brush her hair at the dressing table, a card propped up against the mirror caught her eye and she smiled, seeing Thomas's familiar doctor scrawl on the gold-edged invitation.

*The Earl of Morton requests the pleasure of your company in the garden summerhouse.*

*TR*

'What are you up to now?' she wondered aloud as she headed downstairs, her curiosity piqued.

Unfortunately, he hadn't left her a map to find her way to the 'summerhouse', which could be anything from an old garden shed to a full botanical garden conservatory.

Everything in this house was a constant surprise to her. From the outside it looked more like a boarding school than a family home. The nondescript grey exterior, complete with standard sash windows, gave nothing away. Stark, stern and functional was how the house presented. Yet inside was a frenzy of colours and clashing patterns. The rooms were smaller than she'd imagined but crammed full of contrasting furnishings and décor. The busy visual of intricately painted ceilings and adorned walls was enough to give her a headache and it seemed as though the layers of Thomas's ancestors had more of a claim on his home than he did.

She navigated her way along the hallway, past the marble busts on plinths and unnecessary velvet drapes on the walls and down the grand staircase. If Thomas was to make his mark on the place, the way she was trying to do in the cottage, she imagined the house would be much more streamlined and bright. He didn't strike her as the sort who liked to show off; he was humble and, despite her previous fears, never lorded his status over anyone.

She kept walking towards the back of the house, through the kitchen where she and Thomas had kept Little Morton's inhabitants fed and watered during the great flood, and let herself out of the French windows onto the patio. Although the paved area and white wrought iron furniture were pristine clean, Daisy couldn't picture Thomas taking the time to sit out here to simply relax or entertain. The magnificent green lawn was interspersed with pink and purple bursts of rhododendrons and camellias and a three-tiered fountain made a beautiful centrepiece. Everything was immaculate and obviously cared for, yet Daisy felt as though she had stepped into a secret garden no one else knew about. It was a shame Thomas kept it all to himself.

She thought about the glamorous garden parties which must have been held here in the past when his ancestors entertained, imagined the sights and sounds of the lawn filled with people and wondered if they would ever happen again. It would be easy to picture herself sitting in the gorgeously ornate swing seat among the blossoms, relaxing and sipping a cocktail. All the things Thomas should be doing instead of treating this place as a museum. She hoped whatever he was up to today was the beginning of him opening up his home as well as his heart to other people.

Since Thomas hadn't given any directions, she followed the stony path winding away from the house, down into the bushy conifer trees at the bottom of the garden. The deeper into the trees she went, the more she felt as though she was walking into a dream.

The sunlight was streaming through the branches, lighting every step leading into a clearing where a small domed building made up of tiny panes of glass sat waiting for her to discover.

'Thomas?' she called out into the ether.

When she got closer she couldn't believe her eyes. The doors to the summerhouse were open and Thomas was sitting at a table beckoning her over. She realised the colourful haze wasn't coming from her rose-tinted glasses but fairy lights hung around the doorframe.

'I thought you needed a treat, as well as something to eat.' He pulled out a chair for her and she drifted to it in a daze.

'How long did I take to get ready?' She couldn't believe he had managed to do all of this in the time it had taken her to shower and get dressed.

'I called in a few favours and waved my credit card around. I had a lot of help putting this together.'

'It's very thoughtful, Thomas, but doesn't it seem in bad taste when the rest of the village is trying to salvage their belongings?' It was such a lovely thing to have done for her, but she was thinking of everyone else out there mopping up.

'All taken care of. I've hired just about every industrial heater there is in the country and brought catering trucks in to feed the residents. If anything, we're the ones missing out.' As he poured her a cup of tea from a china teapot, she knew beyond doubt she was the luckiest person in the village.

'It all looks so inviting.' The porcelain cake stand set in the middle of the table was filled with dainty sandwiches, delicious scones and mini desserts and she couldn't wait to get stuck in.

'I thought we could still have a civilised meal in the

midst of all the chaos. Afternoon tea is just what I'm prescribing.' Thomas took a hearty bite from his cucumber sandwich, almost devouring it in one mouthful. This was a man with a healthy appetite and, given her recent graphic fantasies, Daisy wondered if that extended to the bedroom.

She was sure it did. He was a man who thought of everyone before himself. Who liked to give and was generous to a fault.

That tingling sensation started within her again. The one he had encouraged for a short while last night. It was too bad the next time she slept in his house she was liable to be put in the room furthest from his.

Daisy slathered half of her scone with jam and cream before popping some into her mouth, swapping sugar for sex. As yummy as it was, it was no substitute for the handsome man opposite. His kisses were every bit as delicious and moreish as the home-baked goodies on display.

Daisy wasn't sure she was being as civilised as she ought to be for the occasion.

'So, Thomas Ryan rides to the rescue again. The villagers will soon be naming the streets in your honour.' She teased him because it was safer than waxing lyrical about how amazing he was. Everything he did reminded her of that, and she didn't need to be any more enamoured of him. Things were complicated enough between them.

'I'm simply doing what my father would have done. Besides, most of the streets are named after the family anyway. Maybe we could introduce a national holiday in my honour instead.' Every bit as mischievous as she was being, Thomas toasted her with a mini strawberry tart from the top tier.

'I'll be sure to mention it to the relevant people. I think a Thomas Ryan day where we hide away from the rest of the world and eat cream teas might prove popular, you know.'

He stuck his tongue out and threw a strawberry at her. Daisy caught it between her teeth and ate it noisily to rile him.

'We used to do this at home. I remember my mum pouring tea into her best china and cutting into petits fours with a tiny dessert fork.' The wistful look on his face told Daisy it was a special memory and one he was sharing with her today, attaching the same significance to this occasion with her.

'You must miss her. I haven't seen my mum since I was a kid. It was hard carrying on without her. Especially when I never knew my dad. I used to have this dream she'd appear at the school gates some day, scoop me up and take me home with her. I think it was more about getting away from my stepfamily than believing she might miss me or want me back. I don't really remember much about her, to be honest.' The thought of her stepfather or stepbrothers showing up in her life again brought an altogether different reaction to the fore. Anger. Fear. She didn't know whether she would want to slap them for the way they had treated that little girl, lost and alone in the world, or be afraid she would regress to that scared, helpless soul. Either way, she would prefer not to see any of them again.

'Don't get me wrong, I'm not sure I'm in any rush to see my mother again either. I try not to think about her at all because it's so painful to consider how she betrayed my father and walked away from her own son. As you know, it's not something you get over easily. It's just a nice memory I have of all of us together at the dining table as a family.'

Although Thomas had obviously suffered as much as she had emotionally, he painted a vastly different picture from the upbringing Daisy had, where family meals were taken on a tray in front of the television. She'd been the exception, often made to eat in a different room away from the family and, though she'd cooked it, didn't always get the same meals. More often than not, she'd been left to eat the scraps. It was no wonder she couldn't resist a spread like this. She still ate as though she couldn't be sure where her next meal was coming from.

'Hopefully this will be another nice memory to add to that.'

'Every day with you is a treasured moment,' he replied, and Daisy's heart soared a little more.

It should have been one of the worst times of her life and yet Thomas had made it something special. For someone who didn't think it was a good idea for them to get too close to one another, he was going out of his way to spend time with her.

She wasn't the only person in Little Morton he had supplied lunch for or given help to, but she was the only one receiving his individual attention. Despite his protestations, she knew he liked her and as more than a colleague or neighbour she was certain.

She liked Thomas too. For his kindness, his thoughtful ways and for how he had opened up to her. Not every man would be willing to show that vulnerability or be that honest. Indeed, she knew he valued his privacy above most things and sharing that personal information about his mother was a precious gift to Daisy. One she didn't want to let go unnoticed.

'Thank you again, Thomas, for doing this. It was amazingly thoughtful.' She reached across the table and covered his hand with hers.

Thomas looked down at their hands, then back up to her face, his eyes darkening to glittering sapphires as he looked at her. It was clear he had felt that same jolt of electricity she had from that simple touch. They had been through so much together, shared more experiences over the past days than some people shared in a lifetime, and it was unsurprising that they had become closer. Still, the sheer impact of feeling his skin against hers said there was more between them than a working relationship. Something which both scared and exhilarated her at the same time and refused to go away.

Daisy could tell Thomas felt it too by the way he pulled his hand away as though he had been burned. 'It was nothing. I simply wanted to make you smile again.'

He stood up and began to clear away the dirty dishes. Daisy knew he was fighting temptation as much as she was, but it seemed a pointless exercise when they clearly had feelings for one another that went beyond those of mere work colleagues.

She watched him walk back towards the house, drinking in the fine sight of him. The long legs, straight back and cute backside did nearly as much for her as his handsome face and chiselled torso. She'd had a good view when they'd been in bed together and could remember every sexy inch of him.

Her skin was suddenly prickling with a heat only Thomas could bring out on her. She no longer seemed to have control over her own body or emotions when she was around him. An exhilarating but terrifying discovery.

It was a long time since she had taken a risk on anyone and it called for courage and conviction. Perhaps it might be enough to convince Thomas to do the same.

She collected the rest of the dishes and followed him back up the path and into the kitchen.

'Hey, this is your day off,' he said, with his hands already submerged in soapy water doing the washing-up.

'I don't think I thanked you properly for today.' Daisy wondered if it was the husky tone of her voice which made him abandon his chore to give her his attention.

As he stood there, bubbles clinging to his fingers, she had never been more attracted to anyone in her life. She took one small step towards him, knowing it was a giant leap forward in their relationship. If he rejected her she was in danger of losing everything she had here, but she also knew the time had come to stop denying this attraction and let things play out. Otherwise she could be missing out on the best thing which had ever happened to her simply because of those who had hurt her in the past. Neither her stepfamily or her exes could ever hope to hold a candle to the kind of man Thomas Ryan was. He was a risk worth taking.

Without a word, she reached up, took his face in her hands and kissed him full on the mouth. For a horrifying moment she thought she had got it completely wrong when he didn't respond, his arms still hanging limply by his sides as she clung to him.

Then Thomas was kissing her back, clutching her to him, his wet hands soaking through her clothes, and she didn't care. All that mattered was that they were finally putting their past heartbreak behind them to live in the moment.

A moment which was getting hotter by the second, burning so fiercely Daisy knew there was no way to stop it now. She could only hope when the fire died down she was not left to sift through the ashes for the remnants of the woman she had once been.

Misplaced or not, her faith and her trust were wrapped up in the kiss. Her gift to Thomas for trusting her with the deeply personal insight into his life.

This was a new experience for both of them.

# CHAPTER EIGHT

THOMAS HADN'T EXPECTED any of this to happen. His seduction technique didn't usually involve dainty sandwiches and mini éclairs. Something had changed between them and he'd found himself opening up about the pain of his mother leaving, a subject he had avoided even thinking about for decades.

Being with Daisy brought out those memories and emotions because he wanted to be open about who he was with her. Talking to her about the painful things he had experienced in his life helped him work through it, so he no longer attached the same significance to those events. He knew it was because being with Daisy, being his true self with her, was more important than anything else. Although today wasn't supposed to have been about him; he had merely wanted to do something to raise Daisy's spirits. Now he had something else raised in return.

The gentleman in him didn't want to take advantage of her during such a distressing time. Yet the way she was kissing him, her tongue dipping into his mouth to tease and tantalise, wasn't the action of a woman who didn't know her own mind.

A point proved further as she unbuttoned his shirt, pushing it off his shoulders so his body was exposed to her hands and mouth. Thomas inhaled a ragged breath as she kissed her way across his collarbone, circled his nipple with her tongue and tugged on the hardened peak with her teeth.

They had shared a lot over these past days. Danger, trauma, a birth and a bed. It was only natural they should become closer. Especially when the chemistry between them was stronger than ever.

By all accounts, Daisy's past had been as tough as his. Perhaps that was why he longed to make things better for her now. He wanted to see her smile, to help her forget the bad stuff too. Although, right now, when she was doing indescribable things to his body, he simply wanted her.

He wasn't going to ask her again if she was sure this was what she wanted when she was being clear about that. Thomas was the one who had resisted, who had tried to convince them both they could ignore this escalating passion. That exploring it would be worse than letting it pass. He was wrong.

There was nothing in this world which could beat the taste of Daisy on his lips or the feel of her against his skin.

Once Thomas's resolve wavered, all bets were off and so were Daisy's clothes. He had some catching-up to do when she had already tossed his shirt aside and was currently working on his trousers.

'You're beautiful,' he said, genuinely marvelling at the soft white skin of her breasts as he uncovered them, the rosy tips of her nipples he was kneading in his hands. The sight of her alone was enough to make him hard as hell, but having his hands on her made him fit to burst.

'Shut up and kiss me,' she demanded, breathless with impatience.

Thomas didn't have to be asked twice, and Daisy's boldness served to increase his own. His mouth was hard on hers, taking everything she was willing to give. Her arms were wrapped around his neck, pressing her body to his. All soft curves and heat he no longer wanted to resist.

Urgently divesting her of the rest of her clothes, he backed her over to the dining room table. She gasped as he pushed her back onto the hard wooden surface.

'It's cold,' she giggled, sitting up again so her legs were dangling off the edge of the table.

'Sorry.'

'Don't be.' Daisy wound her arms back around his neck and she kissed him so fully, so completely, reminding him it didn't matter where they were. Only that they were together, finally letting themselves revel in this animal passion.

This blinding need to have her was overwhelming, his senses completely overtaken by thoughts of Daisy. He laid her back, kissing her neck, the cleft of her breast, before licking circles around her nipples. When he sucked the pert tips she arched her body off the table.

'Thomas—' The plea to end her frustration as well as his own made him throb until he could hold out no longer.

Although it had been some time since he'd needed one, he kept a condom in his wallet and was glad of it at this moment. In no time at all he had himself sheathed, his wallet and the condom wrapper abandoned on the floor in his haste to get back to Daisy.

Taking his erection in hand, he positioned himself between her soft thighs and thrust inside her. He let out a groan of satisfaction to match hers and knew immediately that their relationship would never be the same again. This was more than sex when he knew he would give up everything he had just to be with her.

Daisy was a trembling mass of emotions. The foremost of which was absolute ecstasy. Thomas must have kissed every inch of her skin as she was burning everywhere he had touched her. Now their attention was focused entirely on one area, Thomas was as thorough as ever in his ministrations. His hands were digging possessively into her hips as he claimed her again and again. Daisy widened her legs to accept him, hooking them around his waist as he thrust into her once more.

She would never have believed he was capable of such wild abandon, but he was thrusting into her relentlessly, giving them both what they needed at this moment. Sending her hurtling towards that final, thought-obliterating destination. That pressure within her was building so quickly it was beyond her control. All she could do was cling on and enjoy the ride. Literally.

She had a fistful of Thomas's hair in her hands as her orgasm slammed into her. Her throaty cry echoed through the house, soon followed by Thomas's equally vocal climax.

He collapsed on top of her, panting as hard as she was, trying to catch his breath.

'I hope no one heard us or saw us,' she said, peering over his shoulder at the open back door. An indication of how reckless they had been and how desperate to have one another at any cost.

'There is no one around to bother us and I don't care anyway,' he said, keeping her pinned down with his arms braced either side of her. Not that she was trying to escape when he was kissing her again, his tongue gently probing her mouth and making her wish they were somewhere more comfortable to cuddle together for a while. Now she was coming back down from the clouds, she remembered they were naked in his kitchen.

'You will when your patients start gossiping about that scandalous Dr Ryan who seduced his co-worker on the dining table.'

'I think you might have that the wrong way around.'

Thomas began to dress, hiding that delicious body of his.

'I suppose it does take two to do what we just did,' she conceded, trailing a fingertip seductively down his chest before he covered it completely. Although she had been thinking about this moment for a long time, if she had thought about it properly she would have picked somewhere warmer, where they would still be lying in one another's arms.

All that had been on her mind was that she wanted him to acknowledge the crazy sexy vibes between them. Job done. Now what?

Thomas rested his hands on her shoulders. 'We've been skating around this for days. It was inevitable.'

'And now?' She looked up at him and swallowed hard, waiting in agony for him to tell her if he still thought this was a mistake. Something which would break her heart when she had risked everything to take a chance on him.

He tucked a strand of her hair behind her ear. 'Now, I think there are a lot more comfortable places than a hard wood table to spend the rest of the day.'

Daisy's heart was beating like a butterfly's wings at all the connotations in that comment. The promise of repeat performances and the prospect of spending the rest of the evening in his bed was all it took for her to abandon her fears about moving in here with him for a while.

This was one time she was willing to give up her independence because it was exactly what she wanted too.

They took some time out to check on the village residents before indulging their erotic fantasies further. Not everyone had been able to salvage their belongings but there seemed little Daisy and Thomas could do for now except patch up those who had sustained minor injuries during the storm.

Selfishly, she couldn't wait to get back to the house to have Thomas to herself. It was admirable that he wished to help everyone as best he could, but they had done their bit and deserved some down time.

'If you need anything at all, call me. We're going to be working out of the house from tomorrow for anyone who needs treatment.' He handed his business card over to one of the locals, making sure everyone knew who to go to for help.

'Are we taking anyone back with us?'

He shook his head. 'A few are going to stay with family and friends, some are booked into hotels and the rest are staying put. It's just us tonight.' He lowered his voice for the last part of his reply, sending shivers of anticipation dancing across the back of Daisy's neck.

'Oh, dear. I hope you're not too upset,' she said, coyly batting her eyelashes at him.

'Not one little bit.' He was looking at her with that fire in his eyes capable of incinerating her on the spot.

'In that case maybe we should—' She tipped her head towards the car.

'Go home? My thoughts exactly.' Thomas made giant strides across to the vehicle, clearly in a hurry.

If it was not for the audience of residents and those Thomas had drafted in to help, Daisy got the impression he would have thrown her over his shoulder and carted her back to his cave.

A completely different person from the superior doctor in the three-piece suit who had looked down his nose at her. Now she knew that was a defence mechanism and self-preservation against people like his ex, she was glad he no longer felt the need to shield from her.

This was the real Thomas Ryan—fun, loyal, passionate and someone she wanted to be around. The sort of bond forming between them was something she had tended to steer clear of, but they were both dealing with similar issues. Venturing into new territory. Though they hadn't discussed where things were going, she was sure they wouldn't want to rush into something serious too soon.

She also thought it wise that they shouldn't engage

in any public displays of affection in case the local gossip put them under pressure.

Once they had driven away from the village she leaned her head on Thomas's shoulder. It was nice. Normal. Anyone could be forgiven for thinking they were a regular couple, minus the emotional baggage wedged into the front seat between them.

'I hope you're not falling asleep on me,' he said, dropping a kiss onto her head.

'No. I'm just enjoying the time out from all the drama.' She could easily fall asleep here when she was so content, not to mention worn out by the events of the past few days. Except she didn't want to miss a second of whatever Thomas had planned for tonight. There was no telling how soon this would end so she wanted to make the most of this can't-get-enough-of-one-another phase.

'Don't worry, you can lie back and let me do all the hard work if you're tired.'

'Why, Dr Ryan, are you trying to seduce me?' Daisy knew the second he touched her, her body would be wide awake and raring to go.

'Trying? Obviously I'm not doing a good enough job of it.' He turned off the engine once they pulled up outside his house, unbuckled his seatbelt and leaned over to undo hers. He was so close she could feel his breath on her cheek. Enough to send arousal rushing through her bloodstream.

Instead of letting the belt retract itself, he slowly drew it up across her chest, deliberately brushing his hand over her breast. Her body ultra-aware of him now, her nipples tightened in response.

'Any better?' he asked, his lips almost touching hers.

'A tad,' she squeaked, waiting with bated breath for him to make a move.

He leaned further across, nuzzling against her neck, and just when she was about to explode with need he reached past her and opened her door.

'Good to see I haven't lost it after all.' The wink he gave her was too much.

'You're in big trouble, mister.' Despite her frustration Daisy was still smiling when she got out of the car. This flirty teasing was exactly what she needed. No stress, no drama, just sexy fun, and this version of Thomas was the man to have it with.

'Good.' Thomas slid his arms around her waist and pulled her roughly to him. Daisy's heart gave that fluttery extra beat it had started doing every time he came near her, the anticipation of his touch sending her pulse and libido into overdrive. Thankfully she didn't have to wait long for her prize.

Thomas bent his head and covered her mouth with his. A leisurely kiss at first, as they took their time exploring one another again, it soon developed into something much more demanding. The lust for one another was too great to be satisfied by one kiss alone. With the knowledge that they had the house to themselves, uninhibited by thoughts of being interrupted, there was no reason to worry about modesty or privacy.

In a frenzy of kissing and undressing, they made their way across the hall. Daisy stumbled back against the stairs, bringing Thomas down with her. Undeterred, he unzipped her trousers and pulled them off, along with everything else until she was lying beneath him in just her bra. Without taking his eyes off her, Thomas stripped off too.

Daisy watched him, her chest rising and falling with every shallow breath she took. This had to be one of the most erotic moments of her life, but it was also one of the most uncomfortable.

'Thomas?'

'Yes?' He was kissing her neck, his body on top of hers, his erection pressing between her thighs. She was wet and ready for him, but not here with the edges of the stairs bruising her back.

'I thought we were going to do this somewhere more comfortable this time?'

Thomas laughed and levered himself up off her. 'You're right. My bad.'

He offered his hand and helped her to her feet. 'Bedroom. Now.'

Giggling, Daisy took off towards his room with him chasing her. They were acting like two hormonal teenagers in the first throes of passion, but that was what was making this so easy for her. She didn't have to think when her body was doing the talking for her. When she and Thomas were having fun she could forget the serious stuff. There was no need to overthink things like what would happen between them at work or the prospect of giving up her independence to start a relationship with another man. For now, this was just sex and that suited her fine.

Thomas caught up with her, grabbing her waist from behind and making her squeal. It was thrilling to be in the house alone, making as much noise as they dared and not caring about anything other than reaching that big comfortable bed. Here they were both free from the shackles of the past and at liberty to revel in their sensuality.

As if to prove the point, Thomas unfastened her bra and let it fall to the floor, taking the weight of her breasts in his hands. He teased the peaks between his fingers and that, combined with his hot breath at her ear and his hardness pressed against her buttocks, meant Daisy was a puddle of arousal. She spun around to kiss him and pulled him down onto the bed.

'I want you, Thomas.' She was begging him to fulfil that aching need for him but, instead of covering her body with his, he lay down beside her.

'Soon,' he said and kissed her on the lips. He grabbed a condom from the bedside table and rolled it down over his erection, Daisy watching his every move with anticipation.

She turned onto her side, pressing herself against him, desperate for that ultimate connection between them. He took her breast in his hand and ran his tongue over the mound, teasing her nipple until it stood proud. The sharp tug of his mouth as he sucked was pleasant torture and she closed her eyes to let the sensation wash over her.

Thomas slipped his hand down between their bodies and dipped his fingers into her very core.

'You're so wet,' he growled, his voice filled with undisguised lust.

Daisy was so wrapped up in what he was doing to her she couldn't find the words to respond. With masterful fingers he massaged and stroked the most sensitive part of her until he had her bucking off the bed with pure want. Her breathing was rapid as the pressure built up inside her. She clutched at his chest, desperate for something to hold on to as she soared away on that feeling of bliss. It pushed him to delve deeper, faster, hastening her climax. It overwhelmed her both physically and mentally that he could do this to her so easily. Commanding her body with so little effort made her fear that she was losing control. The warning flashing in the distance disturbing her euphoria brought her abruptly back to earth. She pushed Thomas's hand away.

'Is something wrong? Did I hurt you?'

'No. I'm simply taking the initiative.' Daisy moved across to straddle his hips, taking charge again.

'Oh, yes? I thought we agreed I was going to do all the hard work tonight?' He was grinning from ear to ear, content about the shift in power. An aphrodisiac in itself if she had needed it.

'I'm all for equal rights,' she said, sliding her body along his length to make them both groan with need.

'Me too,' he gasped, taking a possessive hold of her wrist as she bore down onto his erection. She was temporarily stunned into silence as he filled her but that need to make a snarky comeback was obliterated by the need to have all of Thomas. To render him speechless, his body at her mercy this time.

Daisy rocked her hips back and forth, bracing herself with a hand on his chest. He was watching her intently as she used his body to pleasure herself. All the time she held his gaze, increasing the pace and stoking the fire within.

Thomas shifted into a sitting position, grabbing the back of her head and kissing her, distracting her from other parts of his body using his mouth and tongue. That control was slipping, that focus on keeping this about sex when he was kissing her so tenderly and trying to make her feel something more than physical need.

She pushed him back down, slid up and down his shaft with renewed determination. Thomas cried out and she grinned, knowing she had got the upper hand again. Then he grabbed her hips and thrust upwards, surprising her into a gasp of ecstasy. They moved together now, both striving to find their ultimate satisfaction. Daisy realised it was better when they were in sync, each wanting to please the other, caring about their partner's needs as well as their own. Somewhere deep inside she knew it meant something, but she was too consumed by this race to bring their release to care.

She didn't even mind when Thomas somehow ended up on top again, manoeuvring her legs over his shoulders so he could plunge deeper inside her. Daisy closed her eyes, gave herself over to the things he was making her feel. Stopped fighting it. When her orgasm came, her eyes were wet with tears.

Thomas couldn't hold back any longer when she was calling out his name with her climax, squeezing him tight as she came. Daisy did things to him he couldn't explain—and didn't want to examine too closely. So far they had been keeping things light, not daring to venture beyond the amazing sex and good times together. As though they were afraid that whatever it was when acknowledged would burst the bubble and remind them that they had to deal with the real world.

Yet when they were lying in bed together, trying desperately to catch their breath, bodies glowing from their exertions, he wanted a deeper connection that went beyond the bedroom door or the kitchen table.

He rolled onto his side and watched her smiling through those panting breaths she was trying to regulate. Daisy was beautiful, sexy and fun and everything he had been missing in his life. He didn't know what he was afraid of any more. She wasn't his ex, she wasn't going to betray him when they were working and living together, albeit temporary. Perhaps it was time he stopped punishing himself for things he hadn't done. Started living life to the full instead of hiding away, afraid of getting hurt. He needed to be honest about what he felt for Daisy.

With a sudden rush of blood to his head, he wanted to share this revelation with her. Tell her how much she had done to help him get to this point and how he felt about her. He was falling for her, beginning to think they could have a future together if only they could move past the reservations they both had about committing to anyone again.

'Daisy, I—'

'Shh.' She put her finger on his lips. Whatever he might have been going to say, obviously she wasn't ready to hear it.

# CHAPTER NINE

THOMAS LEFT DAISY sleeping to get a head start on the day. He'd been thinking about the evolution of their relationship, what it meant to him and how they were going to proceed. Following his old pattern, he should draw a line under what had happened between them and halt any progression. He'd been wary of women and relationships in general because of his mother's actions and Jade had only cemented that belief that he couldn't trust anyone, that it would only lead to heartbreak.

Daisy was making him reconsider that belief. At least to the point where he was willing to take a chance that things could be different. He thought they could have a real chance of something special when they had already pushed through some of their fears to be together. She had given him the impetus to want to make changes in his life because he wanted her in it. If only she felt the same.

When she had so many scars from the past yet to heal, Thomas was aware that taking the next step into a proper relationship would be a big deal for her. He wanted her to feel safe, to know that he was willing to

share everything he had and take that risk to his heart
and his home if he could be with her.

Thomas set to work making arrangements so that
Daisy would know he was serious about her. They had
already talked about working out of his house until the
clinic was safe again, so he organised that while she
slept. It was no wonder she was exhausted after everything she had been through these past few days, so
he let her sleep while he set up her office in one of the
front rooms. He cleared away the ugly antiques, garish
statues and drab paintings he'd lived with as a tribute
to his father and put them into storage. In an effort to
make Daisy more at ease so she could treat this as her
own space, he dotted her things around. The houseplant
someone had given her as a gift, the knick-knacks and
stationery he had rescued from her desk and the London
cityscape she'd had hanging on her wall now adorned
the walls of her new office.

It was his way of telling her she was part of his life
and he welcomed that development rather than fearing it.

They still had a long way to go. Thomas couldn't say
what would happen long-term between them. He wasn't
sure if he would ever find the courage to completely
open up his heart and his life to the point of marriage or
children. There was no way of knowing if Daisy would
even want that, but this was a gesture to tell her he was
willing to begin that journey with her. That he trusted
her enough to try.

'What is going on?' Some time later Daisy wan-
dered into the room he had allocated as his office. His

last patient had just left so he was filling in some notes when she walked in.

'Morning. I opened the clinic early for walk-in patients but now you're here we can split the list between us.'

'That explains all the coming and going. I thought I was imagining it.' She yawned and took a sip from the cup of tea sitting on his desk.

'Take it. Eunice keeps making tea for everyone to keep herself busy.' He pushed the cup back towards her, knowing she needed that first cup before she started her day.

Daisy wrapped her hands around the cup and breathed in the steam. 'Eunice is here too?'

'I've set up a waiting area with her desk in it so she can point people in the right direction. It's not an ideal set-up but hopefully it won't be for long.'

'In that case, I suppose I should get started. Where should I go?'

'I've allocated you the other front room for your office. If there are any problems just let me know.'

'I will need to swing by the cottage to get some more of my work clothes and toiletries to see me through.'

'No problem. Although it's going to take a while for the cottage to dry out, never mind the time it will take to get the place redecorated and furnished. You're going to need to bring most of your personal things.'

'It would probably be easier for me to just move in,' she joked, but Thomas didn't think that was a bad idea at all when she was living with him anyway.

'Right, I must go and get ready to face the day. Thanks for the tea.' Daisy raised the cup before she walked away. It wasn't the warm reunion he might have been hoping for, but she was likely trying to process last night's events too.

Thomas would do everything he could to make Daisy comfortable in his home and she had given him the perfect idea. Once she saw the lengths he was willing to go to in order to welcome her into his life, he was convinced any wariness she had around their current situation would soon evaporate. This was going to be the start of something great between them.

There was something about having the contents of her office suddenly appear here which unnerved Daisy. She knew Thomas had only been trying to make her feel comfortable, but she wasn't used to people doing things for her. It automatically put her on edge. Invariably when her ex, or even her stepfather, had done anything remotely nice for her, there was usually a motive behind it. In the case of her stepfamily, they used to humiliate her afterwards.

Like the time when her stepfather had built up her hopes for weeks, telling her he had got her something special for Christmas, something no one else would have. At ten years old she had believed him, and told all her friends about this amazing present she was getting. Only to unwrap a chocolate Easter egg on Christmas morning, her disappointment caught on camera and shared as a source of amusement, making a laughing stock of her.

It was not by any means the cruellest stunt pulled on her but one which had stuck in her mind. Mostly because her stepfather had let her believe that he genuinely cared, that she was special and that life might be getting better for her. Only to receive expired chocolate while her stepbrothers enjoyed the latest games console, which she wasn't allowed to touch.

Then there was her ex. Aaron would buy her gifts to make her feel indebted to him. If she wanted to see her friends or do anything with anyone other than him she was met with sad eyes and, 'No one loves you the way I love you. Who else buys you the things I buy you? No one. You don't need anyone but me.'

Of course there were also the gifts after he had lashed out at her in temper. Flowers and chocolates to make her forget about the cuts and bruises.

Thomas was neither of those men who had emotionally abused her for their own agendas, but it was difficult to change her mindset after all this time of living on her own. In order to protect herself she had learned to be wary. She was still afraid that he might be doing these things for her in a subconscious attempt to control her. He had made it known he had issues with trust, and she could understand to some extent that he had a need to take charge to prevent himself getting hurt. However, she was not prepared to lose herself simply so that he could feel protected.

It was likely that all they needed was a conversation to explain her need for some space without offending him. He had a kind heart. She had seen that for herself. And it wasn't his fault that she felt unable to reap the benefits of that. Nevertheless, that feeling of needing to protect herself was valid and there for a reason—so she didn't end up in the same predicament she had been in with her first serious relationship. If she and Thomas decided this was going to become more than sleeping together he would have to understand her need to take things slowly.

Although they had made love again last night Daisy had slept in the spare room, telling him she needed a full night's sleep and wouldn't get that if they were in the same bed. It was partly true. She had also needed a bit of space to herself. The early days of a new relationship were a challenge for her, and she didn't want to seem ungrateful when Thomas was simply trying to help her adapt to the new surroundings. Even if she found it a tad overwhelming so soon.

It was plausible that the nerves she had about getting into a relationship had caused her to catastrophize when he had only hoped to put her at ease. That she was projecting her issues from the past when he had made a loving gesture to show her he was ready to share his living space.

At least Daisy had her patients to fill her day and the sense of uneasiness she initially experienced seeing her new temporary office gradually subsided.

'I will chase up that consultant appointment for you at the hospital, Mrs Cooper, and in the meantime I'll continue to see you every couple of weeks.' Daisy stood up to see her patient out and wished as she always did in these cases that waiting lists for hospital treatment were not so long.

The elderly woman took some time to get across the floor on her walking stick. Daisy had done everything she could to relieve the pain in her knees, but she really needed surgery to make any long-term difference.

'Thank you, Dr Swift. I'm so glad you and Dr Ryan are still able to see patients.'

'So am I,' Daisy said, and she meant it. She needed some sense of normality, to be in her comfort zone, when things around her seemed to be out of her control.

Her libido in particular, whenever she happened to see Thomas. He was at the door of his office saying goodbye to his patient too. She took her chance to satisfy her thirst for him.

'Dr Ryan, could I see you in your office for a moment, please?'

'Sure—'

She barely gave Thomas the time to answer before she pushed him back through the door, kicking it shut behind her. It didn't take him long to get with the programme, taking her face in his hands and kissing her passionately on the lips. Daisy nearly slid down onto the floor in a puddle of arousal and would have let him take her there and then if Eunice hadn't buzzed through on the intercom.

'Dr Ryan, your next patient is here to see you.'

Thomas slowly peeled away from her, a smile on his lips now instead of her. 'No rest for the wicked.'

'I guess not,' she said, wiping the smudges of lipstick she was sure were round her mouth, giving away exactly what they had been up to.

'Can we pick this up later, after work?'

'Of course, Dr Ryan. I am here at your disposal,' she said with a coy wink, putting any doubts about what was going on between them behind her for now to enjoy the flirtation.

It wasn't Thomas's fault she had been displaced from

her house. He hadn't arranged a devastating flood just so he could get her under his roof. No, he had offered her a place to stay, regardless that up until the night of the storm he had been reluctant to let anyone cross his threshold. He had done his best to make her feel comfortable. She should be grateful to Thomas for his kindness. Everyone else in the village was certainly enamoured with him. Any time she saw him with one of the residents, they were enthusiastically shaking his hand or slapping him on the back, thanking him for all of his help. Now that she and Thomas had taken the next step in their relationship, it would be a shame for her paranoia to creep in and ruin everything.

Daisy made the decision there and then to simply enjoy being with Thomas and not to let the past steal away her future.

It was crazy to think of his family home being used as a makeshift surgery, but there was also something incredibly natural about winding down with Daisy after work. With the staff and patients gone, this was their time and Thomas had been looking forward to it all day. Along with more of those delicious kisses they stole any time they had a break in their schedule.

'Dinner?' he asked as she kicked off her heels at the front door once they had waved Eunice off for the night.

'Yes, please, but can we have something here? I don't really feel like going out.' She wrapped her arms around him and planted a leisurely kiss on his mouth.

It was nice not to be facing a night alone with nothing but the TV and paperwork to keep him company.

'No problem. I'm sure I can fix us something to eat. I'll see what we've got in the fridge.'

'You cook?' Daisy's incredulity was evident as she followed him through to the kitchen.

He laughed as he set to work making dinner for two, a novelty for him since losing his father. 'I'm a grown man. Yes, I can cook.'

'I just assumed you would order in or, you know, have your own private chef on call twenty-four hours a day.'

Thomas rolled his eyes as he passed the contents of his fridge to Daisy to set on the kitchen worktop.

'I like to cook. I haven't done much of it since Dad died. This makes a nice change.' He held up a bottle of white wine and Daisy nodded her approval.

'For me too. I can't remember the last time anyone cooked for me.' Daisy was about to make herself comfortable when Thomas poured two glasses of wine and put some mood music on in the background. He wanted her to feel more at home than simply a dinner guest.

'Who said I was doing all of the cooking? You can be my sous chef.' He pushed a chopping board and knife towards her, along with some garlic and vegetables.

Daisy let out an exaggerated sigh before setting to work chopping the ingredients.

'I hope a stir-fry is okay for you?' Thomas diced some chicken and added it to the hot pan on the stove. Once it was seared, he added the vegetables, some soy sauce and chilli and tossed in some noodles.

'Definitely. I'm starving.'

Thomas dished up the meal while Daisy carried their glasses of wine to the table. It was nice, normal, to be making dinner as a couple, looking forward to spending the rest of the night chilling out together. A routine he could get used to quite easily.

'Here's to us,' he said, raising his glass to hers. 'We make a good team.'

Daisy was smiling as she joined the toast. 'And a good stir-fry, apparently.'

They ate in companionable silence, content to fill their bellies and simply enjoy winding down from their working day. Thomas went to top up the wine glasses, but Daisy covered hers with a hand.

'I've had enough. If you don't mind I'd like to go to bed.' She got up from her chair and left her dishes in the sink.

'No problem.' He knew all the upheaval had probably exhausted her and it would be selfish of him to ask her to stay with him merely because he wanted more of her company.

She moved to the kitchen door and glanced back, her hand outstretched towards him. 'Aren't you coming?'

Thomas almost kicked over the table in his haste to join her. When Daisy was taking him to bed he knew it would involve more than sleep. That was something she apparently preferred to do on her own, and though he would prefer to wake up next to her in the mornings he was prepared to wait until she was ready to share his bed all night. Whatever it took for her to be comfortable and remain in his life. Daisy was one habit he didn't want to break.

# CHAPTER TEN

'Wakey-wakey.'

Daisy was shaken from her slumber by the sound of Thomas's voice and a hand on her arm.

'What time is it?' she mumbled into her pillow, her eyes and body refusing to wake.

'Early.'

'I thought so,' she said and rolled over to get comfortable again.

The rustle of the sheets and a sudden blast of cold air on her skin told her he wasn't taking no for an answer as he pulled away her covers. She groaned. She was not a morning person.

'Come on. I have something planned for us.' He sounded like an excited little kid, which at any other time of the day she would think was adorable.

'What?' She still refused to move her face out of her pillow to look at him. It would have to be something pretty special to make her want to leave this bed if she didn't have to.

'Look,' he coaxed.

When she didn't move he kissed her cheek. That wasn't playing fair when he knew she couldn't resist his touch. Daisy brushed her hair from her eyes and squinted over at him. 'What is it?'

He was holding up something black and wearing what seemed like a skin-tight all-in-one. She blinked furiously, trying to focus so she could see what on earth he was trying to get her to do.

'It's a wetsuit. I've already got mine on.'

'Ugh.' She collapsed back into her feather haven when he failed to convince her there was somewhere better to be than here. It definitely was not in freezing-cold water making a fool of herself doing whatever it was Thomas had in mind.

'You helped me face my fears by inviting people into my home, now I want to help you tackle one of yours. Put this on and meet me down by the harbour.' The wetsuit landed on top of her and Thomas left the room, apparently confident that she would acquiesce to his demands and go to him rather than leave him standing there waiting. He was right.

She knew he was only trying to do something nice for her and since he had set aside his fears when she'd asked him it was time she did the same. She was afraid of the water because she couldn't swim but she was certain Thomas wasn't about to let her drown. It would take a lot of trust on her part, but that was an important element in a relationship. If they were ever going to make it she had to learn to have faith in him. After all, he had proved his worth these past weeks, to her and the rest of the community.

With a lot of puffing, panting and swearing, Daisy wriggled her way into the tight costume, knowing her reward would be seeing Thomas in his. She hadn't taken the chance to ogle him properly, but that would soon be rectified now she was awake and missing his presence in the bedroom. If she did this for him, showed willing, maybe she could persuade him to come back for an afternoon nap…

If she'd gone with Thomas when he'd asked, there would have been no need for her to take her car down to the harbour too. It seemed scandalous to be driving to the village wearing so little, yet it was acceptable dress around here with the locals and their love of water sports. Still, she opened the barrier and drove down to the harbour rather than parade through the streets in her figure-hugging outfit which left nothing to the imagination.

The village was slowly getting back to normal, though most days the air was filled with dust and noise as builders and carpenters set to work repairing that which had been lost or ruined in the flood. Given the early hour of the morning, though, everything was quiet now. Everyone but her apparently had the luxury of sleeping in on a Saturday morning. She couldn't complain, not really. These past couple of weeks with Thomas hadn't been a hardship. They worked together, relaxed over a bottle of wine as they made dinner at night and made love before they went their separate ways to sleep. It was a life she could easily get used to.

This morning was out of the norm from their usual routine but at least she had the sight of Thomas, barechested, his wetsuit hanging open to his waist, all to herself. He was walking across the small strip of the sandy shore at the harbour's edge with two large boards under his arms. Daisy groaned as she parked the car and got out to join him, knowing this was the last time she was going to be safe on dry land for a while. What was it about this man and water?

'Morning,' she said, enjoying the view of her gorgeous man coming towards her, so happy to see her he had broken into a run.

'Morning.' He grabbed her around the waist and swung her around and kissed her on her lips.

'That's some welcome.' She was breathless and giddy and unsure why she had wanted any time apart from him when she felt so good in his arms.

'You're in better form too, I see. I didn't realise you were so grumpy in the morning.' His teasing earned him a playful slap on the arm.

'Only when people wake me up at a ridiculous hour with the sole intention of trying to drown me.' She glanced at the boards. Surfing? Surely he was not expecting her to be comfortable with that? Trepidation crept in and she suddenly wondered why she thought keeping Thomas satisfied was better than keeping herself safe. Surely that was the old way of thinking which had got her into trouble before?

Before she could worry herself into a state, Thomas started to laugh.

'I assure you what I have planned is nothing as dangerous or dramatic as that. I thought it would be good for us to get out and do something that didn't revolve around work. Have fun. Remember that?' That twinkle in his eye was just as alluring as the unzipped wetsuit just waiting to be stripped all the way off his body.

'What have you got planned?' She sighed, resolved to do whatever it was he was so keen for her to take part in.

'Paddleboarding.'

'Paddleboarding?' she repeated. 'What if something takes a huge chunk out of me or I fall off and drown?'

'We'll be doing it in the harbour, where nothing is going to bite you and you will be wearing one of these.' He let go of her and reached for one of the lifejackets laid out on the sand.

'In the harbour where there are millions of pounds' worth of yachts I can crash into,' she huffed as she donned the bulky buoyancy aid.

Thomas zipped up his wetsuit and put his on too. 'You are not going to crash into anything, drown or get eaten by a shark. The point is to have fun and learn something new. Now, no more excuses. Get on your board.'

Daisy eyed him with suspicion. 'Here? How exactly are we going to paddle on the sand?'

He resisted rising to her sarcasm and passed her a paddle. 'I'm giving you your first lesson before we get in the water. Trust me, you'll thank me for it.'

Daisy doubted it. Nothing about this was her idea of fun, except for the fantasy of peeling that rubber suit off him later. Only then might she be grateful to him for suggesting they do this.

'I'm on the board, I've got my paddle—now what?'

'Get on your knees.'

'Ooh, Dr Ryan, you're so masterful.' If he wanted her to have fun he had to expect some teasing on her part too. Especially when they could be enjoying each other's company back in the comfort of a bed.

'You need to start off on your knees so you can get your balance right.' He demonstrated the move without acknowledging her childish innuendo. In the end she gave up fighting his attempt to teach her how to paddleboard and literally got on board.

'Okay, so I'm on my knees. Now what?'

'That lowers your centre of gravity so you can stabilise yourself. Once you're comfortable enough to take the next step, place your oar across the board, move up onto one foot and then the other so you're in a squatting position.'

'I think I can manage that.' She watched Thomas do it first and though the moves were easy enough to emulate now she knew it would be a different story when she was out there on the water.

'If you keep looking out across the water instead of looking at your feet it will help you centre your balance as you stand up.'

'What happens if I overbalance and fall off?'

'You get back on. Your board will be tethered to your ankle so it won't float away from you.' Thomas went on to show her the basic strokes she would need to get her board moving and how to use the paddle to turn her around.

'Is that the first lesson over? Can we go home now?' she asked, dreading what was coming next and praying he would show some mercy. No chance.

'This is just the start. All the fun is still to come.' He was grinning as he picked up his board and walked towards the water, beckoning her to come with him.

'I wouldn't do this for anyone else, you know,' she grumbled, joining him in the shallows.

'And I appreciate it. I might just forget about the dunk tank incident after this.' He reminded her he had done a lot to keep her happy over these last weeks and now it was her turn she didn't want to disappoint.

'Okay, now, how do I get on without toppling the whole thing over?' Daisy was looking at it like a hammock scenario where the wrong distribution of weight could see her capsized and flailing about like a helpless turtle on its back.

'Get on it here where it's not too deep and paddle your way out. Don't worry, I'll be beside you all the way.' True to his word, Thomas waded out with her as she managed to get onto her board and on her knees and made her way further out into the harbour.

This was all new for her. It was terrifying and exhilarating that she was facing one of her fears without over-analysing the possible outcome. A process she should apply to her other issues if she ever hoped to move on. She had taken that first step by accepting Thomas was here to stay in her life but making that next risky move would take all of her courage. It was the fear of being left floundering on her own which prevented her from trying.

Thomas jumped athletically onto his board and paddled out alongside her. 'See? Easy-peasy. Now, when you're ready, try and get up onto your feet.'

She wondered why she couldn't just coast along like this, where she was comfortable, but Thomas would only tell her she was missing out on so much more. A metaphor for her entire life. It gave her the impetus to strike out and take a risk for once in her life and damn the consequences. What was life if she didn't experience new adventures once in a while?

Very slowly, she unfurled one leg from beneath her.

It had started to go to sleep so it was better she did it now before her entire lower half was numb and she toppled into the harbour like a drunken sailor on shore leave.

'That's it. Keep looking ahead and get that other foot up there too.' Thomas called his encouragement to her, but she was too busy trying not to look at her feet to spare him a glance or nod.

The second foot was much trickier.

'Woah!' The board was wobbling about under her as she attempted to master that sit-down crouch which was so much easier on dry land. Everything went into slow motion as she tried to stop the inevitable. Try as she might, she couldn't get her balance and she felt herself falling into the abyss.

The water went in her mouth and up her nose, leaving her gasping for breath. She was splashing around in distress even though common sense told her she was wearing a life jacket and close to shore.

'You're okay. I've got you.' Thomas's calm voice broke through her panic as he jumped into the water beside her.

'I told you, I can't do this,' she blubbed, hoping no one else was watching her epic fail. It was bad enough Thomas had witnessed it and she probably looked like something that had been washed ashore in a storm with her wet hair and mascara-stained face.

'Yes, you can. It wasn't long ago you were underwater helping to rescue old Jimmy. I'm sure you're not going to let a paddleboard beat you.' Thomas appealed to that stubborn streak inside her and he was right. She had held it together through all their trials during the storm, at least until she had seen her own place, so a stupid lump of fibreglass wasn't going to defeat her. It wasn't the end of the world because she had fallen into the water; she was still alive and still spending the morning with this lovely man.

'Well, give us a hand up then,' she said, wiping the water from her eyes and grabbing her paddle before it drifted too far away from her.

'Yes, ma'am.' Thomas obliged with a helping hand on her posterior as she clambered back onto her board in a more ungainly fashion than she had first time around.

'Okay, let's do this,' she whispered to herself before she could overthink things and chicken out. One foot. Two feet. She wobbled but managed to steady herself again and very carefully stood up from her crouching position. It was tempting to cheer or punch the air in celebration, but she didn't want to risk toppling over again. Thomas did it for her.

'Woo-hoo! Go, Daisy!' He slapped the surface of the water with the flat of his hand, sending a celebratory shower over her.

'Thomas! Careful before you knock me off-balance again!' She fought to stay upright as the board rocked against the motion of the disturbed water. Though this time the thought of falling in again wasn't nearly as terrifying. It hadn't killed her, only wrecked her hair. Even if she did get into trouble, she trusted Thomas to save her.

If only she could find the same courage to believe in them as a couple they might have a future together. That meant she would have to stop overthinking all the different ways she could end up getting hurt and show the same trust in Thomas as a partner as she did in him as an instructor.

Thomas was pleased he'd been able to convince Daisy to come down here this morning. He'd left the decision entirely up to her, not wishing to push her too far when he knew how difficult it was to face one's fears. If it had not been for the flood, his neighbours' distress and Daisy's nudging, he might never have invited another living soul back into the family home. He was glad he had, as now it seemed as though the gloom had lifted from the house so the sun shone in every corner once more. All he wanted for Daisy was that same freedom. To release her from whatever pain she still held from the past to enjoy every day fully.

Thank goodness the paddleboarding had turned out to be a good idea. That early fall had made his heart stop and his breath catch, fearing that it would trigger whatever trauma continued to wreak havoc in Daisy about the water. He should have known her bravery would win through and she would push herself to the limit, as she had done since she'd first arrived in Little Morton.

Indeed, they had both fallen into the water a few times during their lesson, but now they were coasting contentedly around the harbour. Daisy was no longer frowning in concentration trying to maintain her balance but smiling and enjoying the feel of the sun on her face.

'Thank you for doing this, Daisy.' Thomas was aware she had only agreed to come here because he had asked her to. It meant the world to him, not only that she had got out of bed for him but because she had confronted her fear simply so they could spend more time together. The fact that they were both willing to make sacrifices for one another was a good omen for their blossoming relationship.

Until recently he had thought himself incapable of feeling anything other than fear and distrust, doing little more than going through the motions of daily life. With Daisy there was genuine affection, passion and longing running through his veins again like electricity, sparking his body back to life and giving him something to look forward to every day. Being with her had given him a new lease of life. He didn't know what he had to offer her in return, but he hoped this was a start. They both needed a little time out just to chill and enjoy each other's company like this. Hopefully it would become a regular occurrence.

'I'm actually glad I came. There's something peaceful about skimming across the water with no one else around. I can see why you wanted to do this so early in the morning. You can't hear anything except the seagulls and the boats bobbing around us.' Daisy looked so at peace in the surroundings it seemed the perfect antidote to the stress and drama working at the clinic often brought. That was why he had taken up paddleboarding himself. Although he had rented Daisy's wetsuit and board, he had his own. He wasn't a surfer or someone who got his kicks on high-powered jet skis and speedboats. This got him out of the house and gave him all the benefits of the fresh sea air without risking any serious injury which could put him out of action at work for any length of time. Now it seemed like something they could do as a couple, with the added bonus of seeing Daisy in skin-tight fabric.

Even with her hair wet and devoid of her usual swipe of red lipstick, he couldn't wait to get his hands on her again. This wasn't like it had been with Jade, when he'd rushed blindly into a relationship without knowing what he was getting into. He and Daisy had fought against this attraction from the start. They had shared a lot about their pasts and the residual issues they harboured as a result. He had agonised over the consequences of them being together, yet he wanted her more than he had ever wanted anyone or anything in his life before. There seemed little point in wasting any more time when he was certain Daisy was the one he was willing to risk everything for.

'And no one to see what we get up to,' he said, moving until his board was parallel with hers.

'What are you doing?' she asked, eyebrows raised as she watched him set down his paddle and set one foot onto her board.

'I have gone too long without kissing you and I need to rectify that.' Once he had himself balanced between the two boards, he made the leap across so he was facing Daisy.

'You're mad!'

He grabbed hold of her and kissed her long and hard as the paddleboard shifted beneath them with his added weight. They were still clinging to one another when they overbalanced and plunged into the water.

Thomas couldn't have been more apologetic when Daisy came spluttering back to the surface. 'I'm so sorry. I didn't mean… I'm such an idiot… I was only trying to… Sorry, Daisy.'

He pulled her board over and held it steady until she was back upright and, thankfully, still smiling.

'It's good to know I'm so irresistible, but perhaps we should take this back onto dry land, lover boy.' When she blew him a kiss and headed back to shore Thomas wasted no time in paddling after her. They had enjoyed their early morning leisure pursuit and put a few demons to rest in the process. There was enough time for them to have a little more fun back home before they were needed elsewhere.

Back on the beach, he untethered his board and went to Daisy so they could pick up where they had left off without the unexpected cold bath. Her lips tasted like the sea, her little satisfied groans like a siren's call, and he would have willingly gone to his death for just one more kiss.

'What if someone see us?' she asked without any real urgency.

'I don't care.' It was the truth. They were both young and single; what they did in their private lives was no one else's concern. He'd been using the possibility of village gossip damaging his reputation as another excuse to avoid getting hurt. Rather than being afraid of people knowing they were together, he'd been more concerned about what he thought would be an inevitable break-up in the spotlight. He'd had no desire to suffer his next heartbreak in front of an audience. Now, though, he was doing his best to be as brave as Daisy had shown herself to be today and throw himself into this at full pelt. It seemed as though they were both ready to start living again and he, for one, was looking forward to all the surprises that would bring.

'It's just as well. I think that's Eunice over there walking her dog.'

Thomas instantly moved out of the embrace to see what Daisy was talking about. Sure enough, his trusty receptionist was up along the promenade with her dachshund tottering alongside her. If she saw them together the whole village would know by lunchtime. His personal life didn't come under the confidentiality clause in her contract.

In an act of bravado or defiance against those who had caused him pain in the past, Thomas pulled Daisy close to him. He bent her back and planted a Holly-wood-style kiss on her mouth so there would be no mistaking what was going on between them.

Beyond the sound of blood pounding in his ears he heard clapping and whistling, followed by the sound of Eunice's voice. 'It's about damned time.'

He leaned his forehead against Daisy's. 'I hope that was okay with you?'

She nodded and gave him another peck on the lips in return, gaining another round of applause from Eunice. A chorus of whoops went up as others had apparently gathered with their receptionist to witness their very public display of affection.

'I guess there's no going back now,' Daisy said, sounding every bit as nervous as Thomas felt.

Daisy was guilty of daydreaming in between appointments. Letting her thoughts drift to the previous night and the incredible time she'd had in bed with Thomas was becoming a habit. At times she even found herself loitering in the hall, waiting to catch a glimpse of him or, if she was really lucky, grab him for a quick kiss. Man, she had it bad.

When it came to the end of another day's surgery, she was bursting to spend some quality time with Thomas.

'See you tomorrow, Eunice.' She waved the receptionist off at the front door, then closed and locked it.

'Has everyone gone now?' Thomas came up behind her, his arms sliding effortlessly around her waist. Daisy leaned back against him, the tension of the day leaving her body to let arousal take its place.

'Yes.' She couldn't wait any longer to take her fill of him, kissing him as though she hadn't seen him for months instead of hours.

'Do you want to get some dinner or—?' He didn't have to say what else he was thinking about when Daisy's mind was already racing upstairs with him.

'Or?' she said, taking him by the hand to catch up with their runaway thoughts.

'We can get takeaway later if you like? When you see what I have for you upstairs you're not going to want to leave.'

'Promises, promises.' She grinned, hurrying up the stairs hand in hand with Thomas, eager to see just what he had in store for her.

Nothing could have prepared her for what he had done. Instead of taking her into his room, he led her to the room next door. 'I know you like having your own space. Although I'm hoping you'll be spending most nights in my bed.'

Daisy wasn't listening to him. She was too gobsmacked by what she was seeing. 'What have you done, Thomas?'

While she hovered at the door, unsure whether to stay or run, Thomas walked into the room and opened the wardrobe door to show her all of her clothes hanging on the rail. *All* of her clothes. Not just the ones she had packed herself.

That was as unsettling as seeing all of her perfume, make-up and jewellery laid out on top of the mirrored dressing table.

'I thought it would be easier for you to have your stuff here so you didn't have to go back and forward to the cottage.' Clearly oblivious to her discomfort, Thomas continued to show her all of her transferred belongings. He had moved her in without even asking if that was something she wanted. It wasn't.

Red flags were waving everywhere. She hadn't been consulted on something as huge as living with him on a more permanent basis and that absolutely freaked her out. It was too much too soon and making her feel suffocated. All those old feelings came rushing in, overwhelming her with thoughts of what this could be leading to. This was how her ex had started out, with little gestures she'd thought were sweet, until she'd realised he had manipulated her, cut her off from everyone else and any sort of independence. With this move, Thomas was making sure he was becoming her whole world when they would be with each other twenty-four hours a day. Even if his motive was altruistic, she couldn't take the chance of falling into that same trap, thinking she had to do whatever it took to make him happy if she was living in his house and working in his practice, with nowhere else to turn.

'I never said I wanted this.'

'It was you who mentioned things would be easier if you just moved in. I thought it would be a nice surprise.' His smile was beginning to falter as Daisy made it clear she wasn't happy about the situation he had forced her into.

'I wasn't being serious. Why on earth would you think I would want you to move my things in without my permission?' She opened one of the neatly stacked boxes to find the rest of her clothes all folded inside. The other boxes were labelled with 'Toiletries', 'Shoes', and 'Underwear'. Her shudder was probably not the response he had anticipated, but it was such an intrusion into her life she didn't think she would ever get over it.

'I got professional movers in. They were all women and very respectful of your belongings,' Thomas explained, as though that made the slightest bit of difference to her.

'I don't care. You had no right to do this.' Her skin was hot and clammy, her pulse racing so fast it was making her nauseated. She had to get away from here and fast.

'Okay, I got it wrong, but don't you think you're overreacting the tiniest bit, Daisy? This wasn't some attempt to take over your life. I was simply trying to make things easier for you.'

He had absolutely no right to be offended by her reaction when he was the one in the wrong. If he had stopped to think about her, what she had fought against in the past, he would have realised this was the last thing she would have wanted. No, Thomas had only been thinking about what he wanted. Now he was over his people phobia he thought he could move her in here for the sake of convenience and expect her to go along with it because he was her boss as well as her landlord.

'No, I don't think I'm overreacting. We might be sleeping together but that certainly doesn't make you entitled to go onto my property and mess with my things.' If he wanted to be particularly facetious he could point out it was his property and as landlord he did have rights to enter the property, but Daisy was counting on him knowing better than to contradict her in the heat of the moment.

'I wasn't trying to force you into anything. It could just be a temporary arrangement until everything gets back to normal.'

'You had no right.' Her fists were bunched at her sides, an involuntary action as she got ready to fight for her independence. Flashbacks were terrorising her with images of her ex locking the front door and refusing to give her a key because she didn't need to go anywhere without him.

'I want everything put back now or, better still, I'll take it myself.' She began collecting her bits and pieces, even though she couldn't possibly carry everything herself, but she wasn't thinking clearly. How could she when her past life was flashing before her eyes?

'I'm sorry, Daisy. I didn't mean to upset you, but it's done now.' Thomas moved and took the large can of hairspray from her, which she was trying to shove into her pocket without success.

It was happening. He was undermining her, taking away her freedom, not even allowing her to think or speak for herself without being ridiculed. She was done. There was no way she was putting herself back in this situation.

'Yes, it is, and so are we, Thomas. I should have listened to my instincts from the start. This was never going to work. I can't be here any more. I can't be with you.' Daisy turned on her heel so she could get out as soon as possible. With Thomas's reluctance to take her fears seriously she was feeling more trapped than ever.

'Can't we talk about this?'

'Apparently not. I'll stay somewhere else tonight. The cottage, the pub, wherever…but I will not spend another night here. Don't worry, I'll show up for work. At least until I can find a position elsewhere. I should never have come.' She walked away, shaking her head and cursing herself for repeating past mistakes. Letting her guard down had only left the door open for someone else who thought he could take over her life and work her like a puppet on a string.

Daisy got into her car and drove away. Somewhere along the way she had lost her independence and become some lovestruck zombie following along without thinking or doing anything for herself. It should have been a relief to shake herself out of that daze but, as she drove to the cottage, the only thing she could feel was her heart splintering into a thousand sharp shards.

Even before she opened her front door, tears were blurring her vision. Time had not eased the pain of having her trust broken again. If anything, this hurt so much more. She wasn't some naïve kid who didn't know any better; she was an adult who had been burned before and had spent years making sure she didn't get herself trapped in this very scenario. It was her own fault for sharing too much, for trusting again, for falling for someone who could hurt her so easily.

Her footsteps on the bare floorboards echoed around the walls as she walked into her living room. She didn't know if it was worse seeing her belongings floating in dirty river water or finding everything gone. Her new life in Little Morton had been obliterated. Including the love and the future she'd thought she had found with Thomas. The house was empty, devoid of anything which held any meaning or sign of being loved. Exactly how she felt inside.

# CHAPTER ELEVEN

EVEN WITH A houseful of patients and Daisy working in the room next door, Thomas was lonelier and unhappier than he could remember. It had been a couple of weeks since she had called it quits. He had tried to convince himself it was an inevitable outcome and he would have regretted letting her move into his home if she was capable of walking away so easily. At night, his empty house and heart said differently.

She would only speak to him on a professional basis, leaving no room for him to make apologies, though he had tried. Even then, she made sure the majority of their correspondence went through Eunice, leaving their intermediate scurrying between their offices wearing a harassed expression on her face most of the day.

He was drained emotionally and physically exhausted, kept awake at night by thoughts of how he had messed things up. If he thought Daisy would have given him another chance, he would have begged to be able to put things right again. He understood that in his enthusiasm to start a life with her he had frightened her off, but he hadn't had any sinister motive in moving her things in from the cottage. All he had wanted to do was make her comfortable in his home and prove to her that she was welcome.

Since his epic mistake, Thomas realised how inadequate he was as a partner. His distrust of strangers and his need for privacy at all costs had severely affected his ability to read what the important people in his life needed from him. He was a good doctor, but when it came to his personal life he clearly had some work to do. Not for the first time he wished his father was around to advise him. He had never had any problems expressing his feelings for Daisy and how much he liked her, and that appreciation had been mutual. Thomas could have done with a few pointers before he had lost the only woman in his life he was ever likely to love.

He didn't even know how Daisy was coping in the cottage after she had lost everything, and he was concerned she might decide to move away and start over somewhere else.

It wasn't supposed to be this way for any of them.

'Dr Ryan? Dr Swift would like to know if you could add one of her patients to your list of house calls.' Poor Eunice tentatively hovered in the doorway once his last patient had gone.

At least he had work and Daisy's presence—albeit at a distance—here to look forward to.

'Of course. Just leave me the details and I'll stop by on my rounds.' He respected Daisy's medical opinion sufficiently to not question her reasons but would have to acquaint himself with the case. Previously, she would have come in to ask him herself, perched her backside on his desk and given him the lowdown on her patient while they drank their umpteenth cuppa of the day. He missed that. He would miss it more if she did resign as she had threatened to do, yet they couldn't carry on working in this atmosphere. It was painful for all involved, just having to see each other, and not see each other, every day.

He could spend all day hoping to catch the slightest glimpse of her, only to have that swell of sickness in his stomach when the sight of her reminded him that she was no longer part of his life. It felt as though she had in some way betrayed him when he had made so many changes to try and make her feel safe. Clearly he had stuffed up, but Daisy wasn't a woman who gave second chances any more. He understood that, but that didn't stop the hurt of losing her.

'Dr Ryan, there's a lady here who urgently needs help. She's not one of our patients, but I think she should really see someone.' A perturbed Eunice showed up again with a woman standing right behind her clutching her midriff and her long, lank hair seemingly matted with blood.

Thomas quickly rose to usher them inside. 'Of course. Come in.'

As he came over to welcome her in, she flinched away from him, sticking close to Eunice. Sensing her uneasiness, he stood back to let the two women into his office without crowding them.

'What's your name, love?' Eunice was the one who pulled a chair over and coaxed her into sitting down.

'Alice.'

Now he could see her better, Thomas would have said she couldn't have been any more than twenty years old. Yet, even beyond her apparent injuries, her general demeanour suggested she was someone already worn down by life.

'And your surname? Is there anyone you'd like me to call?' Alice was clearly a vulnerable person, and it would be better for her if she had someone she knew with her.

'No, I don't want anyone to know I'm here. It's just Alice.'

He and Eunice exchanged concerned looks. This was more than a simple injury. She was frightened and they would have to tread carefully in case they scared her away.

'Okay, Alice. I'm going to take a look at those nasty cuts on your face. Do you want to tell me what happened?' Thomas made sure his hands were clean before donning some surgical gloves and let Eunice comfort her while he got some cotton balls and antiseptic to clean her wounds.

'I fell.'

He didn't believe that for a moment. Especially when the injuries appeared to be on both sides of her body and he could see the shadow of an old bruise under one eye. No doubt if he questioned her about that she would tell him she had walked into a cupboard door. Excuses he had heard from victims of domestic abuse before. It sickened him to think that someone was capable of doing this to Alice.

'It must have been a bad fall to cut you like that. If that had been any closer to your eye you might have needed surgery.' The skin above her eyebrow was split, blood trickling into the corner of her eye and down her face, but she said nothing.

Thomas went to dab at the cut but she shrank away from him, reaching out for Eunice's hand.

'Perhaps you would prefer it if Daisy, my colleague, tended to that?' He could see that she was fearful of him, and if it had been a man who had inflicted these injuries she would probably feel safer with a female doctor treating her. Despite their personal issues, he knew Daisy would want to help this young woman.

Alice nodded, suddenly tearful.

'It's fine. Don't you worry, Alice, you're safe here. I'll be back soon.' He took off his gloves and discarded them with the cotton balls to go and get Daisy's assistance. It was not unusual for female patients to request her; likewise, sometimes the men preferred to have Thomas treat them. In this instance it was important that they kept Alice calm and made her feel safe so she could get whatever help she needed after her ordeal.

He hurried next door where, thankfully, her door was open and she was sitting alone at her desk. For a split-second Thomas took in the picture of her sitting by the window, the sun creating a golden silhouette of the beautiful woman he knew he had lost his heart to. She rubbed the back of her neck, reminding him she was not some ornamental statue he had commissioned to remember her by. For now, Daisy was still here, flesh and blood, and he wondered if it was too late to fix things between them. He didn't wish to wander these halls with even more ghosts to haunt him when he was alone in the house.

'Are you going to stand there gawping all day or are you going to tell me what you want?' Daisy didn't as much as glance in his direction, yet she had known he was there.

Thomas coughed away his embarrassment at being caught staring. 'I…er…was hoping you could help me with a young woman next door. She has a head injury and possibly some damage to her ribs.'

'Shouldn't you advise her to go to the hospital?'

'I don't think she wants to be seen somewhere so public. She says she fell but there are old bruises still healing. I don't want to scare her off and I think she would be more comfortable with a female doctor.' He didn't have to say any more to get Daisy onside. Most GPs had some experience dealing with victims of domestic violence and the most commonly used excuses.

'What's her name?' There was a grim determination in Daisy's manner now as she draped her stethoscope around her neck and walked the short distance with him.

'Alice.'

As soon as they entered his office, her demeanour changed, a smile replacing the thin-lipped expression she'd worn when Thomas had told her what he was dealing with.

'Hi, Alice. I'm Daisy, one of the GPs here. Now, Dr Ryan tells me you've had a nasty fall?' She donned a fresh pair of gloves and scooted a chair over to sit with the young woman.

Their patient nodded but she wasn't scrabbling to get away as Daisy took a look at the cut on her eye.

'Eunice? Perhaps you could go and make some hot, sweet tea and Dr Ryan and I will see to Alice.' Daisy took control of the situation, sending the receptionist away to keep anything Alice told them in confidence.

'Yes, Doctor.' The way she took off said she was only too happy to leave them to it.

Thomas sat back and let Daisy take the lead since the young woman was more likely to open up to her. He stayed in the room not only to witness anything which happened or was said, but to be here as support for Daisy. These cases were never easy, and he knew it could bring up difficult memories of the troubled relationship Daisy had told him about with her domineering ex.

'This might sting a little bit, Alice. It's quite a deep wound and I need to make sure it's clean, so infection doesn't set in.' She set to work dabbing the cut with the cotton and antiseptic, Alice wincing with the first application.

'I think you should really get that checked at the hospital. It's going to need stitches.'

'No. Can't you do it here?' The wide-eyed panic in the girl's eyes was heartbreaking when she clearly felt it wasn't safe to get the help she needed.

Daisy looked at him and he nodded before going to get the sutures to help close the wound for her.

'Alice, you seemed to be in some pain when you first came in. If you don't want to go to the hospital, maybe you would be okay with Daisy taking a look to make sure you didn't hurt yourself anywhere else when you fell?' He diverted attention away from the most obvious injury, which Daisy had now patched up, and towards the right-hand side of her body, which she clutched at every now and then.

'If you want to pop up on the bed I can pull the curtain around and give you some more privacy?' Daisy offered and Alice eventually agreed. If Thomas thought his presence here was making her unduly uncomfortable he would leave, but for now he was going to sit in to see what steps they could both take to get Alice to a place of safety.

Eunice knocked before bringing in a tray with three cups of tea and set it on the desk.

'Thanks, Eunice.'

'Is everything okay?' she mouthed back to him.

He winked and nodded, praying it would be.

In the background, Daisy was gently persuading Alice to let her examine her injuries. 'If you could take your top off, or even lift it up for me… That's great… That's a bad bruise you have there… I'm going to press gently… Let me know where it's tender…'

When Alice let out a pained yelp, Thomas winced in sympathy with her.

'The ribs are very badly bruised. I'd prefer it if you had an X-ray to make sure there's nothing broken but I will recommend you take it easy for a while. Rest up and take some painkillers.' Daisy came out from behind the curtains and pulled off the disposable gloves. A frown wrinkled her forehead and disapproval was there in the tight line of her mouth. Thomas felt the same way about whoever had caused those injuries.

Alice appeared again, pulling down her top and covering whatever injuries Daisy had been privy to.

'You know, Alice, I used to have a lot of…falls. My life was so much better once I got help and moved out of the toxic relationship I was in.'

Daisy's admission stunned Thomas and Alice into silence. He had been aware that she'd had trouble with her ex but he hadn't realised that extended to physical harm. It made his stomach knot to think of her in a similar position to Alice, broken and frightened. Not the confident, self-assured doctor who had firmly put him in his place from the moment she had arrived here.

It was difficult to marry those two versions of Daisy and he could see how hard she must have worked to get where she was today. And why she was so fiercely independent and determined to do things her way. It was her way of protecting herself from ending up in the same situation. He could relate to that when his emotional scars had caused him to shut himself off too, afraid of making the same mistakes again.

Thomas thought back to their tiff when he had accused her of overreacting to him moving her stuff in without her consent. He was such a dolt. Too caught up in what he wanted, he had been oblivious to her plight. He had taken over, disregarded her feelings and invaded her privacy. Everything she had feared by getting involved with someone again. He had shown all the signs of being another controlling partner and that was exactly why her shutters had come hurtling down, blocking him out of her life. Even if it was too late to explain his actions and accept responsibility for making her uncomfortable, Thomas would find some way of making amends so she could at least see he was not a complete monster.

Daisy was desperately attempting to hide her own emotions while she tried to cajole Alice into accepting help. She knew from experience it was not easy to make that big life change and leave that kind of relationship when it was your whole world. Being in this position, sharing her abusive past, was bringing up a lot of emotions for her too. Things she hoped she had moved past and would never have to deal with again, but recent events with Thomas had brought a lot of those unresolved issues to the fore again. It would be worth it though if she could persuade Alice to escape from her toxic relationship too, paying it forward after the help she had received from the Earl all those years ago.

'How…how did you get away?' Alice's voice was small, as though afraid to say the words aloud, and Daisy's heart went out to her and all the other women like her, still trapped with men who abused them to make themselves feel better.

'I was lucky. I heard about a lovely man who helped me. Then I went to college, studied really hard and was determined I would take care of myself from that moment on.' She could feel Thomas's eyes on her and knew this was coming as a revelation to him too.

Perhaps if she had shared more of what she had gone through they could have avoided the scene in his house altogether, but the damage was done. Even talking about her ex now made her realise Thomas was nothing like Aaron. With some space she was able to look at the two different situations and see the motives for his actions had been completely different to the man who had treated her so badly in the past. Not that it mattered now, when they had both retreated to their individual corners, clinging tightly to that emotional baggage which kept them safe from predators. At least if they could make arrangements for Alice to live independently from her abuser, something good would come out of all of this.

'Do you have any family we could call for you? Perhaps a loved one could take you in and give you somewhere to stay?' Thomas interjected. Though he meant well, family was not always the best option in these instances. They would have been the last people Daisy would have turned to for help.

'My mum would let me stay, I know she would, but I haven't seen her in so long. Arty stopped letting me call her, didn't like her coming to the house and eventually we lost contact.' Alice was shredding the tissue she had pulled from the box on Thomas's desk, her anxiety showing in every tear.

It was typical manipulative behaviour, cutting her off from anyone who might tell her to leave, convincing her that her partner was the only one who had her best interests at heart. All the while grinding her down until her confidence was at an all-time low and she didn't think she deserved any better. At least it sounded as though Alice did have a parent who loved her and might be able to get her out of her boyfriend's grasp.

'I'm sure your mother would be only too glad to hear from you. Why don't you give her a call? Or myself or Dr Swift could do it for you?' Thomas pushed his phone across the desk towards her, keen to get Alice to take that first step.

There were refuges and safe houses they could contact for her too, but if Alice had a real home to go back to it could make all the difference. Daisy almost envied her having somewhere safe she could retreat to for her recovery. She had never had anywhere except the home she had made for herself. The only time she had really felt as though someone was looking out for her was during the storm when Thomas had taken everything in hand and comforted her when she had needed it. Then she had gone and ruined everything by freaking out when he had made one kind gesture too many. Now she had nothing.

'I… I think I should be the one to call. I don't want her to worry.' Bless Alice, for thinking that her poor mother was already frightened to death for her daughter who was living with a dangerous man, capable of hurting her. Still, it would be better for her to start a dialogue now and make that connection in case she had second thoughts and thought going back would be the easier option.

'We'll give you some privacy, but we'll just be outside the door if you need us.' Thomas rose from his chair and Daisy followed him out into the hallway.

They stood awkwardly together, not really knowing what to say to each other. It was Thomas who finally made the first move.

'That must have been hard for you in there.'

She swallowed down the sudden ball of emotion trying to block her airway. 'It was important Alice knew she had someone she could confide in. Who wouldn't judge her or tell her she'd been stupid to put up with it for so long. It's not as easy to get out of a situation like that as people think.'

'You really helped get through to her. Hopefully this will get her the help she needs.'

'I hope so too.'

Thomas had been right to come to her for help in the first place. Some might have turned Alice away. Daisy remembered plucking up the courage to go and see a doctor once, not knowing where else to go. He'd accused her of wasting his time and being a silly little girl. It was an age before she'd even contemplated asking for help again.

Thomas was compassionate to anyone in need, and she could only conclude that the dark light she had cast him in recently was mostly down to her own issues. Yes, he had overstepped the mark, but it was a mistake he had tried to apologise for repeatedly. She was the one who'd continued to hold a grudge because it was safer than admitting she had fallen for him. A good excuse for her to keep her distance instead of letting the relationship blossom and put her heart on the line for him. Even though Thomas already unwittingly held it in his hands.

That realisation had freaked her out more than his interference in her living arrangements and deep down she knew that was why she had run out on him. What she had to decide now was whether or not she wanted to stay in Little Morton, pull up her big girl pants and tell him how she felt, or keep running away from those feelings. Should she open her heart or protect it at all costs?

'Daisy, I had no idea you'd gone through so much yourself. I'm truly sorry if my actions brought you more pain. That was not my intention.'

'I know,' she conceded. 'I should never even have joked about moving in. I guess we could call it a mutual misunderstanding.' Letting him continue to think the whole debacle was his fault wouldn't be fair to Thomas when they had both made mistakes.

Before they could discuss the matter any further or

consider what this meant for them now, Alice opened the office door.

'Mum says I can go and stay with her,' she said with a heartbreaking smile. It must have come as such a relief and a revelation to know she was still wanted and loved, despite any disagreements in the past.

Daisy longed for the same. Would Thomas accept her half-apology and be willing to try again when she had hurt him so cruelly by walking away when he had made room in his life for her? Was that what she even wanted? On her part at least the answer was yes, but she couldn't be one hundred per cent sure she was brave enough to take that step again.

'That's fantastic, Alice.'

'That's the first step. I'm so pleased for you.' Daisy agreed with Thomas's sentiment. This was the best news they could have hoped for.

'I hate to ask but I might need to borrow my bus fare. Mum doesn't drive and I don't have any money. I don't want her to see me like this. Maybe I should go back and get some of my things…' Alice glanced at her blood-stained shirt and Daisy could see why she was worried, but going back for any reason was a bad idea. Making the break was the biggest step and there was no way of knowing what she could be returning to in that house.

'Listen, Alice, if there is nothing really important back there, I would walk away. I can drive you wherever you need to be and we can stop and get you a change of clothes on the way.' Someone had stepped up to help Daisy start over and she would be only too happy to do the same for Alice.

'I could come with you too…or just give you my

credit card to get whatever Alice needs...' Halfway through his offer Thomas seemed to have a change of heart, no doubt afraid he was overstepping the mark again. Daisy appreciated that he wanted to support them both, especially if there was a violent partner involved, but there was no need. As she had to keep reminding herself, she wasn't the helpless young girl she had once been. Hopefully the same would soon be said about Alice too.

'Thanks, Thomas, but I think we can manage. Besides, you will need to hold the fort here.' She gave him a smile to convey her thanks, that there was no ill feeling on her part, and hoped the same was true for him.

'No problem. You know where I am if you need me.' Thomas walked away, leaving her and Alice to fend for themselves, just as Daisy had asked him to.

If she had made it clear from the beginning what she did or did not need from him they would likely still be together. All Thomas had done was try to make her feel a part of something, even if he had gone about it the wrong way. The notion of sharing her life again had terrified her. Thinking the worst about Thomas's well-intended gesture had given her a good reason to back away. She hadn't known what she would do if the same happened again somewhere down the line, if forgiving one transgression left the door open for more to occur. So Daisy had taken the easy option and retreated back into her safe, lonely shell.

The problem was she had enjoyed being with Thomas and could picture them as a couple. If she hadn't screwed things up with him altogether, she had to decide once and for all if she was willing to trust, to love again, or let the bad guys win by continuing to live alone and miserable.

Daisy had to struggle to focus on the road. Dealing with Alice had brought back so many bad memories for her to deal with she was exhausted. Plus there were no streetlights on the lane back to her cottage. Not that she was in a rush to get home. There was nothing waiting for her there except empty rooms and memories of Thomas and everything she had turned away from.

She yawned as she drew up towards the cottage and was forced to slam the brakes on when she nearly ran into the car parked outside.

'What the hell?' An unexpected visitor was the last thing she wanted to deal with tonight.

A cold chill ran in her veins when she considered the possibility that it could be Alice's partner come looking for her. He might have heard she had been at the clinic and hunted Daisy down to find out what had happened and where she had gone. With Alice gone, he might take out his frustrations on her.

She grabbed her bag but her phone was dead and the only thing inside she could use as a weapon was a compact umbrella. Armed with her makeshift cudgel, she got out of her car and walked tentatively towards the dark figure sitting in the car in her driveway.

Just as she was getting ready to make vague threats against the intruder, on closer inspection she realised it was Thomas slumped in the front seat. He was fast asleep, his breath steaming against the window. If he was waiting for her he could have let himself into the cottage until she came home, but he probably hadn't wanted to risk her wrath again by intruding onto the property. Knowing she couldn't leave him out here in the cold all night, Daisy rapped on the glass.

'Thomas? Come in out of the cold.'

He startled then saw her, smiled and got out of the car clutching a manila folder.

'How long have you been sitting out here?'

'A couple of hours. You weren't answering your phone and I wanted to make sure everything went well with Alice.' He followed her into the cottage as she turned on the lights and the central heating.

'A couple of hours? You must be freezing and out of your mind.' Although she was touched he had waited that long to make sure she was okay.

Thomas shrugged. 'I realised what dealing with Alice meant to you and couldn't stop thinking about everything you must have suffered in the past.'

Daisy shuddered, trying not to think about it too much and focus on Alice's progress. 'I've tried to put it behind me but sometimes it does sneak up on me. I'm sorry if I transferred some of those residual issues onto you. As for Alice, it all looks promising so far. We got her some clean clothes and drove to her mum's. Naturally she was over the moon to have her daughter back and managed to talk Alice into going to the hospital for a check-up, telling her to get it on record. The ribs were just bruised, as we suspected, so she should make a quick recovery.'

'I'm glad. I was thinking that perhaps we could look into setting up a charity to help other women in similar situations.'

'I would love that; it's a great idea. We could fund

a safe house and help get them into employment, so they would be working towards their independence.' She'd got a buzz helping Alice break away today and it would give her a real sense of purpose to help desperate women make a new start. Thomas's father would have approved too, she was sure.

'Does that mean you're staying?'

'I think so.' She was content here. It was only the ghosts of her past which continued to make her miserable. Daisy guessed that would go on for as long as she let it. It was about time she took back control and dictated her own happiness. That included having Thomas in her life.

'In that case, you might need these.' He handed over the folder he had tucked under his arm. When Daisy opened it she found legal documents relating to the cottage.

'What's this?'

'The deeds to the cottage. I want you to be comfortable here, and if that means giving you this place, so be it. I know my father would have wanted you to have this anyway.'

'I would never have accepted it off him either. I told you I never came here with any ulterior motive. I simply loved your father for the special man he was. The male role model I never had in my life.'

'It was stupid of me to say those things about you at the festival. I don't think you came here for his money, but I do want you to have the cottage. It's your home. You don't owe me anything in return and it will give you peace of mind that I will never set foot in here again without your permission.'

Daisy was speechless. Not only was this an unbeliev-able gift but it was a spectacular display of trust on his part. If she was so inclined, she could sell the cottage and do a runner. He was willing to risk that sort of be-trayal again in the hope she would stick around. Even if he didn't know it himself, only a man who truly loved her would take that sort of chance. Thomas deserved the same recognition in return when Daisy knew she had fallen in love with him from that first day, when he had carried her shoes and handbag without saying a word.

'There's really no need to do this, Thomas.'

'There's every need when I want you to stay. You mean the world to me, Daisy. I know I messed things up between us and I'll understand if you can never forgive me for that. I just want you to know I wasn't trying to take over, or make you feel insignificant. It was my stu-pid way of showing you I cared. Maybe I should have just told you I loved you and saved all the trouble.' He mumbled the last bit as he turned back towards the door.

If Daisy let him leave now she knew she would lose him for ever. This was the time for her to have a say in what was going to happen next in her life. She had to make that move forward or remain stagnant for the rest of her days.

'Thomas, wait.' She reached for his hand and pulled him back towards her. He looked at her hand then at her face with such hope in his eyes Daisy's heart gave an extra flutter.

'Say that again. The bit where you muttered some-thing about loving me.'

'I love you, Daisy, and if you'll let me I'll spend the rest of my days proving it to you.'

'I think you've already done that. There is such a thing as overkill, you know.' She smiled at him and saw the relief on his face that she was finally hearing him out.

Thomas smiled back. 'As long as you don't hate me any more.'

'I could never hate you. What on earth would make you think that?' Daisy took the bold move of slipping her arms around his waist, hoping an embrace wasn't too much to expect after everything.

'I don't know. Maybe it was the not speaking to me for what seemed like for ever, or perhaps it was when you said you wanted a transfer.' Thankfully Thomas appeared to have forgiven her for her past transgressions as he took her in his arms.

'I'm sorry. I got it all wrong. I know you would never hurt me. I was confused about how I was feeling and afraid everything was going to go wrong again. It was easier for me to run away from it all than face it.'

'And now? How do you feel about me? About us?' Thomas bent his head so his mouth was hovering a mere whisper away from hers, waiting for her permission to close that tiny gap.

'I love you, Thomas Ryan. I love us and I want to try again.'

'That's all I needed to hear.' He set his mouth on hers and kissed her so gently Daisy knew she had made the right decision. Thomas was someone who would take care of her the way no one else in her life ever had.

She had finally decided to take a chance on her Prince Charming and she prayed they would both get their happy-ever-after.

# EPILOGUE

*One year later*

'ARE YOU FINISHED in there?' Thomas called through the bathroom door, waiting for Daisy to come out.

'Patience is not your strong point, is it, my darling?' She put him out of his misery by coming out to join him in the bedroom.

'No? I'm still waiting for you to accept my marriage proposal, aren't I?' He sat down on the bed and patted the space beside him. Daisy went to him, clutching the pregnancy test in her hand that he was so desperate to see, even though they wouldn't know the result for another few minutes.

'That's marriage proposals, plural.' It had become something of a standing joke between them now that he would get down on one knee at any given opportunity and ask her to marry him, even though she had said no every time.

'I live in hope that one day you will say yes and make me the happiest man in the world.'

Despite the fact that she had moved in with him several months ago to show how serious she was about the relationship, Daisy had not been ready to go all in and get wed. She was still clinging onto her independence and she had no idea why, other than that residual fear that she would be handing over control of her life to someone who might abuse that trust. It was ridiculous when Thomas had proved repeatedly that he was nothing like the men who had hurt her in the past.

After getting it so very wrong by moving her things in without telling her, he had made a conscious effort since to ensure she was comfortable with every step they took as a couple, consulting her about each room in the house as he'd begun to make the place into a home for them both. He had redecorated and sold a lot of the family heirlooms to fund the safe house they had created for vulnerable women at the cottage.

She couldn't have asked for a more considerate partner. He told her he loved her every day, showed her that in his every action, and she knew he would never have asked her to move in if it wasn't the truth. Of course she loved him with every fibre of her being too and couldn't imagine life without him now. There was just that one hurdle to get over…

'What if the test is positive?' she asked. They hadn't planned to have a baby so early on in their relationship, but they had not been as careful as they should have been where contraception was concerned. Daisy liked to think it was an unacknowledged part of their commitment and trust that if she did fall pregnant they would both step up and be there for one another, as they always had been.

'Then I will be absolutely over the moon. I never thought I would be a father and the chance to raise a family with you feels like I'm in a dream. I had a great relationship with my father, and I hope for the same with my own children. This baby would have a happy, loving home with two parents who will want only the very best for him or her.' He was already beaming at the prospect and Daisy knew he would be a great dad when he had so much love to give. They had both grown up in a broken home, so they knew how important it was for a child to feel safe and happy.

When they had done so much soul-searching before committing to their relationship, Daisy was positive Thomas was 'the one' she was going to share the rest of her life with. Which begged the question why she hadn't agreed to be his wife yet. A piece of paper wasn't going to change anything except to give them that sense of belonging. Her heart and soul were already Thomas's and accepting his surname wasn't going to suddenly turn him into the controlling monster she feared. Being his wife didn't necessarily mean she would be giving anything up, but she would be gaining a family in him and any children they might be lucky enough to have.

'What if I'm not pregnant?' It was one thing contemplating marriage knowing there was a baby on the way and wanting to 'do the right thing', but if this was a false alarm she was afraid the disappointment would overshadow the engagement she was now contemplating.

'Then we can try again when we're ready. It won't change the way I feel about you, Daisy. I love you and I'm yours for ever.'

Every time he said the words he claimed another piece of her heart and made her fall in love with him even more. She was only hurting them both by refusing his offer of marriage when it would cement their relationship for ever.

'Ask me the question.' Right now she was surer than she had ever been that this was what she wanted. Thomas. A family. Even if she wasn't pregnant now, she hoped that some day they would be looking forward to the arrival of their child. In the meantime she was happy to put the past behind her and focus on the future she could have with Thomas.

'*The* question? Why, when I already know the answer?'

She gave him *the look* which he knew meant there was no point in arguing. Thomas was no doormat, but he would do absolutely anything for her. That worked both ways, which was why they had such a great relationship. They were a team, at work and at home. Hopefully as parents too.

He sighed but still got down on one knee and took her hand. 'Daisy Swift, would you do me the absolute honour of being my wife?'

'Yes.' She beamed, enjoying the complete shock registering on his face.

'Really? This isn't a wind-up?'

'No,' she said, laughing. 'I love you, Thomas Ryan, and I can't wait to be your wife.'

'You won't have to wait. Name the day and I'll be there waiting at the end of the aisle for you.' He hugged her and kissed her hard on the lips. Daisy was the happiest she had ever been in her life and there was just one more thing that would make everything perfect.

'Time's up. Should we take a look at the results?' She opened up her hand to check the plastic window which would reveal if they were going to be parents soon or if they would have to wait a little longer.

They were both holding their breath as they checked the results.

'Positive.' Thomas confirmed what she had seen for herself but didn't quite believe it.

'We're going to be parents,' she said aloud as it began to sink in.

'We're going to be a family.' Thomas was clutching her hands, his eyes filled with happy tears, and Daisy finally knew what it was to be loved.

It was everything.

*  *  *  *  *

# COMING SOON!

We really hope you enjoyed reading this book.
If you're looking for more romance, be sure to
head to the shops when new books are
available on

## Thursday 26th May

To see which titles are coming soon, please visit

**millsandboon.co.uk/nextmonth**

# MILLS & BOON®

## Coming next month

SURGEON'S SECOND CHANCE IN FLORENCE
Kate Hardy

Sam was still smiling when she walked into the Michelangelo Hospital. At the reception area, she picked up the lanyard with her ID card, and asked for directions to Ricardo Fanelli's office.

When she reached the maternity department and pressed her ID card to the reader, nothing happened; clearly her card hadn't been activated yet. Not wanting to be late on her first day, she pressed the buzzer.

There was an answering buzz, and a few seconds later the door opened.

And her knees buckled for a moment when she saw who'd opened the door to her. She almost dropped the flowers she'd bought to thank Lidia.

It couldn't be Angelo. How could he be working in Florence, when she knew he lived in Rome?

But the name on the lanyard round his neck was very clear: Dottore Angelo Brunelli.

The love of her life. The man who'd told her he didn't love her any more.

'Hello, Sam,' Angelo said. 'Welcome to the Michelangelo Hospital.' He held out his hand, offering her a formal handshake, as if to prove that they'd both got over the past.

The second her palm touched his, her skin felt as if it was fizzing. Memories bubbled over, of how she'd touched him in the past. Linked her hand with his as they'd walked along, talking. Wrapped her arms round him as they'd danced together. Slid her hands through his hair as he'd kissed her. Stroked his bare skin as they'd made love...

She hadn't been prepared for this. She'd thought she was working in a brand-new unit with Ric Fanelli and Henri Lefevre. She'd been so busy over the last three days, packing and sorting out her flight and accommodation and saying goodbye to everyone, that it hadn't even occurred to her to look up the rest of her new department.

But clearly Angelo had known she was coming here, because there wasn't the slightest trace of surprise in his expression.

'I didn't realise you worked here,' she said, forcing herself to sound calm and collected—even though seeing him again had sent her into a spin. 'I thought you were in Rome.'

He inclined his head. 'I moved here a year ago.'

And he looked just the same as she remembered. The same unruly hair that he tried to keep neat for work, but it insisted on curling and tended to stick out everywhere by the end of a shift. The same dark, soulful eyes with their incredibly long lashes. The same beautiful mouth that had made her heart feel as if it had done a triple somersault whenever he smiled at her.

*Continue reading*
SURGEON'S SECOND CHANCE IN FLORENCE
Kate Hardy

*Available next month*
www.millsandboon.co.uk

# MILLS & BOON

## THE HEART OF ROMANCE

## A ROMANCE FOR EVERY READER

**MODERN**

Prepare to be swept off your feet by sophisticated, sexy and seductive heroes, in some of the world's most glamourous and romantic locations, where power and passion collide.

**HISTORICAL**

Escape with historical heroes from time gone by. Whether your passion is for wicked Regency Rakes, muscled Vikings or rugged Highlanders, awaken the romance of the past.

**MEDICAL**

Set your pulse racing with dedicated, delectable doctors in the high-pressure world of medicine, where emotions run high and passion, comfort and love are the best medicine.

**True Love**

Celebrate true love with tender stories of heartfelt romance, from the rush of falling in love to the joy a new baby can bring, and a focus on the emotional heart of a relationship.

**Desire**

Indulge in secrets and scandal, intense drama and plenty of sizzling hot action with powerful and passionate heroes who have it all: wealth, status, good looks…everything but the right woman.

**HEROES**

Experience all the excitement of a gripping thriller, with an intense romance at its heart. Resourceful, true-to-life women and strong, fearless men face danger and desire - a killer combination!

To see which titles are coming soon, please visit

**millsandboon.co.uk/nextmonth**